THE
BETTE DAVIS
CLUB

Center Point
Large Print

**This Large Print Book carries the
Seal of Approval of N.A.V.H.**

THE
BETTE
DAVIS
CLUB

JANE LOTTER

CENTER POINT LARGE PRINT
THORNDIKE, MAINE

This Center Point Large Print edition
is published in the year 2016 by arrangement with
Amazon Publishing, www.apub.com.

This is a work of fiction. Names, characters, organizations,
places, events, and incidents are either products of the
author's imagination or are used fictitiously.

The text of this Large Print edition is unabridged.
In other aspects, this book may vary
from the original edition.
Printed in the United States of America
on permanent paper.
Set in 16-point Times New Roman type.

ISBN: 978-1-62899-936-5

Publisher's Cataloging-In-Publication Data
(Prepared by The Donohue Group, Inc.)

Names: Lotter, Jane.
Title: The Bette Davis Club / Jane Lotter.
Description: Center Point Large Print edition. | Thorndike, Maine :
Center Point Large Print, 2016.
Identifiers: ISBN 9781628999365 (hardcover : alk. paper)
Subjects: LCSH: Middle-aged women—Fiction. | Automobile travel—
Fiction. | Large type books. | LCGFT: Humorous fiction.
Classification: LCC PS3612.O7777 B48 2016 | DDC 813/.6—dc23

For my children, Tessa Marts and Riley Marts.
And for my beloved husband, Robert Marts.

Dear Whoever-You-Are,

I don't know how you came to hold this book in your hands. Perhaps you're browsing in a bookshop while waiting to meet up with a long-lost high school pal. Is she late? Are you early? Maybe you received this book in a white elephant gift exchange. Maybe you're reading it on your phone. Maybe you heard something somewhere about this novel or its author, and decided just to give it a go.

My mother, Jane Lotter, wrote this novel. Shortly after she completed it, she left this particular plane of existence. And since *The Bette Davis Club* is being republished posthumously, I have been tasked with introducing it.

I feared at first this forward would sound too similar to the eulogy I gave two years ago, in 2013, when I spoke mainly of my deep admiration and love for a woman who raised me and bestowed upon me her sense of humor (and love for all things Bette Davis and road trips, as this book demonstrates), and for a woman who was truly the greatest I have ever known. She was fun and interesting and smart and sometimes judgmental and sometimes bossy and always loving. She was human. And superhuman to me. She was everything I hope I turn out to be, and perhaps I will, if I am very, very lucky.

The truth is my mother's death and the publication of her first and only novel are inextricable. She spent her last months trying everything possible to publish what she had spent so many years working to create. But she ran out of time. She needed to see her creative passion come to life before she faced the end of her own, and so she turned to Amazon's self-publishing services. Her last day on earth, she held a copy of the book she had written, reflecting on what she had accomplished. She held her book, and she cried. And we all cried with her.

And then, many, many months later, our family was contacted by Lake Union Publishing. They wanted to publish Mom's book for real. And here we are. It's what she dreamed would happen, and it's a real bummer she never got to see it. Though I think she knew this would happen all along.

I can't remember a time I didn't think of my mother as an author. She wrote and she read and she took care of my brother and me. She read to us and she proofread our homework and she made us memorize our spelling words and she made sure we could relate to Dickens and Twain and Shakespeare and Ephron and Capra and Hitchcock—all those whom she considered so singularly excellent at the craft of storytelling. Mom loved a good zinger, loved a good turn, and she loved a good story.

And she watched a lot of classic movies. And she made us—and any of our school friends who happened to be over on a Friday night—watch a lot of classic movies too. My mother loved watching classic movies the way some mothers love trying a new recipe. For us, dinner was always a variation on four different types of pasta. But we were served an endless array of Cary Grant and Katharine Hepburn and Bob Hope and, of course, Bette Davis. This book isn't about Davis. But in a way, Bette Davis is the reason it exists.

My mother treated writing like something that had to be done. She loved it; it was for fun and for her soul and it was something completely her own. And now she has her chance to share it with the world. With you, dear reader.

My mom was one of the special ones. Anyone who ever met her knew it. And now, you'll get to meet her too. I hope you enjoy the ride.

Most sincerely,

Tessa Marts

Daughter, Friend, Classic Film Fiend

THE
BETTE
DAVIS
CLUB

CHAPTER ONE

MALIBU

It is late morning, and I am drinking a double martini.

I'm sitting on a marble bench, on a bluff high above the Pacific Ocean. Nearby is the large Spanish-style house—a sort of mansion, actually—that was once my father's, but which now belongs to my older half sister, Charlotte. The sun is shining, the water is blue, the lawn is the color of money. Perfection.

Or at least it would be, if it weren't for all the people standing around. Unfortunately, there are about six hundred of them.

Like me, they're guests at the wedding of my nineteen-year-old niece, Georgia. Unlike me, many of them are Hollywood filmmakers and celebrities. Everywhere I look it's designer dresses, tailor-made tuxes, and the predatory gaze of the rich and vacuous.

Restless, waiting for the ceremony to begin, many people have crowded under several large tents pitched on the lawn, where they're helping themselves to free liquor.

Well, why not? God knows they can sleep it off tomorrow.

As for me, by tomorrow I hope to be headed home to New York. I am bored and I am lonely and I realize my friend Dottie Fielding was right when she warned me that coming out to Georgia's wedding was a bad idea.

"I can't believe you're going to that circus," Dottie had said to me, back in Manhattan. "Not now, not with things the way they are. Besides, from what you've told me, you're not overly fond of your sister."

"Half sister," I said. "Anyway, her daughter's sweet."

Dottie's my oldest, dearest, and, believe it or not, kindest friend. And as my closest friend she's earned the right to be, well, blunt.

"You can't even afford a decent wedding present," Dottie said. "Nothing that would go over with that crowd. You could take something out of your inventory, I suppose. Ship the happy couple a chunk of old Pennsylvania Station. Ha! There's an *objet* one doesn't stumble over every day."

Dottie, I should tell you, is in her late fifties. She owns a chic little shop in Greenwich Village that's filled with French Art Deco antiques. As an antiques dealer, she has quite an eye and makes a good living selling the overpriced to the over-indulged. I, too, have an eye and a shop full of old things, but lately my eye wanders—with the result that I don't much care if I sell anything or not.

14

"Please tell me you're not going to Georgia's wedding," Dottie said.

I shrugged. A few days later, I boarded Amtrak. (I love flying about as much as Indiana Jones loves snakes.)

Of course, unlike most of the mistakes I've made in life, I know why I've come to California. To this impressive residence in the hills of Malibu.

I'm here because I'm broke—insolvent, in debt, in trouble—and my half sister, Charlotte, Georgia's mother, offered me a train ticket and a place to stay, which at least meant a break from my financial worries. I'm here because I always liked Georgia when she was a little girl, though it's been years since I last saw her. And I'm here because it's a rare opportunity to visit this beautiful estate, a property that currently belongs to Charlotte, but which was once, briefly, our mutual childhood home.

I suppose I'd pictured Georgia's wedding as an all-expenses-paid vacation, like winning a trip in a raffle. But nothing's really free, is it? People always make you pay one way or another.

A tall, gray-haired gentleman in a tuxedo stands near me, lighting a cigar. His midriff contracts as he sucks in air, but the moment the tobacco is lit his stomach relaxes into its natural position, resting contentedly against his waistband. His clean-shaven face is vaguely familiar to me, though I can't think how I know him. He's aging and careworn but not unattractive, and he savors his cigar in a way that says he's pleased with the world and his place in it.

I peg him at sixtyish, which would make him a decade-ish older than I am. Behind a pair of dark-rimmed glasses he has what they used to call bedroom eyes, and he looks like someone who has definitely rumpled his share of sheets over the years.

"Lovely day," he says. He has a British accent, which I imagine means that—like me—he grew up in England. He gestures toward my bench. "Might I?"

I tell him he may.

He seats himself, sticking one foot out a little and jiggling his trouser leg to get comfortable. "You don't mind?" he says, holding up the cigar.

I shake my head. I'm of a generation that is not necessarily repelled by the smell of burning tobacco. Besides, at the moment I'm smoking a Pall Mall, so I can hardly object to this fellow's own bad habit.

"Party of the bride or party of the groom?" he says.

"Bride," I say. "Maternal aunt."

"Groom, father of. Well, truth of it is, I'm Tully's former stepfather. Course, his mum left

16

me long ago. Haven't seen much of the boy since." He coughs. "Thought I'd show up just the same, memory of happier times and all that. Family is everything, isn't it?" He holds out his hand. "I'm Malcolm Belvedere."

That's it, I knew I recognized him. Even I know that name: Malcolm Belvedere is probably the most powerful studio head in Hollywood, one of the last of the old school. I reckoned Georgia ran with the glitterati, but I had no idea she was marrying into royalty. This man is responsible for hit movies playing at malls and multiplexes all across America.

I'm dying to tell him—that when it comes to Hollywood filmmaking—I'm tired of all the computerized rubbish and cartoonish action pics, but instead I take his outstretched hand and simply say, "Margo Just."

"Shall I call you Miss Just?"

"No," I say. "Just Margo."

He smiles. "Then call me Malcolm."

I look again at his eyes. They're soft and intelligent and a touch tired.

I'm wearing a borrowed Donna Karan—strapless, ochre-colored, cocktail-length—and suddenly wonder how I look in it. Good, I hope.

"When I came up just now, you were gazing out there," Malcolm says, gesturing with his cigar toward the ocean. He peers into the distance. "Something in the water?"

"Not really," I say. "Only a very old . . . sea monster."

"A refreshing change from whales, I'm sure," he says. He gazes a moment more at the Pacific. "I don't remember seeing you at the rehearsal dinner," he says finally.

I decide to leave out the truth—that I wasn't invited—and tell a half-truth instead. "Couldn't make it," I say. "I was tying up some business in New York."

"Ah. That sounds important."

"It wasn't, I'm afraid."

"You're English," he says.

"Sorry, no, American. Born here in California." I flick the ash of my cigarette onto the ground, as if to note the spot. "However, I spent the second half of my childhood at a boarding school in England. It left a mark."

"Not too Dickensian, I hope?"

"More *Jane Eyre*."

"Still, they must have got a few things right," Malcolm says. His green eyes sparkle. "You turned out beautifully, if I may say so."

"Oh, you can say it," I reply, taking a drag off my cigarette before stubbing it out on the ground. "Whether or not I'll believe you is something else entirely." He laughs good-naturedly, which makes me want to go on talking with him.

"What about you?" I say. His pronunciation is

upper class, so I take a guess. "I should imagine you're from London."

"I was born within the sound of Bow Bells—"

"Cockney?" I say, laughing. "I don't believe it."

"Within the sound of Bow Bells," he repeats. "My mum was a charlady, my dad worked in the fish market. Always thought I'd follow in his footsteps. But when I was just a lad, a friend got me a job at Twickenham Studios, and I discovered I liked the film business. Soon after that, I came to the States, found a tailor"—he fingers his lapel—"and got my teeth fixed." He has brilliant white teeth and he flashes them my way.

"Oi," he says, "an' I dropped me bloomin' Heast Hend haccent." He puffs on his cigar. "That, my girl, was over forty years ago. And in all the years since, all those years of making movies in America, I have never ceased to profit from this country's endless appetite for amusement, coupled with its astonishing weakness of intellect."

"Well," I say, "since I'm a Yank, I'll have to watch myself or you'll think I'm dim."

"Not at all," he says. "You are a delightful exception to the rule. There will always be exceptions to the rule. Though mind you, never enough to have any effect whatsoever on the entertainment turned out by Hollywood."

He has me there.

"You live in New York?" he says.

"Yes, for many years."

19

"I enjoy Manhattan. I have a place in SoHo where I stay sometimes. Perhaps we could have lunch one day?"

"I'd like that," I say. And anyway, as my friend Dottie would point out, the first rule for a woman in financial difficulties—a woman such as myself—is to accept any and all offers of free food and drink.

"I also have a beach cottage in the Hamptons," Malcolm ~~says. "Ever get out there?"~~

"Sometimes. At the invitation of friends."

"Well, consider us friends, and consider yourself invited." He takes a card from his wallet and holds it before me, pointing at various numbers. "Cell phone, landline in Manhattan." He slides his finger farther down the card. "This number is my beach place."

He hands me the card. It is a thick, creamy vellum, the very weight of which says money. It is not, I suspect, the card he distributes to men and women with whom he does business. Rather, it's the valentine he hands out to unattached women with whom he desires monkey business.

I can't help myself. I picture dinner for two in a cozy house at the beach: cracked crab, oysters on the half shell, candles flickering on the table. Malcolm and I sipping cocktails while we wait for his Viagra to kick in. Later, we'll roll around on the sandy shore of the Atlantic, a middle-aged version (well, late middle age) of Deborah Kerr and Burt Lancaster. Oh, Malcolm, I find myself thinking, *From Here to Eternity*—or possibly From Here to Next Tuesday.

Even when I'm feeling sad, I'm susceptible to an intermittent optimism. It's like when you drive down a street looking at houses, saying to yourself, I'd adore living there. Or there. Or maybe in that one over there. Tudor, Victorian, American Bungalow. They all look good because you know nothing about them. You don't know if the plumbing's bad or the roof leaks or the neighbors are snake handlers. Yet you can't help picturing yourself moving in, snugging up to the fire, and being suddenly very happy.

Malcolm glances at his wristwatch. A flicker of concern crosses his face.

"Everything all right?" I say.

He runs a hand through his hair, or what's left of it. "I'm afraid I don't know the answer to that question," he says. He stands and again flashes that smile. "I hope you'll excuse me, Margo. It's been so very pleasant chatting with you."

Chatting me up, is more like it. Nevertheless, when Malcolm goes I turn and watch him walk away across the broad lawn, headed toward one of the tents.

I spy Charlotte at the opposite end of the house, near the swimming pool. She's pacing back and forth, waving her arms at a collection of servants.

Malcolm may not know if something's amiss, but it's obvious to me that disaster looms. Charlotte is like an aurora borealis of bad vibrations; even from here I can see her shimmering with anger and frustration.

I turn around and again focus on the wonders of my martini and the Pacific Ocean. Minutes later, I hear footsteps and look up to see Charlotte's thin little butler, Juven, standing before me. I like Juven, though perhaps what I feel for him is more pity than affection. I'd feel sorry for anyone employed by Charlotte.

"Thanking you in advance," Juven says, bowing. "Señora Illworth asks if you would please come up to the casa. If it's no trouble."

Of course, it's trouble. Lately, my whole life is trouble. Anyway, does Charlotte think I'm furniture to be moved about? Am I blocking someone's view? Because most of the time, Charlotte doesn't have much to do with me. I'm an embarrassment to her. Her only possible reason for summoning me now is that she needs something.

Well, I think, the joke's on you, Charlotte.

For the unhappy truth is that I am the survivor of a shipwrecked life. I'm a castaway who has washed up on your shore without craft, without hope, and without the one person I ever really loved. In other words, my dear half sister, I have nothing left to give.

CHAPTER TWO

I LEAP FROM
A RUNAWAY TRAIN

B y the time I finish my drink and walk back to the house, Charlotte has disappeared from her place by the pool. I'm ushered into the library by another servant and asked to wait. Library, indeed. What nonsense. When our father was alive, this was a real library with real books. When I first came to stay at the house at the age of eight, I'd curl up for hours in a club chair, reading *Stuart Little* or *Winnie-the-Pooh*.

But the leather-bound volumes of my childhood are all gone. In their place are rows of DVDs, a giant television screen, and a well-stocked bar.

Almost nothing left in the room is familiar to me. The French doors leading out to the terrace are still there, slightly ajar, their white silk curtains moving gently in the breeze. A large antique globe of the world, about four feet high, stands near them. I don't recall the globe from my childhood, and I can't imagine why Charlotte, who probably still believes the world is flat, would have such a thing. I go over to inspect it.

"Hello, world," I say, bending down to take a look. "What's new?"

I reach out to give the globe a spin, but something prevents it from turning. It won't budge. I wiggle the North Pole pin when—oof!—the entire Northern Hemisphere pops up like a jack-in-the-box, bopping me on the nose. I freeze, and it takes me several seconds before I understand I'm all right, my head has not exploded.

After I catch my breath and rub my nose, I examine the globe and see that it's hinged at the equator so it can open up like a clamshell, or a treasure chest. I seize the upper half and push it farther back. Inside, nestled in the earth's center, is a lacquer box containing . . . what? Money? Diamonds? Love letters?

I lift the lid off the box, but find no currency or precious gems. What I do find is a small stash of white powder. Hell-o, kitty, I think. So this is what you find if you dig through to China.

I dip my forefinger in the powder and regard the white specks that cling to it. Well, I've lived a long and sometimes sinful life, and I can recognize cocaine when I see it. It's funny, but when Charlotte was a teenager, Daddy nicknamed her "Cokie" because she drank so much soda. Now I realize our father wasn't being playful. He was foretelling Charlotte's future.

Feeling like Pandora, but without finding the hope that remained in her box, I replace the lid and put the world back together. Then I sit down on a leather sofa and flip through a copy of *Entertainment Weekly*. You'd think I was in the waiting room at my doctor's, only the magazine selection is less promising.

Moments later, Charlotte comes sweeping into the room. Her body is as thin and straight as a panatela. Her lips, on the other hand, are so swollen from collagen injections she looks like she plays first trumpet for the Los Angeles Philharmonic. She's wearing a jet-black Chanel suit, black leather pumps, and her dyed black hair is lethally styled, as if Joan Crawford's hairdresser has had his way with her. The overall look is more harried funeral director than mother of the bride.

"Little Mar," she says by way of greeting. She plops down next to me and takes my hand. Her fingernails are immaculate and painted a deep plum. "Thanks for meeting with me."

"You're welcome," I say, putting my magazine aside and leaning back against the leather. "It's not like I was doing anything."

She sighs, then regards me closely. "You look good," she says, without an ounce of sincerity. "Stylish, slim. That's a killer dress."

"Thank you. I've received several compliments on it today."

"That color flatters you. The fit is to die for."

"You're too kind."

"Is it Donna Karan?"

"Yes," I say. "From the spring collection." With

my free hand, I smooth the hem and finger the expensive fabric. "Actually, Charlotte, I took it out of your closet."

All is silence, broken only by the gentle grinding of Charlotte's teeth. Then she speaks. "I figured," she says, squeezing my hand a tad tightly. "Little Mar and her jokes. Well, let it go."

Let it go? When we were children, Charlotte wouldn't lend me a bobby pin, never mind a dress. *What in the world do you have up your sleeve?* I wonder.

There's a knock at the door and sad-eyed Juven enters, carrying a silver tray holding a decanter of port and two glasses. He brings the tray over to where we're sitting and places it on a low table in front of the sofa. After a nod from Charlotte, Juven picks up the decanter and pours wine into the glasses. At this stimulus, Charlotte, like some sort of mad Pavlovian dog, drops my hand and reaches for the alcohol.

"*Gracias*, Juven," she says, handing me a glass and taking one for herself. "Now *por favor* go take care of that other thing we talked about."

The two of them look first at me, then at each other, with such obvious collusion that I can only imagine the "other thing" is the assassination of one of the crowned heads of Europe.

The second Juven leaves the room, Charlotte begins gulping down port.

I taste it myself. It has a dry, woody flavor. "This is quite good," I say.

She waves a hand dismissively. "Donald gets it by the crate from one of his buddies over at Paramount."

Donald, her husband, is an agent who represents several successful screenwriters. He's employed by one of the larger agencies, WME or CAA or . . . somebody. It's hard to keep track. I haven't spotted Donald among the wedding guests today, but that's not surprising. After all, he isn't Georgia's father. That hapless fellow was two or three marriages back, and we lost track of him long ago.

I suppose I should mention that Charlotte—like her husband, like Malcolm Belvedere, like most of the wedding guests—is in the motion-picture business. She's a movie producer. Her latest project, *Muscle Man*, is a mega-million-dollar extravaganza shot at great expense in exotic locations and featuring a galaxy of big-name stars.

All of which sounds good until you find out it's an action picture based on a comic book. Or perhaps a comic strip. Come to think of it, maybe it was inspired by one of those Saturday morning cartoons for children.

The script is by one of Donald's clients. Malcolm Belvedere's studio will release it. (Why does that always sound like the unleashing of some sort of toxic bacteria?) Naturally, everyone involved expects a giant hit, a real blockbuster. And no doubt *Muscle Man* will ultimately receive numerous Oscar nominations for things like Makeup, Special Effects, and, you know . . . Very Loud Noises.

As I say, Charlotte's a professional. She's had hit movies before and knows what she's doing. But from the little I've heard about it, *Muscle Man* isn't anything I'd care to see. Nevertheless, I make an attempt at small talk. "So how's the film coming?" I say. "In the can and all that?"

"We wrapped three months ago," Charlotte says. "Finished up in post, test screenings start this week." She gives a short laugh. "That's a formality, believe you me. Licensing, merchandising, all inked. This one's so in the bag, I told Donald to start researching property in Spain. I love the idea of a pied-à-terre in Barcelona, don't you?"

I don't know how to answer that. Yes, I'd like to own a fashionable little flat in Spain. Who wouldn't want to be rich like Charlotte and travel the world, eating in expensive restaurants and staying in posh digs? But the reality is, right now I'd be happy just paying my electric bill.

"Anyway," Charlotte says, "on a project like this, we can't lose. It's mathematically impossible. The comic-book rights alone are worth a boat-load of money."

"Comic-book rights?" I say. "I thought the story was based on a comic book."

Her eyes widen, as though she can't quite believe my stupidity. "Well, it is. And now there'll be a *new* comic book—except we call them graphic novels—based on the film. Honestly, Margo, have you forgotten how this town works?"

"I'm not sure I ever knew," I say.

"Maybe not," she says thoughtfully. She swirls port round in her glass. "You really were just a kid."

This, I admit, is unexpected. It's one of the rare times I've heard my older half sister acknowledge that I was once a child who needed looking after, that I was ever anything other than an adult.

There's a lull in the conversation as Charlotte grows reflective. Her eyes glaze over, but whether that's from drinking Donald's port or from the thrill of envisioning a freehold in Barcelona—or even from remembering our unhappy childhood—I cannot say. Then, deep within her, something switches back on. She returns to the here and now.

"Well!" she says. "How'd we get off on that? That's not what I want to talk about at all."

Cocking her head like a robin, Charlotte views me over the rim of her glass as if I were a promising earthworm. "I had Juven round you up for a reason," she says. "There's a family matter I want to discuss."

Family matter? *Family?* All right, yes, we're half sisters. Though, frankly, it feels more like one-eighth or one-sixteenth. And all right, our parents—her horrible mother, my beloved mother, and our dear mutual father—are dead, and we're the only siblings each of us has. Meaning there's precious little family left.

But what could Charlotte possibly want to talk about concerning our family? Childhood memories? Holiday gift-giving ideas? I think not.

Perhaps Charlotte wants my opinion as to whether she and Donald should have a child. The fact that she's pushing sixty is irrelevant—with sufficient hormone injections, anything's possible in Southern California. But no, I doubt that's it either.

If we're going to talk family, somehow I don't think Charlotte wants to consider her life or mine. I have the distinct feeling she wants to confer about someone else altogether. I believe she wants to discuss the one and only living blood relation the two of us have left in common: her nineteen-year-old daughter, Georgia.

"Let me get right to it," Charlotte says. "You were always a bright girl, Margo. You've probably figured out what's going on."

I sip my port and remember the look on Malcolm Belvedere's face when he read the time on his watch. "I believe I know what's *not* going on," I say.

"Which is?"

"Georgia's wedding."

"Bull's-eye," Charlotte says. She pours herself more wine, this time up to the rim. "Georgia's run off!" she declares, anger flashing across her face. "Last night, apparently, though I just found out half an hour ago." I watch as she shuts her eyes, hugs herself, and takes a deep cleansing breath, tricks I think she may have picked up in yoga class. Unfortunately, they do not produce the desired calming effect.

The anger bubbles up once more and, in a way I remember vividly from our childhood, Charlotte releases it via her mouth. "Those ripe little girl-friends of hers!" she says. "That gaggle of tattooed bridesmaids! They've been covering for her the whole time."

She drums her fingers on the arm of the sofa. "Big joke. Ha-ha. Very funny. Georgia gone and Mama stuck with six hundred guests, a river of champagne, and a catering bill the size of Rhode Island."

"I'm sorry," I say. "I—"

"*Run off!*" she repeats, as though informing me of a serious drainage problem. "It's a cliché, I know, the disappearing bride. But then, nobody will ever accuse Georgia of originality. Not to mention, cold feet run in the family, don't they?"

This last remark is accompanied by a slight smirk, a touch of half-sibling superiority. That's because it's a reference—a dig, actually—to my own wedding day, long ago. It's true that I left

31

my fiancé, Finn Coyle, standing alone and embarrassed in front of the judge. It's true that I jilted Finn.

But that was over thirty years ago and under very different circumstances. At any rate, too many years have passed for me to rise to the bait. I ignore Charlotte's question and instead submit a couple of my own.

"But why did Georgia leave?" I say. "Doesn't she love the boy?"

Charlotte looks blank, as if I'd just asked her to recite the Pledge of Allegiance. "Boy?" she says.

"The groom. Doesn't she love him?"

"Oh! You didn't meet Tully, did you?"

"Not yet."

"Well, he's unique. He's . . ." She pauses, as though she can't quite remember what it is that's unique about Georgia's fiancé, Tully. Then again, perhaps I heard wrong. Perhaps Charlotte isn't saying Tully's unique. Perhaps she's telling me he's a eunuch.

At last she throws up her hands in exasperation, as though I'm a willful child who refuses to cooperate. "Tully has a very high IQ," she says, as if that explains everything.

I can't help thinking that, in Charlotte's world, IQ probably stands for Icky Quotient.

She picks up the decanter. "More?"

"Why not?" I say. "It's a specious occasion."

She attempts a smile, but it ends up a little

frown. She refills our glasses, and we perch in awkward silence a few moments, imbibing Donald's excellent port.

"Here's the story, Margo," Charlotte finally says. "I have a proposal for you. Ha-ha. Bad choice of words. Proposition is what I mean. I want you to go after Georgia and bring her back. Right away. Today, in fact."

Clearly, Charlotte is in the early stages of mad cow disease. Any minute, she'll begin crawling round on the carpet, mooing like a Guernsey.

"Are you *completely* gone?" I say. "I'm not chasing after some little popsie—sorry—some confused young person who doesn't know her own mind. Can't you hire a private detective or someone?"

"No, I can't. There isn't time, and there's nobody in this backstabbing town I trust. I want a family member to go, someone I can rely on. You're the only family I have. There's no one else." She says this last not with warmth and affection, but more in the defeated tone people use when they look in the refrigerator and realize they're out of pretty much everything.

"It's bad enough," Charlotte says, "that the entire film community will go to bed gossiping about what's happened here today. But if the news media and tabloids catch up with Georgia before we do, it'll be a public relations disaster.

The paparazzi will be snapping those awful photos, interviewing busboys, digging through garbage cans . . ."

What of it? Charlotte's problems are not mine, and I have no intention of pursuing Georgia. As Charlotte drones on, my mind drifts and I find myself distracted by a bowl of cashews. I reach for a handful of nuts—

"Dammit!" Charlotte shrieks.

I jump, dropping the cashews back into the bowl.

"I need damage control!"

I watch as Charlotte again tries the yoga thing: Breathe in, breathe out. This time she has some success. A little calmer now, a new thought comes to her. "Do you know who Tully's ex-stepfather is?" she asks.

"Yes, as a matter of fact," I say. "Malcolm Belvedere, the studio head. We met out on the lawn."

She raises the penciled arches that pass for her eyebrows. "No kidding? What did you two talk about?"

"England, Charles Dickens, and the American cinema," I say, exaggerating the tenor of the actual conversation just a tad. While she's taking this in, I decide to add a zinger. "I think you could say we hit it off. He more or less invited me to the Hamptons."

"Well, well." She again drums her fingers on

the sofa. "The men always did go for you. But if you fool around with Malcolm, it'll have to be on the side. There'll be hell to pay if his wife finds out."

"He's married?" I say. This catches me unawares, and I hear my voice grow uncertain. "I thought he was . . ."

I hesitate, trying to find the words to express whatever it was I had thought earlier when I was flirting with Malcolm. "That is, I got the impression he was divorced from Tully's mother."

"Well, he is. No, wait. She died. Oh, I can't remember. All I know is, she's not here. And anyway, Malcolm's remarried several times since."

Amused, I suppose, at my ignorance regarding Malcolm's marital status, Charlotte laughs. "Margo, sweet Margo. Daddy's fave. Even in middle age, you've kept your girlish innocence. But let me tell you something, kid. When it comes to wealthy, powerful men, they're *all* married. Malcolm hires people to promote his films, but he pays those same people to keep his private life out of the media. He never had children of his own, so he's sensitive about matters concerning his ex-stepson. I don't know why, but he has a soft spot for Tully." She glances down at the floor, as though trying to envision one human being having a soft spot for another.

"Look," I say, "I'm sorry Georgia's gone

missing. I'm sorry if it's an emotional hardship for you or Malcolm or anybody at all. But I fail to see how it concerns me."

"Well, it does," she says. "It will. Let me circle back. First of all, did you know Georgia's hoping to cut a movie deal?"

"Really? As an actress?"

"No. Yes. Sort of." She spreads her hands. "What I mean is, her acting career didn't exactly gel, so she redesigned herself, widened her range with a completely new concept. She's become a total package!"

She beams with pride, as though having revealed some amazing fact about her daughter. High marks in school or a special award for community service. But I don't have a clue what she's getting at. What does she mean "total package"? Has Georgia been shipped off via UPS?

Charlotte gives a little shiver of delight. "Georgia's branched out into screenwriting!" she crows. "Donald and I are so happy, our bragability factor has gone through the roof. Even more amazing when you consider that for years her teachers kept telling me she was dyslexic." She pauses, letting this image sink into both our brains.

"Donald's representing Georgia's work," Charlotte says. "Or he will, when she completes her first script. Georgia's determined to write a huge hit, something targeted to her own demographic—teens and twenties. Obviously, with her looks there'll be a part for her as well. That's what I mean by total packaging."

I get the feeling I'm expected to comment favorably on all this. I do the best I can. "Sort of a female Ben Affleck?" I say.

She slaps her palm against the sofa. "Exactly! You may or may not know this, Margo, but Hollywood is desperate for product these days. Stories are . . ." She gestures vaguely.

"Hard to come by?" I say.

She shakes her head. "I was going to say superfluous. Nowadays, it's all marketing, names, computer graphics."

She gulps down wine, then adds, "Granted, you need a framework, something to hang it all on, a sort of, I don't know—"

"Plot?"

"You could call it that. But, oh, there's money to be made with the right concept and the right players, believe you me. Which is where you come in. This drama-queen behavior of Georgia's. Running away on her wedding day! I won't accept it. She's booked to marry Malcolm Belvedere's former stepson. Can you picture the doors that will open for her when she does that? For all of us?"

"But you already know Malcolm," I say. "I thought you've done five or six pictures with him."

"Knowing someone powerful," she says, "isn't like joining his family. Didn't you see the *Godfather* movies? *The Sopranos*? In the end, it's all about family. If Georgia marries Tully, our futures will be set."

Charlotte laughs as though she just remembered a joke. "Tully adores Georgia!" she says. "And she's so . . . fond of him. I'm only thinking of everyone's future happiness."

And, I imagine, future income.

"Minutes ago," Charlotte says, "I paid one of those trashy blonde bribesmaids—ha-ha—I mean, bridesmaids—to tell me where my daughter is. Lord, you should've seen this member of the wedding. It's her navel that's pierced, but the metal has obviously worked its way into her brain."

"Charlotte, I—"

"In exchange for a used Louis Vuitton travel bag, a discount coupon for Lasik eye surgery, and a voucher good for a two-night stay at the Beverly Hills Hotel, this little stalk of celery ratted out her good friend Georgia. She says Georgia flew to Palm Springs—though whether she's staying with friends or at a hotel, nobody knows. Well, it's a small enough burg, Georgia won't be hard to find. And Georgia won't have much money; she can't go far. So now, will you go after her?"

"I'm sorry, but I don't—"

"I'll pay you," she says flatly.

I give a sharp laugh. "Pay me? In what? Used luggage and hotel vouchers?"

"Cash. A lot of it."

Charlotte knows I need money, but this is too much. No, absolutely not. I will not be sucked in. I will not put myself in the employ of my half sister; I will not make myself the female counterpart to Juven. I'd rather leap from a runaway train; I'd rather disco dance in hell; I'd rather—

"How much?" I ask, surprising even myself with the question. "How much will you pay me?"

"Forty thousand dollars."

I gape at her, my reluctance to pursue Georgia brought to a screeching halt by the image of the number forty followed by three fat zeroes. But Charlotte misinterprets my hesitation. She thinks I want more money.

"Okay," she says, holding up her hands. "I don't have time to negotiate. Fifty thousand, plus expenses." She belts back more port. Then she picks up the nearly empty decanter and stares at it. It's crystal. Waterford or Baccarat. Like so many things in this house, it cost, I'm sure, a great deal.

"Fifty large isn't so bad," Charlotte muses as she fondles the decanter. "I spent nearly that much on the wedding dress. If you bring even that back, let alone Georgia, I'll get something out of my investment in you." She puts down the decanter.

"What if she refuses to see me?" I say.

"That won't happen." She pats my knee. "Georgia likes you. You're her favorite aunt."

"I'm her only aunt. And she hasn't laid eyes on me since that time when she was thirteen and the two of you visited New York for about fifteen minutes and we all had lunch at Le Cirque."

Charlotte laughs in a chilly sort of way. "She thinks you're fab. She loves the 'Brit accent' you do."

Okay, that was a *really* annoying remark, and I can't let it go by.

"This is my natural voice, Charlotte," I say. "It's not an affectation. I had to pick it up to fit in, to survive the pecking order in that wretched school I was sent to. I was so young when I got packed off to England, when I was . . . banished. After a while, talking like the other girls became a permanent part of me."

"All right," she says. "I hear you. Being sent overseas was hard for you, and I'm sorry about it. You probably suffered Post-Dramatic Stress Disorder. Excuse me, I mean Traumatic. But none of that was my fault."

"No, it wasn't." I hesitate, then I plunge in the knife. "It was your mother's."

"God, here we go!" Charlotte says. Discussion of Charlotte's mother has never been a pleasant topic between the two of us. "That was years ago," she says. "We were children. If you're going to start . . . well, you're just wasting time!"

"Wasting time?" I say. "If your mother had done the decent thing and divorced Daddy, *my* mother might still be alive today. My whole life would have turned out differently."

Silence.

I take out a cigarette and light it, not bothering to ask Charlotte if she minds. She is, after all, the person who gave me my first smoke, back when I was nine years old. I put the pack down on the table.

"Pall Malls!" she says. She picks up the pack and studies it. "I thought you kicked these years ago."

"Did," I say, taking a deep drag off my cigarette. "Started up again."

"When?"

I let out a curl of smoke. "Last year."

"Oh. You mean because . . ." She clears her throat. "But even so, it's incredibly unhealthy. It's practically illegal, isn't it?"

I don't answer. I tilt my head back and blow three perfect smoke rings. Something else she taught me to do.

Charlotte puts down the cigarette pack, gets up, and walks over to the globe. She positions herself there, spreading both hands over the Arctic

Ocean and patting the world with her fingertips, its cocaine-filled interior no doubt calling to her. Charlotte may have given up smoking, but she's retained other vices.

"All I'm asking you to do is find Georgia," she says. "Find her and talk to her. Talk to her kindly, sympathetically—then ask her what the hell she thinks she's doing!"

"What if I fail?" I say. "What if I get to Palm Springs and I can't find her or something goes wrong?"

"Half."

"Just for trying?"

"Yes."

"Plus expenses?"

"Yes."

I think about the money Charlotte's offering. It's really all I can think about. Fifty thousand dollars disappears surprisingly fast in Manhattan. But it would buy me time. I could pay my creditors. And I'd have a month or two of not worrying about my shop or what to do with it. There'd be time to sort out my life, time to have drinks with Dottie. My treat.

It's in thinking about the money, picturing what it would be like to have that much ready cash, that I feel myself tumble down the rabbit hole. Charlotte, standing there, watches me fall, wills me to fall.

I put down my glass of port. "Let's say I do this."

"You will, won't you?" she asks. She leans forward over the globe.

"Let's say I do. You know I don't fly, so the fastest way for me to get to Palm Springs is by automobile. Which means I'll need a car."

I watch Charlotte for her reaction to this statement. I'm worried she might challenge me on it. My driving record is a joke. Surely, my own half sister is aware of my reputation behind the wheel. She must know I no longer possess a valid driver's license. A minor detail, but some people take these things seriously.

"*Can* you loan me a car?" I press.

"Yes. You can use Daddy's." She looks away. She's embarrassed, I know. Though not about the car.

"I don't understand," I say. For the first time today, I'm genuinely taken aback. "You can't . . . you don't mean the MG?"

"I do," Charlotte says. "Ha-ha. Poor word choice again. I should have said, Yes, the MG is exactly the car I mean."

Toward the end of his life, our father drove a red sports car, a classic 1955 MG TF. But when I was ten and Charlotte fifteen, our dad died from a heart attack. Since my own mum had passed on two years earlier, I was officially an orphan. Charlotte's mother wanted nothing to do with the daughter of her dead husband's dead mistress. So she sent me to live with my great-aunt Fiona, in England.

Only Aunt Fiona and I did not get on. I was packed off again, this time to St. Verbian's School for Girls, just outside London. There I lived in miserable exile for the next eight years, a free-spirited California girl who picked up an English accent simply to survive. And there I lived a bleak, lonely existence like . . . like Cinderella or Jane Eyre or young Princess Diana stuck with Charles.

In the meantime, Charlotte and her mother, Irene, occupied the Malibu house. And all these years, I'd assumed the MG, like so many pieces of my childhood, was gone. I thought Irene had sold it. My shock is enormous. It's as if Charlotte were telling me she had a time machine.

"You have Daddy's car?" I say.

"Actually, it's mine now."

"Yes, understood. But, I mean . . . my God, his car. Does it run?"

"Certainly it runs. Do you think I expect you to push it to Palm Springs?" She inspects one of her plum-colored nails. "Mama hung on to all of Daddy's things after he died. Not because she loved him. She didn't. She kept everything out of plain old Catholic guilt. She honestly believed they'd meet in the afterlife, that he'd walk up to her in heaven or purgatory or some damn place and demand his golf clubs, a Tom Collins, and the car keys. Anyway, she always kept the car in perfect condition."

Perfect condition. I only wish someone had kept me in perfect condition. Still, the car, I'll get to drive Daddy's car!

But wait a minute. What am I getting myself into? What is it exactly I'm agreeing to? Putting aside the car, certain other practicalities come crashing down. "I don't have any cash," I say. "I'll need an advance or something."

Charlotte looks relieved to be off the subject of our father. She crosses to a writing desk and motions for me to come over. She picks up a leather handbag that's lying on the desk. Rootling round in the bag, she pulls out several impressive credit cards, including an American Express Black Card, and hands them to me.

She puts down the bag and reaches for her smartphone. "What's your cell phone number?"

"I haven't one," I say.

The frozen look on her face tells me how inadequate this response is. Putting down her phone, she leans across the desk and retrieves a tiny clamshell phone from its charger. "I keep this old one as a spare," she says. She hands me the phone and charger. "You never know when an emergency will turn up."

Or, I imagine, a clueless, cell phone–impoverished half sister.

I turn the phone over in my hands, examining it. "I've never liked these things," I say. "I know

I'm old-fashioned, but I've always avoided having one. And if you call when I'm driving, I won't answer. Driving and talking at the same time is not only illegal in many states but also dangerous. They've done studies."

Her mouth twitches. "Don't worry, you won't have to do that."

Something else occurs to me. "My bags—"

"I sent Juven for them," she says, not missing a beat. "He's getting the car out too."

I realize what the "other thing" was that she asked Juven to take care of earlier. It was the car. For me.

I look down at my dress. "I have to change," I say.

"There isn't time. You can do that when you stop for gas."

Always a flair for theatrics, my half sister. Fine, I think, remember I'm wearing *your* Donna Karan. See if you get it back.

Charlotte steps over to the French doors and opens them wide. The ocean air rushes in, filling the room with the scent of the sea. With a nod for me to join her, she passes through the doors and out onto the broad flagstone terrace. I drown my cigarette in my glass of port and follow her out into the sunlight.

It's there, as I'm standing on the terrace with Charlotte, that I look down and see it. Just like that, I see it. Looking past the terra-cotta planters and the marble balustrade, I catch sight of something so beautiful it takes my breath away.

Below us, parked on the circular drive, is my father's two-seater MG. Top down, candy-apple red, absolutely gorgeous. Rakish and wonderful, its wire wheels and chrome work gleam in the sun.

I haven't seen that car since I was ten years old. I forget that I'm broke and three thousand miles from home, that my half sister is a cocaine addict and my niece some sort of fugitive bride. Instead, I remember how our father looked at the wheel of his favorite automobile—elegant, laughing, full of life.

"Oh, Charlotte," I say. "It's beautiful. What fun it must be to own it."

"I wouldn't know," she says impatiently.

I turn to her, but she avoids my gaze.

"I mean," she says, "I never drive it. Even though Mama's been dead for years, the only reason I keep it is because she did. I have Juven take it in regularly for service."

She pulls at one of her diamond earrings. "You know, Margo, Daddy's car doesn't hold the same memories for me that it does for you. I see it, and I think, There's the little toy my father drove away in on all those bright sunny mornings— when he went to cheat on my mother."

Well, I think, *that's your version.* But this is no time to begin arguing again about our parents.

I'm about to descend the stone steps, when Charlotte touches my arm. "There's something else I want you to do. Georgia took things that belong to me. I want them back."

"You mean the wedding dress?" I say.

"That too. But besides the dress there are other things. Tell her I want my possessions returned immediately."

"What are these items?" I say.

"Doesn't matter, she knows." Charlotte's voice is controlled, but insistent. "Make it clear I'm not kidding around about this."

I sigh. "Tell me something, please. Are you sending me to Palm Springs to retrieve your daughter or your property?"

"The whole kid and caboodle. Ha-ha. I believe I mean kit and caboodle." She frowns. "What I mean is, for fifty grand, I expect it all." We start down the steps.

We're almost at the bottom of the stairs when a man—fortyish, pale, not terribly tall—comes hurrying round the side of the house. He's wearing an Armani tux and clutching a pair of suitcases.

Even in a tuxedo this fellow has the tweedy, self-absorbed look of the professional college student. The rumpled hair, eyeglasses, and befuddled gaze of an absentminded professor. He comes to an abrupt halt, apparently confused by . . . other people? Life? His own thoughts? His eyes dart round like a possum considering how best to cross the road.

I laugh at the sight of him. "Who's that?" I say.

"The groom," Charlotte says. "Tully Benedict. He's going with you."

I knew it! I *knew* Charlotte would play dirty.

"No!" I say. "I won't. I absolutely won't!"

"Yes, you will. Number one, because if you don't, I won't pay you. Number two, because Tully is your driver. And number three, because you and I both know, Little Mar, that you don't have a valid driver's license in the state of California, the continent of North America, or anywhere else in this godforsaken world."

We go on like this a minute or two, though I know it's pointless. Charlotte will have her way. When, at last, there's a break in our bickering, I glance back at the MG and get a shock. Despite the fact that no wedding has occurred, a group of drunken wedding guests are spraying shaving cream all over my father's car.

"Stop!" I cry. "Please, stop!"

Too late. Shaving cream hearts decorate the car's hood, pink rose petals dot the tan leather seats, and a bouquet of red and white balloons floats from the spare tire mounted at the rear. Vinyl clings on the car doors proclaim "Just

Married!" and "Love Machine!" The effect is oddly festive considering, when you think about it, that we're in the midst of calamity.

I decide *not* to think about it. Charlotte's sense of urgency is contagious. So is the temptation to earn fifty thousand dollars for what, presumably, will be a day's work. There's also the fact that I've consumed two double martinis, two glasses of port, and, all right, yes, the teensiest snort of cocaine when I had my head inside that globe in the library. So you could say I'm not altogether sober. Though I fear sobriety may come all too quickly.

I therefore have the impulse to leave immediately, certain that if I don't, God, or possibly Steven Spielberg—didn't I see him among the guests?—will direct the earth to open up and swallow the entire wedding party.

With Charlotte waving me on, I make my way to the car, open the passenger door, and get in. I have the distinct impression this is what it's like to suffer a near-death experience.

Tully Benedict gets in as well, on the driver's side. There's a hint of beard stubble on his face, which doesn't surprise me even though it's his wedding day. Already I can tell he's the sort of person who has to put up Post-it Notes to remind himself to shave.

Now that I see him up close, I note that Tully

has a kind, interesting face. The sort of face that, ordinarily, I would find intriguing. But at the moment, his expression is extremely . . . tense. Well, I expect he's upset. The poor man has just been jilted. He doesn't introduce himself or in any way acknowledge my presence, except to ask where the seat belts are.

"There aren't any," I say.

He frowns.

"This is a classic MG TF," I say, trying to be helpful. "Manufactured in 1955 and kept in its original condition."

The frown deepens.

Meanwhile, Juven has appeared and is strapping our luggage to the shiny metal rack suspended over the spare tire mount. He might as well be strapping Tully and me into twin electric chairs.

Juven finishes with the bags. Tully leans forward to turn the key in the ignition. I reach out to stop him.

"These old MGs are temperamental," I say, remembering every word my father ever said to me concerning his car. "Don't worry about the choke because Juven probably warmed up the engine. But you have to use the starter switch." I point to a small octagonal-shaped knob on the control panel. "This thingy here, with the *S* on it."

Tully stares at me like I'm raving mad. I blunder on. "First, you turn the ignition key. Clockwise, if I remember. Then pull out the starter switch.

The instant the engine turns over, release the starter. And you have to do all those things quite smoothly, I'm afraid, or you'll kill the engine."

Tully looks a bit like he wants to kill *me*. Nevertheless, somehow, he gets the car running. The sound of the engine idling causes people to turn their heads. A crush of wedding guests gathers round us, gawking. There's something aggressive in the way they surround the car, like wolves or killer bees. I'd be happy if we could get going now.

Tully releases the hand brake and slips the transmission into first gear. We lurch forward.

As we pull away, still in first gear, the crowd surges toward us. God knows who these people are. I've never met any of them. They're all fashionably dressed and brilliantly bejeweled, yet they're following us with outstretched arms, like characters from *Night of the Living Dead*.

They draw closer, waving at us, snapping photos, and touching the car as if we were movie stars at a premiere. They blow kisses and shower us with rice. "Good-bye!" they cheer. "Good luck!"

A wild-eyed young man steps forward. I recognize him as the star of one of those TV forensics shows. He's very handsome—in a plastic surgery–enhanced, Aryan kind of way—and very drunk. When he spies the vinyl cling on my side of the car, he jumps onto the running board next to me and pounds on the hood, shouting, "Love Machine, baby! LOVE MA-SHEEN!"

I push him off.

The TV actor isn't the only one who's inebriated. They all are. The entire bunch is under the influence. Simply for this—that these people have access to alcohol and, at the moment, I don't—I envy every one of them.

As we proceed slowly through the crowd and round the circular drive, I glance up at the top of the house. The sun is in my eyes, but if I squint, I can just make out a tall man standing at one of the balconies. He's smoking a cigar and looking down at the crush of people. Malcolm Belvedere?

Yes, I think so. He's watching us.

Well, what of it? No time to dream about oysters on the half shell and romantic beach cottages in the Hamptons. No time to reflect on the disappointment I felt when Charlotte told me Malcolm was married.

So Tully and I drive off in the Love Machine— I in the strapless Donna Karan, he in the Armani tux—looking for all the world like the honeymoon couple. Only we are hopelessly mismatched, and any fool can see the honeymoon is over.

CHAPTER THREE

TERRA INCOGNITA

We pull away from the house and head down the long private lane. At the bottom of the drive, Tully pushes in the clutch, checks the traffic, and then—gears grinding a tad loudly—merges onto the Pacific Coast Highway. We travel south along the narrow, twisty road, the ocean to one side of us, rolling hills on the other. It's early spring. There's not a cloud in the sky, and you can smell the sea. It's a perfect day for riding in a convertible. That is, it *would* be perfect. I mean, you know, under other circumstances.

At one point, when I look over the side of the car, I get a jolt. The edge of a cliff is only a few feet away, and the ocean—white waves breaking against jagged rocks—is far below us. When you're riding like we are, in a low-slung English sports car, the cliff seems even closer.

If I had a seat belt, I would tighten it. Instead, I hunker down and grip the chrome passenger bar in front of me.

To pass the time, I begin making a mental list of all the people I'm annoyed with. Angry at myself, first of all, for getting caught up in this scheme of Charlotte's, even if I do stand to make a large sum of money. Annoyed with Charlotte, just because I usually am. Cheesed off with young Georgia for running away. Irritated with Malcolm Belvedere for . . . for what? Flirting so attractively, I suppose, when it turns out he's a married man.

The only person I'm not cross with is Tully Benedict. I feel sorry for him. Despite his full head of hair and college-boy manner, he must be twenty years older than Georgia. Old enough to know better, though evidently not old enough to *do* better.

Tully holds tight to the steering wheel. I glance at some brown dots on the back of his right hand. Are those freckles . . . or age spots? Perhaps twenty-five years older than Georgia is more like it.

What kind of person is Tully Benedict? He has just been jilted. His bride-to-be has fled. She might as well have put up a billboard on Sunset Boulevard declaring, "Tully has cooties!"

Yet here he is, chasing after her. So am I, come to think of it, but at least I'm getting paid. Poor Tully. What does he imagine he'll do when he finds Georgia? Go down on one knee and beg her to come back? How sad.

Of course it's true, as Charlotte said, that I ran away on my own wedding day. I jilted my fiancé, Finn Coyle. But that was over thirty years ago, and the situation could not have been more different. Still, if Finn had come after me, even in a pretty little sports car, I would not have gone back to him, I would not have married him. Never. No matter how much I adored him.

We follow the highway south to Santa Monica, where I expect Tully to get on the Santa Monica Freeway. He doesn't. He avoids the freeway entirely. He goes east on Santa Monica Boulevard, ultimately steering us through the mansion-lined streets of Beverly Hills and over to West Hollywood.

I can only assume that Tully is uncomfortable at the thought of taking a very old, very small car—with which he is unfamiliar and which has no seat belts—onto a superhighway. The MG could easily do sixty miles an hour or more, but plunging this roller skate, this 1950s relic, into the modern world of tractor-trailers and sport-utility vehicles does seem . . . chancy. Perhaps, along with the credit cards and cell phone, I should have asked Charlotte for the loan of a crash helmet.

When Charlotte said she had our father's car, I thought, *It's as if she's telling me she has a time machine.* And that wasn't so far off. Because it looks like Tully intends on driving the slower-paced back roads that existed long before there ever were freeways, all the way from Los Angeles to Palm Springs.

Fine. We are in an old car, we will follow the old roads. Although the other side of the coin is that Palm Springs is roughly one hundred miles east of Los Angeles. Taking the back roads will make our journey that much longer.

After a while, we leave Los Angeles behind completely. We're heading away from the coast now, inland toward the desert. A brown-and-cream-colored sign announces we're on Historic Route 66. More time travel? Yes. Because despite the modern mania for freeways, parts of the legendary two-lane blacktop known as Route 66 still exist. The most famous road in America has not disappeared. Not all of it, anyway.

That old song "(Get Your Kicks on) Route 66" comes into my head. "It winds from Chicago to L.A." Although Tully and I are going east, not west. We're traveling in the opposite direction from what's described in the song. And thank goodness we're not going all the way to Chicago; thank goodness we're headed only to Palm Springs.

We cruise through one town after another. Once, these were nothing more than villages surrounded by orange groves. Now they're more grown-up. All the same, gliding down Route 66 you get glimpses of what life was like fifty or sixty years ago in Southern California. White stucco motor courts bake in the sun. Mom-and-pop grocery stores hawk cigarettes and cold beer. A fruit stand in the shape of a giant orange peddles fresh-squeezed juice.

I can't get that song out of my mind. "Get your kicks, on Route 66." Oh yes, I think, shifting in my seat to get comfortable, I'm really getting my kicks now.

The hardest thing is that I'm nearly sober. The glow I felt from the alcohol I knocked back earlier in the day is gone. I sneak a look at Tully whom, I realize, I don't know at all. That unruly hair, that distant gaze. Serious suitor—or serial killer? Oh, what have I gotten myself into?

An hour after leaving Malibu, Tully and I haven't spoken a word. It's the shock, I suppose. Neither one of us feels chatty. But what do people think when they see us speed past them in the MG? Tully in his tux, me in Charlotte's Donna Karan, the words "Just Married!" and "Love Machine!" emblazoned on our car.

Well, it's obvious, isn't it? Every motorist, every truck driver, every hog farmer we pass assumes we're newlyweds. Cars traveling in the opposite direction honk when they go by, their occupants smiling at us and waving enthusiastically. You can't really blame them, what with the decorations and the balloons tied to the spare tire. The balloons! I forgot about the balloons. I turn round and see them bouncing along behind us in the breeze. Why don't they burst? They must be made of some miracle new-millennium material. In the event we're rear-ended, I hope they'll function as miniature air bags.

Balloons or no balloons, a 1955 MG TF will always command attention. I remember my father telling me that the first TF was made in England in 1953. The car was in production only until 1955, and many people think it's the prettiest vehicle MG ever built. I could share this trivia with Tully, but somehow I don't think he's in the mood to hear anything about British motorcars or my family.

Route 66 does not go all the way to Palm Springs (it veers north), so we eventually cut over to a two-lane state road. We drive on, deeper into the desert. I'm dying for a drink: gin, brandy, eau de cologne, anything. But we left Malibu so fast, I didn't have time to pack even a thimbleful of spirits.

Finally, from out of nowhere, Tully speaks. "You know about this blue light?"

I jump at the sound of his voice. "Sorry?"

"This light." He taps at a tiny blue glow on the instrument panel. "It came on. Do you know what it means?"

How should I know what the light means? I've been lost in my own thoughts and now Tully's asking about a blue light. I haven't a clue what the blue light indicates. I don't—oh, wait. Oh! OH! The blue light!

"It means we're low on gasoline," I tell him. "It means we'd better get fuel as soon as we can." I scan the horizon for a station.

"I wondered about that," Tully says. "I noticed there wasn't a gas gauge. This is some buggy."

Several anxious minutes go by during which we pass little except sand and sagebrush. Then Tully cranes his neck and declares, "Here we go." He nods at a ramshackle service station up ahead that looks like it probably hasn't changed in half a century. When we reach the station, Tully turns in and eases the car up to an aged pump. He shuts down the engine and everything becomes very quiet.

The station is small and dusty, with a little house set at the back. Off to one side are a sun-bleached picnic table and a rusty swing set, both presumably put there long ago for hungry travelers and their fidgety children. The elderly station owner shuffles out and asks Tully if we want gas.

While Tully and the owner are talking, I step from the car and go to the luggage rack at the rear of the car. The sun is bright, and there's a scent of sage in the air. Battling aside the balloons, I yank one of my cases off the rack. I'm carrying my case to the ladies' room when I nearly collide with a tiny old woman coming round the corner of the station, toting a basket of laundry. The owner's wife, I imagine. She smiles up at me.

"Honeymooners?" she asks, a bit out of breath.

"Pardon?" I say.

She puts down the basket, wipes her brow, and inclines her head toward the MG. "Off on your honeymoon?"

I take in the car—the shaving cream, the "Love Machine" and "Just Married!" clings, the bouquet of wedding balloons—and realize what she's getting at.

"No, no," I say. "It's a mistake."

"Can't say that, hon. Too soon to tell."

"No, no! I mean, we're not husband and wife."

"Maybe don't feel like it yet," she says. She nudges me with her elbow. "But just you wait."

"But I . . . I don't want to wait."

She giggles. "In a hurry for him?"

"Certainly not!"

"Oh, hon. First-night jitters?"

"No! Sorry, but you don't understand. No one on this entire highway understands!"

At that moment, a pickup truck comes roaring down the road. Several young men in blue jeans and cowboy hats stand braced in the back of the truck, holding tight to the roof of the cab. The instant they spot the Love Machine they break into a chorus of hooting, coupled with some highly imaginative sexual pantomime. "Whoo-hoo!" howls a repulsive teenaged boy, waving his hat in the air. "Good lovin' too-nite!"

The old woman clucks her tongue at the pickup as it speeds away, dust in its wake. "Nobody understands," she says. "That's how I felt when I got hitched. I expect you miss your ma. That it, hon?"

This is hopeless. She's never going to get it.

"No," I say. "The problem is . . ." She doesn't seem to twig to the fact that I'm not exactly a blushing bride, that I'm old enough to be a mother myself.

"The problem is . . ." I repeat. Oh, what's the use? I drop my case and throw up my hands. "I can't take it anymore! I want a divorce! The minute we get to Palm Springs, it's over! Finished!"

"Hon, why? What's wrong?"

"He's seeing another woman," I say. "A teen-ager!"

Her mouth drops open in horror.

"It gets worse," I say. "She's my niece!"

The woman gapes at Tully, who's standing next to the car, casually stretching while the old man checks the tire pressure. "But he looks so sweet," she says. "Like a teddy bear with glasses."

I jut out my chin and sniff. "He's a complete stranger. And I'm quite sure he *never* loved me."

She clutches at her chest. "Surely—"

"Never. Not the entire time I've known him."

"But—"

"Nevermore."

"Oh, hon! What a misery!" She takes my hand and pats it. "My ma always said it's the bookish ones who go tomcatting. Well, get what you can from him. Ask the judge for that little car—it'll come in handy when you go hunting for a new beau."

The old woman snatches up her basket of laundry and trundles off in the direction of a frayed and sagging clothesline.

I pick up my case, cart it over to the restroom, and pull open the heavy metal door. I step inside, letting the door clang shut behind me. The room reeks of disinfectant and cheap air freshener, but the thick concrete walls make it cool and silent. Mercifully, I'm alone.

I stand there, resting my back against the door. Well, I think, I'm nearer Palm Springs than I was two hours ago. That's something. And if all goes well in finding Georgia, I'll soon be fifty thousand dollars to the better.

I put my case down on the cracked cement floor. I go into the stall and pee. After I come out, I bend over the rust-stained basin, wash my hands and face, and dry off with a paper towel. Then I take a look at myself in the mirror.

I have my father's eyes and my mother's full mouth and good skin. My hair remains light brown, without a touch of gray, because there are these marvelous chemicals you can buy that keep it your natural color in perpetuity. Short of a plot at Forest Lawn, it's the closest thing to eternal care I can think of.

Like my mother, I wear my hair short and use a minimum of makeup, though I'm never without my lipstick. I believe in God and fair play, and I like old movies and old things.

I'm fifty—

Well, around fifty years old. In my youth, I was considered quite pretty. Nowadays, I'm happy if someone refers to me as handsome.

I open my makeup kit and take out a bottle of C'est la Guerre anti-aging serum. Anti-aging serum. What is that, precisely? They make it sound like life-giving fluid delivered in a blizzard by Balto the sled dog. "You've got to get this through, Balto, old boy. Millions of women are depending on you. If they don't get this serum by nightfall, they'll *age*."

The stuff sells for three hundred and fifty dollars per quarter ounce. My friend Dottie swears by it, but I can't afford it, so I nicked this particular bottle off Charlotte's dressing table earlier in the day, about the same time I lifted the Donna Karan. Ordinarily, I'm neither a thief nor a kleptomaniac, but something about my relationship with my half sister compels me to help myself to her possessions.

I read the directions on the label: "Apply daily to fine lines around eyes, mouth, and chin. Reversal should be apparent in three to four weeks."

Fair enough. Though what you really want to do is pour gallons of the stuff into the bathtub and soak in it. More to the point, if there's truly such a thing as an anti-aging serum, why can't they discover a way for a woman my age to apply it directly to those areas where she needs it most—like her brain or her liver?

Resisting the urge to dump the entire bottle on my head, I put a dollop on my fingertips and rub it over my face. This I follow with a light application of liquid foundation containing a SPF of, roughly, 450.

Then I take off the Donna Karan. I fold the dress carefully and place it in my case.

I pull on a pair of black capri pants, a white cotton shell, and a matching lightweight cardigan, complemented with a darling pair of brand-new Ferragamo flats (Charlotte's, but I swear they were the last thing I pinched).

I brush my hair, fix my lipstick, and throw a royal-blue chiffon scarf round my head and tie it under my chin. I take out a pair of wraparound tortoiseshell sunglasses and put those on too. I fancy I look a bit like young Audrey Hepburn in *Breakfast at Tiffany's*, but the effect is probably more middle-aged, sex-crazed Ava Gardner in *Night of the Iguana*.

I push open the restroom door and step out into the sunlight.

The old woman stands there. She appears to have been waiting for me.

"Hon," she says, "I been thinking. You gotta give your man another chance. Try and patch things up."

She thrusts a faded book at me. It's a vintage marriage manual, easily fifty or sixty years old. The title is *Starting Your New Life Together—A Modern Guide for Modern Newlyweds*.

"That book helped me considerable," the old woman says. "And excuse me being forward, but makin' whoopee can be a high old time. I know. Had six kids."

Don't even try to set her straight, I think. I choke out a thank-you.

The old woman moves slowly away. I stuff the marriage manual into my case.

Tully has pulled the car off to one side of the station. It's dripping wet. The vinyl clings and shaving cream are gone, and Tully's using a rag to shine up bits of the chrome.

"After the guy filled the tank," Tully says when I come up to him, "I asked him to hose off all that junk."

"Where are the balloons?" I say, peering over my sunglasses.

He points behind me. I turn and see a curly-haired little girl, about five years old, standing by the swing set. She's holding the bouquet of red and white balloons.

I laugh. "She looks as though she might float away."

Tully doesn't say anything. I'm aware that he's changed out of his wedding clothes into jeans and a short-sleeved shirt. For the first time, I see his bare arms. His biceps are surprisingly firm.

But where's that tuxedo he was wearing? The one he hoped to be married in. Did he toss it into the garbage can in the men's room? Or did he fold it up and put it in his suitcase—the same way I'm saving Charlotte's Donna Karan for some future occasion. Could it be, even now, that Tully hopes for a second chance at walking up the aisle with Georgia?

For Tully's sake, I hope he threw the tuxedo away. But his chapfallen expression and sloping shoulders tell me it's more likely tucked away in his case.

Oh dear. Oh damn. Poor Tully. Perhaps he really can't stop himself from chasing after Georgia. Perhaps love has caught him in its net.

CHAPTER FOUR

CARY GRANT AND ICE-CREAM

There's a hamburger stand across the road. Not a modern-day franchise, just an old shack with a tin roof.

Tully's eyes flick across the highway. "Food," he says, like some sort of caveman. "You want anything?"

What I'd like is a glass of gin. But we're in the desert in more ways than one. "No, thanks," I say. "I'm fine." Only I'm not. I'm considering lying down in the dirt, kicking my feet, and crying like an infant. To relieve the tension.

"Suit yourself," Tully says, as though agreeing with my thoughts on throwing a tantrum. He looks both ways for traffic (there isn't any), then strolls across the blacktop.

Alone now, I strap my case to the luggage rack and climb back into the car. The minute I sit down, the cell phone rings. I fish it out of my leather tote bag.

"Where are you?" demands a woman's voice. Charlotte.

"I'm in the car," I say, leaning back in my seat

and gazing up at the blue, cloudless sky. "I'll remain in the car until we get to Palm Springs. Then I shall exit the car."

"Have you located your quarry?"

"Just a moment," I say. "I'll look."

I hold the phone to my chest. The curly-haired little girl is at the picnic table, still clutching the balloons Tully gave her. While her mother lays out food on the table, the child ties the balloons to a baby carrier containing an infant swaddled in pink. The baby sister, I presume. The curly-haired girl stands back, waiting for her sister to float off into space. The carrier doesn't budge.

"Rotten luck!" I call to her. In a gesture that reminds me of Charlotte in younger days, the girl folds her arms and sticks out her tongue at me.

I return the phone to my ear. "I looked, but Georgia isn't here," I say. "Perhaps that's because she's in Palm Springs."

"Contact me as soon as you have any data," Charlotte says. "Let me know when you achieve your objective."

Is there some reason she's talking like a CIA operative? I can't imagine. Then it hits me that Charlotte's paranoid. She probably thinks the tabloids have hacked her phone.

"I'll do that," I say. "I'll be sure and telephone you when I locate Miss Georgia Illworth, the nineteen-year-old runaway daughter of film producer Charlotte Illworth, of the wealthy and important Illworth family, key players in the Hollywood film industry, who reside in an oceanfront mansion high in the hills of Malibu, California, at—"

She hangs up.

I put the phone in my bag. My long legs are cramped from sitting. Without thinking, I reach down and feel for the adjustment lever at the front corner of the seat. There it is. I press the lever to release the catch, and slide the seat back so I can stretch out my legs.

How long has it been since I did that? I remember my father helping me adjust the seat when I was a child. Only in those days, we were sliding it forward. A dozen memories come to me. Of the car, of my father and mother.

My father was the screenwriter Arthur Just. You may have seen his name on a few old black-and-white films from the 1940s and '50s, although he started out in New York, working as a very young assistant to Orson Welles. Early in our friendship, I mentioned this family history to Dottie. "Really, darling?" she said. "*The* Orson Welles? What was he like?"

"A whirlwind," I told her. "That's what my dad said. But he also said Welles was a genius, that nobody else had his talent or zest for life."

In 1940, Welles went to Hollywood to direct

his classic film, *Citizen Kane*. My father and his wife, Irene, came west a few years later, and my father began writing for the movies. He and Welles talked about doing a project together, but nothing ever came of it.

For many years, I've put a lot of energy into *not* thinking about my parents. Into not thinking about how, due to the death of my mother when I was eight and, two years later, the death of my father, my childhood came to an abrupt and heartbreaking end. Now, I sit in my father's car, flooded with memories. And when I reflect on all that I have lost, a lump rises in my throat and settles there.

I look up to see Tully bending over the driver's side, clutching two ice-cream cones. "Got you something," he says. He holds out a cone.

I can't help myself. Tully's offer of ice-cream triggers a memory so sharp that tears well up inside me and push their way out, like people fighting for the exit during a real-estate time-share presentation.

"Oh jeez," Tully says. He gazes at the cone as though it were a wilted flower. "Did you want a hot dog?"

I shake my head, I can't speak.

"Don't English ladies like ice-cream?"

In spite of myself, I laugh. "I haven't lived in England for years," I say, wiping a tear from my cheek. "And I am *not* a lady. I'm just having a rotten day."

"Yeah? Me too." He slings a leg over the car door and drops down in the driver's seat, still holding the cones.

"Sorry," I say, sniffing back tears. "Obviously, your day has been far more wretched than mine."

"It's not a contest," Tully says. He licks one of the cones. "Okay, sure, I'm bummed about what happened, but I'm not so emo as to fall apart over an ice-cream cone."

"It's not only the ice-cream," I say. "It's . . . other things." I touch the dashboard. "This car belonged to my father."

"Did he used to take you for ice-cream in it?"

"Never." I sniff. "He was allergic to dairy. But he bought this vehicle used—it was already something of a classic—when I was seven. He was working again, after a long dry spell. One day, when he'd had the car a few weeks, Cary Grant dropped by—"

"The movie star?"

"The movie star. Mr. Grant came by, and Daddy said he could take the car for a spin if he wanted. So Mr. Grant—"

Tully stops eating his ice-cream cone. "Cary Grant drove this car?" he says.

"Yes, he sat right where you're sitting."

Tully takes that in and then glances at the second ice-cream cone he's holding, the one he bought for me. "Won't you please take this before it melts all over the ghost of Cary Grant?"

I accept a paper napkin and the cone, licking the rivulets dripping down its side. After I get the ice-cream under control, I say, "Mr. Grant was very athletic. He was older, had already stopped making movies, but even so he vaulted over the car door and got behind the wheel. This was at our house in Santa Monica, and—"

"I thought your family lived in Malibu," Tully says.

God, where to begin?

"My father owned the Malibu house, yes," I say. "His wife lived there. So did their daughter, Charlotte—your intended mother-in-law."

"Yeah, but—"

"My father never married my mother, all right? Daddy's *wife,* Irene—Charlotte's mother—was . . . well, she was Catholic, among other things. She was also not a nice person, not a kind person. In any event, she and my father didn't get along. When he was fortysomething, my dad fell in love with a twenty-three-year-old English actress. She brought grace into his life. She also rather quickly got pregnant with me. But Irene refused to give my dad a divorce. I think, legally, maybe he could have gotten one, but it was about so much more than legalities. So Daddy wound up keeping two homes: one in Malibu with Irene and Charlotte, the other in Santa Monica with my mum and me. And that's what I called her, by the way—Mum. She liked me to call her that. She was from England."

"Your father kept two households at the same time?" Tully says.

"Yes."

"Very Continental of him. Must have been pricey."

"It was."

"Was he rich?"

"Not really, he was a writer. Screenplays. He made excellent money in the 1940s, before I was born, hence, the Malibu house. But by the time I came along, he'd been through the Red Scare, the blacklist, all of it, and his career had suffered. He ended up writing for television, which he hated, just to pay the bills. When he bought this car, he was writing for television."

Tully has draped himself sideways in the driver's seat, his back resting against the car door. He munches his ice-cream cone, eyeing me over the top of it. "What about your mom? Is she still alive?"

"She drowned in the ocean when I was eight."

"Oh jeez, I'm sorry," Tully says. "I didn't . . . you mean . . . like an accident?"

I shrug. "She was unhappy. She wanted to be married. She wanted to work again—she sometimes played small parts in films. She adored my father, but so many things had worn

74

her down. I think one day Mum made up her mind to go for a swim and . . ." I'm going to start crying again, I know it.

"Anyway," I say, backing off the topic of my mother. "Cary Grant. So there I was on the lawn in Santa Monica, watching my father and Mr. Grant. When Mr. Grant got in the car, he noticed me standing there. He winked and said, 'Hiya, kid.' Then he asked my father if I could come along and go get ice-cream. My dad laughed and said sure, and lifted me up and plunked me down in this very seat. And I, seven-year-old Margo Anna-Louise Just, drove off in a red convertible with Cary Grant."

"And he molested you?"

"Certainly not! Absolutely, unequivocally no!" I wave my ice-cream so hard, the top scoop goes soaring off into the desert. "In those days, only Joan Crawford was gaining a reputation for child abuse. Mr. Grant was a wonderful man. He loved children. I always understood he wanted a large family, but that didn't happen for him."

"He was gay," Tully says.

"No, he wasn't."

"Gay," Tully repeats. "It's like an open secret. He was at least bisexual."

"If you mean those old photos everyone's always going on about—the ones with Randolph Scott—that could have been a one-off. Anyway, Mr. Grant's sexual orientation is beside the point."

"You think?" Tully says. "Then what is the point?" He tongues what's left of his ice-cream into a curving white peak.

"The point—and I don't necessarily expect you to get this, but give it a go—the point is, don't you see how an adventure like that could imprint on a little girl's brain? How driving off at the age of seven in a red MG driven by Cary Grant would be difficult to top in later years? You don't get over it; no woman could. To some extent, it's influenced everything I've ever done. Millions of women melted from just seeing him on the screen, and I . . . I rode with him in a convertible. And that's why I cried when you brought me ice-cream. Because once—when my parents were alive and I was young and happy—I sat in this very car and was offered ice-cream by—"

"The greatest male star in the history of American motion pictures."

"Precisely. Thank you for understanding that."

I lick my cone. Tully watches me. His eyes are a deep, compelling brown, a bit crinkly at the corners. In his rumpled way, he's rather nice-looking. I suddenly feel protective toward him. "Look," I say, "I'm sorry about just now, becoming emotional. I'm not always so sentimental, but recently I've been going through—"

"Menopause," Tully says, with the same know-it-all tone he used in outing Cary Grant.

I lift an eyebrow. "No," I say slowly, "as a matter of fact, my medical practitioner tells me I have a few more years to go in that department."

I'm still working on my ice-cream cone when Tully finishes his. He wipes his fingers on a paper napkin, then twists round so he's sitting properly in his seat. He starts up the car. We get back on the road, once again feel the wind in our faces.

"Go on," Tully says, raising his voice so I can hear him over the hum of the MG's engine. "What happened with Cary Grant?"

I decide to let Tully's menopause remark go by. After all, he's having a rough day. And he and I share the common goal of tracking down Georgia. When we do find her, and I get my fifty thousand dollars, perhaps Tully and Georgia really will make up; perhaps they really will get married. That would make him my . . . what? My nephew-in-law. There's no reason why we shouldn't be chums. There's no reason I shouldn't tell him my Cary Grant story.

"We went for a drive by the ocean," I say. "After a while, Mr. Grant pulled up to a place like that one back there." I point behind us, at the hamburger stand we left down the road. "He bought me ice-cream, yes. But it was more than that. He gave me the gift of himself, his time and attention. He was charming, completely focused on me—a little girl—and the moment. It was like spending the day with a handsome, debonair Santa Claus. He taught me that day how to take a compliment. He said—in that delightful, clipped way of his—'Whenever someone says you're pretty, Margo, or that's a nice frock, always smile and say thank you.' He told me I should remember that because I'd get a great many compliments in life. He asked me about my friends and if I liked school, and he said I'd grow up to be very beautiful, like my mother."

"And you did," Tully says.

Oh, that was sweet. I smile, the way Cary Grant taught me. "Thank you," I say.

"I was seven years old," I continue, "and it was the first time I'd ever considered what I looked like. Mr. Grant was the first man who ever made me feel pretty. When he took me home and returned me to my father, something about my life had changed. For the next three years, until I went away to England, I never missed seeing a Cary Grant movie whenever they showed one on television. I'd fallen in love with Cary Grant, or at least the idea of him. Watching those old movies—dreaming over his style, his wit, his sophistication—just made it worse."

"Must have set the bar kind of high for guys you met later on."

"You have no idea."

"Do you work in the industry?" Tully says.

"Films?" I shake my head. "When I was younger, I did some modeling. Now I own a shop in New York."

Tully momentarily switches his gaze from the road to me. "Manhattan?" he says. "We're neighbors. I grew up in Los Angeles, but nowadays I live in Brooklyn. What kind of shop?"

"Architectural salvage," I say. With my free hand, I retrieve a card from my bag and offer it to him.

Tully takes the card and glances down at it. He reads aloud: "Manhattan Architectural Salvage. We Pick Up the Pieces." He laughs, but he doesn't sound all that amused.

"If ever you want a chunk of old Pennsylvania Station," I say, thinking of Dottie and wishing she were here, "I can fix you up."

"You have some of that?" Tully says. He hands back the card.

"Yes. But do you even know what it is?"

"Sure." A jackrabbit shoots across the road. Tully downshifts to avoid hitting it.

"Penn Station is legendary," Tully says. "They tore it down in the 1960s, even though lots of people felt it was important. Felt it should be saved. But it wasn't."

After he says this, I find myself warming even more toward Tully. Few people these days remember Penn Station, which was located in midtown Manhattan and was one of the most beautiful Beaux Arts structures of the early 1900s.

"I know something about architecture," Tully says. "And I have to tell you, I don't care for your line of work."

A chill shoots through my body, but it isn't from eating ice-cream.

"'Architectural salvage' is an oxymoron, okay?" Tully says. "It's ghoulish, gives me the creeps. You salvage people don't do anything at all to preserve history. You stand around, hands in your pockets, while they knock down some great old landmark. Then you rush in with price tags and a wheelbarrow."

My ice-cream is nearly gone. I crunch down hard on the cone.

"You carve up these incredible old places and sell the body parts to whoever has the dough," Tully says. "And they always end up in somebody's stupid McMansion or in the boardroom of some big law firm. That's not salvage. It's sacrilege." He glances at me as though I've just been revealed as a torturer of small furry animals.

"It's slightly more complicated than that," I say.

"Yeah?" Tully says. The car picks up speed. "How'd you get into that business?"

"Long story," I say, determined not to tell it. Who is this person with the five o'clock shadow, plonked down in my father's car? Why should I explain my life to him?

"So tell me," I say, "while I'm looting America's treasures, how do you occupy your time?"

"I'm a writer."

A light goes on, and I picture both Malcolm Belvedere and Charlotte's husband, Donald, who works with scriptwriters. "Screenplays?" I say. "You write for the movies?"

"I'm writing a book," Tully says. "That's how I met Georgia. I came out here to do research, and we met at a party."

"What's your book about?"

"Miniatures. Dollhouses and things."

I laugh. *Dollhouses?"*

"Yeah," Tully says defensively. "Something wrong with that?"

"You have to admit," I say, "it's an unlikely subject for a grown man to take an interest in."

"Not for me it isn't," Tully says. "It's a collection of interviews and essays, with some history thrown in."

The topic seems silly to me. I can't keep amusement out of my voice. "I didn't realize there was any history to dollhouses," I say.

"No?" Tully says. "Then read my book when it comes out. That is, if you can read."

Is Tully taking his anger at Georgia out on me? Well, look out—because I have anger of my own.

"Oh, I can read," I say slowly. "The question is, can you write?"

"Forget it," Tully says. We bounce over a pothole. "It's obvious you're clueless about dollhouses—just like you're clueless about architectural salvage and clueless about Cary Grant."

I no longer care if Tully's having a rough day.

"And you," I say, "know nothing about architectural salvage, nothing about Cary Grant, and nothing about me."

He glances over at me. His eyes are blazing. "Your name's Margo, right?"

"Correct."

"Well, maybe you don't live in England anymore, Margo, but you're sure an uptight Brit."

I toss what's left of my ice-cream cone out into the desert. "Stop the car," I say.

"What?" Tully says.

"Stop the car." I claw at my scarf, ripping it from my head. "I need air."

"We're in a convertible," Tully says.

"I'm suffocating," I say. "I can't breathe. I need a cigarette."

Tully swings us to the side of the road and brings the car to a sudden, squealing stop. Our bodies rock backward, then forward. We sit there, in the middle of nowhere, engine idling.

I fumble for the handle and push the door open. I swing my legs out onto the ground and stand up.

"Aw, come on," Tully says. He pushes his

glasses back up on his nose. "We've got to keep going. I didn't mean—"

I hold up my hand. "I know we need to keep going," I say. "But right now I need air, I need a smoke, and I need a few minutes alone." I'd also like a drink, but forget that. I reach back into the car for my tote bag, which contains my cigarettes.

Tully switches off the engine. When I grab for my bag, he puts his hand on my arm. "Margo, don't go. Stay here and I'll . . . open a window."

"Ha-ha," I say, pulling away from him. I turn and walk away.

"Why do women run from me?" he calls. He gives a bitter laugh. He's laughing at himself, I know, not at me. Laughing even though there's nothing funny about being dumped on your wedding day, nothing funny about sitting alone in a bright-red Love Machine on a deserted highway in the California desert.

I walk off toward a cluster of rocks. One large rock, bigger than the rest, has a scooped-out area, almost like a seat, and I rest against it. The stone is gritty and warm from the sun. I reach into my bag for my cigarettes and lighter, but my fingers brush Charlotte's cell phone. I stop. I forego the tobacco. I pull out the cell phone instead.

I punch in the number of Dottie's shop in

New York. The phone rings twice, then Dottie answers. "Older Than Sin, French Art Deco and Collectibles."

"It's me. I've been kidnapped."

"Margo! I've been thinking about you. How was the wedding?"

"There wasn't one. I've ended up honey-mooning with the groom."

She laughs. "Right. Really, how are things?"

"I will tell you. Georgia jilted her fiancé and fled to Palm Springs. Charlotte hired me to go after her. So now I'm riding around in my father's 1955 MG. Actually, the car part is nice. Oh, and the bridegroom is my chauffeur."

There's a moment's silence. "*Chérie*," Dottie says at last, "you aren't by any chance on a bender?"

"I wish. More like I'm being held sober against my will."

"*Merde.*"

"Exactly," I say.

"Merde," she repeats. "Darling, I'm sorry, but we're about to be interrupted. There's a young couple looking in the window. Bags of money, if I'm not mistaken."

"Why bother?" I say. "Young people are all broke now."

"Not the ones who own start-ups," Dottie says.

Dottie is a wizard at discerning disposable income. I imagine her straining to look out the window, giving the young couple the once-over. "Yes," she says, "these two are cash cows, coming into my barn. Can you hold?"

I hold. Dottie puts the handset on the counter, and I hear her talking with the customers. From the sound of their voices, I don't need to see them to know what they look like or where they're from. Seattle, probably. I picture the corduroy pants, the cotton turtlenecks.

"Well," the man says, "our accountants say we better start a collection."

"Something world-class," the woman says. "Paul Allen already did rock and roll. That's antique and all, but we want to do something really, really *old*."

"I see," Dottie says. "Of course, this establishment specializes in French Art Deco of the early twentieth century. Did you have a specific period in mind?"

"We like the chocolate period."

"The . . . chocolate period?"

"Fancy stuff. Princes and princesses."

"The *fancy* chocolate period. No plain vanilla for you." By the strain in Dottie's voice, I imagine the wheels turning in her head. "You don't by any chance mean . . . no, you couldn't. You don't mean, rococo?"

"That's it, row cocoa."

I can almost feel the air rushing out of the room. Then I hear Dottie's voice again, deflated:

"Other side of the street, half a block down. Good day."

There's the sound of the shop door opening and closing, then Dottie is back on the line. "Did you hear that, darling?"

"I did," I say. "I've told you before. The television screens are getting larger, but the heads are getting smaller."

"Yes, but I'll have my revenge. I sent them to Starbucks. Anyway, we're alone now. Tell me about your niece's fiancé. Do you like him?"

"Not particularly." I slump against my boulder. "His name is Tully, and I wish he'd fall out of the car."

"And why is that?"

"He has a chip on his shoulder."

"That's understandable, isn't it? You say he was left at the altar—"

"He's a know-it-all. He said Cary Grant was gay."

Dottie laughs.

"It's not funny."

"It is a little. But I can see that it's not the best topic for the two of you to start off on." Dottie sighs. "Still, he must have some charms, or your niece wouldn't have agreed to marry him."

"He probably held a gun to her head. The minute Georgia went to change into her wedding dress, she saw her chance for escape."

"Does the man have any interests? Besides getting married."

"Miniatures or something. Dollhouses. He's writing a book about them."

"I see. Well, it's not that far from Los Angeles to Palm Springs. How long have you been in the car?"

"Days. We're turning into the Donner Party. I'll have to toss out my luggage as we cross the desert. We'll end up drinking water out of the radiator or eating each other for lunch. And he's so small, it'd be more like brunch."

"Margo—"

"About two hours."

"Then you're nearly there. It's a lovely town, have you ever been?"

"No, it's terra incognita. I'm hoping a miracle happens and I don't have to go."

"It's the epicenter of mid-century modern," Dottie says. "All that 1950s and '60s glamour and Rat Pack retro. It's also the playground of movie stars: Dietrich, Gable, Harlow. Of course, those people are all dead. And some things have changed."

"Such as?"

"I don't want to harp on this topic. But it's no secret that Palm Springs has one of the larger homosexual populations in the country."

"Goodie," I say. "I'll drop Tully at the first leather bar we come to. They can stretch him on one of those racks."

"Margo, be serious. Is he really that small?"

"No." I poke a Ferragamo-clad toe in the sand and make circles with my foot. "He's medium height, nice hair. He's good-looking, actually. If you ignore the rest of him."

"Uh-huh. Be careful."

"About what?"

"*Je ne sais pas.* It's an all-purpose alert."

A short time later, Tully and I are back on the road. There's an uneasy, unspoken truce between us as we head east on Highway 111.

The San Jacinto Mountains are not high, and the MG crosses them easily. On the other side of the mountains, the Coachella Valley opens up before us. The landscape once again becomes the scrubby flatland of the desert, dotted with cactuses, sagebrush, and yucca plants.

We soon reach the outskirts of Palm Springs. The first real building we pass is the city's official tourist center, a 1960s space-age structure with a soaring triangular roof.

"I suppose we should find a hotel," I say. These are the first words I've spoken to Tully since we had our spat at the side of the road.

Tully shakes his head. "Charlotte booked us into a place downtown. La Vida Loca."

We cruise farther on, and then we see it: La Vida Loca Resort and Spa. It's a large mid-century modern building, two stories tall, with a flat roof. Sunlight bounces off its white angular walls and striped awnings. Tully turns us onto a circular drive lined with palm trees. We pull up to the valet parking.

A young woman in a polo shirt and neatly pressed slacks rushes to open the car door for me. Another woman attends to our luggage. I thank them both. I step onto the carpet that leads into the resort. Tully comes round to my side and together we walk, rather like the honeymoon couple, into the main building.

The lobby glitters with starburst chandeliers, terrazzo floors, and candy-colored 1950s-style furniture. Off the lobby, through a wall of glass, there are well-tended grounds, tennis courts, a swimming pool.

It's been three hours since we left Los Angeles. Now we're in one of America's most popular vacation spots, bathed by sun and luxury. But none of it has the slightest appeal to me.

I want only one thing: to find Georgia and get this business over with. After I do that, I will walk away with a large sum of money, walk away from Southern California, and walk away from Tully Benedict. That's all the incentive I need.

CHAPTER FIVE

DREAMY MONKEYS

It is not true that misery loves company. What misery loves is a double martini. When Tully goes to the front desk to register, I straighten my clothes and smooth my hair. Then I walk across the lobby, headed for the hotel bar. My top priority—my number one goal—is to track down Georgia. But first I need a pick-me-up.

Like the rest of the hotel, the lounge dates from the 1950s, but it has an added dude ranch twist. Spurs and lucky horseshoes hang from the walls. A bowlegged cowboy in a large framed cartoon drawing waves out at the world saying, "Howdy, Pardner!"

The room is small and crowded. And when I say crowded, I mean it's jam-packed with women, nothing *but* women. The air hums with the high-pitched buzzing of dozens of females all talking at once. It's a sound that reminds me of meals in the dining hall at St. Verbian's.

The only vacant seats are at the bar itself. That would be all right except the bar stools aren't stools at all. They're saddles. Western-style saddles, made of highly polished tooled leather. To get served, you have to swing one leg over and mount up. And now, because I very much want a drink, I do just that.

The bartender, a young man in jeans and a cowboy shirt, is down at the end of the bar, taking glasses out of the dishwasher. He turns and sees me and gives a little hi-howdy wave. But when he comes over to take my order, I realize he's not a man at all. He—she—is a woman. A flat-chested, twentysomething woman with short hair.

"What can I get you for?" she says in a friendly drawl.

"An English saddle," I say.

The bartender hesitates, as though considering whether I've requested some sort of cocktail. Then she takes my meaning. "Right," she says. She grins. "Had a gal in here today who claimed she only rode bareback. Course, she drank so many dreamy monkeys, in the end she fell off her mount. Her *compadres* had to carry her to her room."

I smile. "And what, may I ask, is a dreamy monkey?"

The bartender leans in, as though sharing a confidence. "It's a dog's breakfast," she says thoughtfully. "You throw everything in the blender—vodka, crème de cacao, ice-cream, bananas, the whole *taquito*. A dreamy monkey is like a boozy milkshake for kids, for young folks who ain't got the hang of liquor."

Myself, I long ago got the hang of liquor.

"Pass on the milkshake," I say. "But I have just crossed the desert, and I'd like a large martini."

"You bet. Gin or vodka?"

I rather like this flat-chested bartender and her cowgirl ways. My leather saddle creaks underneath me as I settle in. "Gin," I say. "Gordon's, if you have it."

Half an hour later, the bartender and I are pals. Her name is Ruby. She lives in a house out in the desert with her partner, Vera. Together, Ruby and Vera own a horse, a dog, and several cats.

Ruby is friendly and easy to talk to and (I'm beginning to realize) possibly thinks I'm gay. Well, why not? After all, I'm convinced she is. Not to mention I'm sitting in a bar that for some reason is chockablock with talkative females, every one of whom appears to be homosexual.

In less than a day, I've been mistaken first for a newlywed and now a lesbian. What other surprises await me, I can't imagine.

"Is it always this busy?" I ask Ruby over the noise.

"Nope. We do a good business, but this"—with a sweep of her hand she indicates the packed room—"is because of the Dinah. That and, you know, the tournament."

I don't know. What Dinah? What tournament?

"Course, they changed the name a while back," Ruby says. She mixes a pitcher of margaritas, draws several beers, and continues conversing with me, all without breaking her stride. "It used to be named for Dinah Shore. But now they call it the Kraft Nabisco Championship, or some such thing. You know about it, right?"

"Afraid not," I say.

She looks at me like she's trying to figure out if I'm kidding. "It's world famous," she says. "It's the Masters of women's golf. You honestly never heard of it?"

"Sorry," I say.

She narrows her eyebrows, like she still doesn't believe me. "They hold it a few minutes from here, in Rancho Mirage. And every year, same time as the tournament, there's Dinah Shore Weekend here in Palm Springs, and I *know* you've heard of that. The Dinah is the biggest get-together of dykes you ever saw, the biggest lesbian party in the world. Last year, fifteen thousand gals showed up."

While I'm digesting this piece of news, Ruby leans toward me and says in a low voice, "Don't tell nobody, but I'd work the Dinah for nothing."

I laugh. Ruby continues filling me in. "Every gal who comes to Palm Springs during Dinah Shore Weekend loves golf or women. Or both." She looks me up and down. "You golf?"

"Sorry, no."

She gives a sly smile, and I realize I've just confirmed for her that I'm gay.

I decide to change the subject. I compliment Ruby on her cowboy shirt with the smile pockets. (You don't often see those in New York, unless you're watching the DVD of *Midnight Cowboy*.)

"Thanks," she says. "Vera bought it for my birthday. It's from one of the used clothing stores, quite a few of them in town."

Ruby eyes my own outfit. "If you like clothes," she says, "you might want to visit the shops. There's one place, near here—Mommie Dearest. It's the best of the bunch. They got gowns and dresses that belonged to movie stars, millionaires, celebrities. Everything in there is secondhand, but people spend thousands on it anyways. Not me and Vera so much, but you know—"

"People with money?" I say.

Ruby nods.

By now I'm on to my second martini. I ought to be looking for Georgia, but the gin has clouded my sense of urgency. Fact is, I'm enjoying listening to Ruby as she rattles on about the sights to see in Palm Springs: Liberace's former home, Frank Sinatra's former home, Bob Hope's former home. Between the used celebrity clothing and the used celebrity homes, it would seem much of the tourist appeal of Palm Springs is in musing on what used to be.

Which is right up my alley. Reminiscence, regret, the tissue of memories that make up the ever-receding past—these I know well. And after the day I've had riding in the MG with Tully Benedict, I feel so relaxed sitting on a leather saddle in a busy lesbian bar I could almost imagine I'm not myself at all. I could almost imagine I'm somebody else, maybe a tourist here on vacation. Blimey, I could almost imagine I'm gay.

"That's my gal," Ruby says.

I jump. Perhaps Ruby can read my thoughts. Perhaps she's decided I'm just her style. Curbing a slight feeling of panic, I make up my mind to explain myself to her. You've got it wrong, I'll say. I'm not homosexual. I'm just a heavy drinker.

But when I search Ruby's face, I realize she's looking past me. I turn to follow her gaze and see she's tracking the progress of a tall, hawk-nosed woman who's come into the lounge.

Ruby nods across the room at the hawk-nosed woman. "Speak of the devil," she says, her face lighting up. "That's my gal, my Vera."

Vera moves smoothly through the crowded room. When she reaches the bar, she mounts the vacant saddle next to mine. She has the ease of one who has saddled up, whether on a horse or in this bar, many times.

Ruby introduces us.

"Pleased to meet you," Vera says carelessly. She turns to Ruby. "Rube, honey," she says in a deep drawl, "I'm having a helluva day. Make me a whiskey sour?" She smooches the air several times in Ruby's direction.

"Now, Vera," Ruby says. "'Member what I said?" She crosses her arms. "No freebies, no more. You're gonna get me in trouble."

"No freebies," Vera repeats, as if learning the language phonetically. Ruby relaxes a bit. There's a beat, then Vera brightens. "I know what, sugar," she says, slapping both palms down on the bar. "Put it on my tab!" She looks over at me as though we're both sharing a joke.

"You don't have a tab," Ruby says. "The whole town knows better than to lend you credit."

Vera shrugs. "The whole town knows I'm alive and they're half-dead."

After several minutes of this sort of wheedling, Ruby yields and reluctantly sets a large whiskey sour on the bar. Vera picks up the glass and takes several swallows.

Thus fortified, Vera begins sharing her troubles with Ruby and, by virtue of proximity, me. It turns out Vera is upset because she's signed on for tonight's dance contest—to be held in the hotel ballroom—but her dance partner has taken sick. Alas, Ruby cannot partner Vera because, by mutual agreement, Ruby has no sense of rhythm.

"Get Sandy," Ruby says.

"I could get her," Vera says, "but who wants her? Two left feet and no conversational skills. I'd not only lose, I'd be bored to death."

"You'll find somebody," Ruby says. "Lots of folks in town, maybe tonight you'll find somebody new."

"Maybe tonight the stars will turn into diamonds and fall down into our pockets," Vera says. "But I reckon the odds are against it."

She twists in her saddle and surveys the mob of women in the room. She gives a small groan, then turns back to her drink.

I'm idly swirling the olive round in my martini, missing New York and Dottie, when I become aware that someone is watching me. I turn my head to look. It's Vera. She's staring at me.

"You dance?" she says, in her deep drawl.

A jolt of surprise goes through me. For some reason, I feel like an imposter who's about to be unmasked. But unmasked how? As a straight woman, I suppose. I've been in Palm Springs less than an hour, yet already my heterosexuality is in the closet. I feel I should announce to Ruby and Vera that I'm straight. Honest, I'll say, they don't come any straighter. But the idea of blurting this out seems presumptuous and silly. The words won't come.

"Sorry, no," I say self-consciously. "I don't dance. Not really, not for years."

"Pity," Vera says, watching me closely. "You have the body for it. Not like some of the cows in here." She waves her glass at the room.

"Vera," cautions Ruby, "don't go trashing the clientele, even in fun."

"Don't fret, sugar." Vera downs the rest of her drink and dismounts her saddle. "I'm moving on now, anyways. Think I'll head over to the Jewel Box and see if I can find a partner there for tonight."

"That's fine," Ruby says. She places drinks on a tray for one of the waitresses. "As long as it's for the dance contest." She gives Vera a knowing look.

"Sugar, you are my one and only," Vera says. She leans over the bar and kisses Ruby on the cheek. "Excepting on the dance floor."

She strides off.

Ruby watches Vera walk away. "That gal's gonna get me in trouble someday," she says. "I just know it. But I love her to bits."

After Vera leaves, Ruby makes me a third martini. Soon I'm experiencing the glow you sometimes get in the dentist's chair, right before they put you under.

The thought occurs to me that, really, it's been a long day. I know I should be looking for Georgia, but . . . I'll worry about that later. I lift my drink to my lips.

Except I feel a hand on my shoulder and turn to see the sober face of Tully Benedict. Gamely, he mounts the saddle vacated minutes before by Vera.

"We're registered," he says. "Your bags are in

your room. Here's your key." He slides a key-card across to me. "The rooms are nice. I went to mine and unpacked, made a few calls."

"Calls?" I say blandly. "There are people who speak to you?"

"Yeah, all right. I shouldn't have said what I said about you being uptight. It was rude. I'm sorry, and I take it back. Okay?"

Tully eyes my martini, then orders a ginger ale from Ruby. If Ruby thinks it's odd that a man is swimming among all these females, she doesn't show it. Neither does anyone else in the room. The world's largest lesbian party is a tolerant group.

"Now we're here," Tully says, "I want to find Georgia."

I swirl liquid round in my glass. "Try looking on a map of the Southern states," I say.

"Yeah, right. Listen, Charlotte thinks you should talk to her first—Georgia, I mean—and I agree."

"Why?" I say. "Wouldn't you rather patch things up on your own?" What I'm really thinking is, Why didn't Tully come after Georgia by himself? It was one thing riding with him today in the car, but now that we're in Palm Springs, I feel redundant. I'm Auntie Margo, for God's sake, a complete third wheel.

"Georgia and I had a huge fight yesterday," Tully says. "Major blowup. She threatened to leave me, and I guess she did. She's mad at everybody right now. Me, her mom. No way she'll see me.

Charlotte thought if you came along, you could sort of run interference—talk to Georgia, get her calmed down. Then she might be willing to see me. Now we're here, we'll catch up with Georgia easy. She can't have much money. Charlotte cut off her credit cards last week."

"Before the wedding?" I say. "Why?"

Tully shifts in his saddle. "The two of them are nuts on the topic of money. There's never enough, no matter how much they have. They bicker and argue over who spent what where. Then they make up and go shopping together on Rodeo Drive."

The one word I hear in all this is "shopping."

I remember shopping. It's sort of fun, isn't it? I haven't gone shopping—real shopping, clothes shopping—in quite a while. Dottie would say it's because I'm not taking care of myself; she'd say it's because I'm depressed. But I'd say it's because I haven't any funds.

I picture Charlotte and Georgia popping in and out of the shops on Rodeo Drive. I imagine them buying perfume, jewelry, clothes. Then I imagine Georgia with no credit cards—cut off from her beloved Gucci, Jimmy Choo, Prada—and then I look down at the end of the bar and see Ruby talking to a customer. Ruby, who has taught me so much about Palm Springs. All at once I have a vision, a sort of lightbulb-going-on-over-my-head inspiration concerning Georgia. At that moment, half-bagged, sitting with a man I barely know in a busy lesbian bar in Palm Springs, the thought of going shopping appeals to me enormously. And for more than one reason.

Well, what's stopping me? Haven't I been sitting tall in the saddle buying drinks with Charlotte's American Express Black Card? Doesn't that card have absolutely no credit limit? Ha! I'm sitting on a shopping gold mine! I perk up, remembering the fifty thousand dollars I hope to earn. I push what's left of my drink away.

I lift my hand to signal Ruby. "Another round?" she asks.

Delightful girl. "Thank you, no," I say. "I'm leaving. But that shop you mentioned—"

"Mommie Dearest?"

"Yes. Where will I find it?"

She points. "Two blocks thataway, this side of the street. Can't miss it. There's a big sign"— she holds her arms wide—"shaped like that old-timey actress Joan Crawford."

I dismount my saddle. Once I'm on my feet my cheeks flush, and I'm a bit wobbly. I stand there, gripping the edge of the bar. Tully watches me. "You okay?" he says.

"Just getting my sea legs," I say. "We were a long time in the car today."

"Maybe you should lie down," Tully says with concern.

"No," I say. "I'm on assignment. It's imperative I go shopping."

CHAPTER SIX

MOMMIE DEAREST

I had hoped to go sleuthing on my own, but Tully insists on tagging along, and I'm too well-oiled to argue. When we step outside, the desert heat hits me hard. A lesser woman would wilt like a head of lettuce, but I soldier on.

We haven't gone far when I get a shock. Glancing up, I see Charlotte's giant, disembodied head floating above Tully and me. But when I blink and look again, I see it's not Charlotte at all. It's a shop sign. As Ruby the bartender described, it's a silhouette in the shape of the head of bygone film star Joan Crawford. We have arrived at Mommie Dearest.

Tully holds the door for me and we enter. Like every retail establishment in Palm Springs, Mommie Dearest is air-conditioned. I begin to revive.

A fair-haired, well-groomed young man sits behind the counter, reading the latest issue of *Vogue*. He looks up. "Good afternoon," he says cheerfully. "Pursuing anything in particular?"

"Not really," I lie. "Just browsing."

"Browse away. Any questions, please ask." He glances at my shoes. "Love the Ferragamos, by the way. If I may be so bold."

"Thank you," I say. I gaze down and admire Charlotte's expensive shoes on my feet.

Ruby was right. The place is filled with fabulous used clothing and designer wear. There's even a section of classic dresses and gowns once owned by movie stars: Grace Kelly, Ingrid Bergman, Rita Hayworth.

Although I'm here on a mission, I can't help myself. My eye is distracted by a perfect pair of women's shoes displayed on a small stand near the counter. They're black satin with stiletto heels, ankle straps, and tiny rhinestones set into the heels. I walk over and take a closer look.

"Vivier?" I ask the young man.

"Goodness," he says, "you know your footwear, don't you? Very much Vivier, in the years he was designing for Dior." Laying his magazine aside, the young man rises from his chair. "They belonged to Ginger Rogers in the 1950s. And I must tell you, I will cry salty tears the day we sell them. *Salty* tears."

"They're lovely," I say.

"They're exquisite," he corrects me. "And when you think they were on the feet of Miss Rogers, even if somewhat late in her career, well . . ." He releases a little sigh.

I nod, feeling a gin-fueled rush of affection for Ginger. "You know what they say," I tell him. "Ginger Rogers did everything Fred Astaire did—"

"Only backward and in high heels!" he finishes. We laugh. Tully looks at us as if we're speaking Mandarin.

"Heavens!" the young man says, wiping his eyes. "I'm such a fan! Who isn't?"

Who indeed. I love Ginger and Fred. Not to mention Cary, Kate, Bogie—all the movie stars from Hollywood's Golden Age. I can't help wondering who has their shoes.

The young man comes over to where Tully and I are standing. He picks up one of Ginger's satin high heels. "One thing I've learned in this business," he says, "is when people feel passion for an object, it's often about something more than the object itself."

He slides a well-manicured index finger along the curve of the sole. "This shoe, for example. It's a work of art, naturally. Vivier was a genius. But what matters as much, if not more, is who wore it. I read somewhere that during World War II, Miss Rogers donated a pair of her dancing shoes to a fund-raising auction and they sold for fifty thousand dollars. Imagine! In those days, that was a fortune!"

It's still a pretty impressive amount these days.

"The same holds true for anything worth collecting," the young man says. "The late Michael Jackson paid over $1.5 million for David O. Selznick's *Gone with the Wind* Best Picture award; it was worth that much to him." He sniffs and straightens his shoulders. "Personally, I'd be over the moon if I could someday handle one of the four Oscars awarded to Miss Katharine Hepburn."

"Handle . . . or fondle?" Tully says low in my ear.

The clerk doesn't hear Tully. He continues on with his little philosophical discourse. "My sister and I are still fighting over our grandmother's original red Fiesta Ware," he says. "It's chipped, cracked, quite possibly radioactive, yet we both want it. Why? It belonged to Gram. I suppose it's all about trying to hold on to someone you loved, to that part of your life you shared with them. You know?"

He looks at me, and it's like I'm gazing in a mirror. A fuzzy, distorted, fun-house mirror, but a mirror nonetheless, and I see my reflection. Because, oddly enough, I do know.

We have something in common, this young man and I, aside from our mutual regard for Ginger Rogers. I'm in the business of architectural salvage; he's in the business of wardrobe salvage. What does Tully make of the used celebrity clothing business? I wonder. Is it even more ghoulish than what I do?

I wander round some more and spy a strapless, ivory-colored couture gown displayed on a headless mannequin. I stop and look.

The gown's bodice is layered in crystal beads, the waist flows into a floor-length silk skirt, appliquéd in lace and gathered in the back. Though new, the dress has the delicate, sensual air of the early 1900s. It reminds me of a gorgeous Edwardian-era painting by John Singer Sargent.

The clerk glides over. "Isn't it delicious?"

"Umm," I say absentmindedly. I check the price tag: $25,000.

"Bit of a story there," the clerk says. "Never worn, for one thing."

"Do tell," I say.

"Young lady brought it in early today. Wouldn't take a check, insisted on cash. Very cloak-and-dagger." The light of gossip glistens in the clerk's eyes, and he lowers his voice a notch. "At the Paris showing, this little bonbon went for over forty thousand dollars. I was determined not to pass it up. Luckily, my assistant was here, and I had him *run* to the bank."

Assistant, he has an assistant. Despite his youth, our young man is not a clerk. We're dealing with Mommie Dearest himself.

Tully looks bored. He rolls his eyes at Mommie Dearest's seemingly pointless story, then leans over a jewelry case and gazes at the baubles inside.

I linger with the dress, examining the lace-work. "Did you see this?" I say to Tully.

Without looking up from the jewelry case, Tully

asks, "Is it one of Katharine Hepburn's statuettes?"

"No," I say. "But it should probably win an award."

Tully crosses to where I'm standing and gives the dress an indifferent glance. Another moment and he'd move off, but something—the bead-work?—catches his eye. He looks again. He touches the fabric.

"Jesus!" Tully says. He grips the gown. "This is Georgia's. It's her . . . her wedding dress. She hocked it!"

Mommie Dearest bristles. "I beg your pardon. This is not a pawnshop. I own the gown out-right."

Tully wheels on him. "Right. And with a few alterations it'll fit you great."

Tully's anger is uncalled for, I think. It's hardly Mommie Dearest's fault that Georgia cashed in her bridal gown. I insert myself between the two men. "Well!" I say to Mommie Dearest, trying to smooth things over. "This is all so fascinating!"

He stares at me.

"I do have a question, though," I say.

Mommie Dearest eyes Tully nervously. Then the merchant in him succumbs to even the chance of a sale. "Certainly," he says to me. "What would you like to know?"

"Can you tell us where we might find the woman who sold you this dress?" I say.

"Hocked it," Tully mutters.

Mommie Dearest isn't sure what's going on, but he knows something's up. His glance flits first to Tully, then back to me. "I'm afraid that's confidential," he says. He backs away slightly. Tully glares at him.

"Yes, but there's a problem," I say. I rack my brain as to what that problem might be. It has to be something persuasive enough to convince Mommie Dearest to give me the information I need. "The woman who owned this dress is my niece," I say, "and she's . . ." What? What? What? "She's pregnant!"

Tully gapes at me as though I've gone off the rails. Then he draws a deep breath, like someone about to dive into a swimming pool, and goes off with me. "Right," he says, bobbing his head. "She's going to have triplets! And if she doesn't get her medication, she'll . . . swell up! I mean, you know, more than usual."

"Medication?" says Mommie Dearest.

"Prenatal vitamins!" I say. "Extra-strength!"

"What's her name?" Mommie Dearest says.

"Her name?" I echo.

"If she's your niece, you must know her name."

"Georgia LaBelle Illworth," Tully says.

Mommie Dearest snorts. "I'd remember a name like that," he says. "That was not the name of the woman who brought in this gown."

"She also suffers from sporadic schizophrenia," I say. "Could be using any number of appellations!"

"And she wants to be a screenwriter," Tully says. "Probably used her, you know—pen name!"

Mommie Dearest is back behind the counter. He stands there, like a soldier taking refuge behind a row of sandbags. He fixes his gaze on me. Gone is the honeyed manner with which he greeted us when we first came through the door. His voice is pure ice. "Madam, I think you had both better leave."

Panic overtakes me; everything's going wrong. I'm *this* close to finding Georgia, and I'm blowing it. I look at Tully. His face is a mixture of anger and shock, like someone who's just crawled from a car wreck. With only moments to turn things around, I get the feeling it's all up to me.

All I can think is I need to ease Mommie Dearest's fears, calm him down. But what shall I do? The poor man is obviously frightened. His hands are out of sight behind the counter, probably fingering a can of pepper spray. I've got to make him see me as friend, not foe. I try a new tack.

"You know," I say in a soothing tone, "I worry we somehow got on the wrong foot." I lean on the counter and smile innocently, in the manner of Pollyanna or the Dalai Lama. Mommie Dearest flinches, but does not spray me with pepper. "We want to find the woman who sold you this gown because we'd like to buy it back for her."

"Buy it back?" Mommie Dearest says. His voice is strained.

"Yes," I say. "You see, my niece is engaged to this young man."

Mommie Dearest looks confused. His eyes dart round the room, trying to spot the young man I referred to. Yes, well, perhaps I should have said my nineteen-year-old niece is engaged to this immature fortyish fellow.

Tully pipes up. "Georgia and I argued," he says to Mommie Dearest. That part of Tully's statement is true. But in another moment he reveals himself as having an unexpected knack for making it up as he goes along. "We fought about the dress. I didn't like the color."

"It's ivory," Mommie Dearest says. "It's a bridal gown."

"Yeah, but it reflected the light. Kinda hurt my eyes." Tully flutters his fingers in front of his face. "Except I was a jerk, I see that now. I was wrong to want red."

"No," Mommie Dearest agrees. "Red will never do, not even in California."

I clap my hands together. "See? Nothing but a lover's quarrel. And now, if you'd be so kind, I'd like to buy the gown."

Mommie Dearest looks at me in amazement. Like someone producing the high card in a game of poker, I take out the ace of spades—Charlotte's American Express Black Card—and slap it on the counter.

The moment he beholds that mighty card, Mommie Dearest is revitalized. His spindly body is all arms and legs as he moves like a manic spider to the mannequin. He removes the gown, places it in a lidded white garment box, then turns back to close the sale.

He picks up Charlotte's card. "You do realize the gown is twenty-five thousand dollars?"

"It's a steal at that price," I say.

He laughs, and we're best friends again. I find with shopkeepers, estranged relatives, and public officials, sometimes all it takes is a large sum of money.

Mommie Dearest swipes the card through the terminal and then turns the screen toward me to sign. I pick up the electronic pen. I look at him. I wait.

"Oh," he says. "Your niece."

"Umm," I say. "Her urgent need for vitamins."

"Indeed." He strokes the front of his neck. "As I say, I paid her cash. She did tell me her first name, which *she* said was Jade."

"You didn't get her full name?"

"No, I didn't." His face reddens. "I should have, but I admit to being dazzled by the couture. The young woman said her wedding was canceled, and I had no reason to doubt her. She was so obviously affluent, so obviously comfortable with large sums of money. Everything about her was so calculated. The Dolce & Gabbana jeans, the ankle tattoo, the designer jewelry, even the way she spoke. All of it was so extremely high—"

"Class?" says Tully.

"Hat." Mommie Dearest's hand flies to his mouth. "Oh! No offense. She was such a film family *type,* we get them all the time in here— daughter of, stepdaughter of, granddaughter of—that I wasn't the least concerned the gown was stolen or anything." His eyes skip anxiously from Tully to me. "It isn't stolen, is it?"

"No," I say. "It's not." Mommie Dearest's shoulders drop with relief. "However, some other things have gone missing."

"Oh," he says. "I see."

He stares at the electronic pen in my hand, my hand that's frozen an inch above the credit-card terminal. I'm not budging. Together, we're stuck in a little glacial moment of time. There must be more, I think, you must know more.

Mommie Dearest's lower lip quivers, the ice melts, and I literally see a thought pop into his head. "Mercy!" he says. "I've just remembered! I do know what hotel she's at."

Tully's head swivels in my direction. Our eyes meet.

"That is, I believe I do," Mommie Dearest says. "We were waiting for my assistant to return from the bank, and just to make conversation I asked the young woman where she was staying. She didn't precisely respond to the question, sort of skirted it. I didn't think much about that. People like their privacy. But a moment later, her cell phone rang. When she opened her bag to search for the phone, she pulled out several items and laid them on the counter. One of the things she took out was a keycard. I saw the name of her hotel on the card."

I lean down over the terminal as if to sign. "Which was?"

"La Vida Loca," Mommie Dearest says.

I sign.

Tully grabs the box with the gown in it. The two of us bolt for the door.

"Good-bye," I say, as we exit the shop. "Thank you!"

"Wait!" Mommie Dearest says. "Matching shoes!"

We're big spenders, and he's not about to let us go. He chases us outside. "For the gown!" he cries. "I have the matching shoes!"

CHAPTER SEVEN

LESSONS

Halfway down the block, we can still hear Mommie Dearest calling. "There's so much more! So many things! I have Marilyn Monroe's panties! Did you know that? I'm the only man in town who can show you the undergarments of Miss Marilyn Monroe!"

Ignoring Mommie Dearest's cries, we hurry back through the heat, headed for the hotel. Tully holds the garment box containing the dress out in front of him, as though it were a take-out pizza or a small coffin.

"You do realize Georgia now has currency," I say. We're moving fast, my words come out breathlessly. "It doesn't matter if Charlotte cut off the credit cards. Georgia got thousands for that dress. She can go anywhere, do anything."

"I know," Tully says. "And that's not counting what she got for the goddamned matching shoes."

Tully's tone takes me aback. It must hurt him to know how quickly Georgia sold her wedding dress. She didn't exactly tuck it away in hopes of a second chance with him, did she? Not at all the way I imagine Tully folded up his own wedding clothes back in the men's room of that rickety old gas station.

We're practically running now, both of us sprinting to get back to the hotel. "Did Georgia have an engagement ring?" I say, puffing.

"Sure. A diamond, like she wanted. My stepfather—do you know my stepfather?"

"Malcolm Belvedere," I say.

"Yeah," Tully says. His face is flushed with exertion. "He's really my ex-stepfather, but that doesn't matter; he's a good guy. He never got over my mom. Anyway, he knows a jeweler. Made sure I got a good deal."

"If Georgia sold the dress *and* the ring," I say, "by now she would have—"

"I know," Tully says. He wipes his brow. "A wad of cash."

We look at each other. We both know the horse is out of the barn and is galloping gaily down the road.

We reach the hotel. We stash the dress in my room. Tully tosses it onto the king-size bed, where it promptly tumbles out of its carry box and cascades over the bedspread. Seeing it there makes me feel odd, like remembering a close call, like finding a snakeskin after the snake has slithered away.

We go to the hotel lobby. We stand there, peering across the room at the efficient-looking female clerk working the reception desk.

"What do we say to her?" Tully asks in a half whisper. "We can't go up and say, 'Hi, we're wondering if there's a girl staying here named Jade, only Jade isn't her real name, and besides she's hiding from us, and we don't really know what last name she's using right now, plus she might be registered under some other name anyway. So you know, is she here?'" He holds up his hands. "We can't say that, we'll look like idiots."

"We are idiots," I say. "I should think that's obvious. It's a handicap, but we'll just have to work with it." With that, I turn and walk off in the direction of the bar.

Tully runs after me. "Hey!" he says.

I stop.

"It's none of my business," he says, looking vaguely embarrassed. "But you're not going to get another drink, are you?"

As a matter of fact, that wasn't my plan at all. But now that he mentions it, it sounds like a good idea. "Perhaps a wee one," I say.

Tully and I enter the lounge. My new best friend, Ruby, is behind the bar. She grins and waves.

The leather creaks as Tully and I mount our saddles. I'm beginning to enjoy sitting on a saddle. It's like riding a carousel. After enough gin, it may even go up and down.

"Howdy, again," Ruby says to me. She's not

ignoring Tully; it's more like she doesn't see him, like he doesn't exist. "Double martini?" she says.

I laugh. "A single, please."

"On a health kick?" Tully says.

"Just pacing myself," I say.

Ruby at last notices Tully. "Get you something, sir?" she says. He orders a ginger ale, and Ruby moves off to get our drinks.

I'm meditating on the good news—that we're close to finding Georgia—when Tully reaches up and touches the back of my head. "You've got a cocklebur in your hair," he says.

There's a mirror behind the bar, and I watch Tully's reflection as he pulls at the offending matter. "Got it," he finally says. He flicks the bur away.

With his hand still on my head, Tully smooths my hair. His gaze meets mine in the mirror. For an instant, we stare at each other.

All right, yes, I admit it. Rumpled, distracted, arrogant Tully may be, but he's also compellingly male. I'm conscious of the closeness of his body, the sweet muskiness of it.

I drop my gaze. I swallow. Tully removes his hand. "Well," he says.

I scramble for something, anything, to talk about. I give voice to the first thing that pops into my mind. "Do you know," I say, "I haven't seen Georgia in years. I'm not sure I'll recognize her. What's her hair like these days? Short? Long?"

"Long," he says.

"Still that incredible red?"

"Yup."

Ruby returns with our drinks and places them on a pair of cowboy coasters. Two athletic-looking women in white Bermudas and polo shirts come into the lounge. They mount up at the end of the bar. Ruby goes to wait on them.

"We know Georgia's here," Tully says, stating the obvious. "What I want to know is, what are your intentions?"

I smile.

"What?" he says.

"It's the way you say 'intentions.' Like you're worried someone will seduce you." I don't know why I said that. I wish I hadn't.

Tully reddens.

I feel clumsy and self-conscious. Any moment, I expect I'll simply slide off my saddle and roll around on the floor, speaking in tongues.

After a while, Ruby returns to our part of the bar and begins mopping the counter with a small towel. Contrary to what Tully believes, the reason I've come into the lounge is not to get a drink—not entirely, anyway—but to winkle information out of Ruby.

"Ruby," I say, "could you tell me if you know a young woman, very pretty, with long red hair?" I bring a hand up even with my shoulder. "Her name is Georgia—or possibly Jade. Though by now it could be Topaz or Malachite. She's staying at this hotel."

Ruby stops mopping and looks thoughtful. "Sounds sorta like the gal who drank all those dreamy monkeys. She's a redhead. Don't know her name, but I told you about her, remember?"

"I remember. You said her friends carried her to her room. What room is that?"

"No idea. They paid cash, so there wasn't a room tab. The two gals who were with her, though, they're sitting over there."

She points to the athletic-looking duo at the end of the bar who came in after we did. I stare at them. I study their buff physiques, close-cropped hair, and no-nonsense body language. It takes a moment, but for once in my life, the truth hits me like a freight train.

I get it. Oh God, I get it. I know why Georgia ran off, I know why she left Tully on their wedding day, and I know why she came to Palm Springs, land of the upscale alternative lifestyle. Ha! Mystery solved! It's as clear as the gin in my glass.

Georgia is gay.

Well, I've just earned fifty thousand dollars. Now all I have to do is meet with Georgia, reassure her that everything will be okay, perhaps help her break the news to Tully. Then I report back to Charlotte and tell her mission accomplished—I found Georgia, and I'll do my best to persuade her to return home. Oh, and I mustn't forget to ask Georgia to return those mysterious items she took from Charlotte. Simple.

I turn back to Ruby. "Do you know those two?"

"Not personally. Course, I recognize them." She looks at me as though I, too, should know who the women are. But I don't. All I can think is they must be two exceptionally famous lesbians, the modern-day equivalent of Gertrude Stein and Alice B. Toklas.

"I'd love to take lessons from either one of them," Ruby says.

Lessons? In what, precisely? What possible tricks could Ruby pick up from these two?

Tully perks up. "What kind of lessons?" he asks innocently.

Ruby laughs. "Golf lessons. That's Billie Gordon and Nevada Pike, two of the highest-rated players on the women's pro circuit. They're here for the tournament."

Golfers! Georgia's drinking buddies—while somewhat butch in appearance—are not necessarily lesbians. They're professional golfers. They might be gay, they might not. After all, singer and actress Dinah Shore, for whom this bloody tournament was first named, was an avid golfer. And wasn't she heterosexual? She was! She had a longtime love affair with that actor Burt Reynolds. A young, virile Burt Reynolds, who, I might add, was twenty years younger than Dinah.

Oh, why, why, why, am I the world's worst at figuring out people's sexual orientation? Must my gaydar be forever on the fritz? Naturally, I believe people's sex lives are their own business. Live and let live, I say. But in this case, Georgia's sexual bent could have a huge impact—fifty thousand dollars' worth—on helping or hindering my efforts in tracking her down. Still, I hesitate to ask Tully if he's ever had an inkling Georgia might be gay. I take another tack, the same one Ruby used on me earlier in the day.

"Does Georgia golf?" I say.

"Yeah, she loves it. That and a few other vices."

I didn't know Georgia golfs, nor can I imagine what her other vices might be. I realize I know next to nothing about my niece. All day long I've been picturing the thirteen-year-old shy lass I saw in New York some years back, but the reality seems closer to a redheaded, vodka-swilling sex kitten, wielding a five iron.

The die is cast. I dismount my saddle.

Clutching his ginger ale to his chest, Tully looks down at me. "And you're going to . . . ?"

"Get to the bottom of things," I say. I wave a hand at the golf pros.

He glances in their direction. "Good luck with that," he says.

The two women look like they're about to leave. One of them throws money on the bar, and they drain the last of their drinks. I come up just as they dismount their saddles.

"Good afternoon," I say. "Aren't you Billie Gordon and Nevada Pike?" I have no idea which is which.

"Afternoon," one of them says, looking round the room as though searching for my keeper. The other one says nothing.

"I adore golf," I lie. "May I ask you a few questions?"

"Press conference tomorrow," the One Who Speaks says. "Appreciate it if you'd wait till then." They start to walk away.

"Wait!" I say. They stop and turn to face me. "I'm not a reporter; I'm not even a fan." Whoops.

The One Who Speaks sucks on her tongue as though it were a peppermint. "Yeah, we give lessons," she says. "But they're not cheap. That what you want to know?"

"Actually, I'm looking for someone. My niece, a redhead. I believe you had drinks with her earlier."

"Her!" the One Who Speaks says. "You're welcome to her! We both of us gave her a free lesson, no charge. She told us she writes for the movies, said her stepdad was an agent and her mom some big-time Hollywood producer. Billie and me have an idea for a film, about two female golfers on the pro circuit, based on me and Billie's true-life experiences. We pitched the whole movie to her, right here in this bar. But she got so hammered on dreamy monkeys, she about passed out."

Billie, who up to now has been silent, joins in. "After enough dreamy monkeys," she says, "there was nothing dreamy about that young lady whatsoever. It was all ape."

"Damned if we didn't have to carry her to her room," the One Who Speaks—Nevada—says.

"That would be room number—" I fish.

"That would be room number zero," Nevada says tartly. "As in, if she's really your niece, ask at the front desk. But no joke, that girl has attention deficit disorder. Definitely not good at keeping her eye on the little white ball."

They both let out a hoot. Then they walk away from me for good.

I go back to my saddle, but don't mount up. I stand there.

"Anything?" Tully asks of my encounter with the golf pros.

"Nothing," I say.

At the far end of the lounge, there's a wall of windows and a door that opens to the outside. Through the glass, you can see the swimming pool, the patio (crowded with women), and a large garden area.

Tully follows my gaze. "Let's take a walk," he says. "I'm pretty sure we've got time for that."

CHAPTER EIGHT

SANCTUM SANCTORUM

Tully and I start down a garden path shady with tall shrubs and low palms. The air is clean and fresh and smells vaguely of citrus. I pull my cigarettes and lighter from my bag. "Do you mind?" I say automatically.

"Yeah," Tully says. "I do."

I stop mid-light. Now he wants to keep me from smoking? Outside? He really is annoying, no wonder Georgia left him.

"But only," he says, "because I hate seeing anybody do that to themselves."

Oh. I see. Yes, I want to tell him, yes, I agree. I hate it when people hurt themselves. But what Tully doesn't know is that at the moment I need to smoke and drink and do unhealthy things. It's all that's keeping me going.

So I light up. I inhale the tobacco, letting the nicotine do its work on my brain cells.

"Something's been bothering me," I say. "Charlotte claims when Georgia ran away she took things that belong to her. Belong to Charlotte, I mean. Do you know what they are?"

Tully chews his lip. "Money, jewelry, cocaine . . . who knows?"

"Georgia does coke?"

He laughs. "Georgia does whatever she wants. But yeah, I wouldn't be surprised if that butler, Juven, brings her blow on a tray, with coffee and biscotti." He gazes down at the ground. "Hollywood's a funny place. And the Illworths are a very Hollywood family."

"I don't know if this is about drugs," I say. "I hope not. But I do think whatever items Georgia took must be valuable, or Charlotte wouldn't be so eager to get them back."

"Well," Tully says, "you know the old saying: 'One man's treasure is another man's trash.'"

Perhaps. But Charlotte's house overflows with high-end furnishings and artwork. It's doubtful anything she perceived as treasure would be considered trash by someone else. Besides, didn't Tully get that backward? I thought the saying was "One man's trash is another man's treasure."

We round a corner and come upon a lizard sunning itself on a rock. The animal's wide mouth and thin legs remind me of Charlotte. I halfway expect it to pull out a phone and strike a deal with Warner Bros. The creature sees us and darts off into the undergrowth.

"Have you no other notion what these missing objects might be?" I say to Tully.

"Not a clue. But you think they're valuable?"

"Quite," I say.

"Then, uh, I should point something out," Tully says. "Every object actually has two values." He holds up his index finger. "Number one is the price it'll bring in the open market. What'll people bid for it at Sotheby's or Christie's?" He holds up a second finger. "But every object also has a hidden value. That's a wild card, totally unpredictable. Could be zero, could be millions."

"And what is this mysterious hidden value?" I say.

Tully smiles and for the first time today looks almost happy. "I've thought about this a lot," he says. "It's part of the book I'm writing."

"Dollhouses?" I take a drag off my cigarette.

"Sort of. The culture of collecting. See, the hidden value of any object is what that object is worth to you. Sentimentality can really drive up the price. Like when we were in that shop today and the guy was going on about his grandmother's china and Ginger Rogers's shoes and Marilyn Monroe's underwear. That's all schmaltz."

"But surely some of that must have historic value," I say. "History of the American cinema and all that."

"What do Marilyn Monroe's panties have to do with the annals of American film?" Tully says. "You tell me."

I'd like to tell him. There must be historical importance to Marilyn Monroe's panties, if only I could think what it would be. Wait a minute! What if they were the panties from that film *The Seven Year Itch*? The panties Marilyn takes out of the icebox and innocently waves under Tom Ewell's nose? That was a classic scene of comic male frustration.

You could say in that film Marilyn's panties were a metaphor for political repression in America during the 1950s, juxtaposed against the awakening sexual freedom of the middle class. Oh, that's good, isn't it? Those panties are of significant historical interest. Those panties should be in the Smithsonian!

But before I can make my case, Tully starts in again. "See, the hidden value can go way deeper than sentimental attachment. Sometimes you feel it down to your soul. Like maybe you're the one person who appreciates a work of art that everybody else hates."

He stops walking and squats down to examine a basketball-size plant growing in the ground. It's a round, cactusy thing with milky-white spines.

"This thing you treasure," Tully says, gazing at the cactus, "this thing nobody else wants, could also be what you'd call organic. It could be alive. Could be, I don't know, a dog. Or a human being. That's what falling in love is, isn't it? Discovering the hidden value in someone."

Tully reaches out and touches the cactus. It pricks him, and he jerks back his hand. He stands there and considers the spot of blood forming on his finger.

I stub out my cigarette under my shoe, then rummage in my bag for a tissue. "Here," I say. Tully holds out his palm to me.

I lay the tissue against Tully's finger. I'm pushing down, applying pressure to the wound, when I glance up and look at Tully's face. I take in his smooth cheeks, his rough chin and jaw, the developing wrinkles at the corners of his eyes.

"We fall in love with somebody who maybe seems like a bad match," Tully says, "and our friends run around saying, 'What does he see in her?' What he *sees* in her is what's hidden from everyone else. He's fallen in love with something invisible."

"Or possibly he's made a common mistake," I say, gazing at Tully. "He was needy. He fell for outward appearances. He projected onto this person whatever it was he'd always longed for in a relationship, whatever he hungered for in life. He fell in love with the idea of love."

"That's a pretty cynical point of view," Tully says. He pulls his hand away and removes the tissue, sucking at the cut on his finger. "Or do you speak from experience?"

The garden path circles round until it comes out by the hotel parking lot. The MG is there, parked in the shade of the building. Amid rows of more expensive luxury vehicles, my father's car shines like a cherry in a bowl of vanilla ice-cream. Two women walk by. One of them pulls out a camera and directs the other to stand next to the MG. She snaps a photo. They laugh and move on.

"The car's a photo-op," Tully says.

"It has style," I say.

"It does. Except style, like value, is a matter of opinion. That reminds me—those shoes in the shop, the ones that belonged to Ginger Rogers. How'd you know who designed them?"

"Oh, well," I say. "Roger Vivier was French, he created women's high-fashion mid-century footwear. If you know his work, it's not hard to spot."

"Still, that was pretty good."

"Thanks," I say. "Of course, I also saw the label."

There's a beat, then Tully gives a short laugh. I laugh too.

We walk over to the MG. It's sleek and inviting, and has an air of speed even when it's standing still. Despite having spent much of the day in that car, I have an urge to sit in it. I turn the chrome handle on the driver's side and get in.

I perch in the driver's seat, my fingers wrapped round the steering wheel. The red dashboard in front of me is curved like a pair of lips. In the center of the dashboard are three old-fashioned instrument dials. They have octagonal-shaped black faces and white numbers and pointers. There's nothing at all digital or electronic or modern about this car. A time machine, yes, that's what it is. Finn would have liked it. I like it. I like being in it, imagining the places I could go. Home, mostly.

Tully rests against the hood, facing me. He talks over the windshield. "Look, Margo," he says, "you want to find Georgia and Charlotte's stuff, whatever that is. Me, I just want to find Georgia. How about we try to get along? Seriously, I'm not a bad guy. We could, you know, join forces."

I gaze at Tully, trying to figure him out. On the plus side: attractive smile, nice head of hair. But the rest of him? Fortyish, dumped on his wedding day, writing a little book about dollhouses. Frankly, I feel sorry for him.

"Well," I say, "Georgia's my niece, but the sole reason I'm pursuing her is because Charlotte's paying me. I need money. I'm broke. What about you?"

"I make a living."

"No, no. Why did you get in this car and come after Georgia?"

"Oh." Tully pokes his thumbnail into the rubber coating along the edge of the windscreen. "Well, I'm in love with her. She's young, I know. And we had a huge fight yesterday. Gigantic. I told her I was sick of all the partying. I want her to dry out, ditch the drugs, grow up. That pissed her off. She threw stuff around, said nobody could put her on a leash."

"All right," I say. "You argued; she bolted. But on her way out the front door she paused long enough to nick two or three items belonging to Charlotte. Again, what do you imagine those objects are?"

"Who knows? The only thing out of the ordinary I know for sure happened is Georgia got into a room over the garage. When Charlotte found that out she was ticked. Nobody's supposed to go up there."

A dim memory floats back to me from childhood. Before I can even think what it is I want to ask, I say, "The sanctum sanctorum."

Tully waits, as if there must be more.

"It's Latin," I say. "It means—"

"Innermost sanctuary."

"Yes. Remember that actor John Barrymore? Drew Barrymore's grandfather?"

Tully lets loose a laugh. "Before my time. But I bet the two of you rode around in this car every day, eating ice-cream."

"He died before I was born," I say. "But my father knew him. Barrymore was a legendary drunk. He kept a room, a private bar, in the attic of his Beverly Hills home. He called it his sanctum sanctorum. When my father bought the house at Malibu, he had his own sanctum sanctorum built over the garage. It was his private clubhouse, but it was also his office. If Georgia took something from that room it was almost certainly, even after all these years, an item that belonged to my father."

This starts me thinking about what Charlotte said, how Irene kept all of our father's things. However, as much as I loved my dad, the only item of interest I can picture him leaving behind, other than the MG, is a bottle of good Napoleon brandy. Besides, whether or not Georgia filched something from the sanctum sanctorum is of minor importance. To get my fifty thousand dollars, I first of all have to find her.

I need to know more, but I'm aware of not wanting to hurt Tully. I suspect he's been hurt enough. "Do you think it's possible," I say gently, "that Georgia might have, well . . . any chance she ran off with someone else?"

Tully pokes some more at the rubber coating. "I thought of that. But if she was with a guy, she probably wouldn't need cash, meaning she wouldn't have hocked her dress so fast. Jilting me was a prank. She wanted to hurt me, and she did. Plus, she gets a kick out of driving her mom crazy."

He looks straight at me. "Georgia's wild, yeah. Immature as hell. But she'd never *really* leave me without . . . It's a stunt. She said she loved me."

I listen and nod as if Tully were right. As if

nobody in the world ever lied about who or what they were. Or whom they were capable of loving.

The tiny dashboard clock reads four. In a couple of hours the sun will disappear behind the mountains.

I open the car door and swing my legs out to the ground. "Think I'll go to my room and change," I say. "I want to go for a swim."

Tully jumps from the hood and holds the door for me. "What about Georgia?" he says, shaking his head. "We should be looking for her. We could walk around the place, see what we can . . . see."

"Walk around all you like," I say. I give Tully my cell phone number so he can call me if he discovers anything. "But just remember," I say, "all we really know is that Georgia is at this hotel. Somehow we have to figure out what room she's in, and what our next move should be. Our 'intentions.' In the meantime, I believe a swim will help me think. Who knows? Maybe Georgia will show up at the pool."

Half an hour later, I've already been for a dip. Now I lie poolside, on a slightly damp lounge chair, watching women splash about in the water. Cocktails are served by the pool. I order a martini.

I'm sipping my drink, reflecting none too happily on the day's events—and thinking hard about how the hell to find Georgia—when a female in a tank suit strides out to the edge of the diving board. She stands there, silhouetted against the late-afternoon sky, taking the measure of her dive. She's slim, sinewy, and unusually tall. When she raises her arms for the plunge, I get a good look at her face. That hawk nose, those penetrating eyes. It's Vera, beloved of Ruby the bartender.

Vera does a respectable front dive off the springboard, then swims over to my side of the pool. She floats there, treading water. She smiles up at me. "All alone?" she says.

"Well, I—"

"I'll join you."

This is the thing about Vera. She doesn't ask, she announces. It's like being in the path of a bad driver, an oncoming train, or a large wet dog.

Vera hauls herself out of the pool. She grabs a towel from a nearby cart and begins drying off. A healthy young woman in a two-piece bathing suit saunters by. "Hell-o, Raylene," Vera says admiringly. The woman smiles and keeps walking. Vera finishes drying, then wraps her towel round her shoulders and drops down on the lounge chair next to mine.

"Always nice to see a friendly face," she says.

"Vera, I'm sorry, but I'm not feeling the least bit friendly. I have a lot to think about, and I—"

"Meant me," she says. She pushes back her wet hair. "I'm the friendly face. Because, darlin', you look like you could use a pal."

Oh.

She focuses on the glass in my hand. "Liquor is mighty pricey at this hotel, but money's no object for you, is it?"

I laugh. "Money—the lack of it—is a huge object in my life," I say. "But I'm here on a sort of expense account. So, you're half right. At this exact moment, at this hotel, money is not an issue."

She looks at me, and I realize I've just declared myself her own personal happy hour. Oh, what difference does it make? She might as well mooch off me as anyone. "May I buy you a drink?" I say.

By the time we're on our second round, Vera and I are cozy as old chums. I have to admit there's something engaging about Vera. She's a steamroller, yes, but a big-hearted, laughing steamroller. She's also a good listener.

Before you know it, I've shared with Vera the whole story of why I've come to Palm Springs. My financial troubles, my runaway niece. I explain that not only have I been hired to return Georgia to the family fold, but also I've been charged with retrieving Charlotte's purloined goods, whatever they are.

Vera takes a swig of her whiskey sour. "There's only one thing to do," she says. "Slip into your niece's room when she's out, see what you find."

I laugh. "Isn't that breaking and entering?"

"Not if you had a keycard," Vera says. "No breaking about it, just turn the handle."

I laugh again. "Right. And where would I get a keycard?"

"From a friend," Vera says. She strokes her chin. "Here's what: I need a partner for tonight's dance competition. You be my partner; I'll get you a pass key."

I feel myself growing nervous. Yes, I need to find out what room Georgia's in. And yes, I'd like to have a look round that room. All that might help me earn fifty thousand dollars. But must I enter the dance contest? The idea of dancing cheek-to-cheek with another woman all evening makes me a tad uncomfortable. It's false, it's not who I am.

And there's something else—a much bigger emotional hurdle to Vera's proposition. The last time I entered a dance contest my partner was Finn Coyle. We won a trophy. I've held on to that night as one of the most sublime evenings of my life. I even told myself I would never enter another dance contest, not unless it was with Finn. I'm afraid that competing in tonight's event might stir up memories, might make me feel somehow disloyal to Finn. I don't think I'm up for that.

I move to put the brakes on. "Look, Vera, I realize this contest is important to you, but I told you before. I do not dance."

"So you say. Trouble is, I need a partner; you

need a keycard." She wags her finger at me. "But if you ain't dancing, then darlin', I ain't opening no doors."

Vera's twang gets thicker with every sip of her whiskey sour. She lays this cowgirl stuff on with a vengeance, but I have a suspicion she never set foot out west until well into her adult years.

"How would you acquire a key?" I say. "Not that I'm serious."

"Rube can get one, easy."

Oh God.

"No!" I say. "Absolutely not! It's one thing for me or you to take a risk, but Ruby could lose her job."

Vera snorts. "If you *knew* the stuff that girl could have lost her job over and didn't."

"Well, even if you got a key, I still don't know what room Georgia's in," I say, thinking this whole discussion is absurd. "We can't go racing through the hotel, opening every door."

"Course not."

"Then how—"

"Didn't you tell me it was Billie Gordon and Nevada Pike who carted your niece off to her room?"

"Yes, but—"

"I'll ask Nevada."

I'm incredulous. "Nevada Pike is a stone wall," I say. "Billie Gordon too. Neither one of them would give me any information. And you can forget about Ruby getting anything out of them because she doesn't know them, she—"

I stop. Vera's watching me as if I were a windup toy destined to run down.

"This isn't something I'd want getting back to certain people," she says sotto voce, "but I've known Nevada since I first came west, before I ever took up with Ruby. Nevada comes to town for the tournament every year, and when she does, me and her always get together and play—"

"Golf?"

"Around. She has a thing for me."

I try to take this in stride, but my face fails me.

"Darlin', don't look so shocked," Vera says. "I love life and life loves me back."

"Well!" I say. "That's a happy definition of infidelity!"

"Call it what you will," she says.

There's a cherry floating in Vera's drink. She lifts the cherry by the stem, slides the fruit into her mouth, then tosses the bare stem over onto some grass.

"If you stuck around here for a while," she says, savoring the cherry in her mouth, "and you and me got to know each other, you'd know I always look on the bright side. It's the secret of my charm. And unlike most folks, I'm not a snob. I judge everyone by how colorful they are, as well as by the content of their character."

"You have no character," I say. "You're a moocher and a cheat."

"Point taken. However, I'm easygoing, I'm kind, and darlin', I can be oh-so-gentle. You have no idea." She smiles at the memory of some love affair, perhaps many love affairs. "Anyways," she says, "if you're picking a lock, you want to do that with somebody respectable or somebody who knows what she's doing?"

I lean back in my lounge chair, clenching and unclenching my toes.

"So now, I repeat my offer," Vera says. "Partner me tonight, and afterward, I swear on my little pinto pony, I'll get you into your niece's room."

"Look," I say, trying to work a compromise, "I'm here with that man I told you about, Georgia's fiancé, Tully. Perhaps he'd partner you."

Vera rolls her eyes. "Tonight is women only," she says. "You know that, don't you? Every gal who comes to the dance is gay." She pulls her towel tight round her shoulders. "Besides, I lead. I need somebody who can follow."

"Follow what? What variety of dance do you compete in?"

"Samba."

"Oh, you're joking!" I say. The samba was the dance Finn and I competed in the night we won our trophy.

"Darlin', I never joke about the samba."

"Well, I don't know the steps," I lie. "So that's that. Besides, I have nothing to wear."

"I can show you the basics; the rest is just coming along for the ride. As to clothes . . . They hang well on you, don't they? I noticed that in the bar. Any old little black dress will do nicely."

"I don't—"

"Please don't tell me you ain't got a little black dress," Vera says. "Your kind always packs one."

I picture the darling LBD tucked up in one of my cases. I'm weakening, it's true, but only because I want to learn what room Georgia is in. I'd like to have a look at that room. But do I really want to compete in this contest? Can I bear to break the promise I made to myself about Finn? Not to mention that Ruby would be risking her job—and if I were caught I'd likely be in a great deal of trouble.

My indecision must show. Vera watches me with a glimmer of a self-satisfied smile. But that smile rubs me the wrong way. Why is everyone always so sure of themselves around me? Why is everyone so certain I'll do what they want?

"I'm sorry," I say. "But what you suggest is out of the question."

Vera's smile turns into a hearty laugh. Not derisive laughter, just amusement.

"You're wrong, darlin'," she says. "You're in this up to your hips and about to go deeper. You won't turn down a keycard, any more than you turned down your half sister's offer to earn fifty thousand dollars. Any more than you're going to turn around, tail between your legs, and head back to LA or off home to New York." She hoists her glass and drains it. "Thanks much for the libations, by the way."

Vera gets up from her lounge chair and wraps her towel round her waist. She stands there in her makeshift terry-cloth skirt, gazing down at me. "Sun's about set," she says, nodding toward the mountains. A few wispy clouds glow pink and red in the western sky. "I'm going home, eat dinner, get ready for tonight. You better get a wiggle on and do the same."

"Now, look—" I say.

"Darlin', please. What? You won't strike a bargain with me?"

"It's just that—"

"Well, I'm no bully. You don't want to do it, don't. You don't want my help getting fifty thousand dollars, no skin off my nose. But didn't you tell me you *have* to raise money or you'll lose your business back home in New York?"

I consider the logic of what she's saying.

"Thought so," Vera says. "Meet me in the hotel ballroom, nine o'clock."

CHAPTER NINE
WHEN IN ROME

I go to my room, shower, and call housekeeping to take my little black dress for pressing. Then I have room service bring me a light dinner. After I eat, I get out my makeup kit and do my face, like I used to in the old days, like I was going on a fashion shoot or a big date.

When housekeeping returns my dress, I slip into it and stand in front of the mirror. The dress features a low back and thin straps and is cut just above the knee. It's always fit me more or less perfectly, and as I slide my hands over my hips, I'm pleased to see it still does. After that, I step into heels, put on some sparkly glam earrings, and I'm ready. Ready to go downstairs. Ready to face the music and . . . dance.

That is, it's nearly nine o'clock. Time to go downstairs and compete in a lesbian dance competition, followed by some sort of unlawful entry. I mean, it's time to meet Vera. It's . . .

I really should get some ice.

I wander out into the passageway. The only sounds I hear are someone's television and a random bit of laughter.

The ice machine is at the end of the hall. I step over to it and begin noisily scooping ice cubes into a little plastic tub. The door to a nearby room opens. Tully pads out. He's wearing a wine-colored Asian-style robe that ends just below the knees. He has a book tucked under his arm. He has nice legs.

He sees me. "Wow," he says. "I mean . . . you going somewhere?"

"Me? No, I'm not. Not at all. No."

"Well, you look amazing." He takes a plastic tub from atop the ice machine. He shovels ice cubes into it.

"Thank you," I say. "I . . . what are you reading?"

He shows me *The Dollhouse Book*.

"Fascinating," I say. "Don't let it keep you up."

"Nah, I'm exhausted. I'm turning in early."

"Me too. I'm just going to have some hot cocoa with"—I glance down at the little plastic tub in my hands—"ice."

Tully, too, looks at the bucket of ice I'm holding.

"So," I say quickly, "any luck with that plan of yours to walk around looking for Georgia?" I do not tell Tully my own plan—the one I've made with Vera.

"Nope," Tully says. "I'm thinking tomorrow I'll talk to the manager." He yawns. "Sorry," he says, covering his mouth. "I'm beat." He looks at me again. "But you . . . you look incredible."

• • •

I go back to my room. I lock the door behind me.

I drop ice in a glass and help myself to a drink from the minibar. After I light a cigarette (thoroughly against hotel rules) and pull out the cell phone, I settle into a purple upholstered armchair. It's close to midnight in New York, but that doesn't matter. I call.

"Darling!" Dottie says. I picture her in her Greenwich Village apartment, talking into the handset of an antique French phone. "I thought it might be you. How's Palm Springs? Found your niece?"

"No, I have not," I say. I sip my drink. "The only thing I've located is the ice machine, the hotel bar, and a bevy of lesbians. I'm up to my knees in lesbians."

"You paint quite a picture," Dottie says.

"I'm speaking metaphorically."

"So I gathered."

"I have a question for you," I say.

"Thinking cap on."

"How do you know what a thing is worth?" I say. "Do you ever get it wrong?"

"Oh," Dottie says, pausing to consider the question. "Well, let's see. Naturally, there's the occasional surprise. I once found five hundred dollars tucked inside the most god-awful vase."

"Yes, all right." I rub my forehead. "But in general, what makes something valuable?"

"Often," Dottie says, "it comes down to essence, a sort of hidden *something*. I mean, what makes anything worth anything? So many times, what we call 'worth' is artistry, the unique beauty of a thing."

"Does it have anything to do with sentimental value?" I say.

"In my experience, it's more about passion. There's a rather crude French phrase some collectors use when they're excited about an object: '*Ça me fait bander.*'"

"Meaning?"

"This gives me an erection."

"Well," I say, "you paint quite a picture yourself."

"Touché," Dottie says. "But let me assure you when a connoisseur expresses that level of interest, he's not describing his grandmother's tea set. For collectors—serious, wealthy, cutthroat collectors—sentiment has nothing to do with whatever it is they're pursuing."

"Then what's the fuss about?"

"They're mad for it. Or terribly greedy. Either way, they feel they'll go insane if they can't have it."

For some reason—probably because she's the best friend I've ever had—talking with Dottie always cheers me up. We chat a few minutes more, but in the end I decide not to share with her the details of my bargain with Vera, not to bring up the women's dance contest or the breaking-and-entering thing. Not now, anyway. Still, after we say our good-byes and hang up, I at least feel game to go downstairs.

When I arrive at the entrance to the ballroom, I'm surprised and pleased to find the well-dressed company is not entirely female. Women *and* men pass by, chatting and laughing and walking arm in arm. Men! Yes! There are males here after all. Not a lot, but some. And everybody's dressed in their very best clothes, which is nice. Some of the chaps are even in black tie.

So I must have misunderstood Vera. This dance is not exclusively for women. It's a mixed bag, a social potpourri, a sort of . . .

Wait a minute. Is that a guy?

Trying not to be obvious about it, I cut my eyes in the direction of a portly fellow standing near me. Like me, he's lingering outside the ballroom, and like me, he appears to be waiting for someone. He's medium height, wearing a dark-blue suit, every inch the gentleman. But when he straightens his tie, I note polish on his fingernails. And his face is smooth, not a trace of beard. The more I look at him, the more it dawns on me he's not a man at all. The more it dawns on me he's a woman in drag.

Well, she has a right. It's a free country, isn't it? And it's her party, so to speak. I'm the gatecrasher. But now that I've figured him—er, her—out, the scales drop from my eyes. I stand at the door, watching people stream into the ballroom, and see that everyone here, whether clothed as yin or yang, is female.

It takes my breath away. The place is wall-to-wall women. There's not a man in sight, though there are some very convincing drag kings.

It all reminds me of something, but I can't think what. Then I remember how, decades earlier, on a summer evening, I wandered alone down Christopher Street in Greenwich Village, back when that was the heart of New York's gay male community. Men were everywhere. Young and old, they smiled at each other from front stoops, they stood entwined in doorways. They called to each other, they cuddled and kissed and drowned in each other's eyes. And not one of them took any interest in me.

At the time, I was nineteen years old and, like every woman in Manhattan, any time I ventured into the street I risked being the target of lewd remarks from a certain type of male passerby. So it was an unexpected treat, a liberating feeling, to stroll through a sea of Manhattan men and find myself ignored. In a way it felt good, almost as though I were invisible.

Tonight, I'm in the reverse situation. I'm surrounded by gay women, but I'm not invisible. Far from it. Indeed, I blush when I tumble to the fact that I'm the focus of more than one admiring glance.

A striking blonde comes up and taps the shoulder of the blue-suited woman near me. Blue Suit turns round, sees Blonde, and breaks into a smile.

"Remember me?" Blonde says playfully. They embrace, kiss, and together melt away into the crowd.

It's at this point that a new thought comes to me. What if Vera shows up in drag? What if she taps me on the shoulder and I turn and find her in a Brooks Brothers suit, silk tie, and wing tips? Whoa, Nellie. Vera was insistent about my little black dress, but I don't recall her mentioning what she would wear.

I'm rooted to the doorway of the ballroom. I stand there, peering at the room and the women in it, at the fantasyland decorations of paper streamers and strings of tiny electric lights. There are candles on all the tables. A female dance band is playing up on the stage. It's all done quite nicely, actually, terribly romantic. Which is why I hesitate.

The truth is, I'm filled with apprehension. For one thing, attending this dance means I'm basically passing myself off as gay. Just being here feels dishonest and deceitful.

More important, I'm having a Finn flashback.

There's only one person I was ever comfortable dancing with, only one person who made me feel graceful. And he's not here. I'm uncertain therefore if I should continue with what, for me, is a masquerade. Uncertain if—

"Darlin'," a voice says low behind me. "I hoped you'd come."

Like Blue Suit did moments before, I turn to see who's at my back. It's Vera, of course, and she's not dressed as a man. On the contrary, she's radiant in a one-shoulder white dress that sparkles when it catches the light.

Is it my imagination or is she even taller than before? Oh, yes. High heels. They've catapulted her into the stratosphere. I'm tall myself and also in heels, but Vera has several inches on me.

Looking at her in her white dress, with her athlete's body and sharp features, I cannot deny that Vera, in her own way—in the way of all human beings who are kind and not cruel—really is lovely.

"That's a fine little black dress," she says to me. "It fits you to a T."

"Thank you," I say. I feel self-conscious and am aware that I have nothing to talk about. I fall back on good manners as a conversational device. "You have a nice dress too," I say, sounding in my mind like a five-year-old complimenting another at a child's birthday party.

"Thanks," Vera says. "It's used, but even so,

Ruby spent a bundle on it. The little guy who sold it to us swore it belonged to Geena Davis. The actress? Not sure I believe that. She and I are the same height, though, six feet. It's from this place called Mommie Dearest. You know it?"

"Yes, I . . . I dropped in once."

"Buy anything?"

"A frock," I say, remembering the twenty-five thousand dollars I charged earlier in the day to Charlotte's American Express Black Card. "Nothing special."

"You're a phony," Vera says, and I flinch, convinced that I've just been found out, that she knows I don't belong at this particular party. "Everything in that shop is special."

Oh, clothes. She's still talking about clothes. I stare at the floor.

"Anyways, doesn't matter," she says. "My, they've decorated the place nice. What are we standing here for? Let's go in."

We enter the vast ballroom, which by now must have three or four hundred women in it. The band is playing a soulful "Night and Day." The dance floor is full.

"I love this place," Vera says, as she shepherds me through the crowd. "Built in 1950. The floor's on springs, you know that? Floats when you dance on it."

I follow Vera to a table at the edge of the

dancers. "You can leave your purse here," she says. "Ruby will keep an eye on it."

"Ruby?" I say. "She's here?" Sure enough, along with three other women bartenders, Ruby is behind the long ballroom bar, pouring drinks from a stainless-steel cocktail shaker. I catch her eye, and she gives me a thumbs-up.

"Doesn't she ever get off work?" I say.

"She usually pulls the noon-to-six shift in the lounge," Vera says. "But they told her to come back after dinner and help with the dance tonight. Just a couple hours, she gets off at eleven. What can you do? They're shorthanded. Besides, we need the dinero; she owes a heap of cabbage on this dress."

Vera pulls a chair out from the table and stands there expectantly, holding the back of it. Oh, what the hell. I sit down in the chair and she helps me scoot it up to the table.

"You want something to drink?" Vera says.

God, yes. "A martini, please. Gin, very dry."

She cocks her thumb and index finger at me like she's taking aim with a pistol. "Got it. Be right back."

I sit alone at the table, watching the dancers. By now the band has moved on to "Taking a Chance on Love." I bob my head to the music and try smiling at the room in general, as if there's no place I'd rather be. I'd like a cigarette, but of course there's no smoking.

Vera, who gets VIP service whenever Ruby's behind the bar, returns shortly with our drinks. She deposits a glass in front of me.

"Thanks," I say.

"Don't mention it," Vera says. "My treat. Got 'em off Rube, but she says after this round we have to pay."

"Lovely."

Once again, I'm aware that my end of the conversation is foundering, but Vera doesn't seem to notice. I sit in my chair, watching Vera salute what seems like half the women on the dance floor. She's electrified by the music, the twinkling lights, and all the females she knows or hopes to know before evening's end. Her eyes shine as she scans the room, taking everything in.

Two women swing dance past our table. One of them calls out Vera's name, but for once Vera's response is cool. She tilts her cocktail ever-so-slightly in greeting and says in a chilly tone, "Sally."

Is it my imagination, or does Sally see me and then flash Vera a look? Is it . . . it couldn't be. But it is. Sally's jealous that I'm sitting with Vera. At least, I think that's it. Sort of. Possibly. Whatever it is, the moment passes and Sally and her dance partner swirl away.

Vera ignores what did or did not just happen between her and Sally. "Good crowd tonight," she says after a moment.

I make an agreeing "umm-hmm" sound.

"You know," Vera says thoughtfully, "lots of twentysomethings, serious partygoers, come to Palm Springs for Dinah Shore Weekend. They drink cerveza, slam down tequila shooters, rock till they drop. Me, I'm more old-fashioned, which is how come I love this dance every year. First half of the evening, they play swing, waltz, whatever. Later, they have the Latin Dance Competition."

She sips her whiskey sour. "Course, in professional competition, couples take turns on the floor while the judges score them. But tonight's strictly amateur. All the contestants cram out there together, and the judges drift around tapping people on the shoulder to eliminate them. Last couple left is the winner."

Did I hear her correctly? What did she say? That this is a lightweight event, that it's not to be taken seriously? You'd think I'd be relieved, but I'm not. I'm annoyed. I didn't want to participate in this contest to begin with and now that I've committed to doing so, Vera's telling me it's some sort of joke.

"Then why bother?" I say irritably. "If it's nothing but amateurs, if it's the equivalent of a high-school prom or senior-citizen social, why does this competition mean so much to you?"

"Why?" She leans forward in disbelief. "Because it's the Dinah! Because it only comes once a year. It's like Christmas, and when I dance it's like . . . getting to open my presents! And if I win the contest, that's the icing on the cake." In the manner of an Italian mobster, Vera puts the fingertips of one hand to her lips, kisses them, and pops her fingers open like a flower. "Anyways, that's how it feels to me."

Sally and her dance partner again swing by our table. Gliding together in perfect unison, they execute some impressive triple stepping. They move like professionals, like they belong on *Dancing with the Stars*. I can't take my eyes off them. Then they pause and sway there in front of us, like boats at anchor. "Hey!" Sally taunts Vera. "You dancing tonight?"

"Yup," Vera says.

"Uh-huh. You going to samba?"

"What do you think?"

"Yeah, but"—Sally tosses her head in my direction—"with that?" The two women snicker and float off.

I comprehend that I've just been insulted. That! She called me "that." What cheek!

Vera finishes her drink. "Come on," she says. "Let's warm up."

"This isn't a samba," I say. "You said the contest starts later, this is a—"

"Fox-trot," Vera says. She seizes my hand, yanking me out of my chair and onto my feet. "Let's cut a rug."

Vera pulls me into the throng of dancers. The band is playing "Cheek to Cheek," which makes me think of Fred Astaire and Ginger Rogers, and of Ginger's rhinestone-encrusted shoes and Mommie Dearest and the value of . . . things.

We're fox-trotting, and I have to say Vera is one smooth dancer.

I, on the other hand, can only be described as awkward. My rhythm's off, I turn right when I should turn left, and my feet get tangled up, which means the two of us aren't dancing together at all. That is, Vera's dancing, and I'm stumbling along after her.

This goes on for many minutes, and I don't get any better. Truth is, I can't concentrate. My shoulders slump, my feet are leaden. After some time, the band takes a break, and Vera and I return to our table. As soon as we're seated, Vera leans back in her chair, crosses her arms, and stares at me. I try to act like I don't notice, but in fact it's exceedingly uncomfortable being scrutinized in this way. Finally, Vera speaks: "What's up?"

"Sorry?"

"Out there." She jerks her thumb at the dance floor. "My grandma's walker has better moves than you."

"I told you," I say. "I can't dance. I don't dance."

"Bull. You're a million miles away. Just wish I knew why." Vera scoots her chair back and stands. "I'm gonna go get something cold for the both of us."

She moves off to the bar.

If I felt self-conscious sitting alone at our table earlier, this time it's worse. This time, I don't bob my head to the recorded music that's playing while the band is on break. I end up staring at my hands, unable to think of anything except Finn. Perhaps the best thing would be if I simply said good-night to Vera and went to bed. If I do that, the deal will be off, and I won't get to snoop around inside Georgia's room, but maybe that wasn't such a fabulous plan anyway.

Vera returns with our drinks. She plonks them on the table. "I told Ruby you're a mess," she says. "I told her it's an effing terpsichorean emergency." She pulls out her chair and sits down. "Rube sends her sympathy, best wishes for a speedy recovery, and one more round for medicinal purposes. So drink up."

I decide Vera's correct about this being an emergency. For the last year, pretty much every day of my life has been an emergency. I sip my martini.

Vera gulps whiskey, then slams her glass down. "Darlin', cards on the table," she says, her eyes fixed on me. "I keep my bargains. I never welsh on a deal. You showed up tonight. We're dancing—HA-HA—and after the samba contest,

I'll get you that key to your niece's room. But, little girl, I won't lie to you. You disappoint me. Can't you loosen up out there? Can't you relax? You're like a pony gone lame."

She's right. I'm not exactly skipping round like a wood nymph. Dancing with me must be more akin to tripping the light fantastic with a well-dressed upright freezer.

"Vera," I say, "I'd like to help you. I would. But I'm having a hard time at this event. I carry a lot of baggage, and—"

Just then, the recorded music stops playing. There's a drumroll, and a spotlight hits the stage. Vera and I both turn to look.

Up on the bandstand a short, thickset woman in a white tuxedo steps to the microphone. "LADIES OF PALM SPRINGS," she says. Her voice echoes over the sound system. "GOOD EVENING!"

She has the oddest, deepest, gravelliest voice I've ever heard come out of a woman's mouth. It's like a cross between Harvey Fierstein and Linda Blair in *The Exorcist*. She's standing on tiptoe, struggling to reach the mike, which is adjusted too high for her.

"It's my favorite time of year," she growls. "Dinah Shore Weekend!" The room erupts in applause and shouts of approval. "In fifteen minutes, La Vida Loca presents its annual Latin Dance Competition. I'm one of the judges. My name is Davita Maroni."

I've never heard of her, but obviously I don't travel in the right circles, because when she says her name there's a roar from the masses. She laughs and takes a bow and waggles her fingers at her numerous admirers around the room. Vera leans over and tells me, "Davita's kind of an institution around here."

"Management wants me to remind you all of the competition rules," Davita says. She peers at a card in her hand. "And they are: No cheating, no shoving, no slapping, no switching partners in the middle of a tune."

She shakes her index finger. "And ladies, remember that the decision of the judges, drunk or sober, is final. The other thing I'm supposed to tell you is that the Latin Dance Competition has three separate categories—samba, cha-cha, and rumba—with three separate prizes. You can enter one category or all three. Samba will be first. So pick a partner, pick up your feet, and let's everybody head SOUTH OF THE BORDER!"

The recorded music starts playing again, only now it has a Latin beat. Amid more applause, Davita shimmies off the stage, as talk and laughter and excitement ripple through the room.

"Did you hear that?" Vera says, panic in her voice. "Samba first! Lordy, this is it. Ship going down!" She stares at the glass in her hand. "I should have told Rube to make 'em doubles."

I feel sorry for Vera. She looks so unhappy, and I know this contest means a great deal to her.

Vera straightens her bare, well-developed shoulders and belts back her drink. "Moment of clarity!" she says, her eyes gone wild. "This possum ain't playing dead! No sir, not tonight! We at least gotta try. Come on, I'll show you some steps."

"No," I say, even as she's pulling me from the table and over to an alcove at one side of the room. "Vera, listen, we need to talk!"

"Darlin', you English girls are so chatty. But just do your best and try to follow."

"No!" I say again, but she's not listening. We're standing in the alcove, facing each other. She has my right hand in her left, a tight grip round my waist, and she's barking directions at me. "Feet together! Weight on your right foot!"

I cock my hip and shift my weight like she tells me, but only to buy a few minutes of time. The moment she calms down, I'm informing her I don't think I can go through with this. It's been too long since I danced with anyone, and it's too difficult for me emotionally. Though I admit it'll be hard getting a word in edgewise because Vera's single-mindedly counting the beat aloud and saying things like, "Right foot back, *one,* left close to right, *and,* right foot stays in place, *two.*"

I feel a headache coming on.

. . .

Vera and I are still practicing in the alcove when the band returns from break, bringing along even more female musicians. Now there's a large percussion section with all manner of Brazilian-style drums. Together with the horns, guitar, and piano they start in on something smooth and Latin-sounding. At the same time, the room lights dim and women ooh and ah as a galaxy of electric stars and planets appears on the ceiling. A glitter ball commences rotating above the dance floor.

Davita Maroni's back onstage. She grasps a cocktail in one hand and the microphone in her other. "Ladies," she rasps into the mike, "this song is 'So Danco Samba'—that's Portuguese, baby, for 'I Only Dance the Samba.' Oh my, yes! It's Carnival time! Let's all go to Rio! Let the games begin, let the best couple win! We begin our Latin Dance Competition with the glorious, meritorious, notorious . . . SAMBA CONTEST!"

Women *flood* onto the dance floor.

My mind's spinning faster than that glitter ball overhead. Now that the contest is starting, the energy and sexual excitement in the room ratchet up enormously. As if in proof, Sally, the woman who insulted me earlier, winks at me as she passes by on her way to the dance floor. But it's not a playful wink. It's a rude, sarcastic gesture. It's a put-down.

That does it. It's Sally's wink that tears it for me,

that somehow puts me over the edge. So I haven't danced in years, so I'll never again dance with Finn. Vera's a good person, and she deserves to have a shot at winning this contest. It's not right that she could lose to the likes of Sally. And me? I *need* to get into Georgia's room, I need to make fifty thousand dollars.

Vera's in the middle of showing me how to do a basic samba move. "Step sideways with your left foot, close right foot to left—"

"Stop!" I say. "Vera, stop, I mean it!"

She ceases moving. She stands there, holding me in her arms and giving me her full attention.

"I'm a fake," I say. "I'm not the person you think I am."

"Well, darlin', who is?" she says matter-of-factly.

"Oh, good point," I say. "But the truth is—" I hesitate. I'm embarrassed. I'm embarrassed that, on some level, I've been misrepresenting myself— my sexual orientation, my dance skills—to both Vera and Ruby from the moment I met them. Nevertheless, I try again. "What I told you before was untrue. I do know how to dance."

"You lied to me?" Vera says. It's hard to tell if she's offended or impressed.

"Yes," I say. "I'm sorry."

"Why would you lie to me?"

"Because," I say, "I was confused, upset,

ambivalent about things that happened in my past. Also, I was nervous. Nervous that, I don't know, you might get angry if you found out I was . . . straight."

"You're straight?" Vera says. Her face is riveted on mine. "Lordy, little girl, you haven't been listening. I don't give a *hoot* if you're straight, gay, bi. I just want you to stop being so damn frigid on the dance floor! Can you do that?"

"Yes," I say, feeling both relieved and excited. "I think I can now. My dance partner and I were . . . well, we were very good. He taught me everything. We even won a trophy. And I do know how to samba. Quite well, actually. I'm rusty, but I can do it."

"Samba whisk, traveling voltas?" Vera says, as if inquiring about Brazilian side dishes.

"Yes."

"Botafogo? Shadow position?"

"All of it," I say. "I know all the moves."

Vera throws back her head and laughs. She has the most perfect set of upper molars I've ever seen in my life. "Darlin'!" she says. "You beautiful fraud!"

She takes me by the wrist, even more forcefully than before, and pulls me away from the alcove, out among the dancers. Carving out space for the two of us in the middle of the floor, she stops, drops my hand, then turns round to face me.

We stand there, looking at each other—she in her sparkling white dress, I in my classic black. Vera's right hand rests on her hip. Her eyes are bright. She holds out her left hand to me. "Come on, Margo, show me. Show the whole damn room what you got."

Funny, but I'm ready to do exactly that. When I put my hand in Vera's, I no longer feel conflicted. I feel like I'm about to do something right for a change.

Vera raises our entwined hands to just below her own eye level. Her right hand reaches round and cleaves to my left shoulder blade. I rest my left hand on her right shoulder. In dance, this is called the closed position, but I don't feel closed at all. I feel open. I feel like myself.

For once, Vera and I are in sync. And when a sultry, long-haired woman in a floor-length gown moves to the microphone and begins crooning "One Note Samba," Vera and I . . . well, that is to say—

We dance.

Except this is better than ordinary dancing. It's more fun. That's because the samba is all rhythm and joy. It's a flirtatious, happy dance, with a sexually provocative hip movement. And as you might imagine, Vera has the hip thing down perfectly.

For the first time all evening, I'm at ease. I'm

comfortable now with Vera, who really is an incredible dancer.

The vocalist is good. After "One Note Samba," she sings "The Girl From Ipanema" and an assortment of other Latin standards.

Davita passes by, clutching a cocktail. She and the rest of the judges move through the dancers, tapping couples on the shoulder and directing them off the floor. Occasionally, there's a short scuffle when an inebriated twosome resists being eliminated.

Dancers are weeded out. The floor becomes less crowded. The singer goes into a tune I recognize from my youth. It has a samba beat, but it's called "When In Rome (I Do as the Romans Do)." Well, I think, that's appropriate.

The song is carefree and upbeat. A lively piano and bass come in. And horns. The spring-mounted dance floor quivers with the movement of the dancers.

Vera's wearing some sort of herbal scent—vetiver?—that drifts through the air. "You're doing great," she tells me. "And you look fabulous, darlin'. You are one gorgeous armful."

Of course, flattery is the oldest trick in the book of dance. The superior dancer always does everything possible to build up a weaker partner's confidence. Nevertheless, Vera's comments have their effect. I lift my head a touch higher.

The singer is at the apex of her song, belting out the lyrics. Pumped up with gin, adrenaline, and the rhythm of the music, I throw myself into the dance. I'm determined to help Vera win her trophy. I also happen to look round at the other dancers. Most of them are dreadful. The word "clumsy" comes to mind. Also "inept," "amateurish," "drunken."

Everyone in the place has consumed vast quantities of alcohol, and there's a great deal of aimless wiggling going on. Many couples have altogether given up attempting to samba and are simply grinding away at each other in an explicit hip-hop manner.

Off to one side, Davita and a disgruntled contestant get into a fistfight. Bystanders pull them apart, but the mood of the contest has changed. It's become more aggressive.

As the remaining dancers struggle to stay on the floor, the competition takes on the ruthlessness of a Roman chariot race. When in Rome, indeed! Elbows, knees, and spiked heels become makeshift weaponry. A dancer intentionally stomps on my instep. I realize it's the obnoxious, insulting Sally. I can't believe she'd physically attack me like that, and I stare after her. She and her partner look back, laughing.

"She hurt you?" Vera says.

"It's nothing," I say, glad there's enough gin in my body to deaden the pain.

"Sorry," Vera says. "It's sorta my fault. I had a one-nighter with Sally a while back. When I sobered up the next day and told her there wasn't going to be no more, she was none too happy about it. Still, she has no call to get nasty with you."

"I'm all right."

"So you say. But let's have some fun anyways." Vera maneuvers us across the room, near Sally and her partner. Then she swings us round, and we do the dance move known as a kick ball change, which—as Vera sways hard to her left and forcefully kicks her left foot—comes off as a sort of body slam into Sally's partner's backside. Sally and her partner go sailing off into a table and chairs.

"Guess they got eliminated," Vera says.

The remaining couples whirl through a few more songs, but it's obvious who's the best dancer in the room, and in her arms I've become the second best.

Soon, all the contestants are directed off the floor except Vera and me. Vera beams as the room fills with applause. A spotlight bathes us in light.

We do a quick victory turn and then one of the judges—not Davita—hands us a large trophy. Vera clutches the prize, as we move in tandem toward the bar. I'm winded, but Vera's hardly ruffled. We make it over to where Ruby stands, applauding. "Lover, you won!" she says.

"You bet we did," Vera says. "Course, the judges are all bombed. Look at Davita over there." She points to where Davita, her eyes spinning like pinwheels, stands clinging to a table, trying not to fall over. Vera gives a throaty laugh. "What the hey. I guess everybody in this place is tits up."

Vera sets the trophy on the bar. "Sweetheart," she says to Ruby, "make me a whiskey sour? Margo's buying. Margo wants a—"

"Double martini," I pant.

Vera slaps me on the back. "Double martini, single woman!" she says. "A wicked combination."

I smile. I'm proud we won the contest. Like Vera, I stare at the trophy as it gleams in the light. It looks pretty much like every big, shiny dance trophy you ever saw in your life. It even looks a bit like the prize I won with Finn. Except there's something special about this trophy that will cheer Vera's heart every time she looks at it: the happy couple on top is one-hundred-percent female.

CHAPTER TEN

AN INNOCENT LAMB

When Ruby finishes work at eleven, she stashes Vera's trophy behind the bar. Eager to enter the cha-cha and rumba contests, dancers still crowd the ballroom. But the three of us—Ruby, Vera, and I—make our way through the crush of women and over to a back stairway. With Vera in the lead, we hurry up the concrete steps to the second floor where we creep along a quiet, carpeted corridor. We come to Room 205. We all three stop in front of the door and stare at it.

"This is your niece's room," Vera says. "Guaranteed. Go ahead and knock, Margo. If your niece answers, you two can tangle right now. If not, Ruby unlocks the door and you go on in, nose around. Either way, Rube and I will stay out here and keep watch."

I look up and down the empty passageway. Then I look from Vera to Ruby and back to Vera. She nods for me to go ahead. So I do. I knock on Georgia's door, but there's no answer. I knock again. Still no answer.

"No one home," I say.

"Maybe she's on a bender," Ruby says. Her voice cracks with nervousness. "She sure wasn't feeling any pain in the lounge today. Maybe we'll open the door and there she'll be, passed out all over the floor."

"How can you pass out all over the floor?" Vera says. "A body only takes up so much space."

Ruby shrugs.

"Well, anyways," Vera says, "if she's out cold, she won't mind callers. So there's nothing to fret about. Go on now, Rube, unlock the door."

Ruby pulls a keycard from her pocket. Her hands are trembling. "I do not believe I'm doing this!" she says in a harsh whisper. "Lover, what are you getting me into?"

"Just keeping my end of the bargain," Vera says. "Besides, you got to once in a while walk on the wild side or life gets mighty dull. Open the door, sugar, and we'll be done with it."

Ruby inserts the card into the electronic lock. It beeps. But when I reach for the door handle, Ruby grabs my wrist. "Promise you won't take anything!" she pleads.

She's running a tremendous risk on my behalf, I know, so like a Girl Scout I raise my free hand and make a solemn pledge. "Promise. Quick look round, then—poof!—I'll vanish. No one will ever know I was here." She lets loose of my wrist.

With Ruby and Vera keeping guard, I slip into the darkened room, closing the door behind me. I feel anxious, but I force myself to move forward and switch on a lamp. Standing there, the heels of my shoes sinking into the plush carpet, I see Georgia's room is something more than your average hotel lodgings. It's a luxury suite, decked out glitzy retro Rat Pack style.

I can't help but admire the care some interior decorator took in choosing the vintage amoeba-shaped coffee table, chrome lamps, and sleek Eames chairs. The walls are hung with original black-and-white photographs of Palm Springs in the 1950s and '60s. In addition, another note-worthy feature of the place is that it's been . . . ransacked! Plundered! Pilfered! Great Jupiter, some other detective has been here before me! Someone's gone through Georgia's things!

It's like opening the Great Pyramid of Giza and finding grave robbers got there ahead of you! It's like making your way to the front of the Clinique counter at Bonus Time and discovering they're out of goodie bags! It's like—

But hang on. Hang on one minute. Georgia's suite hasn't been ransacked. That's not it at all. There's another explanation for why this place looks like it's been looted: Georgia lives like a pig.

By my calculations, she's had the room a little over twenty-four hours, yet it's complete chaos. Bath towels, lingerie, half-eaten meals from room service lie about. Single-serving liquor bottles from the minibar, drained of their contents, peep from sofa cushions.

Reassured now that no one has broken in before me, I move through the suite, looking for God knows what. I'm careful not to disturb anything, though in all honesty, who could tell if I did? A brief inspection of the pink-tiled bathroom and lime-green bedroom reveals nothing more than the lingering scent of Dior Pure Poison. I go back out to the living room, wondering what it is I think I'll find.

I move to look at something of interest—drug paraphernalia scattered across the top of that amoeba-shaped coffee table—when I bump into a pile of magazines resting on the floor, next to the table. The pile tilts and topples over onto the carpet. Now I've done it! I promised Ruby I wouldn't touch anything, and now I've made a mess. Or at least, you know, I've added to the general confusion.

I go down on hands and knees, hurriedly scooping things back up. I'm picking up a bunch of magazines when something sandwiched between them—a black binder—catches my eye. Though it's not really the binder I take heed of, so much as the label on the front of the binder.

The label intrigues me because the typeface is unusual. For one thing, it wasn't computer printed. It was produced on a typewriter. And judging by the aging, yellowed look of it, somebody typed that label—which says "Thalia Television Productions," by the way—a long time ago.

I get up off the floor and sit down on the sofa, thumbing through the binder. It contains a typewritten script, the title page of which reads "Spy Team Final Episode—Story and Teleplay by Arthur Just."

Spy Team. Lots of people are old enough to remember this series, or to at least have seen reruns on late-night TV. My father created Spy Team. The main characters were a sophisticated black man paired with a gorgeous milk-colored blonde woman. It also had that catchy, unforgettable theme song—they still play it on the oldies radio stations.

Spy Team's premise was that the man, Saxe, and the woman, Ariana, were high-school gym teachers by day and international spies on evenings, weekends, and holidays. Saxe and Ariana had perfect teeth and wore fabulous clothes. They had electronic gadgetry; they were highly skilled in the martial arts; they looked fantastic in gym shorts. Saxe and Ariana were never openly linked romantically, but part of the show's appeal was that there was a constant undercurrent of sexual tension between them. Nearly every episode worked in a suggestive joke around Saxe's name: Saxe appeal, great Saxe, Saxe before marriage.

Spy Team ran for only three seasons. It was what my father came up with at the end of his life, at the end of his creativity, and I feel he was embarrassed by it. I think he thought the show was trash. Whenever it was time to turn in a new episode, he had to get himself drunk just to write it.

Why, I wonder, does Georgia have this old script? Why would she even want it? I close the binder, and my gaze travels down to the rest of the magazines littering the floor. A line of black pokes from beneath a copy of *Us Weekly*. With the toe of one shoe, I push *Us* aside. Underneath is a second black binder.

I put *Spy Team* down and pick up this other binder. It, too, has the look of age. It, too, contains yellowing pages that were long ago composed on a typewriter. But as I flick through it, I see this script wasn't written for television. No, this is the script for a feature-length film.

I flip to the title page. It's called *An Innocent Lamb*, and at the bottom of the title page there's a quotation:

> "Is not this a lamentable thing, that of the skin of an innocent lamb should be made parchment? That parchment, being scribbled o'er, should undo a man?"
> —William Shakespeare,
> *Henry VI*, Part 2

Below the title are the names of the script's coauthors: Orson Welles and Arthur Just. A thrill goes through me. Orson Welles! I'm holding a script by the late Orson Welles! And also by my father—apparently he cowrote it.

But Orson Welles! The man who created *Citizen Kane*, the motion picture the American Film Institute calls the greatest American movie ever made. I'm enough of a movie fan to know Welles not only directed and starred in *Citizen Kane*, he cowrote it with Herman J. Mankiewicz. And didn't they each take home an Academy Award for Best Screenplay?

I weigh the script in my hands and think about what it is, the history of such an object, the rarity. My pulse quickens, and I remember the French phrase Dottie used: "Ça me fait bander." Well, okay, not exactly. But I am excited.

And now I know what happened. I comprehend this whole big mess. Georgia must have discovered these two old scripts—*Spy Team* and *An Innocent Lamb*—in my father's attic office, his sanctum sanctorum. Charlotte found out; perhaps they argued over ownership. Either way, when Georgia ran off, she took the scripts with her.

It's also obvious that these are the mysterious and unnamed "things" Charlotte wants returned to her. The *Spy Team* script is basically worthless. I imagine Charlotte wants it as a memento, because our father created the show. Plus, she was a fan of the series. She had a teenage crush on the actor who played Saxe. So the reason Georgia took the *Spy Team* script is because, like Tully said, she gets a kick out of driving her mom crazy.

But *An Innocent Lamb* is priceless. It must be. If this story by Orson Welles and my father is even half as good as *Citizen Kane*, it's worth an incredible amount of money.

It's apt that the title, *An Innocent Lamb*, is from Shakespeare. If someone discovered a long-lost play by William Shakespeare, what would it be worth? Millions! Well, Orson Welles was the Shakespeare of film. He crafted the greatest American movie ever made, and finding an unproduced script by him, even one written with a coauthor, is a big deal.

But I remember what Tully said about the hidden value of things. I thumb through the script and see that it's a period piece full of murder, mayhem, and swordplay. I realize the hidden value of *An Innocent Lamb* is that nobody knows it exists.

Orson Welles and my father are both long dead. Georgia, who fancies herself a screenwriter, could tweak the story a little, update it, then put her own name to Welles's genius. After that, she could peddle it to any studio she chose.

Holding the script, looking down at it, it's as though I'm inside Georgia's head and can see her whole dirty scheme laid out in front of me. I know what she's plotting; I know what she's planning to do. And I'm livid at the thought of it. I'm angry because she has no right to appropriate Welles's work.

So what do I do? Do I take *An Innocent Lamb*? Do I steal the thing? Every impulse in my body says to nick it and run.

But I remember my promise to Ruby, my solemn pledge not to take anything. Reluctantly, I bend down and scoop the magazines back into their pile, slipping the two scripts in as well. *Relax,* I think. *You know what room Georgia's in. You know what she's scheming. Tomorrow morning, you can return and confront her face-to-face.*

So that's it. I keep my vow to Ruby. But even so, I feel good because I have a plan. I know my next move.

I switch off the lights and step out into the hotel corridor.

Vera and Ruby sit on the hallway floor. Ruby's eyes are closed, and her stocking feet rest in Vera's lap. Vera kneads the soles of Ruby's feet. Both women look up when I exit the room. "Good hunting?" Vera says.

"Not bad," I say, thinking I'll keep my discovery to myself. "Thanks so much for your help."

To this cryptic statement, Vera makes no comment other than a yawn. She stands, then helps

Ruby up. Ruby puts her shoes back on, and a moment later we three say good-night.

Just before the two of them disappear through the stairway door, Vera stops and blows me a kiss. Instinctively, I reach up and catch it.

It's midnight when I reach my room, but I'm not sleepy. My mind races with thoughts of Orson Welles, my father, Georgia.

I open the minibar and pull out two single-serving bottles of gin. Tomorrow, I'll deal with Georgia in person. In the meantime, I put gin in a glass and sink down into the sofa.

The coffee table holds numerous advertisements for spa services in Palm Springs: hot stone this, aromatic that, mud facials, detoxification, exfoliation. I pick up a brochure and take a look. "We pamper you," it says. I sip gin and envision a whirlpool spa filled with men and women drinking white wine and wearing disposable diapers.

"Let yourself go," says another pamphlet. "Depend on us." There it is again, that image of incontinence.

I wonder about the sort of people attracted to this type of thing. Then again, if I'm honest, I know I myself am attracted to it. In a whirlpool spa, you don't have to think or be sad or grow old. You just float there, an amoeba with credit cards.

Eventually, I get into bed with my brochures and my drink. I lie there, half reading about herbal body wraps, half reflecting on all that's happened this day, on all that's happened in my life. I lie there, as I do every night, remembering Finn Coyle. After a while, I fall asleep.

In the morning, I wake up hungover and shaky. It's early. I'm eager to confront Georgia, but there's no way I can do that on an empty stomach. I decide to take a quick breakfast in the hotel dining room.

An older woman—well, older than I—sits at the next table. She's expensively dressed in silk cropped pants and a silk top. A cashmere sweater is thrown over her shoulders with the indifference that comes from having money. She's definitely not in Palm Springs because she loves women. I'm guessing she's a well-heeled matron who's here because she loves women's golf.

In a curt Midwest accent, she harasses the waitress. "My coffee's cold," she says. "These eggs are hard." (They look fine to me.) The woman goes on like this for several minutes, relentlessly bullying the waitress. She threatens to withhold a tip, threatens to complain to the manager.

I don't believe the woman is that dissatisfied with either the food or the service. I think she's upset about something in her own life, and she's releasing that anger onto the waitress. People do that all the time in restaurants.

"Take these back," she commands the waitress. "Tell that cook to try again."

I feel for the waitress. There was a time in my life when I waited tables. I was in my late thirties, old enough that the little success I'd had as a model was drying up. I had few marketable skills, and it seemed like I'd never have what you might call a career.

"This is the worst service I've ever had," the woman rants to no one in particular.

I can't stand it any longer. I'm both hungry and nauseated. My head is pounding. I'm annoyed that this woman has advantages, yet no appreciation of those advantages. I resent that she obviously has money, real money, but the waitress and I don't and most likely never will. There's even some-thing about the woman—the superior attitude?—that reminds me of Charlotte. Something that makes me want to reach out and hurt her, make her feel as lousy and damaged as I feel at this moment, as I have felt much of my life.

I twist round in my chair and face the woman. "Really?" I say. "In your whole life, this is your worst restaurant experience? How awful for you."

She responds with a slight smile.

"I hope you don't mind my asking," I say, as if

she were a famous movie star and I one of her fans, "but how old are you?"

She hesitates. "Not that it's anybody's business," she finally says in that Midwest accent, "but I'm seventy-five."

"Seventy-five years old," I repeat.

She nods in a brittle, condescending way.

"Well, if you're seventy-five," I say, "you'll be dead soon, won't you?"

Her mouth makes a large O.

I'm an awful person, I know it. But there's no stopping me now. I'm a loaded gun, and I'm going off. "You'll be deader than the proverbial doornail," I say. "Deader than the bleached bones of some long-deceased cow lying out in the desert. Deader than that lifeless pile of bacon sitting before you."

She looks down at her side dish of bacon.

"And when that blessed moment comes," I say, buttering a piece of toast, "why then—joy and jubilation!—the rest of us can enjoy our breakfast in peace."

The waitress, who's overheard all this, turns to her brightly. "More coffee?" she asks.

CHAPTER ELEVEN
THE WINDY CITY

After I finish breakfast, I'm anxious about meeting with Georgia. On the one hand, I should probably let Tully know what I'm up to. Then again, he made it clear that Georgia is furious with him. So perhaps the smart thing is to stick with our plan and make initial contact with her by myself.

Of course, I haven't seen Georgia in years. And now, having spent last night breaking and entering her suite, I'm about to knock on her door and tell her . . . what? That I was passing by? That I was out taking a stroll on the second floor of La Vida Loca hotel?

Well, that's ridiculous. I can't pretend I'm here by accident.

I remind myself I'm in Charlotte's employ, and I'm here to speak with Georgia on Charlotte's behalf. There's nothing for it but to approach the situation as a professional. I'll rap on Georgia's door; she'll open it, and we'll exchange a few pleasantries (*"Auntie Margo! How young you look!"*). Then, in the manner of an experienced gumshoe, I'll lay out the facts in evidence. *"You really should go home. Your mother wants her things back. Have you considered the Betty Ford Clinic?"*

. . .

Minutes later, I'm walking along the second-floor hallway. There's a high-pitched whine that gets louder the farther I go, and when I get to Georgia's room, the sound is at full volume. I don't rap on the door because it's already wide-open. A maid is inside the room, vacuuming.

I double-check the room number. Sadly, I'm in the right place. I stand in the doorway and stare. The mess of last night has all been cleared away. The maid sees me and turns off the vacuum cleaner. The whining sound ceases.

"Yes, miss?" she says. Her face is as round as the moon.

"I'm looking for my niece," I say. "She was here—in this room—last night."

The maid puts a hand to her cheek. "Oh, my," she says, her round face filled with sympathy. "Maybe ask the desk. Okay? They will know." She doesn't wait for my reply, but starts up the vacuum again and pushes it off toward the bedroom.

I step back into the corridor and stand there, stunned. This can't be happening. Georgia has slipped through my fingers, taking *An Innocent Lamb* with her. Well, I never said I was a detective. Quite the opposite. I'm usually the last to know anything of importance whatsoever; half the time I can't even follow the evening news.

Nevertheless, this is a miserable development.

Charlotte and I agreed on a set fee of fifty thousand dollars, which was fine because I envisioned finding Georgia in twenty-four hours or less. Here it is, day two, and I patently haven't found Georgia. That means my daily wages have been cut in half, from fifty thousand to twenty-five thousand. At this rate, I'll soon be earning minimum wage. Worse, I haven't a clue where Georgia might have gone. Another hotel? The home of a friend? Back to LA?

What, what, *what* do I do now? I slump against the wall.

Just then someone comes walking round the corner of the hallway—and oh God, I can't believe it! It's the old lady from the dining room, the one who was rude to the waitress. True, her behavior in the dining room was awful. But that's no excuse for my own bad manners. I should not have said the things I did, should not have taken my unhappiness out on a stranger. I feel remorse at the way I treated her. It's not the old lady's fault that lately I drink too much or that I'm hungover or that . . . well, lots of things.

She comes closer. I nod to her. "How are . . . you?" I stammer.

She snorts. "I'm not dead yet, if that's what you're asking. Though you'll probably tell me I could go any minute."

"Umm, yes," I say, fumbling for words. "I mean, no! No, I wouldn't!" I take a breath. "It was inexcusable of me to say such a thing, and I very much apologize." There. At least I've made an apology.

She pulls a keycard from her purse, all the while keeping an eye on me. "Is there some reason you're standing near my room?" she says.

"*Your* room?" I say. I gesture toward the open door. "I'm looking for my niece. This was her suite."

The woman raises her eyes to the ceiling. "You're related," she says. "Of course you are."

"You know Georgia?" I ask, utterly confused.

"Is that her name? All I know is that child kept me up half the night. I'm here, right next door." She waves her keycard at the room next to Georgia's. "She made enough racket to raise the dead, not to mention those of us who've been told we're next in line."

"Quite," I say. "I'm sorry she bothered you. I do know she's no longer here."

"Small blessings," the woman says. "She and her playmates came home in the wee small hours, laughing and turning up the music REAL LOUD. I had to get out of bed, put my robe on, and come over and tell her that in Chicago, where I come from, we're considerate of our neighbors. She didn't hear a word I said. Except 'Chicago.' She heard that. She threw her arms around me and said, 'I'm going to Chicago in the morning!' I said, Honey, it *is* morning. It's three a.m. Why don't you and your friends toddle off right now, so I can get some sleep? Either she took my advice or she had an early plane, because when I got up at seven, she was gone."

I walk downstairs to the lobby. I'm dying to discuss this latest development with Tully, when I look up and spot him across the room, buying a coffee at an espresso stand.

Tully sees me, grabs his drink, and comes over. "You should turn on your cell phone once in a while," he says. "I've been looking for you."

"Sorry," I say. "Anyway, I have bad news. Georgia has left Palm Springs. I just found out she's gone to Chicago."

"Chicago?" Tully says. "I wonder what that means." He lifts the round plastic lid off his coffee and blows on the hot liquid inside the cup.

"It means she had enough cash to buy a ticket to O'Hare," I say.

Tully looks at his watch. "Okay. New day, new plan. We better get out to the airport, catch the next plane."

"I'm not flying anywhere," I say, my face flushing. Thinking about airplanes and airports always makes me nervous.

"You're giving up?" Tully says.

"No," I say. I smooth my hair and gaze around the room.

"Then why wouldn't you—" Tully slurps his

coffee and watches me. "Oh God," he says, looking at me with sudden insight. "Christ. Are you . . . you're not . . . are you afraid of flying?"

"Of course not," I say. Tully continues watching me, and I know I've been found out. "Yes, all right. I have a phobia of air travel. But that's not the only problem. I won't leave my father's car."

"We'll put it in a garage," Tully says.

"No," I say. "That's not good enough."

"Well, you can't have it both ways," Tully says. "If you won't warehouse the car, we'll have to drive." He considers this scenario a moment. "That'll take way longer than flying, but you know . . . maybe that's not such a bad thing. We've been chasing Georgia in a rush, like it's an emergency—when maybe what she needs is some space, some time to cool off."

"You want to travel all the way to Chicago in the MG?" I say. "It doesn't have any seat belts."

"We won't go on the interstate," Tully says. "We'll take the back roads, like before. We'll cut over and pick up Route 66. Look, I get why you don't want to abandon the car. It's a classic. Cary Grant drove that roadster, it belonged to your dad—"

"Careful," I say. "You'll find a hidden value in the MG."

"I already have," Tully says. He gazes at me intently. "Plus, I need you."

Needs me? For what?

"We need *each other* to find Georgia," Tully says. "And I need you to tell me about the blue light, the starter switch, all that stuff."

"You know about the blue light," I say. "And the starter."

"But you know more than me. About the car, I mean."

I'm fifty-some years old. By this point in life, I'm expected to have attained a degree of maturity, some worldly wisdom that eluded me in my youth. But looking at Tully, imagining a road trip with him in the MG, I feel about nineteen.

I remember Vera telling Ruby that life gets boring if you don't occasionally walk on the wild side. Is that what I'm feeling? Because despite my age, perhaps because of it, I feel a strong urge to walk—ride—on the wild side with Tully Benedict. Ride with him all the way to Chicago, Illinois.

And there's more to it than that, much more. If I don't go to Chicago, I lose the chance of earning fifty thousand dollars. I need that money. I need it if I'm to have any hope of hanging on to my shop in New York.

"All right," I hear myself say to Tully. "We'll drive to Chicago."

An hour later, we head northeast out of town, toward Route 66.

We've been on the road only a few minutes

when Charlotte calls. In an open convertible, it's a tad difficult to converse on a cell phone. But I manage to explain to Charlotte that Georgia has decamped to Chicago. Tully and I are in pursuit.

"Ye gods and little fishes!" Charlotte says. "It will take you three or four *days* to get to Chicago by car. Can't you—just this once—fly?"

I tell her no, I can't. Of course, Charlotte knows why I'm frightened of air travel—it began for me at the age of ten, when I was torn from my home in California and flown overseas to exile in England. Does Charlotte, I wonder, ever think back on those events? How could she not?

"Tully and I are driving," I say. "End of discussion." Charlotte hangs up. I put away the phone.

I lean my arm on the car door and admire the passing scenery. Low plants, brittlebush, and flowering desert chicory punctuate the dry, purplish soil. I breathe in the warm, fragrant air. I feel restless and adventurous.

Over the next three days, Charlotte phones repeatedly to check on our progress. Most of what she says is so idiotic, I find I can converse with her while thinking about other things entirely.

One topic I ponder is how, this time, it's different riding with Tully in the car. We get on well. We talk. Tully tells me about his interests, his philosophy of life. I share stories about my friendship with Dottie, even some bits about my financial troubles. I tell Tully I love the novels of Charles Dickens. He offers that he has every Beatles recording ever made.

The goal of finding Georgia unites us. Yet I notice Tully and I talk around Georgia, not about her. Our conversation remains largely superficial. It feels like we're both holding back.

Of course, once again, it's as though we're time traveling. Not all of Route 66 still exists, but we follow the parts that do. We cruise past abandoned shacks and ghost towns, motels and run-down filling stations, red neon signs and vintage diners.

Each night, Tully and I engage separate rooms in whatever respectable motor inn we come across. Each morning, we climb back into the MG and drive until the sun goes down.

On our third day of travel, Tully and I cross the state line from Kansas into Missouri. We stop for dinner at a roadside eatery. I ask Tully to go on inside, I'll follow in a minute. I want a cigarette.

When I do enter the diner, there's Tully parked in a wood booth. I sit down opposite him. He looks up from the menu and studies me.

"Okay, it's none of my business," he says. "But I've been thinking this since the first day we got in that car: I can't believe you smoke. I can't believe you treat your body the way you do."

I open the menu and scan the entrées. Pretty much everything on offer is beef.

"I didn't smoke for a long while," I say. "I started up again last year."

Tully leans forward. "And what happened last year that was so awful it made you want to smoke tobacco and drink martinis?"

"Oh, you know how it is," I say. I close the menu and lay it down on the table. "I accidentally missed the spring sale at Saks."

The waitress comes over. Tully and I both order steak. While we wait for dinner, I look round at the Formica counter, the chrome stools, the jukebox in the corner. It puts me in mind of a vanished Manhattan diner I used to frequent, which makes me think of home.

"I know you were raised in Los Angeles," I say to Tully, "but you haven't told me how you ended up living in Brooklyn."

"No?" He picks up a straw and rips one end off the paper cover. He blows on the straw and the paper flies off. "After high school, I got into New York University, which was great," he says. "But about the time I graduated, my mom died, which was hard. I didn't see much point in going back to LA after that, so I stayed on the East Coast. Before college, when I was a teenager, I lived with my mom and Malcolm Belvedere.

They were married for a few years, you know."

"Malcolm told me your mother left him," I say.

Tully taps the straw against his water glass. "I think that's his way of saying she died. He was pretty broken up. He's always been good to me, but the real reason he came to the wedding was in her honor."

"Your mother must have been very special."

"She was," Tully says. "She was beautiful. She had style." He leans back against the booth and looks at me carefully. "Like you, actually."

"More like the MG," I say. "Oh! I meant to show you."

I reach into my tote bag and produce a 1950s sales brochure for the MG TF. "I found this in the door pocket next to my seat, when I was having a smoke," I say. "It must have been in the car forever."

I flip through the brochure, reading aloud about the MG's features and benefits. "It has rack-and-pinion steering. Synchromesh gears. Also, it grips the road like a limpet."

Tully laughs. "Like a what?"

The waitress appears with thick steaks, mashed potatoes, and homemade biscuits and gravy. Tully and I forget all about limpets. I put the brochure back in my bag and we tuck into dinner.

After we finish eating, the waitress removes our plates. She returns with the bill and two pieces of apple pie. We haven't ordered dessert, but the waitress plunks it down in front of us even so. "Cook thinks you should have pie," she says.

When we leave the diner and get in the car, I gaze back at the long, narrow building silhouetted against the open sky. Tully pats his stomach. "Cook thinks you should have pie," he drawls.

I laugh, and so does Tully. For a moment, we look at each other, giggling. We forget about Georgia, Charlotte, the terrible mess our lives are in. For a moment, it's a kick being alone together in the middle of America, just the two of us— away from everybody else, away from our troubles.

Tully and I follow the Mother Road through seven states until, at last, on our fourth day of travel, we cross into the eighth and final state traversed by Route 66: Illinois.

Early spring in the West had been hot, pleasant. Early spring in the Midwest is chilly, blustery. After we stop for fuel, Tully eases the car over to one side of the station and shuts off the motor. He rubs his hands together.

"It's cold," he says, and you can see his breath. "I don't suppose you know how to put the top up?"

Actually, I do.

We exit the car and Tully comes round to my side. We stand there, both of us peering down at the MG's interior like it's a crib containing a newborn infant. A rather scary newborn. Possibly something out of *Rosemary's Baby*.

"Putting the top up is a bit like doing a puzzle," I say.

"I don't care if it's Rubik's Cube," Tully says. "I'm freezing."

"Well, first we have to get these seats out of the way," I say. I lean into the car and tilt the seat backs forward toward the dashboard, exposing the white box that contains Georgia's wedding dress. It's crammed into the shallow storage space behind the seats. "And we need to take out that box."

"Why?" Tully says. He gapes at the car's interior.

"Because the sidescreens—the side windows—are stored underneath. Putting the top up to keep out the cold won't do us much good unless we put the windows on as well."

"Fine," Tully says. "Swell. Except now I get that this isn't a real car. It's a Tinkertoy."

"Not a classic?" I say.

Tully lifts out the garment box and puts it on the asphalt next to the car. Once the box is out, you can see the flat horizontal compartment behind the seats. I undo the snap that secures the compart-ment and push back the lid. Inside, neatly stowed in the felt-lined interior, are the four sidescreens: two for the front, two for the rear.

Tully contemplates the sidescreens. "I take it back," he says. "It's not a Tinkertoy. It's an onion. We keep peeling away layers and finding more and more car."

We unfold the soft top and tease it out and up, marrying it to the connectors at the uppermost corners of the windshield. Then we attach the sidescreens. It's a delicate job fastening them to the car. Each of the two front side windows has a metal pin that hangs down and which you have to fit just so into a socket in the door. There's also a bracket that slides down, hooks over another pin, and gets clamped into position with a wing nut. Plus, there are snaps that secure the sidescreen flaps to the door trim. The rear windows are more or less the same. I hear Tully swearing under his breath.

When the fourth and last sidescreen is attached, Tully picks up the garment box and stuffs it back in behind the seats.

I get in the passenger seat and try to tighten the wing bolt, in the corner above the windshield, that holds the top to my side of the car. But the bolt is stuck, it won't budge. Tully, once again in the driver's seat, watches me struggle.

"Here," he says, and reaches over to help.

In the close quarters of the MG, Tully stretches across me and I'm pressed back into my seat. I can't help but be aware of his physical presence, how good he smells. I'm staring at the upper right corner of the windshield, watching Tully turn the wing bolt. He finishes, but his hand remains where it is, not turning the bolt anymore, just holding it, his body more or less suspended over mine. I shift my gaze from the corner of the windshield to him. His face is only inches from mine.

"I gotta tell you," he says. "You have great eyes."

"Yes?" I say, my throat gone dry.

"Yeah," he says sincerely. "They're so blue."

For a moment, we stare at each other. Then Tully lets loose of the bolt and plops back into his seat. "We're done," he says.

Are we? Oh right, he means the car. Our shiny red roadster now has windows and a tan-colored top.

"That wasn't so bad," Tully says. He reaches up and taps the fabric over our heads.

"Done and done," I say, equally pleased with our success.

Tully slides the key into the ignition. "Now all I need is for you to show me how to turn on the heater," he says. This reminds me of the moment—just days ago, but it feels longer—back in Malibu, when Tully and I first got in the car and I had to explain to him that there weren't any seat belts.

"There isn't one," I say.

Tully frowns. I rush to explain that in the 1950s, when the factory at Abingdon, England, was

195

producing MG TFs, heaters were not standard. "But the cockpit is quite compact," I say. "Now that the top and sidescreens are on, our body heat alone will . . . warm things up."

He looks at me skeptically. I prattle on. "However, then the problem will be interior moisture. Because I'm afraid we don't have—"

"A defroster," Tully says, defeated.

A few hours later, we're on the outskirts of Chicago. The sun has gone down; the air has grown even colder. Luckily, I found a wool blanket nestled in with the sidescreens, and I wrap myself up in it. The blanket, like everything else about the car, is another relic from my shattered childhood.

When my mother drowned herself, I was eight years old. Some weeks later, having nowhere else to take me, my dad brought me to live with his other family—his legal, sanctioned-by-the-state-of-California family—in the big Spanish-style house at Malibu, on the bluff overlooking the Pacific. He parked the MG in the circular drive. He relieved me of the car blanket I was clutching, folded it up, and put it in the side-screen compartment. Then he took me inside. We climbed some stairs and went down a long hall.

"This is your place, here, kiddo," he said, showing me into a room. It was clean and sunny and smelled of the sea. Most of my things were already moved in, a photo of my mother stood on the dresser. We went out on the balcony. My father lifted me up to take in the view. "Look," he said. "You can see the ocean."

"I don't like the ocean," I said.

We lingered, gazing at the water, my father's cheek snugged up against mine. I felt something wet by my ear. "Daddy, are you crying?" I said.

"Nah." He rubbed his face. "Well, you know."

"You're remembering about Mummy," I said.

My father introduced me that day to the female housekeeper, but not to his wife, Irene. Then he told me he had business in town, kissed me good-bye, and left. With nothing to do, I wandered down by the swimming pool. A skinny, flat-chested girl in a two-piece swimsuit was floating on her back in the water. She was about thirteen years old. I knew I had an older half sister because on the ride over my father had told me about her for the first time. Suspecting this might be her, I sat down on a lounge chair to watch.

The girl rolled over, thrashing like a crocodile. "Hey, you little creep!" she said. "Get off my towel!"

This was how I met my big half sister. This was Charlotte.

Route 66 goes more or less to the heart of Chicago. By the time Tully and I enter the city, it's late evening. We're cruising through the down-town area when a beeping sound emanates from my bag. The cell phone. Charlotte again.

"Breaking news!" Charlotte says. "It cost me a Kate Spade clutch and a gift certificate for full-mouth dental veneers to find out Georgia's staying with her best friend, Kelsey. Kelsey moved to Chicago last month—but Tully knows her. They met when Kelsey came back to LA for the wedding."

Charlotte sounds even more manic than usual, and I wonder if she's had her head inside that globe in the library.

"After your odyssey in Daddy's little car," she says, "that is, when you *finally* reach Chicago, I want you to go to Kelsey's."

I gaze up at the lights of the Willis Tower, formerly the Sears Tower, the signature skyscraper of the Windy City.

"I have the address," Charlotte says. "Wait—" She drops the phone on the desk, and it clanks in my ear. I hear her talking to herself and rustling through papers.

I worry Charlotte may wander off, forgetting about me altogether. But moments later, there's more rustling, the clink of ice cubes in a glass, and she's back.

"Sorry," she says. "I'm a little woo-woo right now. I've been doing deep medication.

Ha-ha. I mean, meditation." She rattles off an address, and I write it on a notepad I pull from my bag.

"Charlotte," I say, "if you have this address, you probably have the phone number there as well. Why don't you ring them? Or text Georgia. Tell her the game's up. Tell her to come home, nothing is forgiven."

"Georgia's not answering her cell," Charlotte says. "She's still not talking to me. Find her, make her understand the mother-daughter healing can't possibly begin until she gives back what she took from me."

It's been four days since I broke into Georgia's hotel room in Palm Springs. I have not yet mentioned this escapade to either Charlotte or Tully, but I decide it's time to take a chance. "You mean that old screenplay, don't you?" I say.

I glance over at Tully, who's preoccupied with the heavy Chicago traffic. After days of Charlotte's incessant phone calling, Tully's become adept at tuning out entirely my endless discussions with my half sister.

"I saw it, you know," I say to Charlotte in a low voice.

"You found Georgia?" Charlotte says.

"No, but I got into her room in Palm Springs. That script she has would make quite a movie."

"If you only knew!" Charlotte says. "It's a very hot property."

"And I imagine it's the item you want returned to you."

"It is," she says after a moment. "Along with one or two other things."

"Charlotte," I say, "I'm weary of this scavenger hunt."

Tully stops at a red light just as three young men come out of a bar. Hanging on each other, they gape over from the sidewalk—pointing and giving thumbs-up to our little car. I wave at them.

"If you want me to continue," I say to Charlotte, as the car starts up again, "you have to let me know exactly what it is you want from Georgia. One item? Two? A baker's dozen?"

"All right," she says. She gives an exasperated sigh. "I'll tell you the truth."

There's a pause as Charlotte and I both apprehend that she's set herself a personal best. Charlotte *tell the truth?* We're half siblings, after all. We share the same DNA—and in our family, DNA stands for Denial Now and Always. The truth never came easily to our father, and it doesn't come easily to his daughters.

I again look at Tully, who continues giving his full attention to the traffic. I press the phone tightly to my ear.

"First," Charlotte says, "how much am I paying you?"

What? This is not what I expected. What's she talking about?

"How much," she repeats, "am I paying you to locate Georgia and retrieve my possessions?"

She's paying me fifty thousand dollars, but I haven't lived in New York City all these years without picking up a few tricks. "Fifty-five thousand dollars," I lie.

"All right," she says.

Bother. I should have said sixty.

"I'll make it sixty, *if* you're successful in getting my things returned to me. Georgia has abused my maternal love. But I do care about the goose. So tell her . . . tell her I'm willing to pay for shamanic counseling or mother-daughter hypnotherapy if it will help us heal the hurt. Do please try."

"I will," I say, amazed to hear Charlotte use the word "please." "I'll do my best." And strangely enough, I mean it.

"There are three things I want back," she says.

"Three things," I echo.

"Yes, three. Although one of them is my lost youth." At this last statement, she breaks into peals of laughter. She's laughing so hard at her own joke, she can hardly speak. "That's funny, isn't it?" she stammers. *"My lost youth."* She goes off into more laughter, snorting and giggling into the phone.

I take the phone from my ear and hold it in my hand, staring at it. I've always had trouble understanding people, communicating with them.

My relationship with my half sister is simply another case in point. Here I am in the middle of North America, searching for Charlotte's daughter and some trio of purloined objects, and here's Charlotte, collapsing into what I can only assume are drug-induced hysterics.

I put the phone back to my ear. Charlotte's still laughing, but her tone has changed. The pitch of her voice has gone lower, there's a hollowness that doesn't seem right. She no longer sounds like she's laughing. Not anymore. She sounds like she's sobbing.

"Charlotte?" I say. "Everything all right?"

She breathes in. "Of course! I'm tired, that's all. *Muscle Man* premieres in a few days. I've been working"—the phone cuts out—"that picture! Dog, I'm telling you. D-O-G!"

"There's trouble with *Muscle Man*?" I say.

"What? No. I'm in complete control!"

Maybe. But her voice is husky, she's sniffling. Is *Muscle Man* shaping up to be a flop? Don't read too much into this, I tell myself. Maybe she's not sad. Maybe she's been snorting cocaine.

"Anyway," Charlotte says, all business again except for the occasional sniffle, "as I was saying, the script. That's the number one item I want returned to me. And then there's the other."

"I know there's another item," I say. "You keep telling me that. But what is it?"

"Hmm?" she says. "Oh, that's not as important. But I'd like it anyway. Sentimental reasons. And if you must know, there's something else Georgia stole from me. Margo, you're my . . . half sister. So I might as well tell you as anybody. But you won't be able to help. I'll have to handle that myself."

"But what *is* it?" I say.

"It's upsetting, is what it is. I have feelings, too, you know. After so many years together, a woman shouldn't feel betrayed by her man, her own daughter—"

And then I lose her. The line goes dead.

"Charlotte!" I say. "Are you there? Dammit!" I beat the cell phone against the dashboard.

"Hey!" Tully says. "Don't do that!"

I cease flogging the phone, though perhaps too late. Its lights have gone as dim as Tinker Bell after she drinks the poison intended for Peter Pan.

"Let me see," Tully says. He holds his hand out, and I pass him the phone. In the darkened cockpit, it glows weakly. *I do believe in fairies; I do believe in fairies.* Glancing away from the traffic for a moment, Tully looks down at the device.

"Battery's dead," he says. "Put it in the charger tonight, and if you didn't kill it banging it around like that, it should be okay tomorrow." He hands it back.

I'm not really listening to Tully, however,

because I can't stop thinking about Charlotte. Her man, did she say? Meaning her husband, Donald, the screenwriters' agent? Her own daughter, meaning Georgia?

Is Charlotte saying what I think she's saying? That Donald is romantically involved with his stepdaughter, Georgia? Wait a minute! Is that why Georgia ran off? To be with Donald? And why wasn't Donald at the wedding, anyway?

It's late. After Tully and I check into a downtown hotel, I call Charlotte from the landline in my room. All I get is her voice mail. I undress and climb into bed, but I can't sleep.

Three things. There are three things that Charlotte wants returned to her. At least now I know what they are. The first item, the most valuable, is *An Innocent Lamb*, written by our father, Arthur Just, and Orson Welles. I'm guessing she needs that to offset whatever losses she incurs on *Muscle Man*.

The second item isn't terribly important, yet Charlotte wants it for sentimental reasons. Well, it's not the *Spy Team* script, is it? She didn't even mention that. So it's Georgia's wedding dress, it must be. That dress is exquisite. And I remember Charlotte saying at the Malibu house that she hoped to get the dress back. After all, it's meant for Daughter's First Wedding—like Baby's First Christmas.

But the third thing? The item Charlotte said she'd have to handle herself? It's not a thing at all. It's her own husband. It's Donald. No wonder Charlotte feels betrayed. No wonder she's ambivalent about her relationship with Georgia. No wonder she was crying for her lost youth!

I wonder what Charlotte ever saw in Donald. Something hidden, I suppose. Something the rest of us will never see. Well, she's right: I can't help her retrieve her husband. And I already have the wedding dress.

So my path is clear. Find Georgia, talk to her, get that screenplay. The one thing I absolutely must lay my hands on is *An Innocent Lamb*.

CHAPTER TWELVE
EMOTIONAL BAGGAGE

In the morning, the sun is out, there's a chill in the air, and the wind is blowing in off Lake Michigan. Tully and I leave the hotel and drive to the address Charlotte gave me. It turns out to be one of those glass and steel luxury high-rises across from Millennium Park. After we park the car and walk to the building, we take a very fast, very smooth elevator to the thirty-sixth floor and press the buzzer of apartment 36C.

The door opens and a young woman stands there. Blonde, attractive, yet somehow a tad world-weary for her years, she wears tights and a sleek, stretchy leotard that make her look like she's on her way to dance class. For a moment, she considers Tully and me both, thinking perhaps that we're salespeople or religious zealots. Then recognition comes into her eyes. She leans against the doorjamb.

"Hey, Tull," she says.

Without a word, Tully brushes past her, and I'm pulled along in his wake. The woman closes the door and follows after us. We pass through a marble foyer and into a living room that's all white walls and floor-to-ceiling windows with multimillion-dollar views of the park, the lake, and the city. There's a lipstick-red sofa, a white Berber rug, and a lot of expensive, modern furniture, but I get the feeling we won't be invited to sit down. The three of us stand there, ignoring the view and focusing on one another.

"This is Georgia's aunt," Tully says to the woman. "Margo Just."

The young woman gives me a childish wave.

"Kelsey Burke," he says to me. "Kelsey and Georgia are best friends."

"Duh," Kelsey declares, hand on hip. "Since we were dweebie little boppers, surfing the breaks together."

Kelsey turns to me and her attitude changes. Now it's as though she's addressing the aging headmistress—that would be me—of a private girls' school and has put on her best manners in an effort to escape punishment for some outrageous transgression. "I lived in LA my whole entire life," she says politely. "Until last month, when I moved out here."

"Right," Tully says. "Listen, Margo and I are here to see Georgia. We're worried about her."

"Don't be," Kelsey says. She leans against a sofa table and pulls a leg up behind her, stretching. "Georgia isn't stressed about you."

"She told you that?" Tully says.

Kelsey laughs. "She told me lots of things. The day before the wedding, she texted me she was going to ditch you. Sorry to say that, but you asked. By the way, that was some wedding reception. Too bad you missed it." She laughs again. "After you left, everybody partied. Danced the whole freaking night! Somebody had disco biscuits."

Disco biscuits?

"Party drugs," Tully explains for my benefit. "Ecstasy."

"Anyway," Kelsey says, stretching her other leg, "too bad you and Georgia weren't there."

"Kelsey was going to be Georgia's maid of honor," Tully says.

"That always sounds so *Robin Hood*," Kelsey says. She does a half curtsy toward Tully, then makes a fawning gesture like a courtier. "Thy maid of honor, my lord. Forsooth!"

Is she mad? Surely no one in her right mind could be so willfully insipid.

"Kelsey is also studying acting," Tully says. He's beginning to sound like a frazzled father, humoring his two-year-old.

"Umm," Kelsey agrees. "And Kelsey is about to get her big break. Kelsey will soon be back in Hollywood. Kelsey is stoked!"

"You got a part?" Tully says.

"Yup. Not supposed to tweet about it yet, but it's big."

"I'm impressed," Tully says, though whether he's commenting on Kelsey's career or her anatomy is a mystery. She continues stretching, and we both watch as she lifts her right foot up to the sofa table and bends forward, effortlessly touching her forehead to her knee. Her spine and flawless back muscles are outlined by her leotard. She turns her head so that her cheek rests on her knee.

"You know," Kelsey says, gazing up at Tully, "Georgia totally guessed you might show up here."

"I want to talk to her," Tully says.

"That's funny," Kelsey says, taking her right leg down and switching to her left. "Because whenever Georgia talked about your wants, it was never, you know, *conversation.*"

She makes this last remark sound terribly suggestive, and I feel myself grow warm. Why? The idea of Georgia and Tully together, I suppose. Together and not conversing.

Tully, the frazzled father, has had enough. "Tell me where she is," he says.

Kelsey stops stretching and stands, arms crossed, staring straight at Tully. "Not here, I promise."

"But she was."

Kelsey laughs. "Sure. After Georgia exited your non-wedding, she checked it to Palm Springs where, I guess, she partied with friends. Then she calls and asks if she can kick it here a few nights. By that time, I'm flying home myself. So

I'm like, No problem, perfect timing, Boone's away on business."

She turns to me again. "Boone's my fiancé," she says, once more addressing me in the tone one might employ with a schoolteacher, nun, or sufferer of senile dementia. "He's in Canada right now. Import, export."

I take it Kelsey means Boone is in the import-export business. Though it could be she's sharing her prescription for dealing with the male sex.

"So, anyway," she says, addressing herself to Tully, "Georgia flew here, and we chilled. She needed that. Her life's been pretty random lately."

Tully impatiently shifts his weight. "Yeah, well—"

"We girl-talked," Kelsey says. "Listened to music, watched DVDs. She stayed with me a couple days, then hasta la vista."

"Where'd she go?" Tully says.

Kelsey sighs. "Out of your life, babe, that's for sure."

"I don't believe that," Tully says. "And I won't, unless I hear it from Georgia."

Kelsey seems amused, like a teenager suppressing a giggle at the expense of a clueless grown-up. "Tull, everybody knows you're a sweetie," she says. "And for two or three weeks, five minutes, whatever, Georgia was amped on you. She was."

She pauses, as though a thought has come into

her head. What an unexpected and spooky feeling that must be for her. "Funny," she says, "how some girls, when they've had lots of dads and stepdads, go for older guys." She looks Tully up and down. "I never got that."

Her brief observation on sugar daddies ended, Kelsey returns to the topic of Georgia. "But you better face it," she says, "you and G are so dunzo."

"If by 'dunzo,'" Tully says, "you mean—"

"I mean," Kelsey says, "you have been kicked to the curb. You are Mister Ex-Fiancé. Any relationship you have with that girl is strictly in your dreams." She taps her temple with an index finger. "Totally imaginary. My advice is get off the L train. L as in loser. Collect your emotional baggage from the rotating carousel of life and move on. Know what I'm saying?"

I'm not at all sure *I* know what she's saying, but Tully seems to understand perfectly. "Is she with somebody?" he says.

Kelsey sighs again. "Like another guy? Look, Georgia's ambitious, she has plans. She doesn't park her butt in the sand and watch killer waves break on the beach without her. She paddles her board out there and takes 'em."

And in this case, I'm thinking, it's possible Georgia paddled her board out and took her own stepfather, Donald. Charlotte's husband.

Kelsey turns to me a third time, obviously

racking her brain for the polite thing to say. "Would you like some herbal tea or something?" she says.

I get the feeling "or something" would be a motorized wheelchair or a gift certificate for assisted living. Like Tully, I've about had it with Kelsey. If he's the frazzled father, I'm the exasperated mother.

I sit myself down on the red sofa. "I'll pass on the tea," I say. "But if there's any gin in the house, I'd love a large martini. Very dry."

Shocked, I suppose, that the headmistress tipples, Kelsey nevertheless goes over to a built-in bar and makes me a cocktail. She also mixes herself something large and fruity and pours Tully a soda. She hands round the drinks.

Through all this, Tully and Kelsey continue squabbling about Georgia, but I'm no longer listening. A dozen thoughts swirl through my brain, not the least of which is that remark Kelsey made a few moments ago seeming to suggest Tully and Georgia had an energetic sex life. I don't like picturing that—it makes me feel sur-prisingly jealous, incestuous, and a trifle sick. Actually, more than a trifle. I down my drink, but my stomach is in knots. From out of nowhere, I hear myself say, "I'm sorry, but I don't feel well."

They both stop bickering and spin round in

my direction. Tully appears genuinely concerned. Kelsey looks like she's suddenly guest starring on a television medical show. She seems to be debating whether to call 911 or to go straight for an Emmy nomination by performing open-heart surgery using the only materials she has at hand: disco biscuits and a swizzle stick.

"Perhaps I should . . . visit the powder room," I say. I lean heavily against the sofa back and place one hand on my stomach. With my other hand, I cover my mouth and let out a small, ominous hiccup.

That's all it takes. Kelsey eyes her sofa, her white rug, and the rest of her expensive, sparkling furniture. In a flash, she's hurrying me down the hall to the toilet. I'm just able to grab my tote bag as we go.

"Take your time," she says, hustling me into an elegant half bath. "Don't rush or anything. Tull and I will hang. Don't worry about coming back until you're . . . done."

I give her a brave smile.

Kelsey leaves, and I shut the bathroom door behind her. The minute her footsteps die away, I open the door again and step out into the empty passageway. I can hear Kelsey and Tully still going at it in the living room.

I wasn't lying when I said I didn't feel well. I don't. But what's wrong with me can't be cured by a visit to the ladies' room. What's wrong with me can only be put right by a look round Kelsey's flat, because what's wrong with me is that I need to know more.

Besides the powder room, there are two additional doors off the hallway. The one nearest me is ajar. I tiptoe over to it. I'm jumpy and nervous because I'm certain the minute I peek into that room sirens will wail or a housekeeper will scream or a giant, salivating German shepherd will leap up and take a bite out of my thigh. But when I push on the door, it swings open, and none of these things happen.

I'm standing in what must be the master bedroom. There's a massive flat-screen television, a king-size bed, and two bureaus topped with jewelry boxes and glossy photos in silver frames, mostly glamour shots of Kelsey. Off to one side, an archway leads to a master bath.

Emboldened by gin, I get to work. This is the second time in recent days I've rifled through someone's things. I'm practically an old hand at it. Once again, like when I searched Georgia's suite in Palm Springs, I don't know what I'm looking for, but I feel compelled to look.

I snoop through bureau drawers and night-stands, finding little of interest except a few bottles of prescription narcotics, some spicy underwear, and several titillating sex toys. Quickly, methodically, I search the walk-in closet, the bathroom, under the bed. Nothing. The clock is ticking, I know, but I need to keep looking.

I creep back out to the hallway and stare at the other door, which is shut tight. My heart beats wildly. If I enter this room, I know I will face the sirens, the screams, the large barking dog.

I turn the handle and open the door.

There's only silence.

I walk into the room. It's smaller than the master bedroom and contains an unmade bed and some sleek modern furniture. Something about the room is oddly familiar. I have a feeling of déjà vu, like I've been here before. But that's not possible. This building didn't exist the last time I visited Chicago. Still, there's something about the look of the room, the feel of it, even the smell—

Oh, oh! OH! Dior Pure Poison! And the instant my nose gets it, the instant I recognize that lingering fragrance, I catch on to something else: what's familiar about this room is that it's a complete mess. Luggage and makeup cases are thrown open, their contents spilling out. Clothing and personal items are strewn about like tinsel on a Christmas tree. This is a decorating approach I associate with just one person: Georgia.

Kelsey lied. Georgia *is* here, she's in Chicago. And this is her room. It must be. My pulse is racing like I imbibed every drink on the menu at Starbucks. Nevertheless, I start poking through

Georgia's possessions the way I did in Palm Springs. I know now what it is I'm looking for. Only this time it's different. This time I'm not bound by a promise made to a friendly bartender to look but not take. This time whatever I find, I'm taking.

I dig through suitcases and dirty laundry, all of it. But only when I get down on my hands and knees do I glimpse something promising. On the floor, shoved under the bed, is a jumble of old magazines and papers. I pull handfuls of the stuff toward me: *Entertainment Weekly*, *Variety*, *Vanity Fair*. I sift through it all.

I come to a back issue of *People*. Malcolm Belvedere is on the cover, photographed at a film premiere. The headline says, "The Most Powerful Man in Hollywood."

Generally speaking, I don't read celebrity magazines. They're a waste of time, major contributors to the dumbing-down of America. Everybody knows that. Still, the photo of Malcolm is good, flattering. Even someone who'd never met him would think this older man was attractive.

The picture shows Malcolm striding, straight-shouldered, up the red carpet. He's wearing a gray suit and scarlet tie, and his green eyes sparkle, just as they did the day he and I chatted on the lawn at Malibu. The day The Most Powerful Man in Hollywood handed me a creamy vellum card imprinted with his private phone numbers.

Even though I'm in a hurry, even though I'm kneeling on the floor surrounded by old magazines and an assortment of Georgia's sexy silk undergarments, I decide to flip through *People* and see if there are any more pictures of Malcolm.

But when I pick up the magazine to examine it more closely, I notice something lying underneath. It's a black folder, an aged thing with a faded, typewritten label. My brain cannot believe what my eyes are telling it. Here, once again, is the elusive and not-so-innocent script of *An Innocent Lamb*, cowritten by my father, Arthur Just, and America's greatest filmmaker, Orson Welles.

For a moment, I do nothing. I don't touch the script, I just stare at it. I wasn't dreaming when I first discovered it that night in Palm Springs. *An Innocent Lamb* exists, and I've found it again.

I can't believe my good fortune. To find the thing twice!

Then, out in the living room, Tully sneezes. The sound—that explosive, achoo yelling noise some men make when they get off a really good sneeze—is so loud it pierces the quiet of Georgia's bedroom. It startles me back to reality, and I realize I've been gone many minutes. Tully and Kelsey must wonder what's taking me so long. How much retching can a person do?

I grab at the pile of papers and magazines in front of me, snatching up not only *An Innocent Lamb*, but also a few things underneath it, including the *Spy Team* script. What the hell, I pick up *People* too. In a frenzy—worried I've been gone too long, worried Kelsey will come looking for me and I'll be caught at the instant of my success—I stuff the whole lot into my tote bag, sling it over my shoulder, and get up off the floor.

I dash back out into the hallway. I cross over to the half bath, flush the toilet, run the tap, and wipe my hands on a towel, all in the interest of creating an alibi, of making it look like I spent the last ten minutes throwing up, rather than ransacking Georgia's room.

I'm so flustered with what I've just done, with the value of the item I've taken, that I'm breathing heavily. You could say I'm having a mild panic attack. Part of me is amazed that I can now add "cat burglar" to my resume. The other part still expects to encounter the sirens, the screaming household staff, the snarling German shepherd.

I hurry out of the bathroom. I turn to race back to the living room, but I run into someone. My heart gives a wallop. I've collided with a large man. He's not fat, just solid, like a bouncer or bulletproof glass.

He catches me by the elbow and steadies me. "Well, hey," he says. "You all right?" His voice is husky.

"Yes!" I say. "I was sick to my stomach—quite sick, terribly sick!—but now I'm fine."

He releases my elbow. "Uh-huh." He stares at the hand he touched me with. "Think I'll go wash up."

"Brilliant! There's a darling powder room." I point at the door of the half bath.

"I know. I live here. I'm Boone."

Boone? Import, export?

"Lovely to meet you," I say. "I'm Margo, Georgia Illworth's aunt."

"Yeah?" He smiles, and his upper lip curls back over his teeth, like a shark. "I guess Georgia's going to—" He stops himself and glances in the direction of the living room. "I forget," he finishes.

"Life is just a bowl of scaries!" I say.

Boone goes off to the powder room. I return to the living room where Kelsey and Tully sit together on the sofa, a pair of suitcases parked on the floor next to them. Kelsey holds a scrapbook, pointing at the pictures in it. "Here's when I was three," she says. "Topanga Tots Beauty Pageant. I took a Grand Supreme win."

"Is that good?" Tully says.

"Oh, sure. My mom bawled her eyes out." She

turns the page and touches a photo. "See? I'm wearing the winner's sash and tiara."

When he notices me enter the room, Tully rises. He comes over and puts a hand on my upper arm. "You okay?" he says.

My heart is racing from all that just happened—and perhaps, a little, from the commanding feel of Tully's fingers round my bicep. I try to pull myself together. "I'm fine," I say.

"Sure?" Tully says.

"You look pale," Kelsey declares. Her tone is blunt, as if she meant to say, "You look, like, totally dead." Her mouth slightly open, she stares at me as though trying to figure out how her day went so wrong that she ended up with a middle-aged female invalid standing in her apartment.

"We were starting to kind of worry about you," Kelsey says. "But then Boone walked in from nowhere, which he does a lot." She thumps one of the suitcases with the side of her foot. "Bam! Just like that, he's back from Canada. His allergies are acting up. He's sneezing all over the place."

"Yes," I say, "we met. He—"

"So, anyway," she says, "when Boone showed up, I guess we sort of forgot about you. Then I got out this old scrapbook, and I don't know, we really forgot about you." She laughs, as though amused at her own capacity for indifference.

"Do you want to see a doctor?" Tully says. It takes me a second to realize he's speaking to me and not, as one might expect, suggesting psychiatric help for Kelsey.

"No," I say. "I'm all right. Really."

Slowly, in a gentle way, Tully lets go of my arm.

A few minutes pass, during which Kelsey lies like her precious Berber rug as she repeatedly assures Tully she has no inkling as to Georgia's whereabouts. In the end, she politely, if stiffly, shows us out. On the way to the front door, she even offers to carry my tote bag—the one containing the script and papers I swiped from Georgia's room. I decline her offer. If anything, I clutch the bag closer to me.

Kelsey opens the front door. Tully and I step out into the hallway and turn to say good-bye. Kelsey stands in the threshold, chewing on a lock of her long blonde hair. She pulls a hunk of hair out of her mouth and wraps it round her finger. "Tull," she says, "I'm gonna clue you one last time. Give it up. You and Georgia are so not getting back together."

There's a smirk on Kelsey's face, as though she's savoring the high-school-like thrill of helping her good chum Georgia dump her boyfriend. "Georgia's my tightest bud. I know for sure she's over you."

Tully seems about to say something in reply, but

from inside the apartment, Boone bellows for Kelsey.

"Gotta go," Kelsey says. She springs backward, closing the door on us.

After Kelsey shuts the door in our faces, Tully and I take the express elevator down to the street.

It's good to be out in the air. The day is bright, but blustery. We bend our heads into the wind and walk back toward the car.

"That was stupid," Tully says. "Waste of time."

"I disagree," I say. "I found it instructive."

"How?" Tully says. "Meeting creepy Boone? Hearing Kelsey's immature take on my relationship with Georgia?"

I hesitate. I wonder if I should tell Tully what I've done, wonder if I can trust him. Then again, if I can't trust Tully, who can I trust?

"I wasn't sick back there, you know," I say.

"You mean, you feel better?"

"I mean, I was never ill. When everybody thought I was throwing up in the bathroom, I was snooping round the apartment."

Tully stops and looks at me like I just knocked over a liquor store. "No way."

"Way. Not only that, I took something."

"Jesus! What? The silverware?"

"Better than that."

And then I tell Tully the story. I tell him how *An Innocent Lamb* was written by Orson Welles and my father, how Georgia took the script and Charlotte wants it back. I also inform him that Kelsey lied; Georgia isn't gone. Everything I saw in the guest bedroom indicates Georgia is staying with Kelsey and Boone.

Tully whips his head round to look at Kelsey's building. He starts walking back.

I grab at his jacket to stop him. "No! You mustn't!"

"Why not?" he says. "I'll get Kelsey to tell me the truth."

"You won't," I say. "She's probably on the phone right now, warning Georgia that we came by. Warning her to stay away. Plus, I don't like the look of that Boone."

"Then what the hell do we do?"

"You tell me," I say. I let go of his jacket and smooth the sleeve. "You're the one with the extreme intelligence."

"The what?"

"Charlotte says you have a high IQ."

Tully laughs. "You're kidding. I have some smarts, I guess. Like anybody. Not hard if you pick up a book once in a while."

"But why would Charlotte make up something like that?" I say.

Tully heaves a sigh. "She thinks I'm wasting my time writing nonfiction. She wants me to churn out screenplays. If Charlotte's going around telling people I'm a genius, it's because she hopes it will impress them, or because she's trying to impress herself. And because—"

"In her world, who could tell?"

"Right. Nobody would ever challenge it."

"Please," I say, "let's go to the car."

We begin walking, and I again ask Tully what he wants to do. Should we stake out Kelsey and Boone's apartment and wait for Georgia to show up?

Tully, still walking, gazes up at the surrounding skyscrapers. "You're probably right," he says. "Kelsey will tip off Georgia. Which means Georgia won't come back here for who knows how long. I vote we take a break. As long as we're in Chicago, I should visit the Museum of Science and Industry."

We reach the MG. Tully opens the passenger door and stands there, holding it for me. "You want to come along?" he says. "Have lunch?"

"I don't understand," I say. "You think Georgia's at a museum?"

"I doubt Georgia's ever been to a museum," Tully says. "I'm not sure she'd see the point." He adjusts his glasses. "No, I want to go to the museum because it has a dollhouse I need to see."

Oh, no. A dollhouse. We're back on dollhouses.

CHAPTER THIRTEEN

FAIRY CASTLE

The Museum of Science and Industry is about fifteen minutes from downtown Chicago. It's huge. You can wander for hours looking at things like a baby-chick hatchery or an authentic steam locomotive from the 1890s. But Tully and I are hungry, so after we park and pay admission, we head to the food court.

"Food court" always sounds sort of silly, doesn't it? Sounds like you're going before a judge while also consuming a cheeseburger and fries.

We get our lunch and settle in at a table. Tully lifts the bread off the top of his sandwich. He looks at the filling inside.

"Do you remember the day we met?" Tully says, all the while inspecting his sandwich. "We were out in the desert, and you asked me what I did, was I a writer or what."

"Yes. Neither of us was very sociable that day."

"Right. Well, your sister, Charlotte—"

"Half sister."

"Your half sister, Charlotte, was the reason I didn't want to talk about what I do. Sure, I felt lousy and I was mad at Georgia, but I also thought that since you were related to Charlotte, you'd take her side. I thought you'd end up telling me I should write for films."

Apparently satisfied with the quality of his lunch, Tully puts his sandwich back together and takes a bite of it.

"For your information," I say, "I almost never side with Charlotte."

Tully holds up a finger to signal that he's chewing. "Yeah, well, now you know," he says after a moment. "I don't write for the movies. I don't want to write for the movies. That's Georgia's fantasy, not mine. Georgia's supposed to come up with a script and put herself and Kelsey and all their friends in it. That's her plan. And speaking of scripts, what are you going to do with the one you lifted from Georgia's room?"

"*An Innocent Lamb*?" I pat my leather tote on the chair next to me. It contains the screenplay and other items I took from Georgia. "I shall return it to its rightful owner."

"Which is who, exactly?"

"I'm not sure," I say.

On impulse, I set the tote bag on my lap and do a quick inventory of the things I pilfered. There's *An Innocent Lamb*, of course. Also the *Spy Team* script, a brochure for the upcoming Tribeca Film Festival in New York, the *People* magazine with Malcolm Belvedere on the cover, and a second entertainment magazine. I page through it and see a brief piece about Malcolm.

"That's funny," I say to Tully. I tap the cover of *People*. "Your ex-stepfather is mentioned in both of these old magazines Georgia had."

"He's a celebrity," Tully says. "He gets written about."

"But he's a studio head, not a movie star," I say. "And Charlotte said he avoids publicity. So it's not like he's in every periodical you pick up. It seems odd he'd be in more than one publication that Georgia had."

Tully shrugs. "Let me ask you something," he says. "Does finding that script mean you're done looking for Georgia?"

What Tully's really asking, I think, is whether I'm done helping him look for her.

"Well," I say, "now that I have *An Innocent Lamb*, seeing Georgia could be awkward. On the other hand, my agreement with Charlotte was that I would at least talk to her daughter. So I'm willing to continue. Do you think we should keep a watch on Kelsey's apartment? See if Georgia shows up?"

"Maybe," Tully says. "We could try that tomorrow."

I put the scripts and magazines back in my bag. I pluck a carrot stick from my plate. "I wonder about Kelsey," I say. "I thought wannabe actresses all had shabby flats. I thought they existed on rice cakes and ramen. How does she live so well?"

"Boone," Tully says, ripping open a bag of

potato chips. "The guy's loaded. He's the reason Kelsey moved out here. They met in LA a couple months back and fell in love—or whatever it is they are in. He's bankrolling her career."

"What exactly does Boone import and export?" I say. I munch on the carrot stick.

"Import—drugs. Export—who knows? Dead bodies, probably. The guy's bad news."

"That's a lovely bunch of coconuts you hang with," I say.

"Yeah, well, some of them are your relatives."

After lunch, we follow the signs through the museum directing us to something called Colleen Moore's Fairy Castle. This, I'm guessing, is the dollhouse Tully is so keen on viewing.

Crowded with tourists and schoolchildren, the museum gives off a comforting air of tradition and normality. I like museums. Finn Coyle and I used to visit the Metropolitan Museum of Art. With Finn as my guide, I learned a lot at the Met about art and architecture.

Thinking about Finn reminds me of how other people always mystify me. For example, what is going on at this moment inside Tully Benedict's head?

"Tell me, please," I say, as we walk along, "what's so fascinating about this dollhouse we're looking for?"

"Lots," Tully says. "It's not just a dollhouse.

It's a slice of history, a notable twentieth-century American miniature. It's a side of popular culture I'm researching."

He's telling me this, and I'm trying to listen, trying to comprehend why a grown man would be interested in such things, when up ahead I see something that gives me a shock. The dollhouse, yes, it's gigantic. But there's something else, something between us and the dollhouse. Something barring our way.

God in heaven, it's her. It's the old lady from the dining room in Palm Springs. Still very much alive. I remember she said she lived in Chicago—but even so, I can't believe she's turned up here. And when I recall how rudely I behaved to her just a few days ago, it feels embarrassing and messy to encounter her again, like discovering gum stuck to the bottom of my shoe.

Her silver hair is well coiffed, and she's smartly outfitted in a white dress and pearl earrings, with a blue Museum of Science and Industry vest thrown over her dress. And what's that on her vest? Crikey. It's a name tag that reads "Kay."

No! She can't be. She can't! But she is. She's a docent. She probably has all sorts of museum privileges and powers. She could summon security if she wanted to, or a squadron of flying monkeys. She could bring us up on charges in the food court—for loitering or breathing or something.

Tully and I come closer. The old lady sees me,

and the instant she does she shoots me a look like one this nun used to give me at St. Verbian's. A look that says, If only we still had corporal punishment.

"Hello," she says. Her manner is chill. "Imagine you turning up here. Come to see if I'm still breathing?"

"Yes!" I blurt. "I mean, no! No! We're searching for dolls!"

She looks puzzled. "Dolls?"

"Miniature dolls!" I say in a panicked voice. "We're researching them!"

"She means the Colleen Moore dollhouse," Tully says.

"Really?" the old lady says to me in her broad, Midwest accent. "Now that's a surprise. The museum has several exhibits I'd think would appeal to you more. There's a Nazi submarine, for instance. Think of the fun!"

Before I can reply, she continues, "Or you could take a look-see at our interactive giant heart. Tell us if it's still beating."

"Ho-ho," I say. "I'm sure it's in tip-top shape."

"But if it isn't, you'll let us know."

Tully looks lost.

"This lady was in Palm Springs," I tell him. "We met in the hotel dining room."

"That's one way to put it," she says. She's tapping the sole of one of her polished white leather pumps against the floor.

"But now," Tully says to her, "judging by your name tag, you're back on home territory."

"Yes," she says. "I live in Chicago." Is it my imagination, or does she put special emphasis on the word "live"?

"And you volunteer at the museum?" Tully says. "Do you like that?"

"It has its moments," she says. The way she's glaring at me, I don't think this is one of them.

"I'm interested in Colleen Moore's dollhouse," Tully says. "I'm writing a book about American miniatures, about their history. And about their creators and collectors."

"Marvelous!" the old lady says. "That's a grand idea. I'm Kay Vanderwalk, by the way." Clearly, Kay can't bear the sight of me—but she seems quite taken with Tully. She offers her hand to him.

"Tully Benedict," he says to her. They shake.

As though it's an afterthought, which I'm sure it is, Kay introduces herself to me as well. That done, she turns back to Tully. "Here at the museum, we don't often call it the dollhouse," she says. "When the museum acquired it many years ago, it was officially renamed the Fairy Castle." She smiles and gives a knowing nod. "You'll appreciate the semiotics of that, Mr. Benedict, I'm sure."

Tully laughs like she's just said something highly amusing, but now I'm the one who's lost. Semiotics? What is that? Some sort of penicillin?

Kay looks at her watch. "Actually, I'm scheduled to give a little introduction to the castle right about now." She points to where a group of people are congregating by a sign that reads "Fairy Castle Talk 1 p.m."

"Great," Tully says. "I'd like to hear that."

Kay excuses herself and moves off to address the group. Tully and I join the gathering, too, standing at one side.

The Fairy Castle is surrounded by protective glass, as though it were the *Mona Lisa* or the crown jewels or the Popemobile. The structure itself is quite large, about nine feet square and twelve feet high, and I admit it's impressive. You could say it's the ultimate dollhouse.

Oh, architecturally, it's not my style. It's all fantasy French rococo, with elaborate rooms and furnishings and precious little turrets and carvings. Basically, the whole thing is overdone. But that's just it. The more you look at the castle, the more you get caught up in the story it tells. It's a complete miniature world that pulls you in, like a drug or a dream.

"Good afternoon, everyone," Kay says to the people gathered before her. Her voice is clear and strong. "I'm so glad you could all come today to see Colleen Moore's Fairy Castle."

The crowd instinctively moves closer. A little girl is in front, holding her mother's hand. She's about six years old, dressed in pink, and wearing a Barbie backpack. "Are you Colleen Moore?" she asks in a small voice.

"No, sweetheart, I'm not," Kay says. She bends down toward the child. "My name is Kay. I volunteer here at the museum. I'm afraid Miss Moore died in 1988, but I'm going to tell you about her castle. Would you like that?"

The little girl nods.

And then Kay launches into her talk. She's surprisingly good at it, and I expect she's done it many times before. She explains that Colleen Moore was an American film star—huge, really—in silent films of the 1920s.

Pretty much forgotten now, though, isn't she? I've never even heard of Colleen Moore. She's certainly not remembered the way most people know about, say, Mary Pickford or Charlie Chaplin. Well, one day, you're the Angelina Jolie of 1926, and the next all that's left behind is your giant rococo dollhouse.

"Did she build the castle by herself?" asks the little girl.

"Good question," Kay says. "And the answer is, no, she did not. It was her idea, but she had lots of help putting it together. Miss Moore hired Hollywood set designers and all kinds of expert craftspeople. She spent nearly half a million dollars financing the project. Of course, Miss Moore had a lifelong fascination with dollhouses. When she was a child, she had one fancy dollhouse after another. So it was something she always enjoyed doing."

Kay goes on to talk about the castle's murals and decorations, inspired by fairy tales and nursery rhymes, and the magnificent rooms and furnishings. The detail really is extraordinary: miniature lightbulbs each the size of a grain of rice, a gold chandelier made with genuine diamonds and pearls, a tiny silver bathtub with dolphin-shaped faucets.

"And then," Kay says, "Miss Moore did a wonderful and altruistic thing." She again addresses the little girl with the Barbie backpack. "Altruism means generosity to others. Like when you give money to charity."

"We give groceries to the food bank," the child says.

"Well, there you are. Miss Moore, who had no children of her own, took the dollhouse on a tour to raise funds for children's hospitals and charities. She traveled with it around the country, and people everywhere paid money to see it. This was during the Great Depression, when most Americans didn't have a lot of cash, but even so Miss Moore raised about $650,000 for charity. More money even than the castle cost to build."

A tourist in khaki pants and a T-shirt raises his hand and Kay calls on him. "But why'd she build it so big?" he says. "So . . ."

"Lavish?" Kay says. She tells us that Colleen Moore's first marriage, to film producer John McCormick, was a great love affair that failed because of McCormick's drinking. Failed so spectacularly in a public, Hollywood kind of way, that it later inspired that 1937 movie *A Star Is Born*, about a young actress on the way up who marries a fading alcoholic movie star on the way down. And that *A Star Is Born* was remade two more times, with everybody from Judy Garland to Barbra Streisand playing the part based on Colleen Moore.

In the movies, the alcoholic husband always dies, but I guess in real life Colleen's ex lived on for some time. John McCormick was a handsome, romantic Irish-American, and Colleen had loved him madly. It was when her marriage was breaking up that she began work on the Fairy Castle.

Kay tells us that in the early days of their marriage, when they were happy, Colleen and John had a secret phrase they used only with each other: "Love never dies." She points to a miniature gold box inside the Fairy Castle that holds the castle's crown jewels. Engraved on the box is an inscription in Gaelic. Kay says the translation is, "Love never dies."

And now I get it.

Like an electric lightbulb the size of a grain of rice, my little brain glows with the truth about

1920s film star Colleen Moore. Now I understand why she employed set designers and lighting technicians and a Beverly Hills jeweler to build her a dollhouse. A dollhouse, for Pete's sake. Now I comprehend why she spent eight years of her life and nearly half a million dollars building this elaborate fantasy.

It was her solace.

It was her distraction. It was her drug of choice. It was how she tried to heal her broken heart. She built a magic castle, a perfect home where no one was ever sad and where love lived forever. She herself called it her folly. But was she talking about the dollhouse or her obsession with John McCormick?

Love never dies. Ain't that the truth? And we all go mad in our own way. Glittering dollhouse or bottomless glass of Gordon's gin, in the end it's pretty much the same.

Kay finishes her talk and the crowd disperses, although a few people linger to ask questions. When the last of them has drifted away, Kay sits down on a bench. Tully announces he's off to the museum shop. I tell him I'll wait.

I park myself on the bench next to Kay. She looks at me a moment, then away, then down at her watch. I have the feeling she won't stay put for long. Despite the awkwardness between us, I'm dying to ask her a question.

"What happened to Colleen Moore?" I say. "That is, apart from the dollhouse. Why did she stop making movies?"

"She lost her looks," Kay says matter-of-factly. "In silent films she always played teenage flappers and ingénues. By the time talkies came along, she was in her early thirties. Hollywood decided she was over the hill."

For some reason I can't explain, now I feel bad and embarrassed all over again. Maybe it's because Kay is not at all young, and I can tell she must have been pretty in her day. Maybe it's because even movie stars lose their looks. Maybe it's just because everyone's life is so terribly fragile.

"Listen," I say. "I want to apologize again for my behavior that day in the hotel dining room. There was no defense for what I said. I don't usually go around telling people—"

"They'll be dead soon?"

"Yes. I'm sorry."

"I know I wasn't at my best that morning," she says. "Had an argument with my daughter on the telephone earlier, and I was taking it out on the waitress. I admit that. Hadn't slept well either because your niece kept me up all hours. If it improves your opinion of me any, I left that waitress a very generous tip. She's probably still counting it."

I shift my position on the bench. "It's no excuse,

but I wasn't feeling well either," I say. "I had a headache."

"You drink," she says flatly.

This brings me up short. "Well, that's not anything I want to talk about."

Kay gives a dry laugh. "No, I don't imagine. Talking about it means you'd have to face it. But I can spot a lush a mile away. You think I'll be dead soon? Child, go on like you are, you'll beat me to it."

Her gaze softens. She pats my hand. "You're not alone, you know. Plenty of help out there. Last month, my husband—second husband, met him at a meeting—took me out for my thirtieth anniversary. Thirty years of sobriety, I should say." She smooths her silver hair. "So, where do you go from here?"

"I appreciate your concern," I say, a bit ruffled by the implications of what Kay is saying. "But the verdict's not in yet."

"Margo, child, I'm not talking about whether you'll admit to a problem with booze. I'm asking where you and Mr. Benedict are headed after you leave Chicago."

Oh.

"I'm not sure," I say, feeling my cheeks flush. "I live in New York, though." And I'd like to go there right now.

Kay again looks at her watch, and I know it's only a moment until she gets up to go. "May I ask you one more question about Colleen Moore?" I say.

Kay utters a weary sigh. "There's a book in the gift shop."

"That huge dollhouse . . ." I begin.

"You can buy the book," she says. "In the shop. Souvenirs too. You should take a look."

"That huge dollhouse," I repeat. "It seems sad she never had any children to play with it."

"None of her own, you mean?" Kay says. I've recaptured her interest. "Yes, I've wondered about that myself. Maybe it was part of why she got caught up with the Fairy Castle for so long. Working something through."

She studies her wedding ring. "Do you have children, Margo?" she says.

"No," I say. "I wanted to, very much, when I was younger. There was a man . . ." I swallow. "I didn't get my wish."

"Miss Moore wanted children—with John McCormick. She didn't get her wish either. But ultimately, after her divorce, she fell in love with a stockbroker, a widower with two children, right here in Chicago. They got married. By all accounts she was a very loving stepmother to those children. It was a role she apparently took to with great heart, great affection. Made up for a lot of losses in her life."

Tully comes into our view, carrying a museum shopping bag.

"And here's your Mr. Benedict," Kay says. "Good. I'm off now myself, meeting a friend for lunch."

She stands and looks down at me on the bench. "So you see, Miss Moore finally found a fella who was right for her. She found the family of her own that she'd sought for so long. I believe we'd have to call that a happy ending. Don't you agree?"

I'm quiet for a moment, thinking.

Kay grabs my hand and squeezes it. "Have a safe trip home, Margo," she says. "One day at a time." She releases my hand and starts to walk away, and I realize I'm sorry to see her go.

"I hope you live forever!" I call after her.

"Already have," she says, giving a backhanded wave. She rounds a corner and disappears from my sight.

I'd like to be alone for a while. I'd like to sit and think. But Tully comes and stands in front of me.

"Have fun at the gift shop?" I say, looking up at him.

"I got a couple books and some other stuff," he says. He hoists the shopping bag. "And a Fairy Castle keychain."

"A keychain?" I laugh. "How about a souvenir T-shirt? Refrigerator magnets?"

Tully doesn't seem amused. "Look," he says, "I know what you're thinking. You think all this is crap. You figure dollhouses fall into the same category as velvet paintings and sofa art."

Actually, that is pretty much what I believed about dollhouses when I first met Tully, when he first told me about his book. I don't think I believe that anymore.

"It might interest you to know," Tully says, "that there's a reason people build miniatures. Doesn't matter if it's guys laying out model railroads or women decorating dollhouses. It's about control. It's about reinventing reality."

Love never dies.

"Some people get a lot of satisfaction in creating a little world they can escape to. In making things turn out the way they want, at least in their dreams."

Love. Never. Dies.

"I'm writing a book about that," Tully says. "It's what I do. I write nonfiction works on unconventional topics. I once wrote an entire book about the history of chewing gum—a volume that had very decent sales, by the way. The project I'm working on now is about people who build and collect miniatures. Coincidentally, for me, writing the book is one way of controlling my own world, my own life. Get it?"

I believe I do.

"And I'm writing it because I have to make a living, and because I have a contract with a publisher who thinks there's a market for it. So what I got in the gift shop"—he rattles the shopping bag—"some of it I got to help me with research. And some of it I got because . . . because I got it."

It's while he's saying this that I see Tully not as Georgia's jilted suitor, or the driver of my father's MG, or even an oddball author of oddball books. No, I perceive him as his own man. I look away and remember how it was traveling with Tully these last few days, just the two of us, to Chicago. I remember that he has his own interests, his own passions. Perhaps even his own demons.

I turn again toward Tully. He smiles. It takes me a moment to realize he's smiling at me. Tully doesn't want to argue. He wants to get along. It's like receiving a blessing—not from Tully, exactly. From life. Timidly, I smile back. I feel the gradual stirrings of desire, a longing for human connection. The same kind of connection I ached for in the days when I first knew Finn Coyle. Is this what happens? Do our lives circle ceaselessly until, at last, we come back to our beginnings?

Finn. It's time I explain about him.

Of course, you're not supposed to do that when you tell a story. You're not supposed to go back and talk about the past. But as I said earlier, I've lived a long life. And you have to know about Finn if you're going to know about me. Because everything I am, for good and bad, everything comes from once being very young and from loving Finn.

CHAPTER FOURTEEN

FINN

I met Finn Coyle at a birthday party on a hot July night in New York City. I was nineteen years old. I had spent the day modeling—catalogue stuff, nothing glamorous—and afterward gone for supper with a couple of the other girls, Amy and Delia. When we finished eating, Amy piped up and said, "I know what. It's Tommy's birthday! Let's go to his party!" So we did.

Tommy was throwing himself a thirtieth birthday party at his SoHo loft. I didn't know Tommy, had never met him, and I thought thirty sounded ancient. But I was young and, given the chance, never missed a night out.

Tommy's loft was impressive. It took up an entire floor of one of those old industrial buildings, and that evening it must have held close to two hundred people. Soon after we arrived, Amy and Delia vanished into the crowd of guests. On my own, in search of something to drink, I elbowed my way through the throng and over to the kitchen area. A tall, clean-shaven man stood at a cooking island that was littered with bags of chips, dirty glasses, and empty beer bottles. He was mixing martinis, giving them to anybody who came by, and he offered one to me. When I took it, he introduced himself and told me his name was Finn Coyle.

A few things you should know straightaway about Finn: He had beautiful manners. He was beautiful to look at. And he had a wonderful voice that was sophisticated and full of amusement. I could have drowned in that voice.

I liked Finn immediately. He was fun to talk to. We stood there together, chatting and laughing about everything and nothing. After a while, we eased ourselves off into a corner, just the two of us, and did little else for the next several hours except sit on the floor and visit and drink and, in my case, occasionally spill gin down my front or excuse myself to go pee. At some point during the evening, Finn let it slip that he was thirty-nine years old, which, mathematically speaking, made him old enough to be my father. But there was nothing creaky about Finn Coyle. Quite the opposite. He came off as charmingly boyish.

Finn was intelligent and educated and had a gift for making you feel smarter than you were. He could have been a teacher; he had that way of taking an interest in people and drawing out their opinions. But he wasn't a teacher; he was an antiques dealer. Part-time, anyway. His real source of income was a small trust fund left to him by his grandparents.

Finn was passionate about the history of Manhattan, especially its architecture. Now this was a coincidence because six months earlier, when I'd returned to America after living in England for eight years at St. Verbian's School for Girls, I had decided, as a legal adult, not to go back to California. I wanted to dwell as far as possible from the West Coast. I chose New York as my home, and moved into a fifth-floor walk-up in the East Village. Like Finn, I fell in love with the city.

New York is a great place for walking. I could wander for hours admiring the cast-iron buildings in SoHo, the row houses of Greenwich Village, the classic lines of the early skyscrapers. So could Finn, as it turned out. That night at Tommy's party, we sat on the floor facing each other and ticked off, one by one, some of our favorite buildings: the New York Yacht Club, the Ansonia Hotel—

"Lever House on Park Avenue," Finn said. "What do you think of that?"

Lever House, built in 1952, is the original glass box: all modern steel, straight lines, sealed glass. It's a New York landmark, absolutely. But you either love it or you hate it.

"I hate it," I said.

He laughed. "And why is that?"

"It has nothing to say." I stifled a yawn. I liked visiting with Finn, but it was getting late.

"It's cold," he said.

"It was in the nineties today," I said, puzzled.

"No, no." He laughed again. "Lever House. It has no soul, no romance."

"Agreed," I said.

"So you're a traditionalist."

"I expect I am," I said, never having thought about it before.

"You're a classicist," Finn continued, giving a slight smile. "An admirer of the Beaux Arts style and the early 1900s concept of the City Beautiful."

His blue eyes were twinkling because he knew he'd gone beyond my range of knowledge, that I didn't have a clue what he was talking about. And I'll tell you, it was that sort of teasing, playful behavior that ultimately made me mad for him—where he knew something I didn't, but in the end he'd share it with me. Beginning that night and in the days to come, it was as if Finn held out a present for me every time we met. Some gift of knowledge or truth, of history or philosophy.

"So if you're a classicist," Finn said, "what do you know about the original Pennsylvania Station?"

Once again, I was baffled.

"Of course you know it was designed by McKim, Mead & White."

I knew nothing of the kind, although McKim,

Mead & White I'd at least heard of. I was reasonably certain that was the old-time architectural firm that had produced the Washington Square Arch, the one that's in all the photos of Greenwich Village.

"Penn Station," Finn persisted, in his schoolmasterish way. "The old railroad station. What else do you know about it?"

"Um, nothing," I said.

"All right." Finn paused a moment, gathering his thoughts. "Well," he said, "it took four years to construct—1906 to 1910—and covered about eight acres from West Thirty-first to West Thirty-third. Between Seventh and Eighth. It was made out of rose-colored granite and Italian travertine. The main waiting room was inspired by the Roman Baths of Caracalla, the ceilings were one hundred and fifty feet high. The grand staircase was forty feet wide. Can you imagine? It was magnificent! The greatest building ever created in New York City. You would have loved it." He ran a finger round the rim of his glass. "They tore it down in 1963."

Finn said that some of the shattered remains of Penn Station had been lying for years in a New Jersey landfill. Amazingly, anybody could go out there and haul away chunks of it if they wanted to. Finn wanted to.

Because when I say Finn was an antiques dealer, he was really one of the first in a new field: architectural salvage. He had a downtown warehouse where he sold everything from nineteenth-century marble columns and terra-cotta finials to carved oak fireplace mantels and ornamental stonework. All of it rescued from buildings that had been demolished.

Finn was driving out the next day, Saturday, to New Jersey to try and retrieve pieces of Pennsylvania Station. He asked me if I wanted to come. I said, Yes, I'd like that. He scribbled my address on a paper napkin, and we agreed he'd pick me up in the morning. Searching for the ruins of Penn Station sounded like fun—though by now it wasn't just ruins I was interested in. It was Finn.

It was three o'clock in the morning, the party was winding down. My two friends, Amy and Delia, came and found me. Time to go, they said, laughing and lifting me off the floor. I said good-night to Finn. He stood and took my hand. His eyes met mine. Then he ducked his head like a schoolboy and kissed me quickly, pleasantly, on the cheek.

As my friends and I descended the stairs to the street, you could hear a few soft voices up in the loft singing, "Happy birthday, dear Tommy." It sounded like a lullaby.

I'd passed the entire evening without ever meeting Tommy, or even wishing him a happy birthday. But that didn't matter. I'd met Finn Coyle.

• • •

Early the next day, Finn arrived with a pickup truck outside my aging five-story apartment building. He exited the truck and stood in the street, one hand inside the cab, pushing on the horn. I stuck my head out the window and waved.

"Hello!" Finn called, looking up and waving back at me. His clear voice echoed in the street. It was a bonny morning, not so hot as previous days. Pigeons cooed on the roof, a loose-limbed Puerto Rican boy rode past on a delivery bike. Gazing down at Finn, I admired his easy grace, his reddish-brown hair, and I knew that I already had quite a crush on him.

Despite my youth, I was not a virgin. While I watched Finn, part of my brain—actually, most of my brain—was working overtime imagining what it would be like to go to bed with him. Heavenly, I was sure.

Moderately hungover as I was, I don't think I've ever dressed faster. I was still zipping up my jeans when I pulled open the door to my flat and hurried down the four flights of stairs and out into the street.

Finn smiled when I came up to him. "Good morning," he said. "Turns out the truck is a bit crowded. And since Alec and Sam have volunteered to do the heavy work, I promised they could ride up front." Two muscular young men in jeans and T-shirts sat in the cab of the truck. They nodded hello.

"I thought you could ride in back," Finn said. "If you don't mind."

This was not exactly my idea of a brilliant beginning to what I hoped would be a brilliant association with Finn. However, in a manner of speaking, it was our first date. And I hoped there would be many more. So I hid my disappointment, and instead turned to look in the bed of the pickup.

There, parked on a blanket with her back resting against the cab, was a woman in her late twenties. She wore sunglasses, tight pants, and a safari jacket. She held a cigarette to her lips and sucked on it as if it contained not tobacco, but life-sustaining oxygen.

Finn helped me climb up into the back of the truck. The woman reached out a hand to steady me. "Bonjour," she said. "I'm the Baroness Blixen. We're on our way to shoot lions in Africa!"

Finn waved in her direction. "Meet Dottie Fielding," he said. "A woman of boundless imagination."

"Hello," I said, wondering if Dottie was my rival for Finn's affections.

"This is my young friend Margo," Finn said to Dottie. "Margo Just. Try not to eat her."

"Try not to eat her—or just try not to eat her?" Dottie said.

Finn shook his head. "Whatever you do," he told me, "don't encourage her."

I plopped down on the metal floor and sat, like Dottie, with my back to the cab. Finn returned to the driver's seat, started up the engine, and the truck roared off. We turned onto First Avenue and jolted our way north.

It was a jarring, uncomfortable ride. To keep my balance, I held tight to one side of the truck. Dottie had some kind of inner gyroscope. No matter how rough the road, she never lost her equilibrium.

We went left at East Thirty-fourth, bumping past the Empire State Building and Macy's. We were headed for the Lincoln Tunnel and over to the New Jersey Meadowlands, a few miles west of Manhattan.

After Dottie finished her cigarette, she reached into a black case next to her and pulled out a cocktail shaker and a small bag of ice. She removed the top from the shaker and inspected its contents—the way you might look inside your purse to make sure you had your keys—then dropped in some ice, replaced the top, and set the shaker in a pile of chains.

The rough ride, my hangover, and the smell of truck exhaust were all making my stomach unsteady. Searching for something to focus on, I stared at the cocktail shaker as it shivered and quaked amid the chains.

"Martinis!" Dottie said.

I smiled halfheartedly.

We stopped at a traffic light. Dottie, who ten years later would swear off tobacco forever, lit another cigarette. "What do you call this in England?" she said, shaking out a match and tossing it over the side of the truck.

I wasn't sure what she meant. The ride? Smoking? Mixing martinis in the back of a truck?

My rear hurt from all the bouncing, I'd barely seen Finn, and I was beginning to wonder why I'd come. I answered her question as best I could. "Madness?" I said.

"No, darling," she said, slightly amused. "The truck. Don't *les Anglais* have a word for it?"

"Oh. It's a lorry."

"Is it? I always thought it was a lolly."

"A lolly's like a Popsicle," I said. The truck lurched. I grabbed again at the side of it. "Lolly also means money, the same way Americans say dough."

"*Merci*," she said. "I'm glad we cleared that up. I have a feeling, Margo, you and I may be good at explaining things to each other."

I smiled. I liked Dottie. She was two or three years older than my half sister, Charlotte, but not at all like her. She offered me a cigarette, and I took it.

I had pictured the Meadowlands as a kind of paradise. Sounds that way, doesn't it? *Meadow-*

lands. Sounds like you're going on a picnic with Alice and the White Rabbit. I imagined dairy cows. I imagined little lambs springing through the greenery.

But when we got there, it was nothing like that. The part of it that I saw, at any rate, was a mess— a rubbish heap in the middle of a swamp, so jumbled it was impossible to tell where the garbage ended and the marshlands began. And all around was the sickly sweet smell of wet earth, rubbish, and rot.

The truck came to a halt. Dottie pulled a strainer from out of that same black case and began pouring martinis into tin mugs.

"Forgive the glassware," she said, handing me a mug. "Olive?"

Finn and the other two men came round to the back of the truck. Dottie gave each of them a gin-filled mug. Apparently, this was breakfast in the world of architectural salvage.

After the men finished their drinks, they conferred among themselves. Then Finn declared, "We're going to have a look around."

Before I could even register what was happening, the three males struck out across the landfill. "You girls stay with the truck, would you?" Finn called back.

Oh, this was too much! Watching Finn tramp off, I felt a complete fool. There was no way this could be considered a first date. How could

I have deceived myself into thinking this was a date?

I gulped down my martini.

Angrily, with no purpose in mind, I clambered out of the truck—and fell face-first into a puddle of ooze and muck.

Dottie gazed at me from the truck. "We're supposed to search for artifacts, Margo," she said. "Not mate with them."

I was wearing my best blue jeans, a white blouse, and under my jeans, knee-length leather boots. The entire front of me was covered in mud. I scrambled to stand up, and my boot scraped against something hard. I looked by my feet and saw a large sparkling pinkish stone, buried in rubbish and sludge. Dottie saw it too.

"What is it?" I said.

"It's what we came for, dearheart!" Her eyes were big. "It's Pennsylvania Station! Part of it, anyway. That granite is unmistakable. Cost a lot of lolly in its day."

Finn and the other two men were already some ways off. We could see them walking along, jabbing with sticks at the mud and garbage.

"Oh, this is rich!" Dottie said. "Little boys hunting for buried treasure. Won't they be surprised when they see what the womenfolk have found?"

She pulled on a pair of work gloves, then lifted

two shovels from the truck bed and handed one to me. "Let's uncover this ourselves," she said. "*Seulement nous*—just us."

An hour later, we had exposed a large slab of rose granite. It appeared to be the ornamented top portion of a Roman-style column. It weighed, I'm sure, over two hundred pounds and was the size of a coffee table.

"*Regarde*," Dottie said, gesturing at the granite. "Look what we've done. Few activities are more gratifying than digging up the past."

I was dirty as a coal miner. Dottie had done her fair share of excavating but had somehow managed to stay considerably cleaner. She again reached into that black case of hers and produced a towel and a bottle of water. She offered these to me so I could attempt to wash up, but my efforts were futile. I remained filthy. Then Dottie pulled out a couple of sandwiches.

We sat in the back of the truck, eating lunch and admiring the hunk of granite on the ground next to us. After a while, the men returned.

"No luck," Finn called. He was walking toward us. "Utter defeat." He came round to the other side of the truck and stopped and stared at the relic we had uncovered.

"Margo found it," Dottie said.

"Did you?" His eyes took in how dirty I was. "And it looks like you put up quite a fight to get it." He bent down and ran his hands over the stone. "It's splendid!"

I didn't say anything. For the first time that day, Finn was paying attention to me, and I was flattered. But I was also frustrated and unhappy, disappointed at how the morning had gone.

Finn looked from the granite to me, studying my face. "You're as silent as this capital," he said. "What are you thinking?"

"Nothing," I said. "Random thoughts."

He smiled. "Those are my favorite kind."

"Then you should meet my uncle Otto," Dottie said. "Those are the only thoughts he ever has."

The men loaded the granite into the truck, and we headed back to Manhattan. We dropped Dottie at her flat in the Village. After that, Finn drove to my street, East Ninth, and parked. Alec and Sam waited in the truck while Finn helped me climb out from the back and onto the sidewalk.

We had just begun walking in the direction of my apartment building when Finn halted. Without a word, he touched my arm and maneuvered himself round to my other side, the side closest to the street. I looked at him.

"Sorry," he said sheepishly. "My grandfather taught me when a man and woman are out together, the man walks next to the gutter. That tradition probably goes back a hundred years—

you know, protecting females from the mud and horses. I must be the last man in New York who still does it. I suppose it's stupid."

"No," I said. "It's not." It was adorable, and it made me like him all the more.

We came to my building. Finn held the street door for me. I stepped inside the vestibule and turned to say good-bye.

Finn was half leaning on the outer door. His eyes were shining. "Would you like to have coffee sometime?" he said.

I couldn't read him. Was *this* the offer of a date? Was he asking me out?

"You mean," I said, "the two of us? Or would other people be there?"

He laughed. "I thought we two. But bring a friend if you'd like."

"No, no," I said, feeling my heart quicken and my face turn red. "The two of us would be fine."

One afternoon a few days later, we met at a café in Greenwich Village. Finn got there before me. When I entered the place and went over to him, he stood and smiled. He took my jacket, held my chair. I sat down. A waitress took our order.

Finn was an excellent conversationalist. He was brilliant and funny and warm, and that day he talked about everything from Shakespeare to politics to old movies. He told me stories about the history of Manhattan. He quoted poetry. But he was also not a boor; he never monopolized the conversation. He asked me questions about my friends, my life. How was it I had come to live in New York?

I told him the story of my childhood. When I did that, Finn's face showed such sympathy, I thought I might cry. For the first time in years, someone *saw* me. I felt whole.

"I'm sorry," he said. "That's a long time for you to be so much on your own. So isolated. It's not easy being an outsider."

"No," I said, "it's not." I looked at my hands.

Finn leaned forward. "But now *you're* in charge of your life," he said encouragingly. "What will you do? Do you intend to go on modeling?"

I said I didn't know.

"You should go back to school," Finn said. He spread his arms, as though embracing the whole wide world on my behalf. "Get your degree. You're bright. You could study history— or architecture!"

We visited for over two hours. When finally we stood to say good-bye, Finn hesitated. Once again, I thought he was going to ask me out. But all he said was, "I haven't enjoyed myself this much, just sitting and talking with someone, in quite a while. Shall we get together like this again? Soon?"

"Yes," I said. "I'd like that."

"So would I." He put a hand to his chest. "*Ab imo pectore*," he said in Latin. Meaning, "From the bottom of my heart."

And so began our association. Before long, Finn and I were meeting at that same café three, sometimes four, times a week. Our relationship, our friendship—whatever you want to call it— was this endless string of coffee dates.

I never did go to college, couldn't afford it. But knowing Finn was, in itself, an education. He was a fascinating, remarkable man. Because of the things I learned from him, the books he recommended, the lectures he insisted I attend, my world grew larger. He was my friend, but also my tutor.

I loved meeting Finn for coffee. I enjoyed his intelligence, his wit, his fine voice. I loved just *looking* at him, for God's sake. But he didn't ask me out. Not on a proper date, anyway. Not to dinner or the theater or the movies.

Of course, I knew why that was. No one had to tell me. It was because I was too young for him. Not just in years, though that was part of it, but I was also wide-eyed and inexperienced. I wasn't as brainy as Finn or as well educated. I was pretty enough, but I wasn't worldly the way, say, Dottie was worldly. I had little knowledge of grown-up living. And despite my English accent, no one who got to know me would ever think I was cosmopolitan.

Even though Finn was kind to me, even though he always picked up the check, held my chair, complimented my appearance, I knew he'd be embarrassed to be seen with me. Embarrassed to present me, a naïve young girl, to his older, more sophisticated friends.

One evening, I was out with a girlfriend and Finn passed us in the street, walking with a friend of his own. Finn nodded hello, but that was all. He didn't stop to introduce his companion or to ask how I was. And I knew without a doubt it was because my friend and I looked so juvenile.

Occasionally, Finn and I would skip coffee. We'd go for a walk in the park or visit a museum or gallery. But most of the time, we met at our same small café in the Village. And actually, I was the one who drank coffee. Finn always ordered tea. Then one day, I realized three things that shocked me down to my knee-length leather boots:

I was living for those coffee dates.

I looked forward to each one as if it were a holiday.

I was falling in love with Finn Coyle.

Okay, yes, I enjoyed learning about architecture, history, philosophy. I would have liked talking about those subjects with anyone. It was around this time that Dottie opened her first shop, and I started spending time with her, becoming close friends. In her company, I absorbed a smattering of knowledge about Art Deco.

But Finn was like no one else. He could be funny, teasing, informative all at once. I was discovering that smart, engaged dialogue with a man is extremely erotic. Cleverness is an aphrodisiac.

Which is why I found myself wanting to learn more about Finn, about him as a person. For instance, I wondered why he always wore a particular ring. It was a gold band set with a blue sapphire.

"My ring?" Finn said. We were sitting at our usual table at the café. Finn twisted the ring round his finger. "It was my grandfather's."

"But you wear it on the third finger of your left hand," I said. For some reason, I jumped on that piece of evidence. "Like a wedding ring."

Even as I said the words "wedding ring," a terrible thought came to me: Finn was married. That was why he wore the ring. That was why he didn't ask me out. He wore the truth on his hand, and I was too blind to see it! He'd been stringing me along for months, and all this time he was a married man.

"In America," I persisted, "that finger is usually reserved for a wedding band."

"Is it?" He gave a wry laugh. "I don't suppose I pay much attention to things like that."

Pay attention to what? To what things did he not pay attention? I panicked. I asked him point-blank if he was married.

He stiffened. "I assure you, I am not. Although I came close once when I was young . . ." He shook his head, and let the subject drop.

I wondered about the woman Finn had nearly married when he was young. Was he still in love with her?

It became increasingly apparent that Finn enjoyed talking, but—unlike most people—he did not enjoy talking about himself.

One afternoon, in a roundabout way, I tried speaking with Dottie about Finn. We were in her shop, the first she'd ever had. I was helping her unpack a crate of French antiques. She was only half listening to my story of a man I was seeing. A man I couldn't quite figure out. I didn't tell her it was Finn.

Dottie reached into the crate and plucked out a bronze statuette of a male nude. "Hello, sailor," she said. "New in town?"

I felt lost, helpless. Dottie was busy and distracted. Did she have nothing to say to me, no advice?

She brushed off some packing material that clung to the statuette. "So this gentleman you're seeing is an enigma?" she finally said. "*Un mystère*? Of course, when we don't know someone, we tend to make up stories about them. Stories that may or may not prove accurate."

At last she'd said something that rang true with me, though I could not have told you why. "I suppose when you think about it, everyone's life is a mystery," she said. "Because every human being is mysterious."

She placed the nude on the counter and patted its behind.

Then one night, around ten, the phone rang at my flat. It was Finn. He was at the corner, calling from a phone booth, wondering if he might come up. The tenement I lived in was ancient, built in the 1880s. There was a lock on the street door, but no way to buzz in visitors. I practically slid down the wobbly wood and metal bannister to meet Finn at the entrance to my building. But when I found him there, I got a surprise.

Finn was drunk.

"I have been out with friends," he said, in that overly formal tone drunks use when they're trying to appear sober. "And I was walking by and said to myself, Isn't this where Margo lives? Young Margo of the smiling face and the offers of a cup of English tea. And so I called you on the pay telephone, and now, as you can see, here I am."

He bowed. "And if I have disrupted your evening in any way, if I have chosen an inconvenient time to visit, *mea culpa, mea maxima culpa.*" Which, as I learned long ago from the nuns at St. Verbian's, means roughly, "My fault to the max."

Finn had not been to my apartment house since that day, months earlier, when we all drove out to the Meadowlands. Even then, he'd seen only the exterior of the building. He'd never been inside. But many times during our many coffee dates, I assured him he could drop by any time. In fact, I encouraged him to do so. More than once, I'd pressed my phone number on him and reminded him of my street address. But now that he was here, I couldn't believe it. Finn Coyle, drunk or sober, come to see me?

I was thrilled. I was flattered. I was bewildered.

"I'm glad you came," I said. He was rather unsteady from the drink. "But I'm on the fifth floor, and there's no elevator. Do you think you can make it?"

At the top of the stairs, Finn caught his breath. I swung wide the door to my flat. I wish I could tell you that my place, the first I'd ever had of my own, was tastefully decorated. But it was not. It was gaudy with cheap travel posters, shiny green plants in pots, oversize East Indian pillows.

Finn walked in and looked around. Seeing the place through his eyes, I was appalled at how schoolgirlish it was. I'd never been to Finn's loft in Tribeca, but somehow I knew it wouldn't have a beanbag chair. I shepherded him from room to room on what I called the Grand Tour: the tenement-style kitchen (with the lift-up metal countertop and well-worn bathtub underneath), the living room, and then back through the kitchen to the water closet, and over to the tiny bedroom with no window, just an air shaft.

It was in the cramped and crummy bedroom that something extraordinary happened. Something I'd long dreamed of, but which at the time seemed to come out of nowhere. Finn kissed me.

It wasn't like the kiss on the cheek he'd given me that first night we met at Tommy's birthday party. No, this was the real thing, smack on the lips. As kisses go, it was impulsive, even clumsy.

And then, just like that, we made love. It was not, I admit, terribly satisfying, but I wasn't worried. That could get better, I knew. Afterward, we lay in bed and Finn kissed the top of my head and whispered that he was sorry. I assumed he meant because he'd been drinking.

He stayed the night, and I cuddled up to him. He was clean and warm and smelled lovely, if a bit boozy. Before I fell asleep, I thought, This is it, Margo. This is the beginning of being with Finn. This is the happiest night of your young life.

• • •

In the morning, we went for breakfast. Later, when we parted, Finn kissed me, told me he'd had a splendid time, wanted to see me again soon. He'd call.

But he didn't. Not for three whole weeks.

Then one Saturday, around noon, the phone rang. It was Finn. He spoke as if nothing had ever happened between us. He went on about his shop, the latest show at the Met, and had I read the new biography of Stanford White. Finally, he asked if I were free and could I meet him right then, that day. For coffee.

By this point, I was sure I was going mad. Nevertheless, I agreed to come.

It was mid-December. It had been raining for days, but that morning the clouds broke and the sun came out. The air was crisp and cold. I threw on my long wool coat and favorite scarf and walked the fifteen blocks to the café. All the way there, I considered what I would say to Finn, how I would tell him that after today I didn't want to see him again. Ever.

But when I walked into the café and my eye fell on him sitting there—his unhurried, pensive self, silhouetted against the light from the window—I thought I would die. I thought I would die because I knew I still loved him, and always would.

No one had ever tugged at my heart the way

he did, no one had ever made me feel so at peace, as though I'd come home. The piercing longing I had for him was immutable, as unchanging as a diamond. And even though I was still a kid myself, the idea came to me, as it sometimes had before, that the two of us could make a beautiful child together. That he would be a kind father.

The place was packed, filled with young couples and groups of friends having brunch. Strings of colored Christmas lights hung on the walls. I skinnied past crowded tables and made my way to where Finn was sitting, pot of tea already in front of him.

Ever the gentleman, he stood and helped me off with my coat. I sat down. The waitress came and I ordered a coffee. "Anything to eat?" she said.

I shook my head.

"Pecan waffles to die for," she said.

I shook my head again.

After she went away, Finn and I made small talk: about the weather, about the holidays. Inside, I was in agony. My heart was pounding, and I wanted to shake him. But I didn't. My coffee came, and I bided my time for several minutes, participating in the meaningless banter. Eventually, there was a lull in the conversation, and I fired my first volley.

"I wrote a poem about you," I said.

In my mind, this was a sort of accusation, but Finn gave a little laugh. "About me?" he said. "Well, that was a waste of your time, I'm sure."

"It was not a waste of time," I said evenly, "because I needed to do it." Before I could lose my courage, I took a breath and began to recite:

> Finn sits and sips his tea,
> Looks out the window idly.
> Margo comes in wet from the rain,
> Wonders why she bothered again.

I paused. I felt diminished. I loved Finn, I would always love him. But I knew my relationship with him, whatever it had been, if it had been anything at all, was over, passing into history. Hurriedly, I went on:

> Then they discuss,
> As is their fashion,
> Such clever things,
> Devoid of passion—

I broke off. "It doesn't scan correctly," I said. "And I'm stuck on the last part. I can't figure out how to end it."

I was trying not to cry. I looked down and fidgeted with my coffee cup. "The poem or our . . . friendship," I said. "I don't know how to end either one."

"Margo," Finn said gently. "I'm not devoid of passion—"

"As far as the poem goes," I said, "it should rhyme. Also, it should conclude in a wa that conveys how miserable I've been these last three weeks. Three weeks in which you never called. Not once."

Finn reached out and took my hand. When he touched me, I swear the room gave a lurch. The planet had tilted, for all I knew people were falling off the face of it. No matter. The only event of importance was Finn's hand on mine. His grip was warm and real.

Don't give in to him, I thought. *Don't.*

I never knew a man to make such intense eye contact as Finn. His blue eyes pulled you in until you slid over some sort of exquisite cliff. He was looking directly at me, and I could feel myself going over.

"I'm capable of passion, Margo. But I'm—"

"Please don't tell me you're complicated."

"I would never tell you that," Finn said. "I don't think I'm the least complicated. But I am . . . isolated. I'm not an easy person to get close to. I know that, I've known it all my life."

He watched me with those blue questioning eyes. Little boy lost. "I've been thinking about you the last few days," Finn said. He went on holding my hand. "Quite a lot."

In spite of myself, a thrill went through me. *He thinks about me. I exist for him.*

"I'm thirty-nine years old," he said in that crisp, soothing voice of his. "Almost forty. And so busy with life and work that I never . . . well, I never committed to a relationship. But maybe *commitment* is what I need. I don't know, maybe it's exactly what I need to get my life on track." He straightened. "Margo, I've been wanting to tell you that I think you and I should get married."

If Finn had told me he was about to give birth to kittens, I could not have been more amazed.

"Married?" I said.

"Yes," he said. "It's the right thing to do. For both of us." He pointed a finger at me and shook it, like he was my dad or something. "I've seen your apartment. You need a decent place to live. And I have a home, but I need someone to share it with. And we . . . we should do it. That's all. We should get married and live our lives the way they ought to be lived. So what about it? Will you marry me?"

I sat there, stunned. Finn was watching me, waiting for a reaction. But before I could speak or even move, alarm came over his face, as if he had just remembered something. "Oh! I suppose I should go down on one knee. And I should get you a ring. Do you want me to do that?"

Moments before, my eyes had been moist with tears I was holding back. Now they brimmed over with waterworks of another type altogether. I was so startled, yet so happy. A woman at the next table stole a glance at Finn and me. She had probably heard every word we'd said. I didn't care. In fact, I started laughing. Laughing with relief and happiness.

Finn laughed too. He inhaled deeply and looked round the café, at all the people in it, as though he'd woken from a dream. In a funny way, he seemed as surprised as I was by what had just happened.

Without even trying, I memorized everything Finn and I said that day in the café. Years later, I can tell you that was our exact exchange. Yet here's the thing: I didn't really hear large parts of what Finn said. Somehow I filtered out several very important words. Words such as:

I don't know.

Maybe.

Should.

What I heard—all I heard—was a proposal of marriage. The man I loved and looked up to had asked me to marry him. With my heart in my hands, I accepted. Through tears and laughter, I accepted.

CHAPTER FIFTEEN

GRIPS LIKE
A LIMPET

After our visit to Colleen Moore's Fairy Castle, Tully and I walk out of the Museum of Science and Industry. Tully carries his shopping bag filled with books and souvenirs.

"You mind if we put the top down?" Tully says when we reach the car.

"Now?" I say. "It's not that much warmer than yesterday."

"Yeah, I know." He looks round at the other automobiles. "But Chicago traffic is intense, and the visibility sucks when the top's up. Anyway, the sun's out."

So we lower the soft top and tuck it away. We leave the side windows in place because they cut down on the chill. Still, when we drive off, headed to our hotel, the air feels cold. I wrap myself up in my coat and the wool blanket.

We merge onto South Lake Shore Drive, which is nothing like the deserted country roads of Route 66. We're surrounded by eighteen-wheelers, delivery vans, SUVs—any one of which could squash us like a bug.

I'm gazing out the side window, thinking about *An Innocent Lamb*, which is still in my tote bag, along with the other items I took. I'm wondering just how much that script is worth—a lot, I reckon—when a huge vehicle, a massive yellow pickup truck with whacking big tires, appears beside us in the right lane. Like anything on the road larger than a motor scooter, it towers over us.

The pickup runs neck and neck with our car, not varying its pace. Some part of my brain registers this as odd, and I glance up—way up— at the driver. He looks down at me, his blank face giving forth a spooky, sharklike smile. Boone.

"Oh, no," I say, turning away and staring straight ahead through the windshield.

"What?" Tully says.

The misery of this, of being pursued by some sort of import-export gangster person who can only be in league with Georgia, causes me to clench my jaw and close my eyes.

"What?" Tully repeats.

Eyes closed, I point at the pickup beside us.

"Oh, no," I hear Tully say.

I open my eyes and observe Tully looking past me at Boone.

"How did he find us?" I say.

"Somebody at Kelsey's place must have seen the car," Tully says. "The janitor, a neighbor, whatever." His eyes flit back and forth between the highway and Boone. "We're not hard to find in this sportster, are we? We stand out like blood on a white shirt."

"Please don't use the word 'blood,'" I say.

The two vehicles—our tiny red one, Boone's enormous yellow one—speed along side by side, like very fast ketchup and mustard. Boone signals to Tully to take an upcoming exit. Tully ignores him and we keep going.

I catch sight of Kelsey, in the passenger seat next to Boone. She has a phone pressed to her ear, and she's leaning past Boone, craning her neck to look over at Tully and me. My own phone rings and I answer.

"Hi," Kelsey says in her infantile voice. "This is fun."

Come to think of it, perhaps I got that wrong. Perhaps she's saying, "This is dumb." Hard to tell.

"Boone says get off at the next exit," Kelsey announces. "Please," she adds, remembering her manners.

"How did you get this number?" I say.

She laughs. "Tully gave it to me when you were . . . you know, sick. He made me promise to have Georgia call you if I saw her. Also, he told me he was going to the museum today."

"You need to turn round and go home," I say.

"SWEETIE, I CAN'T DO THAT!"

There's an outburst of swearing in the background. "BECAUSE I CAN'T SAY THAT. IT ISN'T NICE. SHE'S OLDER THAN MY MOM!"

I hear a sound like water rushing as Kelsey covers her phone. Then she's back. "Boone says get off at the next exit or he'll bust Tully's, umm, love spuds. You better believe him. He broke this guy's thumb once, and all the guy did was wave at me."

"Violence is never the answer," I say. "Gandhi taught—"

"WHAT? WHAT? OH! Boone wants to talk to you."

There's the shuffle of the phone being handed over, and then Boone is on the other end, shouting at me. "You took something from my home, and I want it returned! Do you understand?"

"No," I say. "The connection's bad."

"You violated my domicile."

"Sorry? Pedophile?"

"Listen to me! Pull over and give me that god-damned script! I will do serious harm to the both of you if you don't."

"He wants that script I took from Georgia's room," I say to Tully. *An Innocent Lamb.* He's threatening us if we don't pull over."

"Don't believe me?" Boone yells. He swerves the pickup toward us, narrowly missing our front fender.

"Tell Boone," Tully says, "his own mother doesn't like him." Boone swerves at us again.

"I think he heard that," I say.

"Good. Now hang up and call the cops."

I hang up. My heart is pounding with panic and fear. I try to conceive of something, anything, that might help us. "Use the horn!" I say to Tully.

Tully blinks down at the steering wheel. "There's a horn?"

"Yes! Under the scuttle!"

"Right," he says. "Under the scuttle—whatever bright-eyed little British notion that is." He speaks in an exaggerated English accent: "Hullo, chaps, here's a thought. Don't let's put the horn in the ruddy steering wheel, like the Yanks do. Let's hide the bugger under the scuttle!"

"It isn't hidden!" I say. I point at a black button on the left. "It's there!"

"Yeah, well, I hate to tell you this, Margo, but it doesn't matter because it won't help." Tully's voice is calm, but he's gripping the wheel so hard his knuckles are white. "We're in a kind of a situation here, you know? It's not easy finding stuff out at fifty miles an hour, while being chased by a psychopath. Besides the horn, does this sportster have any useful features? Ejector seats? Machine guns? What were you saying the other night at that diner? In Missouri. You read me something from a brochure."

276

"It grips the road like a limpet," I say.

"Limpet, right. That's a kind of clingy sea mollusk, like a snail. I'm not sure why that's good."

"A limpet never lets go," I say. "The MG T was designed to hug the road the same way."

"Anything else?"

"It has a low center of gravity; it's extremely maneuverable. These cars are famous for their maneuverability."

"Okay." Tully straightens. "That might help."

Boone's giant pickup again veers dangerously close to our little car. This time, Tully pounds on the horn. But when he does that his steering wavers, and for an instant we stray into the next lane. A sedan coming up on our left honks and goes round us.

I look at the cell phone in my hand. "Even if we call the authorities, I don't see how they could get here in time," I say.

"All right," Tully says. "It's up to you."

"We don't have seat belts or air bags or . . ."

"Just tell me what you want to do."

I draw my blanket up to my chin.

"The good news is, it would all be over real quick," Tully says. "Let's face it, maybe that's what you and I have both been looking for from the get-go." He takes his eyes off the road long enough to observe me clutching my blanket. "Then again, maybe not."

He brushes his hair back from his forehead. "So you want to give them the script?" he says. "After all you've been through? After all your dad and Orson Welles must have gone through to write it?"

"No," I say. "I'm scared—but I don't want to do that."

"Sure?"

"Yes. I'm damned if I'll give in to these hoodlums."

"And you're telling me this car is really maneuverable?"

"Extremely."

"How fast can it go?"

"I don't know, about eighty."

Boone swings his yellow truck behind us, into our lane. He's on our bumper now, so close we're nearly touching. My phone rings again.

"Let me talk to the man of the house," Boone says.

"Sorry," I say. "He's occupied."

"Put him on the goddamned phone!"

"I can't," I say. "It's dangerous to talk on a cell phone while you're driving. They've done studies."

"I'll give you dangerous," Boone says. "I'm gonna roll up over your car and crush it like scrap metal. You and the geek can converse with me from the hospital."

"Could you hold a moment?" I say. I turn to Tully. "Boone's going to crush our car."

"No," Tully says. "He's not."

I turn round and look at the pickup nipping at our heels. Boone glares down at us with the fury of Zeus atop Mount Olympus. But instead of brandishing one of Zeus's thunderbolts, Boone grips a cell phone in one hand and the steering wheel in the other. Kelsey, sitting next to him, wears a vapid, eager expression, like a princess on a parade float.

"I want you to give Boone a message," Tully says. He's adjusting the rearview mirror and hunkering down in his seat. "Will you do that?"

"Yes," I say. At this point, there are quite a few things I'd do for Tully.

"Tell Boone we're not giving him the script. Tell him he's a brainless bastard. And tell him"—Tully shoots me a look—"we've got a sports car."

With that, he floors it.

The MG takes off like a shot. I'm thrown back in my seat. I shout, "Sports car! Bye-bye!" into the phone, then hang up. I toss my wool blanket to the floor of the car. With my right hand, I hold tight to the grab bar. Tully races us among the automobiles, weaving in and out of lines of vehicles. We're like those mad motor-cyclists you see in Los Angeles, the ones who shoot along the freeway traveling *between* the lanes of traffic.

I ought to be afraid, but I'm not. I've never seen anyone operate a motorcar with such confidence. Tully's jaw is set and his face displays perfect concentration, as though he has complete awareness of everything around him. He handles the MG like he was born to it.

I glance at the speedometer. The needle hovers near eighty.

Tully's eyes are focused on the highway ahead, taking in his next move. "You okay, baby?" he asks, without looking over at me.

You bet I'm okay, I—baby? Did he just call me *baby?* I twist round and for one glorious moment watch Boone's pickup receding behind us. It's working! We're getting away!

I turn back to Tully. "You're brilliant!" I say. I clap my hands together. "You're Stirling Moss! You're Jackie Stewart! Wherever did you learn to drive like this?"

"Go-karts, dune buggies, drag races," Tully says. "When I was a kid."

"God bless California car culture," I say.

But then something changes. The pickup moves to the far right and goes off road, knocking through barriers and bushes. It comes roaring up on the shoulder. The shoulder! They're using the bloody shoulder!

For all its maneuverability, in a flat-out road

race a 1955 MG cannot possibly outrun Boone's twenty-first-century vehicle. The pickup rapidly gains ground. Soon, Boone and Kelsey are again parallel with us. The cell phone rings.

"Final chance," Boone says. "Pull over, or I swear to God I will ram you. In ten seconds, you will be roadkill."

"You're a terrible driver," I say. "You should be ticketed!"

Tully and I are in the middle lane. Boone moves from the shoulder to the right lane, next to us. Like some sort of demented mission control, he begins counting backward in my ear. "Ten . . . nine . . . eight . . ."

Up ahead, traffic slows for no apparent reason. Automobiles hit their brakes and reduce speed. But Boone's not paying attention. He continues squinting over at us, ticking off numbers into the phone. "Seven . . . six . . . five . . ."

The highway is becoming a sea of brake lights. "Four . . . three . . . two—"

Unlike Boone, Tully sees what's happening. He downshifts, abruptly decelerating. Boone— for a split second, before he can react—goes tearing on past us, into the abyss. A terrible noise comes through the cell phone. It's the shattering sound of Boone's pickup rear-ending the silver SUV in front of him.

The SUV spins round and caroms into another car, which bounces off a minibus. In front and all around us, automobiles begin smashing into each other. Finally, a tractor-trailer jackknifes, blocking the road entirely. Tully stomps on the brakes, and we barely miss the tractor-trailer. Amid a mad symphony of colliding, crunching, and horn honking, traffic screeches to a halt.

When the dust settles, the entire expressway is at a standstill. Tully switches off the engine. The road is littered with crumpled automobiles and scattered car parts. The driver of the silver SUV, a very fat man, exits his vehicle, shaking his head. He lumbers toward Boone's pickup.

But when the fat man gets there, the door of the pickup flies open, knocking him down, and Boone comes crashing out. Ignoring the man on the ground, Boone races at our car. He's running like he's on fire.

Tully and I are trapped by the stalled traffic. We sit in the MG and watch Boone hurtling toward us.

"Uh-oh," I say.

Tully's head whips round to me. "What are you doing? Go! Take your bag! Take the script! Run for your life! And, Margo"—he grasps my hand—"I enjoyed knowing you. You're swell. I name you executrix of my estate." He releases my hand.

I do what Tully says and grab my tote. But it's too late. Boone reaches us. Shouting obscenities, he flings open the door on the driver's side. He wrenches Tully—who's clinging like a limpet to the steering wheel—from his seat. Boone throws Tully onto the front of the car and begins slamming him against the hood.

Sitting in my seat, watching this, I feel sick. "Stop it!" I cry. "You're hurting him!" I dig in my bag and snatch up the script of *An Innocent Lamb*. "Here! You can have this! It's what you want!"

Boone ceases assaulting Tully and turns to look. I hold out *An Innocent Lamb* to him. Boone drops Tully and lurches round to my side of the car. He draws closer, extending a large hand. He comes closer still. His fingertips touch the manuscript.

At that moment, the SUV driver appears behind Boone. He's carrying a detached car door. I watch as this humongous man raises the door up in the air, then slams it down on Boone's head.

Change of plans.

I don't give Boone *An Innocent Lamb*. In the lane to our left, some people push their damaged BMW off the highway and onto the median strip. A gap—a way out—opens up next to our car. I shove *An Innocent Lamb* back in my bag and slide over to the driver's seat.

I turn the ignition key and pull out the starter switch. The MG rumbles to life.

"Come on!" I shout to Tully, who's rubbing his shoulder and looking dazed. He opens the passenger door and tumbles in.

I steer us left—off the highway and onto the rough, uneven median. Somehow Boone, blindsided and wobbling, is still standing. Mouth hanging open, he stares at us as we slowly bump along.

"I warned you," I call back at him. "Talking on the cell phone while you're driving is dangerous. They've done studies!"

In the rearview mirror, I see the fat man chuck the car door aside and throw himself at Boone. The two of them fall to the ground, fighting. Kelsey comes running up and looks on helplessly, pulling at her hair in frustration.

We cruise carefully down the median until we've passed every stalled and wrecked automobile. Then we get back on the expressway.

Tully gazes at my hand on the gear lever. "I thought you couldn't drive," he says, still rubbing his shoulder.

"Can," I say. "Just not supposed to. Little problem with traffic violations." I shift into high gear. "How do you feel?"

"Like crap. I haven't been in a fight like that since high school. Always lost then too."

"We got away, didn't we?" I say. "That's a sort of winning."

●　●　●

I drive us back to our hotel in downtown Chicago and pull into a stall in the hotel garage. I turn off the engine, and remove the key from the ignition and hold it in my hand. Tully and I sit a moment in the car.

"It's not over," Tully says, and I don't imagine he's commenting on my parking job. No, he means Boone will make another appearance.

I'd been wondering if Georgia had made copies of *An Innocent Lamb*—photocopied it, perhaps, or scanned it into a computer. Clearly, she did not. Because if she had done that, if a facsimile or two existed, Boone and Kelsey would not have bothered coming after Tully and me in pursuit of the original. Which means I possess the one and only copy of *An Innocent Lamb*. Which means Boone will be back.

"Remember earlier today," I say to Tully, "after we left Kelsey's apartment? You voted we take a break. Well, I'm thinking something similar— only on a larger scale. How about we get our bags, check out of here, and drive home to New York?"

Tully gives a sharp laugh. "That's a ways."

"Not so far as we've already come."

"You're done trying to find Georgia?" he says.

"Not exactly," I say. "But things have changed." I tap the car key against the steering wheel. "And it's because of *An Innocent Lamb*. A lot of people want it. Crafting that script with Orson Welles was the best work my father ever did, I'm sure. There's a dealer in Manhattan—my friend Dottie knows her—who's an expert on all things Hollywood. I'd like to show her *An Innocent Lamb*. Get her opinion on it, some sort of appraisal."

"Margo, listen," Tully says. He sounds serious. "We took this trip because we both wanted to find Georgia. Only we each had different reasons for doing that."

I feel a pang in my chest, combined with a sort of pity for Tully. I know why he came after Georgia, he told me that first day. He's in love with her.

"But we came up empty-handed," Tully says. "When Georgia left me, I knew she was pissed off, but I thought we could patch things up. With what's happened today, though, after what Kelsey said—"

"You can't believe Kelsey!" I say. "You have to speak with Georgia yourself."

Why am I bucking up Tully about his girl-friend? Why am I encouraging him to believe the two of them might still have a future together? Because I care about him, I suppose. I want him to be happy. I don't want to see him hurt by Georgia any more than I wanted to see him pummeled by Boone.

"Let me ask you a question," Tully says. "Do

you think Georgia sent Boone after us? After that script you swiped?" He takes off his glasses and rubs his face. "Because, jeez, if she did that, it was a lousy thing to do. All this time I've been chasing Georgia, worrying about her. Well, maybe you're right, Margo. Maybe it's time to give it a rest. Maybe it's even Georgia's turn to look for me. Because now she knows the script is gone, she and her lunatic posse will come after it."

"We can't be certain what Georgia will do," I say. "But it's obvious that pursuing her has become a dangerous game. Which is another reason I'd like to be on home territory."

"I hear you," Tully says. "But it could be tricky getting there. Boone will get another car, you know. He'll show up. Like I said, we're not hard to find in this little red sportster."

"If Boone comes after us," I say, "he'll look on the interstate. It would never occur to him to search anywhere else. All we have to do is tak the old roads, the two-lane roads—like when we drove Route 66."

"Maybe," Tully says. He puts his glasses back on and gazes at the concrete wall of the garage. "Or we could just get ourselves out to O'Hare, grab the next flight to JFK."

"You know I don't fly," I say. "And I won't leave my father's car."

He sighs. "Right. Mustn't abandon the ghost of

Cary Grant. Okay. We get on the road, go home to New York. I want to make sure you get there safe."

Early in the morning, after a good night's sleep, Tully and I begin the two-day drive to New York. I leave Charlotte a voice mail, telling her that I have her possessions—though not her daughter—and that Tully and I are headed home to New York. Charlotte calls me incessantly, but I don't answer.

These last two days of our trip, Tully and I are quiet with each other. Not sullen, not angry. Reflective. I imagine Tully is thinking about Georgia, thinking over his life.

I meditate on my own existence. There's lots of time to gaze out the window and look back at my youth.

Lots of time to remember Finn.

CHAPTER SIXTEEN
THE BETTE DAVIS CLUB

On the day Finn asked me to marry him, I was scheduled to meet Dottie late in the afternoon at her Greenwich Village flat. No special reason, just gossip and girl talk. But when I arrived outside her hundred-year-old brownstone and pushed the buzzer, I was giddy with love.

I was light-headed over Finn's proposal, gleeful, filled with joy when I pictured the two of us spending the rest of our lives together. By the time I got upstairs, I had to lean against the wall for support. When Dottie opened her door, I couldn't stop smiling.

"You look like you're stoned," Dottie said.

"Nope. Just happy."

"Drugs can produce that effect," she said, peering at my pupils.

I laughed. "I'm not high."

"Well, come into the kitchen and talk to me." She wore a rose-colored apron. "I'm starting a sauce for tonight's dinner. Gerard is coming over."

Gerard—who would later become Dottie's husband—was her new beau.

Dottie knew I'd been spending time with Finn—I often mentioned I was meeting him for coffee—but she thought he and I were friends. I had never told her how I felt about Finn, never told her we'd slept together. I didn't tell her because I knew she'd say he was out of my league. I knew she'd worry that I'd get hurt.

We weaved our way through her apartment (already, even in those days, filling up with French antiques) and into her cozy, cream-colored kitchen. She poured us each a glass of red wine. "*À ta santé*," she said.

Dottie moved to the sink and started rinsing tomatoes. "So," she said. "Explain to me why you arrived on my doorstep grinning like you're on acid."

She didn't know the half of it. I was so happy I could have hugged myself. "Well," I said, "I'll tell you. It's Finn!"

"Finn Coyle?"

"I know, I know. He's older than I am. But it doesn't feel that way, so please don't lecture. Whenever I'm with him, I'm so perfectly content. It's like all the pieces of my life finally fit together."

"The pieces of your life, darling?" She drained the tomatoes and put them on a cutting board. "You make yourself sound like a jigsaw puzzle." There was a half-mocking, half-patronizing tone to her voice that I didn't care for and didn't understand.

She picked up a knife and began chopping tomatoes, all the while laughing a little to herself as if I'd told the biggest joke. This was the most important news I'd ever shared with Dottie, my most earthshaking announcement ever, and I couldn't see why it even remotely amused her. Since that day in the pickup truck when Finn introduced us, Dottie had quickly become my nearest and dearest friend, but at that instant, I felt myself growing angry with her.

"I'm telling you how I feel," I said. "I don't see what's so bloody hilarious about it."

She stopped chopping and took a sip of wine. "You're right," she said. "It's not funny, and I apologize. It's the shock, I suppose."

Now I really was annoyed. "The 'shock' of finding out Finn likes me?" I said. "A person such as myself, so obviously not on his level?"

This was unfair, and I knew it. Unlike, say, my half sister, Charlotte, Dottie had never tried to make me feel inferior or ashamed. On the contrary, she always encouraged me.

"I didn't say you weren't on his level," Dottie said. "However, yes, imagining Finn with—as you put it—a person such as yourself does surprise me."

"Well, get over it. Finn and I are dating." I was trying to sound grown-up and experienced, but the second the word "dating" flew from my mouth I knew I sounded about thirteen years old.

After this announcement, Dottie regarded me coolly. "I'm sorry," she said. "I've hurt your feelings, and I didn't mean to."

Garlic, onions, and peppers were simmering in a pan on the stove. Dottie picked up the cutting board, slid the chopped tomatoes into the pan, then stirred everything together with a wooden spoon. "I'll say this for you, Margo"—she moved the spoon round in the pan—"you've evidently gotten more attention from Finn than any female in many a moon, and that's the truth."

"But women must fall all over him," I said.

"They do, darling, *absolument*. They collapse. They'd line up if someone were selling tickets. However, this does not signify that he returns their interest." With the back of her hand, she pushed a strand of hair off her face. "I've known Finn for, oh, seven or eight years, and he's a jigsaw puzzle himself. Though there are people who would say he's missing one or two pieces."

"What is *that* supposed to mean?" I said.

"Darling, you must have noticed. You must—"

She'd been going on rather breezily, but now she stopped and took a long look at me. She stirred the contents of the pan. "You are of course aware," she said carefully, "that Finn has many friends."

"Everybody has friends," I said.

"*C'est vrai*. But Finn's come and go. They are young and unattached."

292

I stared at her blankly.

"With—" She wavered, then rushed ahead. "With broad smiles, slim hips, and well-toned muscles. Particularly the abs."

A picture came into my mind of that summer day, months ago, when we all drove out to the Meadowlands. Those two young men in the cab of Finn's truck.

"So?" I said, feeling my face redden.

"I've had this conversation before, you know," Dottie said. "Other people have stood right where you're standing and poured out their hearts to me. Other people who couldn't fathom why Finn runs hot and cold in his affections, other people who were head over heels in love with him."

"Other women?" I said.

"No, sweetie. Other men."

For a moment, nothing was said. I thought I might cry, but I swallowed some wine instead. Dottie glanced at my hands, which were wrapped tightly round my glass.

"Oh, dearheart," she said. There was a sort of jaded, big-sister exasperation in her voice. "I mean, really! Finn Coyle! That man's so far in the closet, he thinks he's a coat hanger."

No, it wasn't true. It couldn't be.

"He loves me," I said.

"He told you that?"

"Yes, basically." A marriage proposal was a

declaration of love, wasn't it? "Things have been said, especially today."

"Well, words won't make him straight," Dottie said. "In that department he can't change himself. No one can. We're each of us born what we are."

"We love each other," I said.

She flicked the burner off and dropped the wooden spoon on the counter. "Margo, listen to me. Affection, in and of itself, does not determine sexual orientation. If it did, you and I would probably be a lesbian couple. Finn may care about you, but—"

"You're wrong," I said.

"I'm so sorry, but I'm not."

"I would know if that—if something like that—were true."

Dottie shook her head. "Not if he won't admit even to himself who he is. Not if you're so infatuated it's made you blind."

I pulled out my last and best defense, the one bombshell I knew would shut her up for good. "I'm sleeping with him," I said.

"Forgive me," she said, "but so are half the men in Lower Manhattan."

The kitchen felt close, the smell of olive oil and vegetables in the pan nauseated me. Dottie must have read my mind because she pushed back some curtains and opened a window. I considered jumping, but why bother when I was already dying right there in the flat?

I thought of Shakespeare's *A Midsummer Night's Dream*. Titania, queen of the fairies, is put under a spell and made to fall in love with an ass. She spends a good part of the play doting on a donkey. But at least Titania's story has a happy ending. When the spell is broken and Titania wakes from her dream, she's freed of her ridiculous fixation. She returns to her husband, Oberon, who loves her.

My eyes were open—Dottie had done that— yet somehow I was still bewitched. Despite all Dottie had said, I knew I was still enchanted, still enamored of my beautiful donkey. Only at the same time, everything was topsy-turvy, and part of me could see how hopeless it all was.

So many things fell into place. Now I knew why Finn kept me at arm's length, why he preferred the neutral surroundings of our café or the park or a museum, rather than meeting me somewhere more intimate. Now I knew why he went three weeks without calling. Now I knew—

But hang on. Hang on a minute.

"Then why in the world," I said, "why in the *bloody* world does he—"

"Go out with you at all?"

"Yes!"

"Because you're young and pretty and intelligent. Because the two of you enjoy the same activities." She raised an eyebrow. "Up to a point. Also because you're sweet and kindhearted, you're fun to be with. And because I imagine Finn often wishes he were straight, that he could blend in. Perhaps he wants children."

I remembered a day, weeks earlier, when Finn confessed how much he hoped to have a child, that he wanted to be a father, but he worried time was running out. I told him it wasn't too late, he'd make a great dad. He smiled and asked if I realized that if the two of *us* had a baby, she would probably have blue eyes. It was one of the many times I felt myself falling more in love with him.

"But what does he want from me?" I said. "Why . . ."

"Darling, in this city there are thousands—tens of thousands—of men like Finn Coyle. Middle-aged gentlemen who've spent their entire lives in the closet. They did that because to admit they were homosexual meant they could lose their jobs, their homes, their families and friends. Not that many years ago, it meant they could be locked away in prison or in a mental hospital. It meant they might get beaten or murdered, simply because they frequented a certain type of bar. So from a very young age they learned to pretend to everybody, including themselves, that they weren't gay.

"Only now there's a sexual revolution going

on, and they're faced with this notion of 'coming out.' Well, for some people, coming out is terrifying. They can't do it. Homosexuals have been living a certain way, living a lie, forever. Suddenly, they're supposed to stand in the street and scream their sexuality to the entire free world?" She put a hand on her hip. "Come to think of it, I know several boys who'd jump at the chance to do just that."

"Don't," I said. "Please."

"Yes, all right. But don't you see that for a man like Finn, gay liberation doesn't feel liberating? It feels scary. Finn doesn't want to come out of the closet. He's so frightened, he's digging farther in."

"But what should I do?" I said.

"Do?" she said. "What do you want to do? You could march yourself over to Finn's place and tell him he's an awful person for leading you on in this disgraceful manner. You could take down his very expensive china and smash each piece on the kitchen floor while he watches in horror. You could get a revolver, like Bette Davis in *The Letter*, and shoot him repeatedly until he's undeniably, positively dead."

Was she mocking me? I looked at her in confusion.

"Or," she said, her voice softening, "you could try to see things from Finn's point of view. You could say to him, Look, I get it, the world's a mean old place. I understand, I don't blame you, and now let's be pals the way nature intended, the way we should have been from the beginning. *Les amis pour la vie*. Friends for life."

Friends? She thought Finn and I should be *friends?*

"He asked me to marry him," I said.

An expression came over her face like a woman who could see an accident about to happen, but who was powerless to prevent it.

"God, no," she said. "You can't."

She was wrong. This was the one thing I could do that no man was allowed to do. I could marry Finn. Moreover, I could have his child.

"I told him yes," I said.

I had at last let fall a bombshell capable of silencing Dottie. She lifted the wooden spoon off the counter and stuck it back in the pan. She traced a pattern in the sauce.

"It's your decision," she finally said. "People do sometimes. Elsa Lanchester and Charles Laughton. Judy Garland and Vincent Minnelli. For that matter, Liza Minnelli and Peter Allen— bit of a family tradition there. But, darling, do you think you could be happy in a sexless marriage?"

"Finn and I have sex," I said.

"Not often, I'm sure. And there'll be even less *après les enfants*. After Oscar Wilde's second son was born, Wilde gave up relations with his wife altogether."

I gazed at the pan. Everything in it had gone cold and oily.

Dottie stood there, watching me. "I'm not trying to scare you," she said, "or rain on your parade."

"Then don't," I said.

"But I hope you know none of this is your fault. And you're not the first woman it ever happened to. It just means you've joined The Bette Davis Club."

"Sorry?"

"The Bette Davis Club," she said. "You've joined, you're a member. It's my metaphor for any female—and there've been zillions—who gets a crush on a gay fellow, dates a gay fellow, or heaven help us, marries a gay fellow. Do any of that, and you're in the club."

"Was Bette Davis in love with a gay man?" I said.

"I have no idea. But if you look at her early films, the best ones are all about Bette wanting a male she can't have: *Dangerous. All This, and Heaven Too. Jezebel. The Letter. Now, Voyager.* They're all about the unattainable. They're all about a woman desiring a man she can never possess."

"I've seen *Now, Voyager*," I said. "At the end, Bette Davis sort of ends up with Paul Henreid."

"You are *such* an innocent," Dottie said. She

stabbed at the sauce. "Margo, 'sort of' is not a prescription for happiness. It means settling for something less than a satisfying union. In *Now, Voyager*, it means Bette Davis's character is offered lifelong companionship with the man she adores —the only problem is the relationship will be platonic and sexless. Is that what you want with Finn?"

I didn't reply. I drank more wine.

"The Bette Davis Club," I eventually said. I stared over at the ruined sauce. "You think I'm a member?"

"One of millions of misguided maidens, marching down through history," Dottie said. "In the time we've been standing here, two or three more probably signed on in this neighborhood alone." She took the sauce and dumped it in the garbage. "I've decided Gerard and I are going out for dinner."

I finished my glass of wine.

"Your official Bette Davis Club hat, pin, and membership card should arrive in next week's mail," Dottie said.

I looked at her.

"Just kidding," she said.

After that, I didn't stay long. Dottie invited me to come along to dinner, but I told her I wanted to be alone for a while.

"Chin up," she said, walking me to her front door. *"La vie continue.* You'll survive this.

After all, we're each the star of our own movie."

"You told me," I said. *"Now, Voyager."*

"Actually, chérie, I think in your case it's been *La Grande Illusion."*

We stood at the doorway a moment.

"If it's any consolation," Dottie said, "I understand why you're attracted to Finn. He's erudite, witty, generous." She sighed. "I don't know why so many interesting men are homosexual. They say it's ten percent of the population, but in my experience, it's half the fellows worth knowing."

I left Dottie's in an utter state. Dazed, I began walking crosstown from her place to mine. As I drifted east, the architecture changed from the genteel nineteenth-century buildings of Greenwich Village to the faded tenements of the East Village. Usually, I enjoyed observing the contrast between the two neighborhoods.

But that day I didn't see my surroundings. I barely noticed passersby. Once or twice, I bumped into strangers. All I could think about was Finn.

Everything Dottie had said about him was true. I knew that. Sort of. But she hadn't told the whole story.

So Finn was gay. Call it bisexual. So he wasn't terribly interested in women. So what? Nothing could break the spell he had over me.

I was Titania. Finn was my midsummer night's dream. Never mind that it was winter, and there was no Oberon in my life to rescue me. I was enchanted—not with a donkey, but with a magical man like no one I'd ever known.

I was immensely attracted to Finn. I adored him beyond all explanation, beyond all reason. Being with him was the thing I wanted most in the world. For nearly ten years, the entire second half of my childhood, I had belonged nowhere and to no one. Yes, Finn was old enough to be my father—but perhaps that was part of why he attracted me so. Finn was smart and wise and worldly. He could give me the home and family I longed for. And the more I pictured the two of us living together as husband and wife, the more I wanted to marry him.

Of course, this is how starving people talk themselves into peeling off the wallpaper and eating it. I rationalized my hunger for Finn. I didn't care if he was bisexual. On some level—despite everything Dottie had said—I didn't even believe it. What I did believe was that he would make me happy.

Dottie had told me I was a member of The Bette Davis Club. But that day, walking along, convincing myself I should marry Finn, I became more than a rank-and-file member. I think you'd have to say I graduated to club secretary, maybe even president. No, more than that. I was *empress* of The Bette Davis Club.

And no matter what Dottie or anyone else thought, I was determined to keep my crown.

CHAPTER SEVENTEEN

I'M NO ANGEL

It takes Tully and me two days to travel the back roads from Chicago to New York. We don't encounter Boone.

At last, we pass through the Holland Tunnel and arrive in Manhattan. It's a lovely spring evening. The city air is like a tonic to me, my veins pulse with carbon dioxide and diesel fumes.

Earlier in the day, I called Dottie and told her we were coming. I also explained about the Orson Welles script, our encounter with Boone, every-thing. She knows I'm hoping she can help me find out more about *An Innocent Lamb.*

Now that we're in town, I fish the cell phone from my bag and again dial Dottie.

"I'm out of my league with your Orson Welles *mystère,*" she says. "So I did what you asked—I've brought in reinforcements. Meet me at Ronnie's as soon as you can."

Ronnie—otherwise known as Veronica—is a friend of Dottie's. She owns a shop in Greenwich Village called I'm No Angel. It's filled with movie posters and books, photographs of film stars, vintage Hollywood props and memorabilia—some of it worth many thousands of dollars.

Veronica herself is a real character. She marcels her platinum-blonde hair, wears shimmering retro gowns worthy of Jean Harlow or Carole Lombard, and has a tendency to lapse into 1930s and '40s slang. In other words, she's a lot of fun.

By the time Tully and I arrive at I'm No Angel, it's eight o'clock, and the shop is closing. We slip inside as Veronica sees out her last customer of the day.

"Dollface!" Veronica says when she spots me. She has a high-pitched, breathy voice. "What's tickin', chicken?"

"I'm well, thanks," I say.

"And how. Dottie says you're getting nowhere fast on your own niece's honeymoon. Talk about your screwball comedy!"

Tully reddens, but I laugh and introduce him to Veronica.

Near the sales counter, there's a reading area outfitted with some overstuffed furniture and mismatched tables. Dottie's there, parked in a velvet armchair and browsing through a book about silent films. When Tully and I come over, she whips off her readers and jumps up and hugs me. "*Mon amie!*" she says. "Welcome back. I've missed you."

I introduce Tully to Dottie. Then Veronica opens up the after-hours minibar she keeps tucked inside a mahogany armoire. She makes martinis and passes them round to everyone except Tully, who requests a glass of water. Tully, Dottie, and I sit down. Veronica positions herself at the end of the counter. She stands there, hand on hip, sipping her martini.

The four of us exchange a few pleasantries. There's a flurry of excitement when I tell Veronica about Palm Springs, Mommie Dearest, and the existence of Marilyn Monroe's undergarments. Then, because time is short, I work her round to the subject of Orson Welles.

"I'm a real Welles fan," Veronica says, "but it's true he had a hard time finishing projects. Some say that was self-sabotage, others swear it was the fault of certain studio bigwigs."

She sets her drink on the counter and picks up a loose-leaf notebook filled with black-and-white glossy photographs of 1940s movie stars. She flips through the pictures. "Here ya go," she says, stopping on one. "Here's the ball of fire himself."

She holds up a photo of a youthful, clean-shaven Welles. "Pudgy, self-conscious—but kind of dreamy," Veronica says. "Sexy." Her eyes flick from the Welles picture over to Tully, then back to the photo, then over to Tully again. "Hmm!"

"Ever meet him, Ronnie?" Dottie says.

"Welles? No such luck. But I heard he was something. A storyteller, a real charmer. Marlene Dietrich said—and I love this—she said whenever she'd been with him, she felt like a plant that had been watered." She puts aside the notebook and retrieves her drink. "Anyhoo," she says, "tell me, Margo, about this screenplay Dottie says you glommed on to."

I tell her—about my father, my stepmother, the sanctum sanctorum, all of it.

"Wait a minute," she says. "Are you kidding me? Arthur Just was your old man? Cheese and crackers, Dottie, how come you never set me straight on that before?"

"I was saving it for your birthday surprise," Dottie says.

"Right. Well, Arthur Just was quite the screen-writer. At the end though, like so many of them, he worked in television."

I know all about my father's career, thank you very much. And I ignore Veronica's remark about television, thinking if she only knew that's what killed him.

"Have you read the screenplay?" she asks me.

I feel a rush of excitement that we're finally doing it, finally discussing *An Innocent Lamb*. "Not really," I say. "Remember, I've only had it for two days. Since Chicago. And everything's been so . . . hectic."

I don't add that last night, when I got into bed, I tried reading the complex historical drama and fell asleep after only a few pages.

"But I looked at it," I say. "There's a note on the first page, addressed to my dad. It says something like, 'Arthur, we're getting closer. I've made a few suggestions.' It's signed 'Orson,' and that signature matches the handwriting throughout the script."

"A *few* suggestions," Veronica repeats. "And how many suggestions did Mr. Welles make?"

"Hundreds," I say. "He scribbled all over the thing. The margins are crammed with dialogue, notes on Shakespeare, directions for costumes and lighting."

She laughs. "Sounds like Welles. So how's about letting me take a look?"

I reach into my tote bag and produce *An Innocent Lamb*.

"I know you have to study it to be certain," I say, getting up and handing the script to Veronica. "But do you think there's much chance it's genuine? That it was written—cowritten—by Orson Welles?"

Veronica opens the binder and begins leafing through it. "Yeah," she says, peering at a page. "I do."

This is excellent news, so good I can hardly believe it. When I return to my seat, I have to catch my breath and down a large portion of my drink.

"But hold the phone," Veronica says. "When Dottie called and told me what you had, I did some research. One thing I found is a list of unproduced films written by Welles. Most of the time he worked solo, but there's at least one unproduced screenplay that was cowritten like yours. So that gives us what you'd call precedent. And when you look at the few flicks he completed, his most famous one—*Citizen Kane*—was cowritten with Herman J. Mankiewicz."

I know, I think.

Veronica waggles her index finger at the three of us. "Please note, cat and kittens, Welles and Mankiewicz each took home an Academy Award for writing that one."

"There's an actual list?" I say. "Of his unproduced films?"

"You bet," Veronica says. "I made a copy." She reaches for a piece of paper on the counter. "Get these titles: *The Smiler with a Knife*, *Don't Catch Me*, *The Sacred Beasts* . . ."

"I've never heard of any of them," I say.

"By this I'm not surprised."

"How many are there altogether?" Tully says.

"No one knows for cert," Veronica says. "Manuscripts keep popping up. Lemme see." She runs a finger down the list, counting. "This shows twenty-eight. Twenty-nine if you throw in the one Margo's got."

"Twenty-nine unproduced films?" I say. "That seems like . . ."

"A lot?" Veronica says. "Yeah, it is. It's an all-you-can-eat buffet of half-baked projects."

"But the scripts—the stories—are they worth anything?" I say.

"Oh, sure. They have value."

"I *knew* it. I knew—"

"Strictly as collectibles, you understand." Veronica laughs. "We all know nobody's going to green light an Orson Welles story in today's market."

Through all this, Cary Grant stands near me, looking on with amusement. So does Bette Davis. They're life-size cardboard cutouts for sale in Veronica's shop. Silent film star Buster Keaton is there, too, wearing a forlorn expression. When I put a hand to my face, trying to process what Veronica's telling me, I must exhibit the same lost look as Buster.

"Sister, you should see your puss," Veronica says.

"You do look let down," Dottie says.

"But I thought studios would kill to get this script," I say. "I thought Orson Welles was a genius."

"He was," Veronica says. "But that doesn't make him box office, does it? Doesn't make him bankable. Not nowadays. Today it's all fart jokes, misogyny, and drug humor. Excuse my French."

"Hold it," Tully says. "This Welles script must be worth something. People want it."

"Yes!" I say. "Tully and I chased halfway across the country to get it, and now we're being chased and threatened, and I don't even know why."

"Hmm," muses Veronica. "I'll have to go over it, consult with some of my dealer pals, before I can give you a final appraisal. But if everything checks out, I could feature it here in the shop for you. I'd put it on my Internet site, too; some collector's bound to want it. Meaning, depending on how the cookie crumbles, I could maybe get you seven or eight thousand."

"Is that all?" I say.

"Afraid so. But let's switch gears a sec. You say you've been chased by people who want this screenplay. Kiddo, that doesn't add up. There's not a fan or collector I know of who's that gaga over Orson Welles. You sure you're not packing something else? Like blind Audrey Hepburn in *Wait Until Dark* when she unknowingly has that heroin-filled doll. Boy, does she end up with some company."

"There's nothing," I say. "I guarantee we're not carrying any white powder. My drug of choice is a dry martini."

Dottie raises her glass.

"Mine too," Tully says.

"You don't drink," I say.

He shrugs.

"What I mean," Veronica says, "any chance you been blind to something? Your niece didn't boost some other item from your pop's sanctum whatchamacallit?"

"Nothing. Except . . ."

"Yeah?"

"Well, when I sneaked into her room in Chicago, I took a couple of magazines—but you could get those anywhere. Oh, and I picked up a flyer for the Tribeca Film Festival, and an old script from *Spy Team.*"

"*Spy Team*?" Veronica says. "The TV show? I love *Spy Team*! Loads of fun, way ahead of its time. Did you know they're rereleasing the entire series in a specially restored high-definition collector's set?"

"No, I didn't," I say. I'm only half listening. I can't get over the fact that *An Innocent Lamb* is worth so little.

"Well, they are, and like everybody, I'm on pins and needles. I already own *Spy Team* on old-style DVD. Way back, I had it on Betamax. Then LaserDisc. VHS, of course. These days, you can also get it on digital download. But I can't wait for the Blu-ray high-def twenty-four-disc ultimate collector's edition. It's going to have pop-up packaging."

"Pop-up packaging," Dottie repeats to no one in particular.

"You betcha. They're going all out with the marketing. Oodles of bonus material."

"I didn't think anyone cared about that old

show," I say. "Why would people even want to watch it?"

"Why? Margo, people dig *Spy Team*. It has a huge cult following. I get requests from all over the world for photos, memorabilia, recordings. A year ago, one of Ariana's jumpsuits—Ariana, the female lead on the show—her jumpsuit sold at Sotheby's for over eighty thousand dollars. My customers are lining up to preorder the collector's edition."

"My father created that series," I say. "He hated it. It's garbage."

"Sister, you're off the beam," Veronica says. "*Spy Team* is popular culture. It's what the entertainment industry is built on. Nobody ever went broke peddling it."

For an instant, I flash on Malcolm Belvedere and something he said to me that day on the lawn at the Malibu house. "And in all those years of making movies in America," Malcolm had said, "I have never ceased to profit from this country's endless appetite for amusement, coupled with its astonishing weakness of intellect."

"Tell me about *this* script," Veronica says. "Did your pop write it?"

"I think so," I say. "It has his name on it."

"Since you're not a fan of the series," she says, "you might not be wise to the fact that during the three years *Spy Team* was broadcast, four different writers worked on it. They were

312

all top-notch scribblers, but the episodes penned by Arthur Just are considered the best of the bunch. Is the script you have from the first, second, or third season?"

"I don't know," I say. "I think it's some sort of final episode. I'm not even sure it was ever filmed."

It's like the room has a mute button, and I accidentally hit it. Veronica gapes at me as though I've announced I not only possess a script by Arthur Just, I have the man himself sitting out in the MG. When at last she speaks, her voice is deeper, huskier than usual.

"Margo," Veronica says, enunciating her words slowly, carefully, "are you saying you have the teleplay for the series finale of *Spy Team*?"

"I suppose that's what it is."

She takes a deep breath. "And where is that teleplay?"

"Here," I say.

"Where?"

"Here."

"There and everywhere," Tully says.

Dottie sits up. "Are we playing a word game?"

"It's in this room?" Veronica says. "With us?"

"Yes. I have it in my bag." I indicate my leather tote, sitting on the floor beside me.

Veronica sighs. "Good," she says. "Swell. Terrific. You know, for years there's been a rumor that Arthur Just wrote a two-part finale to wrap up the *Spy Team* series. I never believed that—figured it was an urban myth, like alligators in the sewers or balancing the federal budget. But gosh, Margo, if the story's true, if you have that script, do you have any idea of its value?"

"As far as I'm concerned," I say, "it's worthless."

Veronica's speech returns to its normal, high-pitched level. "Jeepers," she says, "you couldn't be more off base. It's aces. It's a lollapalooza. It's priceless!"

"How in the world," I say, "how could it possibly—"

"Two reasons. First, the right collector would pay fifty grand or more to own it. Second, and this is way more important, there'd be terrific interest on the open market."

"But how—"

"As a screenplay," Veronica says. "Studios would go wacky bidding for this."

"How wacky?" Tully says.

"The most insane kind of madness there is," Veronica says.

"You mean—" I say.

Veronica squeals. "Hollywood, California, USA crazy!" she says.

Veronica's off and running. "Let me lay out the racket for you," she says. "You know about branding, right?"

I picture cowboys and livestock, but I know she means quite another matter. "It's something to do with sales," I say.

"And how. In Hollywood, the marketing execs build customer loyalty to a series of films and film-related merchandise. Haven't you ever wondered why studios make so many sequels?"

I never thought about it before. But it does seem odd how often there's a second, then a third, of even the most mediocre film.

"It's like the sequels become a brand," Veronica says. "A franchise. The characters and situations are already known to the public, and it's that brand recognition that sells movie tickets. Which is the same reason Hollywood has been systematically filming every TV series you ever heard of. It started years ago, and it's still going on.

"Look, Margo, I know for a fact there's been talk of turning *Spy Team* into a feature film, but the project was jinxed, nobody could put together a decent script. Now you show up with an original two-part teleplay by Arthur Just, which is what—about ninety minutes of screen time? Well, a little tweaking, a little updating, and your old man's pages become the hottest screen-play in Tinsel-town. Literally worth a million dollars, maybe two. Maybe more. Not only that, a *Spy Team* pic would be a shoo-in for franchising. It would spawn sequels, promotional tie-ins, merchandising, video games, DVD sales, the works!"

"I don't," I say, "I can't . . ."

"Take it all in?" Veronica says. "Understandable. There's always a gap between the way the world operates and the way we wish it would operate. That, cousin, is why everybody goes to the movies."

"Hold it," Tully says. "What good does this do Margo?"

"Here, here," Dottie says.

"So the script's worth a million or two," Tully says. "So some studio turns it into a big-budget film. So what?" He looks at me. "It's not like Margo wrote it. She might not even have a claim to it. When her dad died, his widow kept Margo from any real inheritance. Why would she get anything now?"

"Geez Louise," Veronica says. "You still don't get how it works, do you?"

"I don't think any of us do, Ronnie," Dottie says. "We haven't your expertise. Could you, would you, explain things to us? *S'il te plait*?"

"Okay, babes in the woods," Veronica says. "Square one." She points at me. "The first thing you do is get yourself an entertainment lawyer. I know a heavy hitter in Los Angeles. Longtime friend and customer of mine, drops in when ever he's in town. Also, you'll need an agent, accountant, possibly a publicist. Then you start negotiations."

"For what?" I say.

"*Spy Team*, kitten! You're going to peddle that property for more dead presidents—"

"Dead presidents?" Dottie says.

"Currency, folding green, moola. More dead presidents than poor old Orson Welles ever got for *Citizen Kane*."

"But I don't own *Spy Team*," I say.

"Wake up, sleeping beauty!" Veronica says. "You're in America. When has ownership ever stopped anybody? It's in your possession. It was written by your father. Look, I get that you had a tough childhood. But as my legal friend will explain to you, you're no longer some little half-pint who can be chiseled out of her rightful inheritance to her pop's intellectual property. So okay, maybe your half sister and her daughter come in for a percentage. But Josh will handle things so you get the biggest piece of the pie."

She opens a drawer and pulls out a business card, then leans across the counter and passes it to me. It reads "Joshua Epstein, Entertainment Law."

"You can trust Josh," Veronica declares. "Like I always say, a girl's best friend is her attorney."

"I don't know . . ." I say.

"What's not to know? You walked in here hoping *An Innocent Lamb* was a pot of gold, right? So there's been a slight switcheroo. The smart money's on *Spy Team*."

I stare at the business card in my hand, feeling like I want to cry. But if I did cry, they would not be tears of happiness.

"You don't understand," I say. "It wasn't just about the money. Or Orson Welles. It was about my dad. After all these years, I felt like I had connected with him. You can talk all you want about popular culture, but *Spy Team* is rubbish. *An Innocent Lamb* made me proud of my father, proud that he collaborated with America's greatest filmmaker."

"You didn't even read it," Veronica says calmly.

"I was . . . busy," I say. "And anyway, that's beside the point. I felt like something good had come out of my father's life, something of value. Together, my dad and Orson Welles might have produced another *Citizen Kane*. They were creating a work of art!"

Veronica rests her elbows on the counter and crosses her arms. "*Spy Team* is art," she says.

I stuff Joshua Epstein's business card roughly in my bag. "It was a paycheck," I say.

"Well, pardon me," Veronica says. "But did no one ever explain to you that in Hollywood there are two kinds of art? There's the art of film-making, and there's the art of the deal. They're like a spider and its web. You can't separate them."

I shake my head.

"Honey," Veronica says, "you own Boardwalk and Park Place. Now what? You don't want to build hotels?" She throws up her hands. "Dottie, talk to her."

"*Moi?*" Dottie says. "I've known Margo for thirty-odd years, some of them very odd indeed. She will do what she wants when she wants, no matter what I or anyone else says or thinks."

"If this *Spy Team* script is so valuable," Tully says, "how come nobody ever went looking for it before?"

"The network probably didn't know about it," Veronica says. "In those days, there was no serial television—not in prime time. Margo's pop would have had to hard sell just the concept of a two-parter series finale. I figure he writes the thing on spec, on his own time. But before he can pitch it, he dies. *Spy Team* was going off the air anyway. As far as the network was concerned, end of story. Years later, the series comes out on VHS, DVD—all that rekindles interest in the show. But Arthur Just's widow didn't mess with his stuff, remember? Wouldn't get rid of it, wouldn't let other people go through it. So the script just sat there, aging and forgotten, up in that sanctum . . . that santa . . ." She flutters her hands. "You know, that secret office."

"Until Georgia found it," I say.

"Right," Veronica says. She fixes a cool eye on Tully. "And the *dish* ran away with the spoon."

Tully clears his throat. "Speaking of spoons," he says, "Margo and I never had dinner."

"Yes, yes," Dottie says. "You two should eat." She finishes the last of her drink. "*Merci*, Ronnie. We've learned so much tonight. I do hope we remember it all in the morning."

"You don't have to," Veronica says. "Excepting Margo needs to remember to call Josh."

I retrieve my bag from the floor and stand up. Tully and Dottie also rise.

"You know," Veronica says to me, "I get that you're disappointed in the lack of a market for the Welles script. To tell you the truth, I kinda feel the same way. But most mugs go to the movies to turn *off* their brains. And when you look at the world, its disappointments, is that so hard to understand?" She bites her lower lip and studies me. "Aw, never mind," she says. "That's what you call a rhetorical question."

It's dark outside. Dottie, Tully, and I step out onto the pavement. I glance back at the window of I'm No Angel. Veronica is inside, tidying up. Her satiny figure is silhouetted against the light of the store, her platinum hair catches the glow of a neon sign that says "Cinema."

For a moment, we could be watching a Manhattan shopkeeper closing up on a night in the 1930s or '40s. Then Veronica switches off the "Cinema" sign, pulls down the window shade, and vanishes.

CHAPTER EIGHTEEN

MANHATTAN ARCHITECTURAL SALVAGE

Margo, I'm worried," Dottie says. The three of us—Dottie, Tully, and I—stand on the darkened sidewalk in front of I'm No Angel.

"I'm quitting again soon," I say, waving away the smoke from my cigarette.

"I don't mean cancer," Dottie says. "I mean, Ronnie knows her stuff. If she says the *Spy Team* script is worth a million or two, it is. No wonder that Boone person and his girlfriend were chasing you. They're after that script. You need to go somewhere safe. I think you should come and stay with Gerard and me."

"Thanks, but I want to go home."

"You lost your apartment," Dottie says.

"You know what I mean."

"The rag and bone shop of the heart?" Dottie says. "Yes, all right. But be careful." She raises her hand to flag down a taxi.

"Aren't you coming to eat?" I say.

"No, I've had my dinner. Plus, I promised Gerard I'd return to the marital love nest at a decent hour. We'll talk tomorrow. If you need me any sooner, call me on that cell phone you've acquired."

A cab pulls up and Tully holds the passenger door for Dottie. She gets in and lowers the car window. "Look after her," Dottie says through the open window to Tully. "And yourself."

As the cab pulls away, Dottie spots the driver's hack license. "Jean-Pierre Alphonse Dubois?" I hear her say. "I bet you speak French!"

After we eat, Tully and I drive through the cobblestone streets of old New York, to an address near the river. We pull up in front of a rundown, deserted-looking warehouse. There's not a soul around.

"This is it," I say. "Manhattan Architectural Salvage."

"Where's the sign?" Tully says.

"It's not open to the public. To the trade only. And we're choosy even about that."

We get out of the car, and Tully gazes up at the darkened building. "It's like something out of Edgar Allan Poe," he says. "This must be the only place for blocks around that hasn't been gentrified."

"Wait till you see the inside," I say.

I unlock the front door. The warehouse is dark, but when I flick on the lights, I catch the amazement in Tully's eyes. The moment someone glimpses the interior of Manhattan Architectural

Salvage always makes me think of when archaeologist Howard Carter first peered into King Tut's tomb. Carter was asked if he could see anything. "Yes," he said, "wonderful things."

Well, all right. Manhattan Architectural Salvage isn't exactly the glories of ancient Egypt. But it is impressive. The loot of lost New York is here. Layers—decades—of architectural treasures rescued from the demolition of notable buildings: bronze statuary, alabaster lamps, fin-de-siècle chandeliers, banisters and balustrades, pedestal sinks and white ceramic tile.

Some of the plunder came from private homes, some from hotels, churches, and public structures, some from places like the old Ziegfeld Theatre and the Roxy movie palace. The worn wood floor holds row upon row of marble and mahogany, of terra-cotta and cast iron. There's a smell of dust and age and the past. A past that, for once, you can reach out and touch.

"Jesus," Tully says. "It's like a museum."

He runs his hand over a marble mantelpiece. "All this time you've been telling me you're broke. But you could sell this stuff."

"Yes, well, I'll probably have to," I say. "The way things are going, before long there'll be a court-ordered auction." But I won't think about that now, won't think about how I have failed in so many ways. "Tonight, though, it's good to be home."

Tully turns from the mantelpiece. "That was a heckuva road trip we took."

"From Malibu to Manhattan," I say.

"I'll never forget," Tully says, "how when Boone was trying to kill me, you distracted him. Then that fat guy came up and hit Boone over the head, and you saw your chance. When you started up the car, you were seriously wild. Your hair was messed up; you were shifting gears like crazy. You were yelling at me to get in."

I laugh.

"I could have kissed you," he says.

I study the wood floor.

"Oh, well," I say at last. "Next time we'll take public transport."

Tully fixes his gaze on me, and I feel my heart beating. He moves toward me, then hesitates, seeming to change his mind. "I'm stuck," he says.

So am I! Stuck in the past, stuck emotionally, stuck—

"I'm caught," Tully says.

Oh. I glance down. The back of Tully's jacket is hung up on a large slab of carved walnut.

"What is this?" he says, inspecting the wood.

"Edwardian-era matrimonial headboard," I say.

We both tinker with the jacket till it's free, but by then the mood has changed, the moment is gone.

"It's late," Tully says. He looks tired. "I better catch a cab to my place."

"You don't have to go to Brooklyn," I say. "I mean, you can sleep here, if you want." I look around. "Although I'm not sure—"

"This'll work," Tully says. He points to an over-size porcelain bathtub that long ago came out of one of the Vanderbilt mansions.

Tully and I go back out to the car a couple of times, retrieving everything from our suitcases to the big white box containing Georgia's wedding dress.

Next we fix up the Vanderbilt bathtub with bedding and blankets. I also show Tully the open loft-style kitchen situated a little forward and to the left of the front door, the bathroom, and the rest of the premises. There's a mezzanine— Finn's old office—where I sleep. I leave my leather tote sitting in a corner of the kitchen, but I carry the rest of my luggage and the wedding dress upstairs to the mezzanine.

Tully parks the MG in a garage a few blocks away. When he comes back to the shop, he brings one last item with him from the car. It's a Museum of Science and Industry shopping bag. It holds the books and mementos he purchased when we visited Colleen Moore's Fairy Castle, in Chicago. Tully sets the bag on the floor.

I'm moving things around, tidying up. I hoist the museum shopping bag and place it on the long trestle table in the kitchen area. But when I do, the bag's contents shift and it splits open. Everything spills out across the table: souvenir T-shirt, books and pamphlets, Fairy Castle keychain.

"Sorry," I say.

"Don't worry about it," Tully says. We both start picking things up.

I reach for a Fairy Castle book and notice that there's another volume exactly like it. "Did you make a mistake?" I say. "You bought two copies of this."

"Meant to," Tully says.

"For research?"

"No, I only need one for that. The other one's for my daughter."

Daughter?

"Her name's Emma. She's too young for a lot of the text, but she'll like the pictures."

Daughter? Tully Benedict, aging bachelor, has a child? A child capable of holding a book and enjoying pictures?

"She lives in Pennsylvania with her mother and new stepdad," Tully says. "But she visits me. I see her. She's the reason I bought all these souvenirs." He rests against the edge of the table.

"How old is Em—your little girl?"

"Seven."

You could, to coin a phrase, knock me over with a Fairy Castle keychain.

"You never mentioned a daughter," I say.

"Not in all this time we've spent together."

"I don't talk about her with everyone," Tully says. His eyes are gentle. "I have to trust somebody before I bring her into the conversation."

"Does Georgia know you have a child?" I say.

"Yeah. But it's also one of our issues. She didn't want Emma at the wedding. Just as well, considering there was no marriage."

It's been a long day. A day in which nothing as turned out to be quite what I imagined. Not *An Innocent Lamb* nor *Spy Team* nor even Tully Benedict.

I cross over and open a cabinet above the kitchen sink. The bottle is where I left it when I went to California. "Fancy a nightcap?" I say. I reach inside the cabinet, my back to Tully. "For once in your life?"

He doesn't answer. I go ahead and retrieve the bottle and pour gin into two glasses. In the same way that Tully once offered me an ice-cream cone in the California desert, I take a glass in each hand and turn and hold one out to him.

"No, thanks," he says.

He looks so uncomfortable, I laugh. "You, Mr. Benedict, are no fun."

Tully doesn't respond. He stares at the floor, as though thinking something over. Then he looks up, and his eyes meet mine. "Margo," he says, "I'm an alcoholic."

I stand there, holding two large shots of gin.

"That's why I don't drink," he says. "I'm a recovering alcoholic."

Part of me is ready to laugh again, because of course this is a joke . . . isn't it?

"I was sober for seven years," Tully says. "Since Emma was born. But a couple months back, I slipped."

I'm gripping both glasses so hard, it's a wonder they don't break. "Why?" I say. "Why did you slip?"

"I'm human," Tully says. "Recovery is not a perfect science."

Not a perfect science. No.

"I was stressed," he says. "My ex-wife had just remarried—and it wasn't that I wanted to get back together with her, because I don't—but it meant that part of my life was really over. My birthday was coming up, and I wasn't happy about getting older. I'm forty-two, by the way. I was having trouble getting started on my next project. I had an overdue library book." He pauses. "That last one was a joke."

"Oh," I say. "Right."

He looks at the two glasses in my hands. "I fell off the wagon because I was feeling sorry for myself. I don't know if you're hip to this, but aside from genetics, the number one requirement for being a drunk is self-pity."

Actually, I was aware of that.

"So, okay, seven years of sobriety down the

tubes. In the middle of that, I go out to Los Angeles on business, meet Georgia at a party. The two of us—"

"Hit it off?"

"Went on a bender. After a week of shared substance abuse, she proposed."

"Georgia asked you to marry her?"

"Yeah. But then I sobered up. That's one reason she's pissed at me. Right before the wedding, I told her I was stopping the booze, the drugs. We had a huge fight about that."

Not to mention she ran off with her own step-father. A fact I still haven't shared with Tully.

"On the day we left Malibu, you seemed so broken up," I say.

"I was down about a lot of things," Tully says. "Getting jilted didn't help."

"But you told me you loved Georgia."

"I did. I do . . . I mean, I . . . Look, you commit to someone, even if it's the worst match in the world, you tell yourself it'll work out. That first day, when you and I got in the MG, I was deter-mined to pull my life together. I didn't want to have messed up again. I was desperate to find Georgia, talk things over. But all this time on the road, I've been talking to Georgia. In my head, I mean. You know what? Georgia's not listening. She doesn't give a damn. She has my number, she never called. She sold her wedding dress, probably her engagement ring. She sent Boone after us—"

"You don't know that," I say.

"I know she's not the person I thought she was. Georgia made me feel young again, made me feel it was okay not to take responsibility for my life. But it's not okay. I know that falling for Georgia was falling for a dream."

Still clutching the two glasses of gin, I climb the stairs to Finn's office on the mezzanine. The office is crammed with papers, filing cabinets, books. There's also a Victorian-era fainting couch pushed up against one wall, which has been my bed for many months.

I sit down at Finn's desk. I put the drinks on the desktop in front of me.

Among the papers and knickknacks covering the desk is a small silk-lined box. I pick up the box and open it. It contains a blue sapphire ring. This is the ring Finn always wore on the third finger of his left hand, the one he inherited from his grandfather. It's the ring he was wearing years ago when I first knew him, when its presence on his finger caused me to worry briefly that he was married. I take the ring from its case and hold it up to the light of the desk lamp. The sapphire sparkles.

I slip Finn's ring onto the third finger of my left hand and gaze at it there. Possibly, just possibly, I'm feeling sorry for myself.

I pick up one of the glasses of gin and drain it. After a while, I knock back the other one as well.

CHAPTER NINETEEN

JILTED

As our wedding day drew closer, Finn took care of everything. He found a judge, hired a caterer, booked the ballroom at the Pierre. He was charming, considerate, gentlemanly toward me. My love for him remained innocent and boundless.

Dottie was right, my relationship with Finn was not terribly physical. But like all young people, I believed in the power of the future. I believed—hoped—that Finn would change. In time, he would desire me. I told myself he would not marry me otherwise.

In the evenings, Finn and I went out—to the theater, concerts, nightclubs. Best of all, we went dancing. Finn was an excellent dancer. I melted at the touch of his hand on my back, the warmth of his body pressed against mine. Finn taught me everything from the fox-trot to the samba. Each time I mastered some new move, he lit up. "Yes!" he would say, almost to himself. "Beautiful."

The two of us moved together like one electrified soul. One being. Dancing with Finn was delicious. It was enchantment. It was heaven. It was the closest thing to good sex we ever had.

● ● ●

Two nights before our wedding, Finn and I dined at a restaurant on the Upper East Side. We were halfway through the meal when an older, well-dressed man, an antiques dealer acquaintance of Finn's, came up to our table. His wife was with him.

The man had delicate hands. His silk tie was perfectly knotted; his fingernails were pale and polished. He was of a type of Finn's friends I'd met before. Men who, perhaps, were not what they tried to appear.

The man presented his wife. Finn stood and shook hands with them both.

The man did not particularly interest me. His wife, however, did. She was stylish, gracious, educated. Her manner was that of a cultured, well-traveled woman who had money and possessions.

But she smiled with her mouth, not with her eyes. She clung to her expensive handbag, rather than her husband's arm. And there was something in the way she held herself that—well, I saw.

I saw the husband. I saw the wife. I saw the marriage.

The man and woman moved on. Finn sat down. The waiter brought more wine.

The morning of my wedding, I woke with a knot in my stomach. I thought, it's the excitement of the day. I took a cab to the Pierre.

As weddings go, ours would be small. On my side, the guest list included Dottie, a few of my modeling chums, and my half sister, Charlotte, who was making one of her rare appearances in my life. In those days, Charlotte was just beginning her career as a film producer. She had taken time off work and flown out specially, from Los Angeles, for the occasion.

On Finn's side, the list was longer: his elderly parents (the grandparents had all passed on), some cousins, various business associates and friends, several young bohemian males.

Dottie and my modeling friend Amy came to the bridal suite to help me dress. It was Amy who, one night after work months earlier, had suggested we go to Tommy's birthday party, the party where I met Finn.

Dottie and Amy began the process of transforming me into a bride. They fussed with my hair, did my makeup. They brought out jewelry and stockings and a garter.

By now, the guests had gathered downstairs. When my two friends finished their handiwork, I slipped into that ivory dress. But when I turned to admire myself in the mirror, I didn't see a bride. I saw a young, pretty girl. And she was lost.

I felt dizzy. My hands were cold. I put them to the back of my neck.

"You all right, darling?" Dottie said.

I sat down on the sofa.

Dottie looked at me. "Amy," she said, "be a dear, go get her a drink."

Amy hurried off, leaving Dottie and me alone. "I feel compelled to point out," Dottie said, "that the bride usually declines a quick one until *après* the wedding."

"I feel sick," I said.

Dottie sat down beside me. "Too sick to get married?"

I swallowed. I touched the lace of my gown. "It's true, isn't it?" I said. "The Bette Davis Club. I didn't want to hear it that day you told me, but it's true. So many women. You can see them, if you look. Oh, Dottie. This is awful. No matter how much I love Finn—and I do love him—I'm getting cold feet."

Dottie clasped her hands together. "I prayed this would happen," she said. "And God knows, I'm an atheist."

Her eyes searched the room. "I'll call for a taxi. You go, get out. Run."

I felt guilty, confused, ashamed, and Dottie knew it. "Don't worry about Finn," she said.

"But what will I tell him?" I said.

"Nothing," Dottie said. She was up and pacing, ready to do battle.

Amy returned and stood in the middle of the room, holding a perfect, glistening cocktail of gin and vermouth.

"I've known that man for years," Dottie said. "I'll talk to him." She snatched the martini out of Amy's hand and drank it down herself.

My head was swimming. It was as if I were bobbing in the ocean and Dottie was bending over the side of a ship, tossing me a life ring. "Margo," she said, "save yourself. I'm telling you straight—as if you were my own sister, my own flesh and blood. Fly!"

I flew. Amy went with me. We took a cab to her place. When we got there, I changed out of my wedding dress into my street clothes. I did not want the dress. I stuffed it in a bag and asked Amy to please get rid of it.

Amy was kind to me. She made sandwiches. We drank half a bottle of wine and watched daytime television. After a few hours, I left her place and went home. I lay down for a moment and fell asleep. When I woke, it was evening. A light rain was falling.

I called Charlotte at her hotel. She was upset, flying out on the next plane. She had missed work, rescheduled meetings, all for this wedding. Did I not understand how valuable her time was? To Charlotte, my breakup with Finn was another disagreeable incident in the prickly, strained relationship we had as half sisters. There was a moment, though, just before she hung up, when her voice relaxed a little, softened. "It must be tough for you, kid," she said. "I do get that. I'm sorry."

After that, I did not want to sit around my flat. I grabbed my coat and went to Dottie's.

"Finally," Dottie said, when she opened her door to me.

We went inside her place and sat down opposite each other.

"What happened?" I said. "With Finn. What did he do when you told him I was gone?"

"The truth or the lie?" Dottie said.

"The truth," I said.

"The lie is prettier."

"The truth."

"Well," Dottie said, "it was interesting. You know Finn. He's all about appearances, how things look. After he took in what I was saying— that you had left, the marriage was off—he was embarrassed. The judge, his parents, all those people. He actually blushed. I'm not sure what he told everyone. Possibly that you'd had some sort of psychotic breakdown. That's what I'd have said in his position.

"But then, after a while, after that initial shock and embarrassment, you could see the relief come into his eyes. He tried to hide it, but it was there. He was like someone who'd been told there was a mix-up at the lab, that he wasn't sick after all. He unbuttoned his jacket and had one of the boys fetch him a glass of champagne. For medicinal purposes, I'm sure. And to be fair, there were jeroboams of the stuff just lying around. Then he—"

"Stop," I said. "I'll take the lie."

She paused, then changed course. "Margo, the man's a wreck, a ruin. You were the only woman for him. I guarantee there'll never be another."

We were silent for a while. Dottie got up and poured us each a drink. "When you think about it," she said, handing me a glass, "it's all part of nature's rich tapestry. The world would be a poorer place without it."

"Without what?" I said. I sipped my drink.

"Homosexuality. There'd never again be a Shakespeare or a Leonardo da Vinci. Never a Henry James or an Oscar Wilde or a Walt Whitman. Never even a Stuart Bingley."

"Who?"

"Stuart Bingley was my first boyfriend."

I lowered my glass.

"Don't look so ill, *chérie*. It was years before I knew you. But yes, I'm a charter member of The Bette Davis Club. How do you think I came up with the club in the first place? Stuart came to me one day, so serious. 'Dorothy,' he declared, 'I have something I must say to you.'" She laughed. "I thought he was going to propose."

"What did you do?"

"Oh, we survived," Dottie said. "Stuart moved

to the West Coast, lives with a banker named Kevin. And now I've met *ooh-la-la* Gerard, so I can't complain." She crossed her legs and leaned back in her chair. "But a world without gays. How dreary. Never again a Gertrude Stein or a Virginia Woolf. Never a Noel Coward or a Cole Porter. There'd be very few decent actors. And oh dear God, there'd be hardly any poetry. Because there'd be hardly any poets."

A few weeks later, I happened through Washington Square Park. The sun was shining and there were lots of people about—chess players, street per-formers, parents pushing strollers. Through a forest of strangers, I glimpsed Finn. He was alone. He was gazing up at the famous arch.

He must have sensed that someone was watching him, because he turned and saw me. I froze. What if he was angry? Worse, what if he ignored me? This man I had loved with all my heart—what if he acted as though we had never met? I did not think I could bear that.

Finn came over to where I stood, near the fountain. He was wearing a tweed sport coat, gray slacks, and a white shirt. I was wearing a green dress.

"Hello, miss," he said. He bowed. "How are you this fine day?"

I stood there, shaking my head, staring at the

ground. I could hardly breathe. I had cried so much the last few weeks, I didn't want to cry anymore.

"Margo," he said. He bent toward me, trying to catch my eye. "Margo, it's all right. I was . . . too old for you. I know that. I'm old enough to be your father. Forgive me."

"I'm so sorry," I said.

"No, no. It was my fault. It usually is. Mea culpa. Mea maxima culpa."

I lifted my head to him. We looked at each other. He smiled the same blue-eyed, boyish smile I had always loved. He asked if there was any chance I'd like to go—right then, that moment—for coffee. Despite all that had happened, I laughed. I said, Yes, I would love a cup of coffee.

We walked to the café. When we got there, we sat and talked for a long while. Without saying so, we forgave each other. But for what exactly? It did not matter, and I did not care. Somehow, in some way, Finn was back in my life. I felt like I had come home. I let myself be carried away by the sound of his voice, the sweetness of his company.

I think there must be times in a young woman's life when she is vulnerable to a sort of romantic imprinting. I imprinted at the age of seven when Cary Grant took me for a ride in my father's MG, and I subsequently fell in love with his old films. I imprinted again at nineteen when I met Finn. Both these men had a style, a sophisticated manner, that I delighted in. Problem is, it was a style—a fantasy—found in classic movie stars and closeted male homosexuals.

I would not, could not, cut myself off entirely from Finn. In a strange way, I felt we were family. Gradually, he and I worked our way round to a different kind of relationship. We would meet, though not so often as before, for coffee or a walk in the park. Occasionally, we went dancing or to dinner. We would laugh because the waiter would mistake us for an old married couple.

At other times, months went by and we did not communicate. This was not because we were angry or tired of each other. I never grew tired of Finn. It was because I would ask myself, *What is the point?* I would stay away for a while. But I always came back.

And if I didn't come back, if I stayed away longer than usual, then fate would throw us together. There would be an art opening or a downtown party, like the one where we first met at Tommy's loft, and there Finn would be.

Of course I had lovers, was involved with other men. Twice, I had proposals of marriage. But none of these men compared to my image of Finn, compared to my dream of him. I began sometimes to look for solace in places you will never find it. I drank, took my share of drugs.

And what about Finn? What did he want from me? Did he still make that incredible eye contact? Still tell me how pretty I was, then reach out to hug me just long enough for me to imagine something in him had changed? Sometimes.

I remained forever curious about Finn because he was forever a mystery. He had told me he was not complicated, but in truth, he was the most complicated person I ever knew. He was still a man who avoided talking about himself. Why did he not come out of the closet? It was becoming commonplace to do so, why shouldn't he? I never asked. If I even came close to the topic, Finn always managed to skitter away from it.

I inquired about his life in other ways. One time at Manhattan Architectural Salvage, I said, "What do you think made you collect all these things, these bits and pieces of the past?"

"Oh, I don't know," Finn said. He heaved a pair of cast-iron brackets off the floor and up onto a shelf. "It seemed a shame to let it all go off to the landfill, the way Penn Station did. That's what happened in the old days. There wasn't any salvage then, only the dump. It seemed sad that people—all of us—we're here a brief time and then . . . we're gone. I wanted to take notice. Perhaps people a hundred years ago were nicer, kinder, than people today. Anyway, it's pleasant to think that."

It was early evening, the shop was growing dark. Finn lit some candles in an old candelabrum. The brass and marble around us gleamed. "I do know," he said, "that the people who came before us made beautiful things. Such lovely buildings."

Then one day, a couple years back, I looked at Finn—really looked at him—and knew that he was growing old. He was sick and his heart was failing. He was no longer lanky and distinguished. He was brittle and thin.

I began spending a great deal of time with him. Some people said I looked after him. Finally, he caught a virus, and it turned into pneumonia. He went into the hospital.

I felt a catch at my heart when I opened the door to Finn's hospital room and saw him lying there on the bed. When I glimpsed his blue eyes and thick shock of hair, now mostly white, but still lush and aristocratic. For the thousandth time, I thought of the child we might have had together.

"Hello," I said.

Finn turned his head to me. "Oh, it's you, Margo," he said. He looked exhausted, worn-out. "I wanted to ask you something."

"What's that?" I said. I stood by the door.

"Have I ruined your life?" His beautiful voice was hoarse. "I mean, did I ruin your life?"

I pulled a chair up by the bed and sat down. "Of course not," I said. "Why on earth would you say that?"

He laughed weakly. "Been thinking about years gone by, I suppose. The rake's progress."

Knowing Finn had enriched my life, I told myself. Not ruined it, never ruined it.

I moved my chair closer to the bed. "As long as we're putting it all out there," I said, "there's something you should know." I paused a moment, choosing exactly the right words. "And it's just this: if I'd been born a man, you'd never have gotten away from me."

"A gay man, you mean," Finn said thoughtfully.

In all the years I knew Finn, that was the one time he identified himself as homosexual. Even after our wedding was called off, the subject of his sexual orientation never came up. The topic was off-limits.

But now he was dying. The truth no longer threatened him. And I understood that at the end of his life he wanted a witness to who he really was. He wanted a friend.

"You, born a gay man," Finn said. "Wouldn't that have been interesting? Although if you'd been born a straight man, you'd have ended up with Dottie."

"As it is, Dottie's sort of ended up with me," I said. "She seems to think she's my big sister."

"Good."

I rose from my chair and went to the window. God knows why. Whatever was going on in the world, I didn't want to watch.

"I'm leaving you the shop," Finn said to my back.

"Please don't," I said to the window. "I don't want it."

"Oh, you won't have it for long." He coughed. "It's bankrupt. The only way I kept the place running all these years is because I drew on my grandparents' trust. I'd leave you that as well, but the money vanishes the moment I do. Want to know where it goes?"

I couldn't look at him.

"An organization dedicated to preserving—and I quote—'marriage as the exclusive sanctity of men and women.' A clause in my grandfather's will."

I watched a man in the street below buying flowers from a cart. It was the only thing I could stand to look at.

"The business is in trouble because you won't sell anything," I said. I put one hand flat against the window. "People ring up and you tell them the thing they want has been sold, even when it's right there in front of you. Or you raise the price and when they meet that, you raise it again."

"*Vincit veritas*," Finn said. He coughed again. "I've been keeping a private museum, not a

344

shop. I still have pieces of Penn Station, including that capital you found years ago. Do you remember that day? You were innocent then. I liked that about you. And you looked so young and pretty. Do you remember?"

"Not really," I lied.

"Then you fell in the mud, and you still looked pretty. But mostly, you looked so very young."

Down in the street, someone bumped into the man who was buying flowers. The bouquet fell from his hands. I watched him rush to pick it up. I was thinking how most people don't make you feel much of anything at all. Don't make you feel like time spent with them has grace, like every moment in their company is a gift. But Finn did. Finn, my midsummer night's dream.

We didn't talk after that. Finn was tired. He fell asleep. I stayed in his room for several hours, watching over him. A nurse brought in a cot, and I lay down on it.

In the middle of the night, I heard a profound sigh and got up to look. Finn's shoulders were slack. His head had slumped forward. I called for the nurse, and they all came running with the crash cart. But it was pointless.

Finn was gone.

CHAPTER TWENTY

BABY, COME TO LONDON

I'm in a deep sleep on the Victorian fainting couch in Finn's office, when a persistent and irritating singsong noise wakens me. I fumble for the cell phone on the table beside me, but by the time I finally pick up, no one is there. Nor do I recognize the anonymous number on the caller ID.

It's the morning after Tully's and my arrival in New York. Now that I'm awake, I lie on the couch, regarding the familiar mess of Finn's office. Sunlight shines through the upper windows, brightening the mezzanine in an encouraging way.

One of my suitcases is on the floor beside me, resting against the couch. A book that I have no memory of owning peeks out from a side pocket of the case. A shaft of sunlight hits the volume's faded spine. I reach down, snatch up the book, and examine its tattered cover. I realize it's the vintage marriage manual given to me by the old woman at that run-down gas station on the outskirts of Palm Springs. I recall the woman saying the book had helped her "considerable."

I open the manual and flip through it. Eventually, I turn to the very last paragraph of the very last page and read: "But most of all, remember that marriage is about much more than mere carnal desire. It's about being good to each other. It's about being kind. It's about seeking the very best within your own soul and sharing that very best, that goodness, with your partner. Only then will you truly start your new life together. Only then will you truly be married."

I close the book. I place it carefully on the bedside table. I get up, find my robe, and go downstairs.

The Vanderbilt bathtub is empty. I call Tully's name, but get no answer.

I walk over to the kitchen area. The Fairy Castle books and mementos are still on the table. There are no eggs and no milk, however I brew a pot of coffee and get down a tin of English chocolate biscuits. (I became fond of this particular brand of biscuits—cookies—when I was at school in England. Ever since I discovered that you can buy them in New York, I always keep a supply on hand.)

I sit at the table, drinking coffee and munching on a biscuit. I'm looking round idly at the shop when I notice a shadow at one of the soaped-over front windows. Tully?

The shadow moves to another soaped-over window. Shadowy hands come up and frame a shadowy head, as though someone is trying to peer in. But who? No one comes to Manhattan Architectural Salvage. Hardly anyone even knows we're here.

I recall what Dottie said last night, that the *Spy Team* script is valuable, that I should go somewhere safe. Well, it's too late for that, isn't it? Too late to worry if the shadow at my window is a confused tourist . . . or Boone.

The shadow moves off. A moment later, though, it looms large through the frosted glass in the front door. For an instant, nothing happens. I don't budge, I barely breathe. Then I feel a shiver as the old brass doorknob rattles and turns a bit.

All right, this is getting spooky. But while I'm aware of being afraid, I also feel myself growing angry. How dare someone come prowling round here!

I rise from the table, tighten the belt on my robe, and reach for a large chunk of marble. Too clumsy. I put the marble back and instead, with trembling hand, grab a wrought-iron fire poker. My heart is pounding. Clutching the poker, I creep toward the front door. When I get there, I wait, unmoving and noiseless.

The doorknob rattles again.

Enough. Poker held high, I whip open the door. In a flash, I perceive the face of someone I know. It's Dottie.

"*Mon Dieu!*" she says. She's standing on the

broad single step up from the street and staring, wide-eyed, at the metal rod I'm brandishing above her head.

"Bloody hell!" I say, lowering the poker. I'm shaking. "You scared me half to death! Why didn't you ring the bell?"

"That bell has not worked since dinosaurs ruled the earth. And I imagined you and Mr. Benedict might be in repose."

"Too much going on for any reposing," I say, blinking out at the morning light. I gaze at the street, the blue sky, and I remember that it's spring. A man and woman pass by, holding hands.

"When I was a child," Dottie says, still standing on the stoop, "my mother heard a noise at the back door. She opened it and found a mongrel puppy. We didn't know it, but someone had deposited a litter of hounds in our yard. One by one, the little things found their way to our door. By day's end, my sisters and I were the proud owners of three roly-poly pups." She rests one hand against the doorpost and the other on her ample, well-tailored hip. "May I come in? Think of me as a puppy."

She comes in. I lead her to the kitchen area, put aside the fire poker, and pour her a cup of coffee.

"*Pas de lait?*" Dottie says, her eye scanning the table for a creamer.

"No milk," I say. "Sorry."

We stand there, like guests at a party, talking and drinking our very black coffee.

"Where is Mr. Benedict?" Dottie says, looking around.

"Out," I say. I hold up the tin of chocolate biscuits. Dottie shakes her head.

"I'm always happy to see you," I say, "but what are you doing here?" I return the tin to its spot on the table. "Did you call me a while ago?"

"No, I did not." She glances down at the table, changes her mind, and helps herself to a chocolate biscuit.

"I am here," she says, between bites, "because I could not sleep. I was too worried about you. I got up early and told Gerard no morning sex, and that he'd have to cook his own breakfast. He took it like a man. By this I mean he announced he was going out for an omelette."

Dottie surveys the vast room and the objects in it.

"God, this place," she says. "I haven't been here in ages. Of course, every dealer in town knows the legend of Finn Coyle. The man who accumulated, but would not sell."

Dottie rests her coffee cup on the table. She wanders over to a pair of stone cherubs and puts on her reading glasses. "So many of these things bring back memories," she says, examining the cherubs. "It's like looking at old photos. You were such a sweet girl, Margo, at nineteen. And after all that business with Finn, well . . . you never really recovered."

"Oh, please," I say. "It's been decades since I fell in love with Finn. I long ago got over him."

"No, I don't think so. You never did. Not completely, anyway." Dottie removes her readers, crosses back to the table, and retrieves her coffee cup. "Even when you sometimes went months without seeing him, everyone knew you adored him. It was like you were under a spell. I don't know why this particular occasion comes to mind—but remember the night you and I went to *La Bohème* and we ran into Finn? He was pleased to see you. Genuinely happy, I think. He hugged you."

I remember.

"The three of us ended up going for a late supper. Finn was charming, amusing, entertaining as always. That man went through life *glowing*. I can still see the way he smiled at you, the way he held your hand. When the meal was over, he insisted on picking up the check. But then he said good-bye and walked away. One look at your face, and I could tell what running into him like that had done to you. I took you straight to the nearest drinking establishment. 'Emergency martinis,' we called it."

I picture the bar Dottie and I went to that night, the table where we sat.

"Then these last few years," Dottie says, "Finn

got sick, got old. And when you heard he was ill, you sought him out anew. You looked after him. At the end, you were practically living with him. But in taking care of him, you gave up your job, your apartment. Over the years, you gave up so many things because of Finn Coyle. Some of them indirectly, I realize."

I laugh. "You make me sound like Miss Havisham," I say. "For your information, I have not wasted my life. I did not fall in love with the wrong man, who then deserted me on our wedding day. I left Finn, remember? I jilted *him*."

"You didn't go far, though, did you?" Dottie spreads her arms at the room.

"Oh, for God's sake! Just because Finn and I stayed friends, doesn't mean I haven't had relationships. I lived for ten months with . . . with . . ."

"Doug Irving?" Dottie says. "So unforgettable you fumble for his name?"

"Never mind him. I spent five and a half years with Michael."

"Michael Gray?" Dottie gives a half frown. "Mister Multiple Personality Disorder?"

"I dated," I say, beginning to feel like someone defending herself in a court of law. "I had boy-friends, lots of them. More than most people."

"That you did. Which, in a way, makes my point."

I'm incredulous. "You think Finn hurt me in

some way?" I say. "You think caring about him kept me from . . . what? Falling in love with someone else?"

"Finn was a good man, a kind man," Dottie says. She sips her coffee. "But his life was not authentic. Huge parts of it were invented to please other people, to fit their image of what they thought he should be. His grandfather was homophobic. Did you know that?"

"Yes."

"Can you imagine how that must have confused Finn, especially when he was young? I believe many people, an entire culture, did wrong by that man. They injured him emotionally, damaged him, and probably, on some level, enraged him. All of which made him . . . *je ne sais pas*. We'll never know. But because of what Finn did to get along in the world, the lies he told himself and everyone he met . . . yes, I think he hurt you. I think you never did resign your membership in The Bette Davis Club."

"Well, you're wrong," I say.

"Of course, I will grant that your own childhood—the deaths of your parents, being sent away to school in England—didn't make you a promising candidate for a healthy relationship with anyone."

"Thank you *so* much," I say. "It's not even noon, but you've already managed to make my day."

"I'm not finished," Dottie says. "Because to top it off, at the end, you and Finn had *folie à deux*, a shared madness. He'd been refusing to sell anything for years, getting more and more eccentric, everyone knew it, and yet during the time you took care of him, you went right along with it. *Folie à deux*! And now, with the bill collectors at your heels, bankruptcy closing in, Finn's been dead a year and you still haven't sold a damn thing. Not so much as a newel post!"

"That's because I'm . . . getting round to it!" I say.

"No, it's not. It's because Finn Coyle couldn't let go of his infatuation with the past. And you can't let go of Finn Coyle."

I look at her. She stares back. We're at an impasse.

There's a knock at the door. "That'll be Tully," I say.

Dottie peers at me over the rim of her coffee cup. "Or a puppy," she says.

I walk to the door and open it, expecting to see Tully. Instead, I find a young woman. Physically, she's gorgeous, really beautiful. And there's a scent of perfume that . . . Oh. Oh, my God. Dior Pure Poison.

"Auntie Margo?" the woman says.

I realize who I'm looking at. It's Georgia, all grown-up. It also hits me that I'm staring at sixty thousand dollars, the finder's fee promised me by Charlotte. I reach out, grab Georgia by the wrist, and fairly yank her inside.

"Whoa!" she says. "Good to see you too!"

I shut the door behind her and we stand there, facing each other. "It is *not* good to see you," I say. "It is close to intolerable. But I need my sixty thousand dollars."

"Whoa, whoa, whoa!" She holds up her hands. "I don't have any money. Not yet. You took everything I had."

"I took? Why, you light-fingered little thief! You mudlark! You spoiled, conniving gutter-snipe—"

She laughs. "God, Auntie Margo, I always loved the way you talk. I guess I just love the Brits."

"I'm American!"

"Whatever." Georgia comes farther into the room, taking stock of the rows of stained glass, the marble columns, the piles of antique fittings. "Wow," she says. "This is like *Beauty and the Beast*—when he was still a beast. What an awesome space for a party!"

Her eye travels to our left. She notes the long kitchen table and the biscuit tin upon it. "Cookies! Can I have one?" She drops down at the table and pulls the tin to her. She also spies the pot of coffee. "Ooh, and can I have a cup of coffee?"

I don't want to give Georgia coffee. I want to

smack her with the biscuit tin; I want to bludgeon her with the fire poker. This is the idiot who bruised Tully's heart, who caused us to drive across an entire continent. Yet when I look at her sitting there, swinging a leg and eating a chocolate biscuit, it reminds me of the few times I encountered her when she was a little girl. I recollect a certain sweetness she had then.

I sigh. I introduce Georgia to Dottie. I sit down at the table.

Dottie busies herself with the coffee. She pours out a cup and sets it in front of Georgia, then sits down herself. "We have no milk," Dottie informs Georgia. The way Dottie says this, it sounds less a report on the contents of my refrigerator than on the state of our post-menopausal bodies.

Georgia shrugs. She reaches for a second biscuit. "These are amazing," she says. "Lucky nothing ever sticks to me."

"*Malheureusement*," Dottie says, "it will."

This inane talk is killing me. I put my hand to my head, feeling it might explode. "What, what, *what* are you doing here?" I say.

Georgia points to herself. "Me?" she says.

"Yes!"

"Well, I called a while ago, but you didn't answer."

I hold up a hand. "How did you get my cell phone number?"

"Mom gave it to me."

"You and Charlotte aren't talking."

"Oh, we are now. Sure we are."

I jump from the table and stand there with balled-up fists. "God, you're both insane! Charlotte hired me to find you. I found you—"

"Didn't I find you?" Georgia says.

"Technicality. I've won whatever game we've been playing, and your mother now owes me many thousands of dollars!"

"Okay, sure. If you say so."

Georgia's youthful indifference is infuriating. I pace back and forth beside the table, then stop and point at her. "You broke Tully Benedict's heart!"

She laughs. "No, I didn't!"

I glare at her, and the laughter dies.

"For real?" Georgia says. She frowns. "Shit. That's so not fair. Tully knew . . ."

"Knew what? That you're a sociopath, that every word out of your mouth is false?"

"That I change my mind a lot. He said I was a big kid. Well, I guess I am. One night we were high, he was telling me about his divorce, his little girl. It was all so sad, and he was bumming me out. I wanted to cheer him up. So I proposed. Just like that!" She giggles at the memory. "Also, I knew marrying Tully would get me closer to his ex-stepdad."

I am always the last to learn anything of

importance whatsoever, but for once, the penny drops. "Malcolm Belvedere?" I say in wonder. "Those magazine articles—that's why you had them. You were studying Malcolm!"

"Hell-o," Georgia says. "Tully probably thinks I left him because we had that big fight. But that wasn't it. I left because the day before the wedding I found out some super-secret news—I found out Malcolm's wife was divorcing him. Even mom didn't know that. So I had this genius idea: Why not dump Tully and marry his ex–big daddy? No offense to Tull, but what a career break for me! Plus, I'd been messing around in Grandpa's attic. I discovered something."

"*Spy Team*," I say. "Did your mother know about that?"

"Yeah," Georgia says. "We argued over it. I think she thought I'd end up giving *Spy Team* to her—but then I split and took it with me. I knew it was a property Malcolm would want. Not only that, I figured *I'm* a property Malcolm would want. All of a sudden, my future was so bright, I was practically self-tanning."

Pleased with herself, Georgia pulls her feet up onto her chair, tucks herself into a ball, and nibbles on her biscuit.

"You thought you'd sell *Spy Team* to Malcolm as your own creation," I say. "All you had to do was update it and put your name on it."

"That was the plan. You have a problem with it?"

"Georgia, I have a problem with so many things you've done. I have a problem with that thug, Boone, you sent after Tully and me."

"Whoa," she says. "I so did not do that. But I heard about it. Boone goes a little Rambo sometimes. He was worried when you took the script, see, 'cause Kelsey's dying to play Ariana."

"The female lead in *Spy Team*."

"Yeah."

"Why did you steal *An Innocent Lamb*?" I say.

"I didn't take any sheep! I—Oh! You mean that old Oregon Welles script?"

"Orson," I say. "His name was Orson Welles."

"Whatever. I read some of it. It's beyond boring. But Grandpa's name was on there too, so I was hoping maybe it was worth big bucks, like *Spy Team*. But it's not."

Dottie, sitting opposite Georgia at the table, has been listening to all this. She leans forward, resting her chin in one hand. "Strictly *entre nous*," she says to Georgia, "what do you foresee as your current career path?"

"Like, what am I going to do now?"

"Like."

"Well, when I split from the wedding, I wasn't in any rush to go back home because, you know, Wrath of Mom. So after Palm Springs, I headed for Chicago to hang with Kelsey, talk with her about *Spy Team*. Then I thought I'd go to New York. The Tribeca Film Festival is this week. I figured that would be the perfect place—away from Mom and everybody—to meet up with Malcolm, pitch him the script." She plays with her hair. "Get him to fall for me."

"Do you know Malcolm Belvedere?" Dottie says, fascinated.

"I've met him."

"Yet you were that sure of yourself?" Dottie says. "Of your own powers?"

"Well, yeah," Georgia says. "Everybody says youth doesn't last. But it's working pretty good for me right now."

"And do you really consider Malcolm Belvedere a wise choice as a marriage partner?" Dottie says. "A man so many years your senior?"

"You've never lived in LA, have you?" Georgia says pleasantly.

Dottie wrinkles her nose and dips a biscuit in her coffee.

Georgia turns back to me. "So anyway, Mom gave me this address and said you might be here. I need my stuff."

"I have nothing that belongs to you," I say.

"Yes, you do!" Georgia says.

Georgia no longer reminds me of a child. Her expression has become that of a determined, even desperate, adult. She untucks her feet from her chair and gets up from the table. If we were dogs, the two of us would be circling each other.

"It's worth a ton of money!" she says.

"So people tell me," I say, feeling my fur go up. "But you're not going to get it!"

"You don't understand—I've got to have it!"

We go on quarreling like this, but a knock at the door interrupts us. Georgia, Dottie, and I all stare at each other. The knocking comes again.

"Better answer it," Dottie says. "Perhaps it's another puppy."

It's Tully.

"I got milk," he says, coming into the room, his arms full of packages. "Eggs, bread, the *New York Times*." He stops. His glasses have slipped down his nose, and his arms are so laden with shopping bags and parcels he has to crane his neck to take everyone in. Then he spots Georgia.

"Oh," he says.

"Hey, babe," she says.

"Babe," he says. "Right. Nice."

She laughs. "Come on, Tull. Don't blame me for being me."

"I don't." He crosses over and plops his packages onto the kitchen table. "I blame me for being me."

Georgia observes him carefully. "Hey," she says, "you sober?"

He takes off his glasses and wipes them with a handkerchief.

"You are," she says. "Wow." She glances at a schoolhouse clock on the wall. "Well, okay, this is pretty weird and awkward and everything. And anyway, I gotta get going. So, Auntie Margo, really, I need my stuff."

"*Your* stuff?" Tully says, putting his glasses back on. "Everything you had, you ripped off from somebody else."

"That is so not true! Mom—" Georgia cuts herself off. She again notices the clock. "Honestly, I've got to go. I'm meeting someone. Auntie Margo, could we talk? In private? Please?"

"Isn't it Tully you should be talking to?" I say.

"Why would she do that?" Tully says. "Why act like a grown-up?" He gives Georgia a look. "You ran off before without saying good-bye, so how about you just scurry off again?" He makes a fluttery motion with his fingers.

"Okay," Georgia says, "all right. I get it. My bad. I never thought—"

"No, you sure didn't," Tully says. "Because if you had, you would have called. Or texted. That also would have sucked—but isn't that how you and your friends avoid doing anything unpleasant?"

"This is so not fair," Georgia says. "Kelsey swears she told you it was over."

"What?"

"In Chicago. At her place."

"Christ," Tully says. "How old are the two of you? Twelve?"

"If you're mad at me," Georgia says, "I'm super

sorry. But the whole time I knew you, we were just having fun. I never, ever meant—"

"Forget it," Tully says. "I can't believe I took you seriously, even for a minute. But now, like you, I get it. You're a child, Georgia. And I'm too old not to have known better."

He waves a hand, as if tossing Georgia out of his life for good. "Game over. You said it all days ago—when you didn't say a word."

He turns and occupies himself with the groceries and his packages.

Under the circumstances, Georgia's request to speak privately, away from Tully, seems the thing to do. I lead both Georgia and Dottie upstairs to the mezzanine.

Dottie parks herself on the fainting couch. Georgia leans against a marble statue of one of the Fates. I stand there, still in my bathrobe, regarding them both.

"Please, can I have my stuff?" Georgia says.

"I'm not giving you *Spy Team*," I say. "I'd rather burn it. Nor, for that matter, am I handing over *An Innocent Lamb*."

"*Spy Team*?" Georgia says. Her eyes are wide. "I'm not talking about *Spy Team*! Or that stupid Oregon Welles script."

I look at her.

"I want my dress!" she says.

"Your—"

"My wedding dress! I called that little man in Palm Springs, and he told me you had it. No matter what anybody says, I didn't steal that. Mom bought it for me, she paid a bundle for it!"

"Your dress?" I say. This is not what I was expecting. "You mean, so you can marry Malcolm Belvedere?"

She rolls her eyes. "You never let me finish. A lot happened when I was in Chicago. A whole lot." She beams. "I'm engaged to Ricky Wallingford!"

"The English rocker?" Dottie says. Dottie keeps up with popular music. "That skinny little fellow who sings 'Baby, Come to London'?"

"Yes!" Georgia says. "I just love the Brits! Ricky's on tour, we met in Chicago. He's coming into New York at noon. Which is why I've got to get going. His tour ends tonight, then we're flying to London and getting married. Which is why I need my dress!"

"But don't you want *Spy Team*?" I say. "Don't you want to put your name on it, pitch it to Malcolm Belvedere, and make millions of dollars?"

"That's what I'm trying to tell you," Georgia says. She waves her hands in frustration. "I've given up screenwriting. I'm giving up the movies. Ricky has tons of money—more than Mom, more than anybody! And anyway, now I'm into songwriting. It's super easy. Ricky says whenever you can't think of any words, you just throw in 'baby, baby, baby.'"

"The dress is all you want?" I say.

"And the matching shoes."

"Oh, the shoes." I picture Mommie Dearest chasing Tully and me out onto the sidewalk, frantically calling after us that he had the matching shoes, not to mention Marilyn Monroe's underwear. "I'm afraid the shoes went on walkabout in Palm Springs."

Georgia shrugs. "The dress is the main thing."

I pull the box containing the wedding dress out from where I shoved it the night before, under Finn's desk. I hand the box to Georgia. She lifts the lid. When she beholds the gown inside, she squeals. "You're a doll, Auntie Margo! A living doll! Thank you!"

Still holding the box, she peeks over the mezzanine railing at Tully below. "In spite of what everybody thinks," she says, lowering her voice, "I'm not a total bitch. That's why I didn't want to talk about the dress in front of Tully. Didn't want to rub his face in it. You were worried I hurt him, I know. But he'll be okay."

I, too, glance over the railing at Tully. He's standing at the kitchen table, holding a mug of coffee and making short work of a chocolate biscuit.

"You like him, don't you?" Georgia says, watching me.

I don't reply. I just go on observing Tully.

"Well, he's more your age than mine. Listen, Auntie Margo, you were nice to me when I was little. I always liked you. I love you even." She lays the box aside. She gazes at me closely. "So, look," she says, "I never slept with Tully, okay? He has kind of a drinking problem, and whenever we were together, we partied so hard, one of us always passed out before anything could happen. Usually him." She gives a wink. "Thank God that doesn't happen with Ricky!"

Georgia raises up on tiptoe and kisses me on the cheek. Then she snatches up her box and makes for the stairs.

"Wait!" Dottie says. "What of the terrible Boone? What if he goes Rambo *encore*?"

Georgia pauses at the head of the stairs. "Boone's in Chicago, he won't bother you. Kelsey says he's recovering from head trauma. He does that a lot."

"What about my sixty thousand dollars?" I say.

"Go ahead and tell Mom you found me. I won't say different."

"But to hear you tell it," I say, "the two of you have already made up. Besides, I was supposed to persuade you to go home to LA. If I don't do that, I only get half."

"Sorry, can't help. Baby, come to London! You're right, though, Mom and me are best friends again. We had dinner last night at her hotel."

"Charlotte's in New York?" I say, bewildered.

"I know!" Georgia says. "It's like a family reunion! Turns out she's got something in the film festival. Which is all the more reason for me to get going. Even when we're BFFs, Mom and me do it better from a distance. Plus, she's mad at me for stealing Juven."

Juven. It dawns on me what *juven* means in Spanish: youth. It's not Charlotte's husband, Donald, that Georgia stole. It's her butler, Juven. Juven is Charlotte's lost youth.

"You took your mother's butler?" I say.

"Yes! He's a gem. I called him from Chicago and offered him more money than Mom ever gave him. She kept promising him a raise, but then she'd just hand him some used luggage and a couple of discount coupons for liposuction. Anyway, he's coming with Ricky and me to England. And I've got a plane to catch. Wish me luck, ladies! I'm off to the land of Will and Kate! Cheerio!"

Still gripping her box, Georgia hastens down the mezzanine stairs. She looks young and beautiful and utterly free. She glides past Tully— who ignores her—and hurries out into the street.

CHAPTER TWENTY-ONE

SOHO

After Georgia leaves, Dottie keeps me company while I slip behind a Chinese screen and get dressed. Then the two of us go downstairs.

Tully is sitting at the kitchen table, drinking coffee and checking e-mail on his phone. He looks up. "I have to see my agent," he says.

I must look surprised because Tully adds, "Won't take long. It's important." He grabs his jacket from a chair, but when he reaches the door, he pauses. "When I come back," he says, "there's something I need to tell you."

"Tell me now, if you like," I say.

"Later. It's kind of a story."

"All right," I say, mystified as to what the story could be.

Before Tully goes, I make sure to give him a spare key so he can let himself back in. Then he leaves. Soon after that, Dottie departs as well.

I'm once again alone in the shop. By now it's lunchtime, and I'm hungry for something other than chocolate biscuits. I pour myself a glass of gin, then get out a pan and a couple of the eggs

Tully purchased. I'm about to break an egg into a bowl, when the cell phone rings.

"Miss Just? Margo?" a voice on the other end says. "Malcolm Belvedere. We met at your sister's house in Malibu."

I remember sitting with Malcolm on that marble bench overlooking the Pacific. I picture his straight back and winning smile. "Hello," I say.

"I'm in town for the film festival," Malcolm says. "And lo and behold, a little bird tells me that not only are you here, but also you have something that might interest me. Something that—well, why don't you come round and we'll discuss it?"

I contemplate this invitation for a moment. Now that Georgia's eloping with Ricky Wallingford, there's no way I'll get my sixty thousand dollars. The most I might hope for is half—thirty thousand. Though I'm not sure I trust Charlotte to come across with even that. Despite what Veronica said last night in her shop—that no one would ever make an Orson Welles movie in today's market—perhaps I could pitch Malcolm *An Innocent Lamb*. Perhaps he'd be the one person left in Hollywood who might be interested in a script cowritten by Orson Welles and my father.

So I tell him, Yes, I'll come over.

I down the rest of my drink. I put the eggs back in the refrigerator. I scoop up my leather tote from where I dropped it the night before in the kitchen. I take a taxi to Malcolm's.

Malcolm's loft is in SoHo. It's on the same street where Tommy had his birthday party, the night I met Finn, all those years ago.

SoHo has changed greatly from when I first knew it. Back then, it was all raw space and artists' studios. Now it's chockablock with expensive boutiques and restaurants. No longer home to impoverished artists, it's the upscale habitat of wealthy businessmen, bankers, and people like Malcolm Belvedere.

The taxi lets me out in front of a landmark cast-iron structure built in the 1870s. I go upstairs. Malcolm himself greets me at his front door.

"How pleasant to see you again!" he says. He takes my hand. "Cocktail?"

While Malcolm mixes martinis, I put my bag down on a chair and look round his place. It has corner windows and high ceilings supported by white columns. The polished wood floors are so broad you could use them as a bowling alley. The furniture is European modern. Huge contemporary sculptures line the walls. I stop and study one.

Malcolm brings me a large drink. "Cheers," he says.

"Cheers," I say. We clink our glasses together.

"You like this?" he asks me about the sculpture.

"I look at it for hours sometimes." His gaze drifts off the artwork and onto me. "You know," he says, "that day we first met, I was thinking you might have had a film career."

I smile. "I think not," I say.

"I think yes. You're a handsome woman. It's only too bad you and I didn't chance upon each other years ago. Though perhaps we can still do business." The light in his eye makes me not altogether certain what type of enterprise he means.

"Business of what sort?" I say.

"Ah. I'll tell you. The day before she was to be married, your niece telephoned me—"

"She found out you were getting divorced," I say. "She intended becoming the next Mrs. Malcolm Belvedere."

"You're joking!" Malcolm says. "I wondered what she was up to!" He puts his index finger to his lips, thinking. "When you and I were chatting the morning of the wedding—remember? There was an odd feeling to the day. I was wondering even then if Georgia had jilted poor Tully. Still, me marry that intellectual dot? I make movies for girls like her; I don't wed them."

"Georgia seemed to think you might," I say.

He laughs. "I'm no saint, it's true. I've had women in my day. But dearest Margo, dear girl, when it comes to matrimony, when it comes to *relationships,* credit me with some discernment."

He gestures at the expensive sculptures surrounding us, as if their presence proves his high
standards in women as well as in art. "As I say,
Georgia Illworth called to tell me she was writing
a screenplay. Out of respect for my business
dealings with her mother, I said I'd take a look.
But I was headed to Europe for a few days, so
we agreed to rendezvous here in New York,
during the film festival."

"And did you?" I say. "Rendezvous, I mean?"

"No, because not one hour ago, she telephoned
again. Today, in what I gather is a soul-cleansing
confession coupled with the joys of young
love—"

"Baby, come to London?"

"Precisely. Today, she gives me to understand
said screenplay was actually penned by her
grandfather, Arthur Just. Which, I confess, piques
my interest enormously. She also says this
long-lost text is now in your possession."

I sip my drink, which is strong. On an empty
stomach, it feels even stronger. "I have two
scripts by my father," I say. "One of them he
cowrote with Orson Welles."

"Orson Welles!" Malcolm laughs heartily.
"Now you're going back! That would be—what
would that be? An artifact, a museum piece!" He
laughs again. "I was acquainted with Welles.
Immensely entertaining at parties, but a quirky
and unreliable man in business. No, I'm not

interested in any-thing by him, even if your father coauthored it. I'm interested in something your dad came up with all on his own."

"*Spy Team*," I say.

"That's the one," he says.

"Trouble is, I'm rather tired of *Spy Team*."

Malcolm smiles. "All the more reason for me to take it off your hands."

"So tired," I say, "that in the last few days, I've considered tearing it up."

Malcolm lowers his drink. "Dear me. In my opinion, that would be a mistake."

"It's what my father would have wanted."

"Interesting you say that. Because by my way of thinking, if Arthur Just had wanted his work destroyed, he would have done so himself. But he didn't. He left it behind."

"That was unintentional," I say. "*Spy Team* meant only one thing to him: a paycheck."

"That's what you believe, is it?" Malcolm says. "Myself, I knew a writer—not your father—who once told me his worst day writing was better than his best day not writing. You follow my train of thought?"

"Not really."

"I'm merely pointing out that perhaps your old man took more pride in *Spy Team* than you credit. He created that series, after all. Years later, it still has a great many fans."

Why do people insist on telling me about my

own father? What can they possibly know or recollect about him that I don't already know?

"*Spy Team*'s fans don't matter to me," I say. "What matters is that my father was made miserable by the demands of Hollywood. And by the demands of his estranged wife, Irene. Writing that ludicrous television series was the last straw. It killed him."

Malcolm gazes into his glass, frowning. "When I was a young man, I knew your father slightly. From what I saw at the time, I'd say it was drink that killed him."

I shake my head. "He drank because Hollywood drove him to it."

"I'm sorry," Malcolm says, "I disagree. Arthur Just drank because he was an alcoholic. Everyone in the entire industry knew that about him."

I move to a window and look across at the building where Tommy used to live, the building where he threw his thirtieth birthday party. Admittedly, I never actually met Tommy. But I'm aware that people like him were driven out of SoHo by people like Malcolm. I take a last swallow of my martini.

"A fondness for drink runs in the family, doesn't it?" Malcolm says. "They say your mum—" He stops himself.

My glass is empty. I set it on a table. I reach for my tote bag and pull out the *Spy Team* script. I take out my cigarette lighter as well. I stand there, script in one hand, cigarette lighter in the other. I begin flicking the lighter on and off, off and on.

"Careful there," Malcolm says. He puts down his drink and spreads his hands, as if attempting to keep his equilibrium. "Miss Just . . . Margo. Just Margo. Be reasonable."

I flick the lighter on and leave it on. The orange flame glows like a tiny candle. My hands tremble a little.

"Steady," Malcolm says. "That's a worldwide box-office potential of half a billion dollars you're holding there."

I move the lighter closer to the script. The paper is old and thin.

"Dear girl," Malcolm says, a note of command in his voice, "I'm serious. I couldn't *be* more serious. Stop and think what you're doing."

"I have thought," I say. "I'm happy with my decision."

"Well, I'm not!"

The truth is, I'm not sure *what* my decision is. I don't know what I want to do with *Spy Team*. All I know is I'm tired of people with money, people with power. I'm tired of being pushed around. And I'm tired of being told what's of value in my life and what's not.

"Domestic ticket sales alone of two hundred and fifty million dollars," Malcolm says. "That's more money than your father—"

"Don't say one more word about my father!" I cry.

Whether panicked by the emotion in my voice, panicked by the flame I'm holding, or simply unhinged by the prospect of all those domestic ticket sales, Malcolm lunges at me, grabbing for the script. But when he does that, it throws me off-balance. In a blur, all I can think is to keep Malcolm from getting the script. Instinctively, I jerk both hands to my chest. The next thing I know, Malcolm backs off, an odd look on his face. I've won! I've got the script and the lighter!

Only thing is, I'm holding them next to each other.

For a nanosecond, I clutch a ball of flame. Then I feel the heat and drop everything to the floor. A throw hangs from an armchair. The ball of flame skitters under it. The throw catches fire.

"Jesus, Joseph, and Mary!" Malcolm says. "You'll burn the place down!"

He tears off his suit jacket and steps forward, beating at the flames. Ash and smoke fly about. I watch, immobile, as Malcolm hits at the fire. It's not a large blaze and he soon succeeds in smothering it with his jacket. When the fire is out, when all danger is past, he stomps on the few remaining embers.

"You all right, dear girl?" he says. He glances my way. "Not burned or anything?"

I tell him I'm all right.

The two of us stand there, looking at the damage: the charred armchair, the pile of ashes on the floor beside it. The *Spy Team* script is destroyed. There's nothing left but cinders.

"Well, that's done it," Malcolm says. He's out of breath. "That chair's wrecked. I've ruined my jacket. Hand-sewn, don't you know, in Milan." He stares at the blackened coat in his hand, then drops it onto the ashes. "On top of everything else, did you notice? The bleeding smoke alarm didn't go off. What am I paying that monitoring service for?"

He rests one hand against a column and bends over, trying to catch his breath. His breathing is labored, and an odd sound comes out of him. It's a sort of gasp, like he's breathing hard. But it's also a sob, like he's crying. The next thing you know, he's choking with it. I'm about to call for help when I realize Malcolm's not choking. Not gasping. Not crying.

He's laughing. His shoulders are shaking and he's holding his sides. He's laughing so hard, he's near tears. He takes off his black-rimmed glasses and wipes his eyes with the back of his hand.

"Christ, what a cock up!" he says, getting his laughter under control. "I've known women in my life. Innumerable women. But never, ever, one like you." He puts his glasses back on. "Never one who incinerated the potential for half a billion dollars in worldwide box-office receipts. Lord love a duck, you must have been a willful child! No wonder the nuns gave you a hard time at that school you went to!"

He looks at the pile of ashes. "I didn't think you'd do it."

"I'm not sure I *did* do it," I say.

"Well, it's done now."

"I know I should apologize," I say. "But I can't. At the moment, I don't know what I feel."

In a little gesture of resignation, Malcolm puts out both his hands, palms up. "A psychiatrist would tell us we're both in a state of shock," he says. "Though each of us for entirely different reasons."

Malcolm motions for me to sit down on the sofa. He seats himself on a wooden chair opposite. "I'm being sacked, you know," he says.

"Sorry?" I say.

"Let go, from my own studio. I have fallen from grace. Forty-eight years in the business, twelve as studio head, and they're handing me my marching papers."

"Oh," I say. "No, I didn't know that. Can't you fight back?"

"Dear girl, for the last hour I've been hoping to—with *Spy Team*! Not sure I want to anymore. Feeling my age, I suppose. Anyway, my number was bound to come up sometime."

He takes a cigar from a box on a table and lights it with a match. "Cleaning lady's going to throw a fit when she sees this," he says, indicating the pile of ashes. "She's not a young woman." He tosses the spent match onto the rubble.

"What will you do?" I ask. "I mean, if you have to leave the studio?"

"Oh, I'll keep busy." He tips back in his chair. "No less than five different publishing houses have asked me to pen my memoirs. They say it could even become a film—one of my life's many ironies, I'm sure. Still, for the immediate future, I shall go on holiday. If I'm to be forced into retirement, then my only ambition for the next few months will be to travel, read, and perfect my knowledge of Italian cooking."

"Sounds lovely," I say.

"Could be. With the right companion." Gently, Malcolm lets his chair legs drop back onto the floor. He gives me a look of great tenderness. "Miss Just—that is, Just Margo—would you like to come with me?"

"Oh!" I say. "I really, I don't—"

He holds up his hands. "I know. Sudden and all that. But you must admit we're simpatico. I felt it the moment we met."

"Yes, yes," I say, blushing. "I won't deny I found you attractive."

"All right then. Fact is, Georgia was right about one thing. My wife has left me. Gone off with the fellow who's taking my job. 'There's glory for you,' as wrote Lewis Carroll. So I'm a free agent. And I would never say you owe me, although . . ." He glances again at the ashes. "My sainted aunt. Half a billion dollars."

"I agree that's a lot of money," I say.

Malcolm grins. "Then agree on something else—agree to come with me! I give you my word I'm capable of behaving like a gentleman. I wouldn't bother you. Unless you wanted to be bothered. Do you enjoy—"

"Being bothered?" I say. "Yes, like everyone. I do. It's only . . ."

"Someone else?" Malcolm says. "Someone since Malibu? But you haven't had time to—"

I bite my lip.

"Wait a moment," Malcolm says. "Not the boy? Not Tully?"

He leans forward, holding his cigar between his thumb and two fingers. "It is!" he says, looking at me closely. "There you see, once again. One of life's many jokes. Do you know, I loved his mother in a way that . . . well, when she died, something of my own self went with her. Suppose that's why I've a soft spot for her son. Course my time with Elizabeth was years ago. Never found anyone to break that particular spell. For a moment there, thought you might take a shot at it, dear girl."

"Malcolm, I—"

"Ah. Well. Not to worry." He makes a vague, accepting gesture. "Some other time, perhaps."

The room grows silent. The only sounds are the rumble of traffic down in the street and the wail of a distant siren.

There's nothing more to say.

I get up from the sofa. I say good-bye to Malcolm and leave him sitting there beside the ashes, dreaming about his lost love. Dreaming about the lost millions of *Spy Team*.

I go downstairs to the street. It's afternoon. I stand outside the building, unsure what to do, unsure about what I just did. The fire didn't touch me, but certain words of Malcolm's had scorched me down to my soul: "Arthur Just drank because he was an alcoholic. Everyone in the entire industry knew that about him."

Haven't I been saying I need money? Don't I want to save Finn's shop? If I want those things, then why was I so careless with the *Spy Team* script? What is it about my father, about my family—about me—that makes me feel so adrift? What is it that makes me destroy things, makes me destroy myself?

Office workers on break, shoppers, tourists, all crowd the sidewalk. I make my way through the people and over to a trash can near the edge of the curb. I reach into my bag for my cigarettes and lighter. I stand there a moment, looking at them in my hand. Then I chuck them in the garbage.

I walk on. I walk for quite a while, until it's dark. Eventually, I figure out where it is I'm going. I dropped in once, years ago, but it didn't take. It's time to give it another shot.

CHAPTER TWENTY-TWO

I'M MARGO

I find the place I'm searching for, walk in, and take a seat. There's a fellow who gives a brief introduction: old business, new business, followed by a short pep talk. Then we break into small groups.

Because we're in the basement of a church, my group of a dozen or so ends up in the Sunday School room. We sit in a circle, perched on little wooden chairs, the kind they have in elementary school. I'm scrunched up on a chair that was designed to hold a kindergartener. My knees are more or less in my face.

We go round the circle, everybody taking turns and introducing themselves.

"I'm Margo," I say, when it's my turn.

"Hi, Margo," returns a chorus of voices. Everyone smiles and nods and is generally cheerful. Naturally, I'm repulsed.

"I'm Margo," I repeat. I'm stalling because this is it, The Moment of Truth. This is when I'm supposed to tell everyone I'm a drunk. This is when I'm supposed to admit to the world that I'm an alcoholic.

Well, I can't do that. How can I possibly do that? Perhaps I could tell a half-truth instead. Perhaps I could start with, I don't know, a prologue.

"My father was an alcoholic," I say. "My mother was a probable alcoholic. My half sister, I'm pretty sure, has a cocaine habit. And my niece is . . . well, she never met a party she didn't like."

There's a murmur of polite laughter. Everyone is on the edge of their seats, or at least on the edge of their tiny wooden chairs. They're watching me. It's like we're all in this together and if I can just admit I'm one of them it will somehow, through some alchemy, help the entire group to heal.

"Anyway, I'm Margo," I say. "And I don't really have a problem with spirits. I'm a social drinker, occasionally. But I'm fine. Although alcoholism does run in my family."

A few people exchange glances.

"Excuse me for interrupting your fellowship," one woman says to me, "but we're all drunks here. Were you looking for the Al-Anon meeting?"

Another woman pipes up. "Al-Anon is for families and friends of alcoholics," she says. She sounds almost happy about it. "It's a special group all their own. They meet next door."

Spit it out, I tell myself. Spit it out!

"I'm Margo," I say again.

The first woman opens her mouth in an attempt to say something.

"I believe I have the floor," I say. "Please don't interrupt."

Christ, this is hard! "I'm Margo," I repeat, and by now the entire room is convinced I suffer from aphasia. They're worried they'll have to listen to me repeating my name over and over for the rest of their lives. I pause, searching for the right words.

"I'm Margo," I say one more time, getting into the rhythm of things. "And there's something I'd like to say."

A man near me mutters, "Not her name again, please."

"I'M MARGO!" I shriek. "MARGO! MARGO! MARGO!"

I have their attention. "AND . . . I . . . AM . . . A . . . RAGING ALCOHOLIC!"

Now I *really* have their attention.

"There, I've said it! All right? Everybody happy? Let me spell it out for you. I'm a drunk, a sot, a boozehound. A dip-so-maniac! Gin, gin, gin! I can't get enough of it! I wish it came out of the water faucet, so I could brush my teeth with it. I'd pour it on my breakfast cereal if only Kellogg's sold something with green olives and vermouth."

The lady who told me they were all drunks gapes at me, dumbfounded. I glare at her.

"Not only that," I toss in, "for years, I was unlucky in love. And did I mention I recently GAVE UP SMOKING?"

I swear she physically recoils.

"So now the whole lot of you know what I am," I say. "For once in my life I've told the actual bloody awful truth. And telling the truth—especially to you pitiful, tippling, red-nosed juiceheads—sucks beyond belief. It burns like I'm on fire, like I'm covered in hot, molten lava. I've told you the truth, the whole truth, and nothing but the truth. Gin! Do you hear me? Gin is what I'm saying!"

Another woman is watching me. She has this expression like she feels sorry for me, like she knows what I'm going through. Oh God, it's pity. Someone is pitying me. I'm pathetic. I feel woozy, and the room begins spinning. Even so, words fly from me like battery acid.

"And now," I say, "if you think I'm going to tell you the story of my life, if you think I'm going to open up and share my troubles with you all, admit to you I'm at the end of my rope, that I need your help because I have nowhere else to turn, that I'm hoping you'll throw me a lifeline. If you think I'm doing that, well, you're in for a rollicking big disappointment because—"

They're all staring at me. "Because I'm not opening up! I'm not sharing my troubles with anyone. I'm not!" Like a woman possessed, I twist wildly in my chair. "I won't, I won't, I won't!" I cry like a toddler. "Never, never, never!"

I glare across the circle and see that woman again, the one with the sympathetic face, a face that reminds me of the kindheartedness of my own dear mum dead and gone these many years. And it's then that something in me shifts. Years and years of stiff upper lips, and I'm all right, don't worry about Margo. For once, it all comes to a head, the hurt comes spilling out like apples rolling madly from an overturned cart.

I crack.

I crack like an ostrich egg dropped into a giant, sizzling pan. I crack like a thousand-year-old sequoia hit by lightning. I crack like Mount Vesuvius erupting all over those poor people in ancient Pompeii.

"God in heaven, help me!" I cry. My body is quaking so hard, I look like I've been strapped to an industrial-grade paint shaker. People around me are poised as if on starting blocks, as if ready to leap up and race to my aid. "Please!" I say. "Are you blind? Can't you see? I'm falling apart! I need a drink!"

There's a man sitting near me, his eyes gone big as saucers.

"Call 911!" I scream at him. I hold out my arms, pleading. "For the love of God, I'm begging you. Call a liquor store! Call a distillery! Call the people at Gordon's gin!"

A smiling Middle Eastern man clears his throat. "We have several tasty varieties of diet soft drink," he offers.

I ball up my fists and beat them against my thighs. "I'm in agony!" I cry. "It feels like I'm being eaten alive by tiny insects. Somebody, please, please, *please*—GET ME AN EMERGENCY MARTINI!"

For a moment, no one moves. The room is silent.

I glance around the circle at everyone. Everyone stares back. I release a long, frustrated moan. Still moaning, endlessly moaning, I slide off my kindergarten chair and onto the floor, where— not unlike a kindergartener—I dissolve into a puddle of tears and helplessness.

A gray-haired woman looks down at me. I lie there, curled up and sobbing by her feet. "Thank you for sharing," she says.

CHAPTER TWENTY-THREE

SELF-DEFENSE
FOR WOMEN

S everal kind and caring people help me up off the floor of Alcoholics Anonymous. I am hugged, I am handed a copious amount of tissues. The meeting goes on for quite a while, and I form new friendships. I get a sponsor; I can check into detox if I need it, but I don't think I will.

I promise to attend two meetings tomorrow: one in the daytime, one in the evening.

Eventually, I make my way back to Manhattan Architectural Salvage. It's nightfall. I have a headache. My cell phone has been off for hours. When I walk through the door, I'm sure I look a sight. Tully and Dottie are sitting together at the kitchen table, the remains of some takeout food in front of them.

"Thank God," Dottie says when she sees me.

Tully gets up. "Where have you been?" he says. "We were worried. Neither one of us could get hold of you, so Dottie came here."

"I had a meeting," I say. I cross to the kitchen

cabinet where the gin is kept. I open the cabinet door. A cockroach scuttles away.

A jar of coffee beans rests on a shelf inside the cabinet. Also, for some reason, a bag of bubble gum. I ignore the bottle of gin sitting there. Instead I get down the coffee beans and the bubble gum. I unwrap a piece of gum and put it in my mouth. I stand at the counter and begin grinding coffee.

"You're making coffee?" Dottie says, over the whirr of the grinder.

"It was a long meeting," I say, grinding coffee and chewing gum.

"Everything okay?" Tully says.

I put the ground beans and some water into the coffee machine. "I saw your ex-stepfather," I say. "He wanted to buy the *Spy Team* script. But then I set it on fire. Accidentally. Sort of. So there isn't a multimillion-dollar property any-more. It's gone."

"She's in shock," Dottie says.

"You're the second person today to make that observation," I say. "I'm beginning to think I've spent most of my life in shock." I push the button on the coffee machine, which sputters to life. Tully stands there, watching me. "Sorry," I say to him. "This morning—didn't you have some-thing you wanted to tell me?"

"It can wait," he says.

I unwrap a second piece of bubble gum and

shove it in my mouth, along with the first. "I've given up cigarettes," I say. I lay the package of gum on the counter. "And liquor."

Tully regards me for a long moment. Then he goes to the counter and picks up the bag of gum. "Bazooka," he says, looking at the bag. "I wrote about them in my chewing-gum book." He unwraps a piece and puts it in his mouth.

"I've joined AA," I say.

Dottie looks gobsmacked. Tully walks back over to the table and offers her the bag of gum. She takes a piece, unwraps it, and studies it. "Flamingo pink," she says. She pops it in her mouth.

"I've admitted I'm powerless over alcohol," I say, turning to face both of them. I lean back against the sink. "Powerless over lots of things, really."

"Well, who isn't?" Dottie says. She chews her gum thoughtfully.

There's a knock at the door. We all three ignore it. The knocking repeats, louder this time.

"Kind of late for visitors," Tully says. He blows a pink bubble.

"I'll get it," Dottie says. "No more puppies. At this hour, it's probably a cat."

It's my half sister. It's Charlotte.

She plunges into the room, looking around. "Jiminy Christmas," Charlotte says. "This place.

It's worse than I remember. *The Addams Family* meets the Metropolitan Museum of Art."

Her eye falls on an impressively large, ornately framed mirror. "Although this has possibilities."

"Ten thousand dollars," Dottie says—a figure she made up on the spot. "And that's the *prix d'amie*." The bargain price for a friend.

"I'll think about it," Charlotte says. She considers Dottie. "I met you once, years ago. You had a juicy little shop."

"*Maintenant*, it's bigger. And juicier."

"I'll drop in."

Tully steps forward. "Hello, Mother Illworth," he says.

"Not unless you've changed your name to Ricky Wallingford," Charlotte replies.

"Hello, Charlotte," I say.

She turns to me. "Greetings, Little Mar. Can you guess why I'm here?"

"*Spy Team*," I say. "But you're too late. It was incinerated."

"Oh, I know," Charlotte says. "Malcolm texted me. What a waste." She admires her reflection in the ten-thousand-dollar mirror. "Actually, I've come to apologize."

"For sending me on a wild goose chase?" I say.

"What? No. That was an illegitimate business proposition. Excuse me, I mean legitimate. I had no idea Georgia would do the things she did."

She cocks her head at the three of us. "Is there some reason you're all chewing gum?"

"We're dieting," Tully says.

"Oh. How retro." Charlotte catches sight of the coffeemaker. "Coffee! God, I could use a cup!"

Dottie pours out four cups of coffee. We all sit down at the table.

"Biscuit?" I say to Charlotte, holding up the tin.

Charlotte takes a chocolate biscuit from the tin and examines it. "Let me tell you," she says, "this is not a biscuit. It's a cookie. And it's about two hundred calories." She sets it down on the table. "I'll pass. Listen, Margo, when you left Malibu, I admit I was hoping you'd bring back *Spy Team*, along with Georgia. But my feelings have changed. I don't want it anymore. I mean, if you hadn't set it on fire, you could have it."

"But don't you need to make up your losses on *Muscle Man*?" I say.

"Losses?"

"You said on the phone *Muscle Man* was a dog."

"God no, you misunderstood. I said I was working like a dog. Woof, woof! Don't you look at television, the Internet? *Muscle Man* premiered last night at the film festival. The audience went wild. They loved it. It's going to be huge! Tarantula! Excuse me, I believe that's gargantuan. Plus, I have several irons in the fire—sorry, you know what I mean. I'm in preproduction on a sequel to *Thelma and*

Louise. The working title is *Don't Look Down*."

"Thelma and Louise drove off a cliff into the Grand Canyon," I say. "They're dead."

"Did audiences see that?" Charlotte says. "Was it shown on screen? No. Always leave room for a sequel. Those two broads landed in the Colorado River and floated downstream. The tagline is: They Survived the Fall." She spreads her hands. "Which reminds me. Speaking of survivors, I brought—I want to show you something."

She pulls an old photograph from her purse and passes it to me. It's a picture of Charlotte, me, and our father. We're sitting together in the MG. We look . . . well, you'd have to say we look almost happy.

"Remember that day?" Charlotte says. "Daddy took us for a ride. You were nine. You sat on my lap. You'd never get away with that now—seatbelt laws. We drove out to the beach and he handed the camera to some man and had him snap our photo."

"He used to do that sometimes," I say, gazing at the picture. "Take us for rides together."

"And when we got back, Mama would yell at me till she was purple. She was furious whenever I spent time with him. Or you."

"I didn't know that," I say.

"How could you?" Charlotte says. "Mama and I lived in a whole other wing of the house. She

394

could carry on all night about how Daddy had betrayed her—and me—and no one heard her but me and the housekeeper. I hated having to choose sides like that. I hated the way Mama treated you, the way she obviously expected me to treat you. It scared me, made me feel bad. I have a load of guilt about that. You were just a little girl."

I remember Charlotte saying something similar back in Malibu, about our childhood, about me being just a kid. Has it been on her mind all this time?

"Ever since Georgia ran off," Charlotte says, "ever since I hired you to go after her, I've been spending time in Daddy's sanctum . . . his sanctimonious . . . his . . . ."

"Private office," Tully says.

"Thank you. I hadn't been up there since I was a teenager. So many things in that room, so many memories. I held on to it all because Mama did. But there's something else Mama held on to: her anger. She never let go of it because she was wounded. Well, we're all wounded. Life cuts up everybody."

"Amen," Dottie says.

"It took me years to understand why Mama never wanted to share with you, Margo. It was because you weren't her daughter. Only I'm not my mother. And after all this time, I want to share with you. I want to share because—" Charlotte stops. She's silent for a moment. She asks Dottie for more coffee.

"I want to share," Charlotte begins again, after Dottie pours coffee, "because—"

"You're afraid of a lawsuit?" Tully says.

"No. I want to share because—aw, hell." She reaches out and puts her hand on mine. "Because you're my sister. Not my half sister, let's forget about that. You're my sister. You're family."

The four of us sit there, as mute as the antiques that surround us.

"You can have the mirror at fifty percent off," Dottie finally says.

"She can have it for free," I say.

"Deal," Charlotte says. "I get the mirror, you keep the car."

"You mean the MG?" I say.

"I do. Ha-ha. We're back where we started. Though where you're going to keep a car in Manhattan—"

"It's not as though she'd need it every day," Dottie says.

"I know a garage in Jersey," Tully says.

"Thank you all," I say. "However, you're forgetting I don't drive."

"*Oui*," Dottie says. "But Mr. Benedict clearly takes you where you need to go."

Tully reddens.

"You tell 'em, honey," Charlotte says to Dottie.

"Oh, and remind me, Margo, to write you a check for thirty thousand. You did try to find Georgia."

"Sixty thousand," Tully says.

Charlotte looks down her nose at him.

"Plus expenses," he says.

"Coffee is pricey in this town," Charlotte says. She sets her cup on the table, stands up, and stretches. "Still, I feel so much better! That was worth two years on the couch crying in front of Dr. Fieldshutter. Where's the sandbox?"

I point her in the right direction.

After Charlotte steps away, Tully takes the bubble gum from his mouth and wraps it in a paper napkin. He asks for a biscuit. I pass him the tin.

A moment later, there's a knock at the door.

"I'll go," Dottie says. "I'm expecting the Humane Society."

Dottie turns the handle on the front door. But when she does that, the door doesn't so much open as explode inward. A man bursts across the threshold.

It's Boone.

Kelsey is with him. Boone points one of his large, meaty hands at Tully. "I'm gonna hurt you," he says. "But first I want that script. And you're gonna give it to me because if you don't, I will not just hurt you, I will seriously kill you."

Tully holds up the tin, and his own chocolate biscuit as an example. "Biscuit?" he says.

"That's not a biscuit," Boone says. "It's a god-damned cookie!" He crosses the room and throws himself at Tully. Tully rises from the table, but Boone puts him in a headlock. They shuffle in a circle, Tully flailing haphazardly at Boone.

"Stop it!" I cry. "For God's sake!"

Dottie and I abandon the table, but all that does is provide Boone with a work surface. He begins slamming Tully against the tabletop, the same way he slammed him against the hood of the MG. Indeed, slamming people seems to be Boone's main mode of communication.

Dottie moves quickly to the coffee machine. She picks up the carafe. Somehow I don't think she's about to offer everyone hot beverages. She approaches the table, where Boone continues battering Tully.

Kelsey screams a warning, but it's too late. Dottie dumps hot coffee down Boone's back.

Boone screams and pushes Tully off the table and onto the floor.

Boone plucks his wet shirt away from his body. He spins round to face Dottie and me. "My code," he says, "is if a woman hurts me, I do not hesitate to hurt her back." He takes a step in our direction.

Tully reaches up from the floor, snatching at

Boone's pant leg. "Leave them alone," he says hoarsely.

Boone stops. He looks down at Tully.

"Just a sec," Boone says to Dottie and me.

He bends, seizes Tully by the collar, and begins pulling him along the floor. Tully's fingers scrabble at the wood planks like Wile E. Coyote being dragged across the desert sands. As Tully is hauled past me, we catch each other's eye.

I'm worried Tully will be hurt, yes. I care about him. But there's something else. In that moment, Tully and I share the truth of our existence. We're twins; we're soul mates. We are life's underdogs. We're the defeated, the conquered, the vanquished.

We were made for each other.

Boone whistles to Kelsey. She opens the front door. Boone tosses Tully out into the darkened street.

With an ominous click of the brass lock, Kelsey bars the door against Tully.

Boone turns back to Dottie and me. "Give me that script," he says.

"I don't have it," I say. "It's gone. There was a fire, and it burned up."

"Liar," Kelsey says. She rakes her hand through her long hair. "Boonie, she's lying!"

Boone comes toward me. He seems about to

demonstrate his personal belief system concerning acceptable violence with regard to women. His hands shoot out in front of him, and he shoves me roughly up against a cupboard, so roughly that I swallow my gum.

Dottie yanks on Boone's coffee-soaked shirt, trying to get him off me. But Kelsey isn't having it. She pulls at Dottie's hair, then pushes her to the ground. Startled, Dottie stares up from the floor. Her legs are collapsed under her, and she's swearing a blue streak in French. She looks like a surprised mushroom.

Boone again thrusts me against the cupboard. This time he knocks the wind out of me. I gasp for air.

"Do not mess with me!" he shouts in my face. He smells of aftershave, liquor, and spilled coffee. "I will tear this junkyard apart, and everybody in it!"

There's a loud pounding at the front door. It's Tully, I'm sure, trying to get back in.

At that moment, Charlotte exits the bathroom, adjusting her suit jacket. She's behind Boone and Kelsey. They do not see her.

Charlotte stops. She spies Dottie on the floor, me pushed up against the cupboard and gasping.

The fire poker rests nearby. It's in the same spot it's been in all day, since when I set it down this morning after using it to menace Dottie.

Charlotte doesn't hesitate. She crosses to the fire poker, picks it up, and raises it high in the air She brings it down on Boone's head.

Boone releases me. His hands drop to his sides. He stands there, teetering.

"Not again," Kelsey wails.

Kelsey advances in Charlotte's direction, murder in her eyes—but Dottie thrusts out a leg and trips her.

In the end, Kelsey and Boone go down simultaneously. Kelsey, like a child falling off a bicycle; Boone, like a felled tree. He lands against the ten-thousand-dollar mirror. It shatters.

"Damn," Charlotte says.

"*On ne fait pas d'omelette sans casser d'oeufs,*" Dottie says. "You can't make an omelette without breaking eggs." She removes the pink bubble gum from her mouth, reaches over, and sticks it in Kelsey's hair.

Charlotte and I are the only people in the room still upright. We stand, shoulder to shoulder, regarding Boone. He lies on the floor, groaning.

"I'm warning you, buster," Charlotte says. "I don't know who you are, or what your game is, but don't you ever again mess with Arthur Just's two little girls."

A while later, the police have come and gone, taking Boone and Kelsey with them. Tully, Dottie, and I are bruised, but otherwise okay. It was

Tully who, when he was locked outside, called the police on his cell phone.

Dottie sweeps up broken glass from the mirror, and Tully puts the kitchen table and chairs back in order.

I approach Charlotte. She's standing to one side, gazing at a hideous, open-mouthed stone gargoyle. "This thing reminds me of the woman who sold me lingerie at Bloomingdale's," she says.

"Thanks for saving my life," I say.

"Balls to that. What did that fathead think? Women can't defend themselves? I'm from Los Angeles. I work in the entertainment industry! I've taken so many female self-defense classes, I'm my own pit bull." She pinches the gargoyle's cheek.

"Charlotte," I say, "there's something I've been wondering about. Why wasn't Donald at Georgia's wedding?"

"My husband?" she says. "I suppose I could tell you he was in Barcelona, scouting vacation property. But I'm done lying to you, Margo. Marriage number four has come to an end. Donald has substance-abuse issues. Did you know he keeps cocaine hidden in a globe in the library? That's bad enough, but then I found out he's been having an affair with his personal trainer. His *male* personal trainer."

From across the room, Dottie overhears this. She and I exchange looks. I know what she's thinking: The Bette Davis Club has a new member.

"I'll tell you what the takeaway is," Charlotte says. "I'm going to fix up Daddy's office. Turn it into a yoga studio. Breathe in, breathe out."

Once things get tidied up, Dottie takes me aside. "You'll be all right?" she says.

"I'll be fine," I say.

"*Bien*. I'm going home and soak in a hot bath. That will make Gerard happy—he can bring me chocolates." She gives me a hug. "What a day it's been, *chérie*! I'll call you tomorrow."

Charlotte also hugs me good-bye. It's the first heartfelt physical contact she and I have shared in years. It feels a little awkward—like being hugged by Richard Nixon—but it's a start.

Dottie and Charlotte decide to share a cab. They walk out the door together, discussing restaurants, shopping, and the finer points of antique mirrors.

For the first time all day, Tully and I are alone in the shop.

"You must feel pretty bad right now," he says.

"No," I say. "I'm kind of happy."

"I mean physically. Quitting booze, withdrawal."

"I think I've been going on adrenaline," I say. "But you're right, I have a headache. And I feel sort of . . ."

"Flu-ish?"

"Yes, like I'm getting the flu."

"That's how it is. I'll fix you some eggs and toast. And orange juice."

It's nearly midnight when Tully cooks me breakfast. He sits with me at the kitchen table while I eat. "It's not enough going to round-the-clock meetings," he says. "You shouldn't be alone."

"Well," I say, "if today's any indication, there'll be armies of people trooping through here. No one visits for years and years and then, all of a sudden, it's busier than . . ."

"Pennsylvania Station," Tully says. "The old one, before they tore it down."

After I finish my eggs and toast, Tully accompanies me upstairs to the mezzanine. The room's antique wall sconces give off a golden glow. I settle on the edge of the Victorian fainting couch and stare at the worn Persian rug.

"Remember that day we talked about hidden value?" Tully says. He stands next to Finn's desk, fiddling with a glass paperweight. "About seeing things other people don't see? Just to be clear, Georgia has no hidden value for me. Not anymore, if she ever did. You, however, have unplumbed depths."

I laugh ruefully. "Like a sunken ship. Which is how I feel. Shipwrecked."

"You're not a shipwreck," Tully says. "You're a lost treasure. And I found you."

I massage my temples. "I'm not good company right now, Tully. I'm so tired. You can go home, you know. I'm fine."

"I'm not going anywhere," Tully says.

"Please just go home," I say. "Really."

"No," Tully says. "I won't. I'll sleep downstairs in the bathtub. If you need to talk in the middle of the night, we can talk. If you need me to wake up, I'll wake up. If you want somebody to rub your head, I'll rub your head."

He puts down the paperweight and comes over to the fainting couch. He sits down next to me. After a while, he slips his hand into mine. It's such a human thing to do, so warm and comforting, I melt. A tear moves down my cheek. I turn and bury my face in Tully's shoulder.

"Hey," he says, holding me, "it's all right."

"It's a big fat mess," I say, wiping my eyes.

"Well, yeah. But it's all right."

He lets go of my hand and scoots himself round so that he's behind me. His back rests against the wall, his legs stretch out on either side of me. He puts both hands on the back of my skull, and begins massaging my head. I do not resist.

"I was wrong about something," Tully says, moving his fingers gently over my head. "I said architectural salvage was an oxymoron. But I've been thinking about it, and it's not much different from when someone dies and we look at their picture or reread a letter they wrote. That's salvage too. If you think about it, people spend a lot of time trying to hold on to things that are gone."

He caresses my head a bit longer. His hands are superb.

"There's something I need to tell you," he finally says.

"Is it what you wanted to tell me this morning?" I say. I feel dreamy from the head rub.

"Yeah, it is. Last night I was restless, couldn't sleep."

"I'm sorry," I say. "Was the bathtub terribly uncomfortable?"

"It was fine," Tully says. "I couldn't sleep because I kept thinking about what Veronica said at her shop. That the *Spy Team* script was worth millions, that you should get an attorney. I was curious. You left your bag downstairs. Excuse me for doing this, but I went over and took out the script. I sat in an old armchair down there, and I read it."

"Could we please not talk about *Spy Team*?" I say.

"We have to talk about it."

"I don't know why."

Tully moves his hands from my head down to the nape of my neck. He begins kneading my neck and shoulders.

"Because for one thing," he says, "Veronica was right. Your father was a good writer. That story has a great ending. I bet your dad was proud of *Spy Team*. I bet he'd be proud now, if he were alive, and he saw that years later people still enjoy that show. Enjoy it so much they're lining up to buy the Blu-ray high-def twenty-four-disc ultimate collector's edition with pop-up packaging."

I'm ill with regret and remorse. Why did God invent cigarette lighters?

"When I finished reading the script, it was late," Tully says. "I went to bed. Then this morning, I woke up early. You were asleep, so I went out. I brought back milk, eggs, groceries. And I brought back something else."

"The *New York Times*," I say.

"Right, I got that. But did you know there's a FedEx office near here? Open twenty-four hours. I took the *Spy Team* script over there." He ceases rubbing my shoulders.

I twist round and look at him. "You—"

"Photocopied it," Tully says. "I figured I better do that in case something happened to the original."

I jump from the fainting couch, turn, and stand there, facing him. "But you didn't tell me! Why didn't you tell me?"

"Margo, you were completely mental about *Spy Team*, your father, all of it. I saw your face

407

when Veronica said the script your dad cowrote with Orson Welles wasn't worth much. I knew how you felt about your dad working in television. You thought television killed him—when maybe it was, you know, other things."

I picture the many people I met today at AA. All of them finally accepting the truth about themselves. "It was other things," I say. "I know that now."

"Okay. So anyway, I decided to wait until you calmed down. When you and Dottie were up here talking to Georgia, I put the original script back in your bag. Then I texted my literary agent. She's here in Manhattan, but her agency has a Hollywood office. I wanted to see if she knows anything about Joshua Epstein, that LA attorney Veronica recommended."

"Does she?"

"Yeah. I went and saw her, we talked. She says Epstein has a good rep."

I'm lightheaded, dizzy. I may swoon onto the fainting couch. "You made a photocopy of *Spy Team*?" I say.

"Actually," Tully says, "I made two."

"You're a genius!"

He grins. "Some people do say I have a very high IQ."

"I could kiss you," I say.

He throws open his arms. "Baby," he says, "what's stopping you?"

I return to the couch, and do what I've wanted to do for a long time. I kiss Tully Benedict. Even more wonderful, he kisses back. He is a fabulous kisser, and he kisses me back many times. In many places. In many ways.

The next morning, I wake up feeling better than I have in years. For someone still suffering the effects of alcohol withdrawal, I have a surprising amount of energy. Sitting at the kitchen table in my bath-robe, I telephone Joshua Epstein in Los Angeles and take him on as my legal representative.

Then I pull out the creamy vellum card Malcolm Belvedere gave me that day we first met in Malibu. The card that lists all his private numbers.

I call Malcolm and tell him he can have *Spy Team*, but he'll have to work with Joshua.

"Done!" Malcolm says into the phone. "With *Spy Team* in my pocket, I have a shot at reclaiming my studio. Hah! You've done me a great kindness! I'm back in the game!"

I tell Malcolm that, as part of the deal, I'd also like a month-long stay this summer at that beach cottage of his in the Hamptons.

"Dear girl," Malcolm says. "Anything. Hardly use the place. Month-long stay every year for the rest of your life if you want."

I tell him, Yes, that's exactly what I want.

CHAPTER TWENTY-FOUR

BEACH COTTAGE

Assuming you live through it, the best thing about falling apart is you get to put yourself back together. I go to Alcoholics Anonymous two nights a week now, more if I'm feeling shaky.

My outburst at that first meeting is legendary. I can't tell you how many people in my chapter have come up to shake my hand. They tell me they thought they'd seen it all, until the night they shared fellowship with me. I'm the benchmark for out-of-control behavior, the poster child for escaping the hellish jaws of alcoholism. And escape it I have. Or at least, you know, as Kay said to me that afternoon at the Museum of Science and Industry: One day at a time.

Charlotte wrote me a check for sixty thousand dollars, plus expenses. And she gave me title to the MG. She was right, you can't keep a car in Manhattan, the garage fees are astronomical. So I store the car out of the city, but Tully and I often take it out on weekends. We go for long drives in the country. Sometimes we stop for ice-cream.

With the cash Charlotte gave me—plus the obscene amount of money I received from the sale of *Spy Team*—I paid off my debts and then some.

I won't have to worry about finances for a long time now, if ever. Dottie is helping me find homes for the things in Finn's shop, many of which we're simply donating to museums and restoration projects.

After we empty the shop, I'm closing the business. I'm done focusing on the past—my own past anyway. I'm looking to the future. And I'm going back to school. Eventually, I want to train to become an architectural conservator. I want to work at saving important buildings *before* they're torn down.

Tully has nearly finished his book on miniatures. He asked me to move in with him, into his flat in Brooklyn, and I did. We plan to be married in the fall—I in the strapless Donna Karan, he in the Armani tux. Georgia has volunteered Ricky Wallingford to play at our wedding reception. We'll see.

In the meantime, it's summer, and Tully; his daughter, Emma; and I are spending a month at the beach. We're staying in Malcolm's seaside cottage—which, to be honest, is a sort of luxury oceanfront home.

Emma, I should tell you, is beautiful. I don't mean physically, though she's nice-looking. I mean, her energy, her exuberance. I love the way she dances by the water, turning cartwheels and laughing.

She and I take long walks along the shore and talk about many things. I'm not trying to replace her mother, and she knows that. But I do hope to be her friend. Together, we worked out that "Margo" was too formal, and "Mom" belongs to her real mother. So I told her about my own mum, who came from England. Because of that, and because of my accent, she decided to call me Mum.

This morning, for instance, while Tully works on his book, Emma and I go for a beach walk. She stops and picks up a smooth white stone and holds it in her hand. Then she looks out at the blue, rolling sea. "Mum," she says, "is everything in the world connected? I mean, you know, except for what's up in the sky?"

I ponder that one for a moment. Now that I'm a mum, I no longer believe in telling half-truths. I believe in giving as honest an answer as I can. Because perhaps if people spent more time being honest with each other, especially with children, there would be less unhappiness in the world.

I know I couldn't love Emma more if she were my own child, and I know it's possible to find heaven on earth, but this is a new kind of philosophy. I mean, really, is everything—*everything*—in the world connected? Finn, Pennsylvania Station, Tully, dollhouses, me, Orson Welles? Every leaf, every insect, every raindrop, every person I ever met in my entire life? Are they all connected?

So finally I tell her, Yes, everything in the world is connected. And in my opinion, what's up in the sky as well.

"I thought so," she says, dropping her stone into the palm of my hand, and running off to splash in the water.

Personally, I can't say I'd given it much thought before, certainly not prior to becoming a mum. But now that I've considered it, now that I've made peace with so many things, and now—to paraphrase brave Bette Davis in *Now, Voyager*—now that I have a home of my own, a man of my own, and a child of my own—

Well. I'm quite sure it's true.

ABOUT THE AUTHOR

Jane Lotter was a Seattle-based writer and humorist whose work has appeared in national publications. Her hilarious column, Jane Explains, ran in the *Seattle Sun*, winning several awards, including one from the Society of Professional Journalists. Jane's only novel, *The Bette Davis Club*, won first place in the Mainstream category in the Pacific Northwest Writers Association Literary Contest.

Center Point Large Print
600 Brooks Road / PO Box 1
Thorndike, ME 04986-0001 USA

(207) 568-3717

US & Canada:
1 800 929-9108
www.centerpointlargeprint.com